**Also available from
Susan Andersen
and Harlequin HQN**

That Thing Called Love
Playing Dirty
Burning Up
Bending the Rules
Coming Undone
Just for Kicks
Skintight
Hot & Bothered

Coming soon

Some Like It Hot

Susan Andersen

Cutting Loose

HARLEQUIN® HQN™

Recycling programs
for this product may
not exist in your area.

ISBN-13: 978-0-373-77784-6

CUTTING LOOSE

Copyright © 2008 by Susan Andersen

Printed in U.S.A.

www.Harlequin.com

Dear Reader,

I don't know what I'd do without my girlfriends. Women forge connections that make crummy days better, breakups a tad easier and bad hair days, well, still bad hair days, but so much less dismal with a pal to make you laugh or lend you her hip new hat to disguise it. So I'm really excited to introduce the reissued first book in my Sisterhood Diaries trilogy, because this series features three women who've been friends since grade school.

Jane Kaplinski thanks heaven for her two best friends. It wasn't easy being the only child of self-absorbed second-rate actors, and there were times growing up when only Poppy and Ava's friendship made all the stormy exits and theatrical reunions in her household bearable.

These days, Jane has her life on track and the only thing on her mind is fulfilling the final request of a dear old lady who bequeathed the Sisterhood her estate. Jane is certainly not looking for love—she's way too familiar with the damage done in its name. Still, if she ever *does* fall in love, she intends it to be with someone stable.

Then Devlin Kavanagh, a footloose international yacht sailor with *steamy* stamped all over him, comes home to help his family business during a crisis. And all Jane's careful plans go up in flames.

It was fun making sparks fly, as well as creating Dev's and Jane's friends and family. As always, I hope you enjoy my efforts. And be sure to check out the sneak peek into my brand-new Razor Bay book, *Some Like It Hot,* in the back of this book.

Happy reading!

Susan Andersen

This is dedicated, with love,
to a woman I've known since I was ten.

To

Marilyn Hansen

Who took the time to sit on her porch steps
to talk to me when I was a kid.
And who has been a warmhearted friend
since I became an adult.

You rock.

~Susie

Cutting Loose

PROLOGUE

Dear Diary,
Families suck. Why can't I have a regular mom
and dad?

May 12, 1990

"JANE, JANE, WE'RE HERE!"

Twelve-year-old Jane Kaplinski leaned out her bedroom window. Below, her friend's chauffeur-driven car was parked at the curb in front of her middle-class house, her friends Ava and Poppy spilling out the vehicle's back door.

"I'll be right down," she called, watching Poppy's cloud of blond curls swaying in the breeze, her filmy skirts plastered against her slender legs. She'd probably bought her outfit at Kmart, but as usual she looked stylish and pulled together, while Ava, who had developed a full year and a half ahead of everyone else in their grade level, looked sort of packed into her pale green dress, its expensive workmanship tugged akilter at bust and hips. But her sleek red hair, brighter than a four-alarm fire, blazed beneath the spring sunshine's sudden peekaboo appearance through the clouds and her dimples flashed as she grinned up at Jane.

Smoothing a hand down her own navy skirt, Jane

flicked off her radio, aborting Madonna's "Vogue" mid-song. The front door banged open downstairs as she picked up her backpack and carefully closed her bedroom door behind her. She smiled as she headed for the staircase, imagining Ava's usual insistence that they knock while Poppy countered they didn't need an engraved invitation.

But it was her mother's voice calling her name that froze Jane in place on the bottom step a moment later.

The suitcase in the foyer should have been her tip-off, but she'd been so focused on her outing with her best friends that she hadn't even noticed it. Now here came her mother, ice clinking a familiar Parent rhythm in the highball glass clutched in her hand as she bore down with frenetic joy on her only child.

Crapdanghell.

"You're back," she said flatly as her mother gathered her to her bosom, and choked when her nose sank into Obsession-scented cleavage. She stood rigid until Dorrie loosened her grip, then edged toward the door.

"Of course I am, darling. You know I could never stay away from you. Besides—" she gave her hair a pat "—your father simply begged me to return." Dorrie slung an arm around Jane's shoulders and looked down at her, the aroma of Johnnie Walker Black wafting from her breath to clash with her perfume. "Look at you, all pressed and shiny! Are you going somewhere?"

Jane twisted away and took a giant step backward. "I've been invited to tea at Miss Wolcott's."

"Agnes *Bell* Wolcott?"

She nodded.

"My little girl is so highfalutin." Dorrie gave her a swift once-over. "You couldn't find something a little more colorful to wear?"

Casting a glance at her mom's neon-hued top, she merely said, "I like this."

"I have some nice red beads we could use to jazz it up." She lifted a shiny brown hank of Jane's stick-straight hair and rubbed it between her fingers. "Maybe fix up your 'do a little? You know how important staging is—if you want to look the role, you need to pay attention to the costume!"

Jane managed not to shudder. "No, thanks. I'm going for tea, not starring in one of your and Dad's productions. Besides, didn't you hear Ava's car pulling up out front?"

"Did I?" Dorrie dropped the tendril and took another sip of her Johnnie Walker. "Well, yes, I suppose I did, now that you mention it. I wasn't paying attention."

Big surprise. Mom was usually all about Mom. Well, that or focused on the drama du jour of the Dorrie and Mike Show.

The doorbell rang and with a sigh of relief, Jane eased around her mother. "Gotta go. Me and Ava are spending the night at Poppy's, so I'll see you tomorrow."

And, boy, was she grateful to be spared tonight's theatrics when her dad discovered Mom was back. It was guaranteed to be filled with passion and fireworks, and having lived through both too many times to count she was just as happy to miss the show.

Ava and Poppy let themselves in before she could reach the door. They immediately surrounded her and, calling, "Hello, Mrs. Kaplinski, goodbye, Mrs. Kaplinski," hustled her to the car.

Daniel, the Spencers' chauffeur, opened the Lincoln's back door. As Poppy dove into the backseat he tipped his neatly capped head at Jane. "Miss Kaplinski."

She always wanted to giggle at his formality, but she gave him a grave nod in return. "Mr. Daniel." She climbed in sedately after Poppy.

Ava plopped down next to her and Daniel closed the door.

The three friends looked at each other as the chauffeur walked around to the driver's door, and, clutching her hair, Poppy mimed a scream. "Can you believe this?" she stage-whispered. "Tea at the Wolcott mansion!" She looked past Jane at Ava and asked in her normal register, "Why did Miss Wolcott invite us again?"

"I told you, I'm not sure." Ava tugged on the hem of her dress to cover her pudgy thighs. "Maybe because we all talked to her at that dumb musicale thing my parents had. They were, like, so psyched that she accepted their invitation. I guess she turns down more than she accepts these days and everyone wants to have the party she comes to. But at the same time my mom says Miss Wolcott's a genuine eccentric and she was a little nervous that she might say or do something Not Done By Our Kind." She shrugged. "Dunno—she seemed pretty regular to me. Except maybe for her voice. My dad says it's like a foghorn."

"I thought she was interesting," Jane said.

"Well, *yeah*," Poppy said. "She's been everywhere and done everything. Can you believe that she's been to places like Paris and Africa and even flew her own plane until a couple of years ago? Plus, she's got that great mansion." She bounced in her seat. "It makes your place look like a shack, Ava, and I didn't think there was *any* place prettier than your house. I'm dying to see Miss Wolcott's on the inside."

"Me, too," Jane agreed. "It sounds like she collects all kinds of rad stuff."

Ava pulled a candy bar from her backpack, ripped the wrapper from one end and offered Poppy and Jane a share. When they declined, she shrugged and chomped off a large bite. "I'm just glad to get out of Cotillion class. Any excuse to avoid Buttface Cade Gallari is a good one in my book."

Upon arriving at the three-storied mansion on the crowded western slope of Queen Anne hill they were ushered into a large parlor by an elderly woman wearing a severely styled black dress. She murmured assurances that Miss Wolcott would join them shortly and backed out of the room, rolling closed a long, ornate pocket door.

The high-ceilinged parlor was dim and cool, the windows all mantled in velvet curtains. Eclectic groups of artifacts cluttered every surface, making a space that could easily contain the entire first floor of Jane's house seem almost cozy.

"Wow." She turned in a slow circle, trying to take in everything at once. "Lookit all this stuff." She edged over to a glass-fronted case and peered at the crowded display of antique beaded bags. "These are awesome!"

"How can you tell?" Ava asked. "There's no light in here."

"Yeah," Poppy agreed. "Look at the size of those windows—I'd keep the curtains open all day long if I lived here. Maybe paint the walls a nice yellow to brighten things up."

"Ladies," a deep, distinctive voice said from behind them, and they all turned. "Thank you for coming." In tailored camel slacks and fluid jacket, with a high-necked blouse as snowy as her carefully arranged hair, Agnes Bell Wolcott stood framed in the now partially open pocket door. A beautiful antique-looking cameo nestled in the cascading ruffle at her throat. She glanced at Poppy. "You may open the curtains if you wish."

Without so much as a blush at being overheard, Poppy ran to do so and the high-cloud pearlescent glow of an overcast Seattle afternoon immediately brightened the southerly facing room.

"Well, now. Would you girls care to explore some of my collections or would you rather enjoy a light repast first?"

Before Jane could vote for option number one, Ava said, "Eat, please."

Their hostess led them to another room that held an exquisitely set table in front of a marble fireplace. A three-tiered pastry stand, set squarely in its middle, held an array of beautifully presented desserts and crustless sandwiches. They sat themselves according to the little name cards at each place setting and Miss Wolcott rang for tea.

She then focused her undivided attention on them. "I imagine you're wondering why I invited you here today."

"We were just talking about that on the way over," Poppy said frankly as Jane gave a polite nod and Ava murmured, "Yes, ma'am."

"This is my way of saying thank you for your company at the Spencer musicale the other night. It's not often young ladies will take the time to keep an old woman company, and I very much enjoyed talking to you." She regarded them with bright-eyed interest. "You girls are very different from each other," she observed. "I wonder if I might ask how you met?"

"We all go to Country Day," Poppy said. Intercepting Miss Wolcott's discreet inspection of her inexpensive clothing, she grinned. "My folks are all love, peace and joy types, but my Grandma Ingles is an alumna. She pays my tuition."

"And I get financial aid," Jane volunteered. Not that her parents had bothered to arrange it. If her second-grade teacher hadn't submitted the original scholarship application Jane would still be attending public school. Nowadays she filled in the annual paperwork herself, so all her folks had to do was sign it.

"I'm just a regular student," Ava admitted. "I don't do anything special for tuition and Jane and Poppy are better at school than I am." She smiled, punching dimples deep in each cheek. "Especially Jane."

Warmth flushed Jane's cheeks, ran sweetly through her veins. "Ava's special in other ways, though."

"I find it lovely to see such a close friendship between girls," Miss Wolcott said. "You're quite a sisterhood."

Jane savored the word as the black-clad woman entered the room, rolling a cart that bore an elegant tea service. Miss Wolcott indicated the rectangular packages lying across the girls' plates as her servant settled the silver teapot in front of her. "I got you a small token of my appreciation. Please open them while I pour."

Jane carefully untied silver ribbon and peeled gold-and-silver paper from her package while Poppy ripped hers off with abandon and Ava unwrapped hers with a just-right show of attention that she'd no doubt learned in one of the Miss Manners classes she was always attending.

Jane smiled to herself. Maybe it truly *wasn't* easy being a rich girl. Heaven knew Av told them so often enough.

Nestled in the paper was a deep-green leather-bound book with her name engraved in gold on the front cover. Poppy's, she saw, was red, while Ava's was a rich blue. Wondering how the older woman had known green was her favorite color, she opened hers, but the gilt-edged pages within were blank. She glanced at Miss Wolcott.

"I've kept a diary since I was your age," the white-haired woman said in her deep basso voice. "And finding you all such interesting young women, I thought you might enjoy keeping one, as well. I find it a great place to share my secrets."

"Awesome," said Poppy.

Ava's face lit up. "What a great idea."

Looking from Miss Wolcott to the friends she'd known since the fourth grade, Jane thought of all the impressions and feelings that were constantly crowding her mind. Things weren't always great at home, but she didn't really like to talk about it—not even to her two best friends. Sometimes especially not to them. Poppy had great parents, so while she could and did sympathize with the way Jane's folks were constantly slamming in and out of her house, she didn't truly understand how shaky that could make the ground feel under a girl's feet. And although Ava's own home life was far from ideal, at least her parents weren't a couple of actors who lived for the drama of constant exits and entrances.

But the idea of writing down how she felt really appealed to her. She smiled.

"Maybe we could call them the Sisterhood Diaries."

CHAPTER ONE

I am so never wearing a thong again. Poppy swears they're comfortable—which probably should've been my first clue.

"OMIGAWD, JANE," Ava screeched. "Oh, my, gawd. It's official!"

Jane pulled the phone away from her ear. Her friend's voice had gone so high she was surprised the leashed dachshund sniffing the light standard down on First Avenue didn't start barking. But she clapped the receiver back to her ear as excitement danced a fast jitterbug in her stomach. "Probate finally closed, then?"

"Yes, two minutes ago!" Ava laughed like an escapee from a lunatic asylum. "The Wolcott mansion is officially ours. Can you believe it? I sure miss Miss Agnes, but this is just too thrilling. Omigawd, I can barely breathe, I'm so excited. I have to call Poppy and tell her the news, too." She laughed again. "We've gotta celebrate! Do you mind coming to West Seattle?"

"Lemme see." Stretching the telephone cord as far as it would reach, she stepped out of her cramped sixth-floor office at the Seattle Metropolitan Museum to peer through the director's open door two doors down. The coveted corner office showcased a panoramic view from Magnolia Bluff to Mount Rainier, with the Olympic

Mountains rising dramatically across Elliott Bay and Puget Sound. Not that she could see more than a fraction of it from her angle, but she wasn't trying to scope out the scenery, anyway. Traffic flow was her objective. "No, that oughtta work. The freeway looks pretty clear your way."

"Good. Let's meet at the Matador in an hour. Overpriced drinks are on me."

She found herself grinning as she changed into her walking shoes and threw her heels into her tote in preparation to leaving. Swinging her butt to the happy dance song playing in her head, she freshened her lipstick, tossed the tube back in her purse and stuffed it into the tote as well.

"You look jazzed."

Jane let out a scream. "Good God!" She slapped a hand to her racing heart and whirled to face the man in her doorway.

"Sorry." Gordon Ives, her fellow junior curator, stepped into the room. "Didn't mean to startle you. What was the little dance for?"

Ordinarily she wouldn't consider telling him. She had a strict policy of keeping her private business out of the office that had worked well for her over the course of her career and saw no reason to change it now.

And yet...

Part of the inheritance was going to impact the museum, so it wasn't as if he wouldn't soon find out anyhow. And the plain truth was, she was excited. "I'm getting the Wolcott collections."

He stared at her, his pale blue eyes incredulous. "As in Agnes Bell Wolcott's collections? *The* Agnes Wolcott, who traveled the world wearing trousers when her generation's women stayed at home to raise the kids and didn't dream of stepping outside the house attired in less than dresses, gloves and hats?"

"Yeah. She didn't wear only trousers, though. She wore her share of dresses and gowns, as well."

"I've heard about her collections forever. But I thought she died."

"She did, last March." And grief stabbed deep for the second time today at the reminder. There was an unoccupied space in her soul that Miss Agnes used to fill and she had to draw a steadying breath. Then, perhaps because she was still off balance, she heard herself admitting, "She left them to me and two of my friends." Along with the mansion, but Gordon didn't need to know that as well.

"You're kidding me! Why would she do that?"

"Because we were friends. More than that, actually—Poppy and Ava and I were probably the closest thing Miss Wolcott had to family." Their original visit eighteen years ago had led to monthly teas and a friendship that had deepened as the fascinating, wonderful old lady took a hands-on personal interest in their lives and accomplishments, treating the three of them as if they were somehow equally as fascinating. She'd always gone the extra mile for them, making a fuss over their accomplishments in a way no one else had ever done—well, at least in her and Ava's lives. Like the celebratory dinner she'd thrown at Canlis the evening Jane had landed her job here.

She rubbed a hand over her mouth to disguise its sudden tremble—then sternly pulled herself together again. This wasn't the place or person in front of whom she wanted to indulge her emotions. "Anyhow," she said briskly, "I'll only be around in the mornings for the next two months. A couple of the collections are being donated to the museum and Marjorie's letting me work afternoons at the Wolcott mansion to catalog them."

"The *director* knew about this?"

"Yes."

"I'm surprised no one else here heard, then."

She looked at him in surprise. "Why would they?"

"Well, it's just—you know. Nothing ever seems to stay a secret in this place."

"True. But this was a private inheritance that came as a complete surprise to me and my friends. Then there were months of probate before it was finalized. It's been all we've been able to do ourselves to figure out how this all works, and I only told Marjorie because one of Miss Agnes's bequests directly affects the museum. I saw no reason to talk about it with people not involved in the matter."

Sensing her curious coworker was about to ask what the bequest was and perhaps even who else had received one, she looked at her utilitarian leather-banded, large-faced watch. "Oops, gotta go. I've got a bus to catch." She grabbed up her tote and ushered him out of her office, closing the door behind her.

Emerging onto the street a few minutes later, she pulled on her little black cashmere sweater against the brisk wind and her sunglasses against the bright October sun. She'd only mentioned the bus to get Gordon out of her office, but after a quick mental debate she decided against going home for her car and hiked up to Marion Street to catch the 55 instead.

As the bus approached the Alaska Junction a short while later she changed back into her heels, smiling down at the leopard-skin, open-toed construction. She loved these shoes and knew this would probably be one of the last times she'd get to wear them this season. According to the KIRO weatherman on the news this morning, their sunny days were numbered.

She beat Ava and Poppy to the restaurant, but even though it was a weeknight and early yet, the Matador's tequila bar was starting to fill up. She bought herself a club soda at the stained-glass-backed bar and staked out one of the few free tables.

She'd never been here before and spent a few minutes admiring the open-concept flow of bar into restaurant and the intricate metalwork on display. She killed another minute perusing the menu, but people-watching soon proved more compelling and she gave herself over to checking everyone out.

It was mostly a twenty-something crowd, but in the restaurant end of the room was a quartet of men who kept drawing her gaze. They ranged from late twenties to maybe forty and were holding what appeared to be an intense conversation across the room. Every now and then, however, they'd all shout with laughter, instigated for the most part, it appeared, by the redhead with the seam-threatening shoulders.

She'd never been particularly attracted to redheaded men, but this guy was something else. His hair was the dark, rich color of an Irish setter, his eyebrows blacker than crow feathers and his skin surprisingly golden instead of the creamy pale she associated with that coloring. Influenced, no doubt, by years of hanging around Ava.

Despite repeatedly redirecting her attention, it kept wandering back to him. He seemed very intent on the conversation with his friends, leaning into the table to speak, those dark brows pulled together in a frown one moment, then relaxing as he grinned and gestured animatedly the next. He talked with his hands a lot.

Big, tough, hard-looking hands with long, blunt-tipped fingers that could probably—

Jane jerked as if someone had clapped hands right in front of her face. Good God. What on earth was she doing thinking—what she was thinking—about some stranger's hands? This was *so* not like her.

And wouldn't you know he'd choose that exact minute to look across the room and catch her staring? She froze as he talked to the other guys at his table while his gaze skimmed her from the top of her head to the tips of her shoes, which he studied for a couple of heartbeats before beginning the return journey. When he reached her face once again, he tossed back a shot without taking his eyes off her, then pushed back from the table and climbed to his feet.

Was he coming over here? *Ooh.*

No! What was she, eighteen? She wasn't here to troll for a date—and wouldn't choose a bar if she had been.

"Hey, Jane, sorry I'm late. Poppy's not here yet, I take it."

She looked up to see Ava approaching the table and noticed that damn near every male head in the bar turned to follow her friend's progress. The redhead across the room was no exception. He checked Ava out for a moment before glancing at Jane again. For just a sec he stood there rubbing the back of his neck. Then he hitched a wide shoulder and headed in the direction of the men's room.

His butt was as nice as the rest of him. But giving it a final lingering glance before turning her attention to Ava, who was pulling out a chair, she noticed the telltale hesitancy in his step of a man who's had too much to drink.

"Well, shit." Her disappointment was fierce, which was pretty dumb considering she'd never even talked to the guy.

"What?" Ava tossed her Kate Spade clutch on the table and slid gracefully into the chair.

"Nothing." She waved it aside. "It's not important."

Ava just looked at her.

"Okay, okay. I was doing the eye-flirt thing with this buff redhead over in the restaurant part of the room and—don't turn around! For God's sake, Ava. He went to the can, anyhow."

"Eye flirting is good—especially for you, since you don't do nearly enough of it. So why are you cursing?"

"He's drunk. I didn't realize it until I saw him walking away."

"Aw, Janie. Not everyone who gets a little lit is a problem drinker. Sometimes it's just a once-in-a-while kind of thing."

"I know," she said, partly because she did but mostly because she really didn't want to argue tonight.

Ava knew her too well, however, and instead of letting it go, she leaned over the table, her bright hair swinging forward. Scooping it back, she tucked it behind her ear. "You've seen Poppy and me indulge a bit too much on occasion and you don't hold it against us."

"Yeah, because I know your history, and I know it's a rare thing for either of you to drink to excess." She gave an impatient shrug. "Look, I know I'm not completely rational on the subject and I don't need to put some shrink's kids through college to understand that Mom and Dad's drinking is the reason why. By the same token, Av, you know you're not going to change my mind. So let's just drop it, whataya say? We're here to celebrate."

Deep dimples indented her friend's cheeks. "Omigawd! Are we ever! Are you as excited as I am?"

"And *then* some. I'm so psyched at the thought of getting my hands on those collections I can hardly think straight. I didn't get a chance to talk to Marjorie this afternoon, but unless something special comes up at the Met—and it's been pretty quiet on the curator front for the past week or so—I'm hoping to dive right in and start sorting them on Monday."

"Sorry I'm late." Poppy arrived breathless at their table.

Ava made a rude noise. "Like we'd know how to act if you were ever on time. Where did you guys park, anyhow?" she asked as Poppy dumped her oversize handbag onto the floor and collapsed into the chair next to her. "Did you find a place on the street or park in the lot above the alley?"

"I'm in the lot," Poppy said.

"I took the bus."

Both her friends stared at her openmouthed, and she blinked. "What?"

"You're crazy, you know that?" Poppy shook her head.

"Why, because I'm a public transportation kinda gal?"

"No, because bus service drops way down in the evening and it can't be safe to hang around bus stops in the dark."

"Oh, as opposed to walking through a dark alley to get your car, you mean? Besides, I can always call a cab. I don't see what the big deal is. Ava said meet in an hour and I didn't think I could make it here in time if I went home first."

"And like Poppy's never on time, you're never late," Ava said.

She shrugged. "We all have our little idiosyncrasies. Shall we talk about yours?"

"We certainly could…if I had any. But I like to leave those to my lesser sisters." Serenely she waved over the waitress and ordered one of the tequila specials.

Poppy ordered tequila, as well, then turned to Jane. "How about you, Janie? Do you want your club soda freshened?"

"No, I think I'll have a glass of wine—whatever the house white is," she added to the waitress.

Her friends whooped and drummed the table and generally made a huge fuss over her unusual selection and Jane leveled a look at them when the waitress left with their order. "Contrary to popular opinion, you two, I do know how to make an exception on occasion." Then she grinned. "And this is definitely the occasion."

"Amen to that, sister," Poppy agreed.

When their order arrived, Ava raised her glass. "To being new home owners."

Jane and Poppy clinked glasses with her. "To new home owners!"

Jane took a sip of her wine, then raised her glass again. "To Miss Agnes."

They clinked again. "To Miss Agnes!"

"Man, I miss her," Poppy said.

"Yeah, me, too. She was like no adult I've ever known."

Then Poppy raised her glass. "To you, Jane. May you speedily catalog Miss Agnes's collections."

"To me," she said while Ava and Poppy exclaimed, "To Jane!" Then in a rare exhibition of uncertainty, she added, "What if I mess up the job?"

They stared at each other as the possibility of failure hovered in the air above them. Then Ava laughed, Poppy made a rude noise and Jane shook her head, her momentary nerves dissipating.

"Nah." If there was one thing she was completely confident about it was her abilities in her chosen field.

"That reminds me." Poppy twisted in her chair to glance around the bar. "I asked the head of Kavanagh Construction to drop by if he had the chance so you guys could meet him. And there he is!"

To Jane's astonishment, Poppy hailed one of the men at the table she'd been watching earlier, then popped out of her chair and sashayed across the bar.

With her usual aplomb, she stooped down next to the bald guy Jane had thought was maybe forty and started talking with the confidence of a woman assured of her reception. After a brief conversation she rose to shake hands with the other three men at the table, then gestured in Jane and Ava's direction and said something.

To Jane's horror, not only did the bald guy get up and follow her back across the room, so did the hot redhead. The latter stumbled over an unoccupied chair a couple tables away and lurched the remaining steps to theirs, where he had to slap his fists down in order to catch his balance. He swore a blue streak beneath his breath.

"Dev!" the bald man snapped. "Cool it!"

"'Scuse my language, ladies." The redhead gave them all a loose, sheepish smile. "I'm seriously jet-lagged."

"More like seriously drunk," Jane said sotto voce.

"Jane, Ava, this is Bren Kavanagh and his brother Devlin," Poppy raised her voice to say over her. "As I told you earlier, the Kavanaghs are going to be in charge of our construction. Bren was just telling me that Devlin here will be the project manager on our remodel. He'll oversee—"

"No." Pushing back from the table, Jane surged to her feet, her heart slamming in outrage. It was one thing to put up with an inebriated man in a bar for a single evening. She'd be damned if she'd put up with one while she was trying to catalog the most important collection of her life.

Devlin, who'd been staring owlishly down at his knuckles where they bore into the rich wood tabletop, raised his hazel-green-eyed gaze and blinked at her. Then, apparently not liking what he saw in her expression, he narrowed his eyes, his devil-black brows snapping together over the thrust of his nose. "Say what?"

"No. It's a pretty simple word, Mr. Kavanagh—what part don't you understand?"

"Hey, listen—"

"No, you listen! I will not have some damn drun— Hey!" She yelped as Poppy grabbed her by the wrist and nearly jerked her off her feet.

"Excuse us," Poppy said as she turned and strode toward the back of the bar.

Leaving Jane no choice but to follow in her wake or be dragged behind her friend like a toddler's pull toy.

DEV WATCHED the uptight brunette being hauled from the table. "Okay, then, I'm outta here," he said, and knuckled himself erect. *Whoa.* He flattened his hand back against the wooden surface. Damn room was starting to sway.

Bren's eyes narrowed as he studied him. "Man, you *are* wasted. You'd better go sit down before you fall down."

Good plan. He started to pull out the chair next to the redhead with the great ti—

"At our table, bro."

"Oh. Yeah. Sure." He gave the redhead with the killer bod an acknowledging nod for her sympathetic smile, then made his unsteady way back to Finn and David.

What the hell was he doing here, anyway? He should have fallen straight into bed to sleep for ten solid hours. He'd sure as hell known better than to let Bren guilt him into going out to discuss how he could take over for his brother while Bren went through treatment. Or, alternatively, having caved, he at least should have been bright enough to forgo the two shots of tequila he'd slammed back after downing a generous dram or two of Da's treasured Redbreast. He was from good Irish stock; he could usually put away his fair share without showing the effects.

Tonight, however—well, he'd been up for more than thirty-five hours, nineteen of which had been spent traveling from Athens, Greece. He'd already been flattened with exhaustion when his brother Finn met him at the airport.

But there was no rest for the wicked as far as the Kavanaghs were concerned. When a chick came home to roost, a celebration was not merely expected, it was a given. And a get-together wasn't a get-together unless it included all six of his brothers and sisters, their respective spouses and kids, his folks, both grandmas and his grandpa, his two uncles, four aunts and their families. Fair enough—he knew the drill.

But he should have paid less attention to Da's whiskey and a little more to Mom's food.

"Way to go there, Dev," his youngest brother said with a sly grin when Devlin made it to their table. "Back in town a few hours and already you've managed to get sent back to the kiddie table so Bren can talk to the grown-ups."

"You're a riot, David, you know that?" Hooking the crook of his elbow around his brother's neck, he staggered slightly, steadied himself against his brother's side, then scrubbed his knuckles in David's brown hair. "You oughtta take it down to open mic night at the Comedy Underground." He turned him loose and dropped into the chair Bren had sat in earlier. "I gotta admit, though, that's kind of what it feels like. Apparently my drunkenness offended one of the potential clients."

"Can't imagine why," Finn said dryly.

He smiled crookedly. "Yeah, me, either. Shit." He rubbed his fingers over lips that felt rubbery. "I didn't realize how trashed I was until I stood up to go with Bren to their table. Had to concentrate like a son of a bitch just to walk a straight line."

Finn looked at him, deadpan. "How'd that work for you?"

"Not so great." He glanced over his shoulder at his oldest brother, still talking to the redhead across the room, then turned back to the others, abruptly feeling a whole lot soberer. "So how's he doing, really?"

"He's got his good days and his bad. I think he'd rather tell you about it himself."

"Yeah, him being such a talkative son of a bitch so far." He gave his brothers a look. "I'm still hacked that I didn't even hear about it until three days ago."

Finn gave him a bland look in return. "You've been a little removed from the family for the past decade, little brother. Maybe we thought you wouldn't be interested."

He came up out of his seat, ready to brawl.

Finn merely looked at him with calm, dark eyes, however, and Dev sat back down. Shifted his shoulders. And leveled a hard look on his brother. "I might be removed geographically, but the last time I checked I was still a Kavanagh. I'm still family." Which, okay, conflicted the hell out of him every bit as much today as it had at nineteen. He loved the clan Kavanagh but couldn't be around them long before he started going insane. Yet while he'd moved to get away from everyone always knowing his business, this was not the usual oh-did-you-hear-Dev's-dating-the-O'Brien girl—I-wonder-how-

May-would-work-for-the-wedding kind of crap—this was Bren, sick with cancer. It pinched like hell that nobody had bothered to pick up a phone to let him know about it. "I'm still family," he repeated stonily.

"Yeah, yeah, Finn knows that," David said peaceably. "But that's something else you have to take up with Bren. It was his decision not to burden you with it when there wasn't anything you could do to help. But now you can. If you didn't blow it with the client, that is. So...what? She took a dislike to you because you didn't hold your liquor tonight? Didn't you explain you were jet-lagged?"

"'Course I did."

"So what was that all about then?"

He thought about the brunette. She'd caught his eye from across the room. She wasn't built like her red-headed friend or model-pretty like the blonde, and in their company he imagined she got overlooked a lot. God knew she wasn't his usual type, but she'd been alone and looking at him and he'd found himself abruptly interested.

It had been the contradictions, he thought. She wore a prim white blouse that showed such a meager hint of lace undergarments it might as well not have bothered and a straight midcalf-length black skirt whose center slit barely made it over her knees, let alone into interesting territory. But her shoes were leopard-print high heels designed to make a man realize that the pale, smooth legs they accentuated were pretty damn sleek. And while her shiny brown hair had been piled up on her head in an old-lady bun, it had listed to one side and looked as if it were about ten seconds from coming undone and sliding down that long neck.

But it was her eyes that had been the real contradiction. He hadn't been able to tell from across the room, but they were blue. And unlike her clothing, there wasn't a damn thing prim about them. They'd looked at him, in fact, as if she wouldn't mind giving him the hottest—

Shit. He shook aside the image that sprang to mind, because who the hell cared? She was obviously humorless and judgmental and he looked at David and shrugged. "Beats me, brother. I have no idea what her problem is."

"YOU WANNA KNOW what my problem is?" Jane wrenched her wrist free from Poppy's grasp and reached behind her to grasp the ladies' room counter at her back to keep from bopping her friend on her elegant chin. She might have thrown caution to the wind and taken her best shot when she was ten, but she had learned control since then.

Hell, she lived and *breathed* control these days.

"My problem," she said coolly, "is one, I don't like being manhandled by you, and two—and this is the biggie, Calloway—you're looking to saddle me with a drunk while I'm trying to get together the most important collection I've ever been asked to head. You know damn well that I'm on a time crunch to get it done for the January exhibit and the last thing I need is to waste time babysitting some lush. *That's* my problem."

"You think you're the only one with something on the line here?" Poppy thrust her nose right in Jane's face. "This is not all about you and you damn well know it. *None* of us want to fall short when Miss Agnes put so much faith in us. At least you have the experience to handle your challenge. Ava has to sell the place without benefit of any sort of real estate experience and I'm responsible for the remodel. And that's not small spuds, Kaplinski, given that I make most of my living designing menu boards!"

"Oh, please." Jane thrust her nose right back at her. "Like you don't know Miss A. requested you decorate because you've been trying to get her to redo the mansion since the first time we saw the place! How many suggestions have you given her over the years for improving the place? One million? Two? And I'm guessing she put Ava in charge of selling because she's the one who has contacts up the wazoo with the kind of people who will be able to afford it."

"All right, maybe you've got a point. But I've busted my butt researching and interviewing contractors, and the Kavanaghs are highly respected in their field. Not to mention that they agreed to work at twenty percent below their usual rate in exchange for the publicity that being associated with the Wolcott mansion will bring them. So get over it! Your hard-on against drinkers is not going to screw this up for Ava and me. Or you, either, when it comes to that."

She could see that Poppy was genuinely angry, and that was a rare enough occurrence to make her swallow her ire and give a jerky nod. "Give me some damn breathing room," she muttered and Poppy stepped back.

Jane smoothed her clothes, brushed back the strands of hair that had slid free of her bun. Then she met her friend's eyes.

"Fine," she said grudgingly, "he stays. But if he

drinks on the job just once, I'm not accountable for my actions."

"Fair enough."

"I'm glad you think so. Because I'll be expecting you to help me bury the body."

"You wound me." Poppy pressed a hand to her breast. "After all, what are friends for?"

CHAPTER TWO

I will do a good job of this. Miss Agnes obviously thought I could—believed all three of us could—and nothing and NO ONE is going to stop me from doing my best.

"LOOKS LIKE you've got your work cut out for you."

Jane tensed, recognizing the voice. The fact that she did after only one meeting made her want to string several nasty words together. Instead she composed her expression and slowly turned.

Devlin Kavanagh, all hard-bodied male in a navy T-shirt, worn jeans and scuffed boots, lounged in the doorway to the Wolcott mansion parlor, his auburn hair gleaming beneath all the lights she'd turned on. Her heart started thundering in her chest and, propping her fists upon her hips, she slammed her mind closed against his appeal. "What do you want, Kavanagh?"

"Oh, that's friendly." Shoving away from the door frame, he tipped his head back, closed his eyes and with wide, sweeping movements touched first his right forefinger, then his left, then his right again to the tip of his nose. Snapping erect, he gave her a level look. "Look, Ma, I pass the sobriety test."

"For now. It remains to be seen how long it will last, though, doesn't it?"

Eyes narrowing to glints of golden green between dense dark lashes, he demanded, "What is your problem? I wasn't kidding the other night when I said I was jet-lagged. Maybe I shouldn't have knocked back those tequilas at the bar, but give me a break. I'd been up for a day and a half and they hit me harder than usual."

Mortification suffused her. Because he was right: she was being a judgmental bitch and it wasn't an attitude that set well with her. She didn't know this guy—it was hardly her place to criticize his actions. "My apologies," she said stiffly.

He made a skeptical sound. "Yeah, that sounds real sincere."

What the hell did he want from her? Her spine ached from holding herself so rigidly against the temptation to get close to him. She didn't understand this crazy attraction at all, but she knew one thing: she was stronger than a few stray hormones. Tipping her chin up, she looked him in the eye. "Then I apologize for that, as well. Your drinking issues are none of my business."

"Jesus, you don't give an inch, do you?"

"I said I was sorry!"

"In the most backhanded way I've ever heard. But you're right about one thing, sister. *If* I had drinking issues they'd be none of your business."

It was one thing for her to criticize herself and something else for him to do so. "Was there something you wanted, Mr. Kavanagh?"

"Dev."

She gave him an *"and?"* look.

"Call me Dev. Or Devlin if you insist on being formal. Mr. Kavanagh's my dad."

"Okay. Is there something I can do for you, Devlin?" She stooped to fiddle with the collection of Columbia River basketry at her feet.

"I'm trying to locate updated blueprints for the mansion. A few of the rooms look off but the place is over a hundred years old and unfortunately I don't have the originals, either. For all I know the joint is riddled with secret passages or other hidey-holes. I'd like to know what we're dealing with before we start tearing things apart, though, because hidden spaces might actually be a selling point, which Bren tells me is your ultimate objective."

The idea of a secret passage intrigued her, but she refused to be sidetracked. The sooner she got rid of Mr. I'm-too-sexy-for-my-boots the better. Yet instead of simply giving him a straight answer, she heard herself demand, "And you're asking me because…?"

"You appear to be the go-to girl for all the odds and ends around here. So would you happen to know where the blueprints are?"

"No, I'm sorry." And she truly was because the more information Kavanagh Construction had, the better the restoration was likely to turn out. And she'd love to see this old mansion fixed up the way it deserved to be. "I'm sure there's more than one set, but I honestly don't know where Miss Agnes kept them. All I know is that she told us Wolcott had been renovated several times. The last was when she had the interior done in 1985."

He nodded. "The year the Wolcott diamonds were stolen by her construction foreman."

Jane quit pretending to pay attention to the work

she should be doing and rose to her feet to face Devlin squarely. "You *know* about that?"

"Babe." He gave her a smile she'd bet her inheritance had gotten him into more than one woman's silkies. "I'm a Seattle boy. Those diamonds are an urban legend in this town. *Everyone* knows about them."

Well, she was a Seattle girl and— "I didn't. Not until recently. Miss Agnes never talked about their theft or the murder of her man Henry." She gave a shrug. "At least not before Poppy heard about it from someone and hounded her for the story." Her lips crooked at the memory. "Poppy can be a bit of a pit bull when she gets her teeth sunk into a subject."

He started to take a step into the room but must have noticed her stiffening, because he stopped where he was. Bracing a muscular shoulder against the doorjamb, he hooked his thumbs in his belt loops and studied her. "Henry, huh? Was that the business manager guy who was killed when the thief came back to recover the diamonds he'd hidden?"

"You're the expert, Seattle Boy."

"Hey, I was a kid when it all went down. I was interested in murder and mayhem but mostly fascinated by the idea of a multimillion-dollar set of jewelry still floating around somewhere."

"Yes, well, Henry was her man for all matters. He was her butler and secretary and advisor and I think probably her lov—" Jane cut herself off, appalled.

What was she doing? She'd already established she didn't know Devlin. And while assigning him dependency problems might have been jumping the gun a bit, there was no reason to offer him blanket trust, either. So why had she almost blurted out that she and her friends believed Henry had probably been more to Miss Agnes than a simple employee? It wasn't as if their mentor had admitted as much to them. But the way Agnes had looked when she'd talked about him and the fact he wasn't even supposed to have been there the night it was popularly believed that Maperton had broken in to retrieve the diamonds that had gone missing the year before, they had all sort of assumed Henry had probably been her lover as well as the man who kept her home and affairs running smoothly.

But she certainly didn't plan on cozying up to Devlin Kavanagh with the speculation.

"Well, listen." She gave him her best businesslike smile. "I have work to do. As I said, I really don't know where the blueprints may be. I'm not even sure any exist. But I will keep an eye out for them."

He looked at her for a moment, then stepped back, his hands shoved into his jeans pockets. "Thanks. I've got a partial set from the kitchen addition that was put on in 1909. I'll head downtown to see if King County records has the originals or any of the updates since then." He gave her a brief head-to-toe once-over, licked his bottom lip and nodded. "See ya around, Legs."

Legs? She stared from the now-empty doorway to the limbs in question, encased in plain old dark Levi's that she'd paired with a black blazer and a white shirt. She had fairly long legs, but they were certainly nothing to write home about. She'd always thought they were on the skinny side herself, which hardly qualified them as showgirl material.

Then she gave herself a mental shake and a stern directive to forget about it. But good grief. The man was a walking, talking Hazardous to Women zone. She imagined that with his confidence and those eyes and that body, females had been dropping at his feet since the day he hit puberty. Maybe even before.

Well, not her. As far she was concerned, he was Mr. Invisible from this point on. She was keeping her distance. Putting him out of her mind.

Getting her butt back to work.

Putting Miss Agnes's collections in order so she could start researching and cataloging them was a huge undertaking, and she was happy as a pig in a puddle at the prospect of getting her hands on them. At the same time she was a little daunted by the scope of the museum bequest, and she needed to get moving on it. She had never headed an undertaking of such scale before, and she was laboring under a deadline.

"So here the clock is ticking and I've been spinning like that Looney Tunes Tasmanian Devil all day long wasting time just trying to figure out *where* to start," she confessed to Ava when her friend dropped by to see how she was doing later that afternoon. "Then, too," she added wryly, "I keep getting caught up in the nostalgia of so many of the pieces—upshot of which is that I haven't actually started anywhere."

"Jane, Jane, Jane." Ava picked up a first-edition book, ran her fingers over the ancient leather binding, then carefully set the volume back on the shelf where she'd found it and looked up to pin Jane in place with her gaze. "It's a no-brainer. When in doubt, start with the jewels."

A startled laugh burst out of Jane and she gave her friend an impulsive hug. "You, Ms. Spencer, are a genius! I've been doing a bit of this and bit of that with all the collections, when I should be concentrating on the Met's stuff. The jewelry is an *excellent* place to start, since that's part of their haul." Grabbing up her slim Apple notebook, she started for the stairs. "Come on. I've got the codes for the safe in here. Let's go see what's in the vault."

It was almost 5:00 p.m. by the time Dev let himself back into the mansion. He probably should have called it a day and headed for the apartment his sister Maureen had rented for him in Belltown. But the skies had opened up, the place didn't feel like home yet and he'd just as soon build a fire in the little study up on the second floor, drink his Starbucks drip and listen to the rain bouncing off the windows while he went over the information he'd gathered from the County Assessor's office and the Department of Development and Environmental Services.

Not that it was much. Before 1936 the records that the Assessor's Office kept for buildings had been compiled in longhand on four-by-six-inch cards with lots of revisions and cross-outs and not a single photograph. Pretty much useless, in other words.

But luckily he'd been able to get a Flexcar from the share-a-ride program he belonged to, and more helpful were the photos taken of the mansion from the late thirties on, which he'd run to ground at the Washington State Archives at Bellevue Community College. They weren't as helpful as blueprints, but they'd at least help him get a handle on the timeline for the various so-called improvements that had been made to the Wolcott mansion.

He frowned as he took the stairs two at a time. Because whoever was responsible for the additions on this grand ole dame ought to be stuffed and mounted. He'd seen some bad do-it-yourself jobs in his day, but he'd never seen a place butchered quite as badly as this one. Few of the structural changes added over the years had been made with the original architecture in mind. And rooms that once must have been spacious and full of grace had been divided to the point they had conceded all personality.

So deep was he in thought about how to undo the damage that he'd nearly reached the study before he realized that feminine voices drifted out of it. He faltered to a stop.

Well…shit. So much for a little time to nurse his coffee in front of a fire.

He was turning away to head back to his apartment after all when the murmur of voices gave way to a woman's deep, raucous belly laugh. The sound cut through him like a hot sword and he found himself following it back to the doorway as if he were one of those old-time cartoon characters wafting in the wake of a beckoning scent.

Since it never occurred to him that little Miss Bug Up Her Butt Kaplinski could be the woman laughing like she'd just heard a deliciously dirty joke, his gaze zeroed in on the voluptuous redhead seated in profile to him across the room. Unless Ava was a ventriloquist, however, the sound wasn't coming from her. A slight smile curved her lips as she sat looking at her friend across the delicate oval coffee table. Dev turned his attention in that direction, as well.

Then he simply stood there feeling as if he'd taken a roundhouse kick to the head.

Jane sat on a velvet love seat perpendicular to the crackling fire, her high-heeled ankle boots tumbled in a heap on the floor and her argyle-stocking-clad feet crossed at the ankles and propped amidst a tumble of velvet boxes and bags on the little coffee table. More neatly arranged containers surrounded her and her left hand curled over the top of an open notebook computer, preventing it from tumbling off her lap while she laughed with her head thrown back as if she'd just heard the raunchiest, most amusing story ever.

It was the first time he'd seen her with her spine fully unbent since stumbling into her table at the bar the other night. Not that he had seen her more than three times total, but on the other two occasions her posture had been rebar rigid, as if she were some secret princess wondering how the hell she'd gotten cast into this world of commoners.

As he watched her start gaining control of herself, a corner of his mouth ticked up. Because the royalty analogy wasn't half-bad, considering she was wearing a queen's ransom in jewels.

She'd removed her blazer and rolled up her shirt-sleeves, and ropes of emeralds and pearls adorned her wrists, looped in strand after lustrous, glittering strand from her neck. A diamond tiara perched at the fore of her listing bun, a cascade of some jewel he didn't recognize swung from her ears and each finger sported a gem-encrusted ring.

Ava was similarly decked out, but he barely spared her a second glance. Adorned with only a couple of select pieces, she had the look of someone who'd been born wearing this stuff. Jane looked like a little girl playing dress-up. And given her sober-puss personality he'd bet a position on the next America's Cup yacht—which, okay, he didn't actually have to wager—that she hadn't played a lot of little-girl games even when she'd been one.

"Your turn," she said, and Ava bent forward to pick one of the velvet containers from the table between them. The redhead's hand suddenly halted midreach, however, and she turned her head in his direction. He had a nanosecond, as their gazes connected, to wish he'd stepped out of sight while he'd still had the chance.

Then she inclined her head and said easily, "Hey, Dev."

Jane's head whipped around and she yanked her feet off the table so fast that several boxes and bags tumbled to the floor. Swearing beneath her breath, she bent to pick them up and her tiara tipped over one eye. She snatched the little crown from her head as hot color flowed up her throat. A minuscule comb that still anchored the tiara on one side ripped a hank of slippery hair free and it unfurled down to the corner of her mouth.

Blowing it off her face, she snapped upright to perch with that ramrod posture on the edge of the velvet seat. Raising her chin, she met his gaze. "Devlin."

He clicked his boot heels together and gave her a clipped bow. "Your highness." Okay, it was a cheap shot. But when the universe handed you an opportunity on a silver platter it was practically kicking karma in the teeth to ignore it. He swallowed a grin.

"What can we do for you, Devlin?" Ava asked.

"Huh?" He pulled his gaze away from Jane's flushed face and looked at her friend. "Oh. Nothing. I was going to build a fire and go over some photos of the mansion that I picked up at the state archives today, but I didn't realize the room was already occupied."

Straightening, the redhead extended an imperious hand. "Let's see them."

He crossed the room and handed her the manila envelope. Taking it, she patted the love seat next to her with her free hand. "Sit."

"Stay," Jane said in the same commanding-the-dog tone, and Dev looked at her in surprise. What the hell— did the woman have a sense of humor after all?

She returned his searching look with a bland one of her own and, rolling his shoulders, he sat down next to Ava. Nah. Probably not.

Ava started to pour the envelope's contents into her lap, but he clamped his fingers over the opening to stay her. "Don't dump 'em—reach in and pull them out," he directed when she bent a queenly look of her own on him. "I'd just as soon not go to the trouble of putting them in order twice."

She did as he bid and a soft sound of pleasure escaped her when she looked at the topmost photograph. "Oh, this is wonderful. Janie, come see what the place looked like before that awful sunroom was added."

Somewhat to his surprise, Jane complied, setting aside her computer and rising to her feet. He felt Ava shift and once again she patted the cushion next to her.

"Scoot over here," she commanded him. "We'll put you in the middle so we can all see."

He felt rather than saw Jane hesitate. But perhaps that was his imagination, because a second later she lowered herself next to him.

On a really small love seat. Now, normally he'd say being sandwiched between a couple of babes on a piece of furniture built for two was a good thing. For some damn reason, however, this was making him edgy as hell. "Uh, I don't think this love seat was designed with three people in mind." Aware of Jane's warmth all along his left side, he added, "Especially when one of us has such impressively curvy hips."

Okay, that didn't come out real suave, even though Ava did indeed have killer hips that cut down on the seating space. Still, he wasn't prepared for both women to freeze on either side of him. And he sure as hell wasn't prepared for the redhead to turn an expressionless face his way and demand with chill civility, "Am I taking up too much room, Devlin?"

"What? No! That's not what I meant at all. I just—" *What, genius?* The truth was, he hadn't been using his head at all, he'd simply rattled off the first excuse that popped to mind in order to get out from between the two. And now his brain, normally facile and quick around the opposite sex, was drawing a big, fat blank.

Jane's breast flattened against his biceps as she craned around to see her friend. "He said 'impressively curvy,' Av. *Curvy.* Not fat."

He jerked in shock and stared down at her for the first time since she'd squeezed in next to him. "Of course I didn't say fat! Jesus. No man in his right mind is going to look at her and think that. Hell, she's built like a walking wet dream." The blue eyes he was staring into widened and he felt like smacking himself in the head. *What the fuck is the matter with you, Dev? You had more savoir faire when you were nine.*

Except it appeared he'd actually said something right, because he felt Ava relax next to him even as Jane smiled slightly and said, "Damn straight she is. And it's your shoulders, Slick, not Ava's hips, that are taking up all the space."

"No, it's probably my hips." Ava handed him the photos with a rueful smile. "I apologize, Dev. I didn't mean to freak on you. I was a fat kid, and I still have a few issues with my weight."

You *think?* With three sisters, one might reasonably imagine he had an inkling into the female mind, but he didn't have a clue. So he merely said, "Well, you shouldn't. There's not a man I know who wouldn't kill to get his hands on a body like yours."

Yet it wasn't Ava who commanded his awareness as the three of them pored over the photographs. It didn't make a lick of sense, but it was Jane who kept capturing his attention.

She might have a chilly personality, but as he'd already noted, the girl pumped out some serious body heat. He felt it radiating along his entire left side and had to peel himself free for a moment to set his coffee on the table. It was hard juggling the cup and the photos in these cramped quarters anyhow, and at this point he didn't need any additional heat from the inside, as well. He was plenty hot.

Plenty. Hot.

Shit.

He focused on Jane's unvarnished fingernails. They were bitten to the quick. It wasn't very big of him, but it gave him a little surge of pleasure all the same. Hah. Maybe she wasn't as aggressively confident as she appeared.

But she had skin like a baby. Not that he could see a hell of a lot of it—she was buttoned up from stem to stern. Still, he couldn't help but notice its soft texture when their fingers brushed as they exchanged photographs. Or how her bared forearms shone more luminous than the pearls twined around them.

He shifted uncomfortably. What the fuck was going on here? This was so not like him. He'd had more women over the years than you could shake a stick at, and he was a sailor and a carpenter, for cri'sake—he didn't think in words like *luminous*.

"Well, hey." He pried himself from between the two females and rose to his feet. "My eyes are starting to cross—I think I'm going to take off. I still haven't caught up with the jet lag. I need to hit the sack."

More like hit a bar and pick up a woman, he thought as he gathered his pictures, said his goodbyes and dashed through the rain to his car a few moments later after letting himself out of the mansion. Someone with cleavage, smiles and red lips. And nails long enough to drag down his back. Someone who'd look at him like he was the hottest stud to swagger down the pike, instead of a lush who was one drink away from oblivion.

Only…

Instead of heading out to one of Belltown's night

spots when he reached his apartment house, he took a shower and went to bed.

Tomorrow, though. Tomorrow night he'd go out and find himself a woman. Because clearly if he was getting all hot under the collar over uptight, disapproving little Jane Kaplinski, it had been *way* too long since he'd gotten laid.

CHAPTER THREE

*Sex is overrated. I for one can live just fine with-
out it. Really.*

JANE SAT in the Wolcott parlor the next evening typing
annotations into her notebook computer for a meeting
with the museum director the following morning. Instead of focusing all her attention on the report, however,
she found her thoughts constantly drifting to a certain
buff redheaded man.

What was it about Devlin Kavanagh, anyway? This
inability to concentrate whenever he popped to mind—
which was far too often for comfort—was ridiculous,
not to mention unprecedented.

Well, there was some precedent, she supposed. It
wasn't as if she'd never been attracted to other men before, because naturally she had.

But not like this. Never had she been drawn to a guy
in such an I-gotta-have-him, out-of-control sort of way.

And *that* was the problem in a nutshell. Because she
didn't do out of control. Having grown up in a household
that was always verging on or in the midst of some sort
of drama, she'd made a firm decision about that before
she was even ten years old.

What had she ever done to deserve parents who were
actors? All she'd ever wanted was a nice, normal family,

but had she gotten one? Oh, no. God was no doubt up in heaven slapping his knee at the thought of the Dorrie and Mike Show he'd sent her instead. It was unfair, that's what it was. Her parents didn't have simple differences of opinion; they had wars, crises of epic proportions. Which she almost could have lived with—had they just *once* not tried to drag her smack-dab into the middle of them.

So, no. She didn't do out of control.

Which ought to make matters simpler now, right? Except somehow this didn't feel simple. And she didn't understand why she was having so much trouble with this particular guy.

"Crap." She stared at her computer screen in frustration. "I have *got* to get a grip."

"Well, this doesn't bode well if the job already has you talking to yourself."

She gave an involuntary start, then scowled at Poppy as her friend strolled into the room. "Jeez, give me a heart attack, why don't you." Even if it was her own damn fault for allowing a man to distract her to the point where someone could sneak up on her.

"Sorry," Poppy said without noticeable contrition. "So *is* it the job that's making you carry on conversations with yourself?"

"I wish," she muttered. "That would be so much easier." Then she gave herself a mental head slap. *Shut up, Kaplinski. Shut up, shut up, shut up.* She wasn't ready to spill her guts, and until she was she knew better than to give Poppy even an inkling that she might have a secret.

But of course it was too late. Because as she'd told Devlin just yesterday, Poppy was a pit bull once she sank her teeth into something. Already her friend, who looked deceptively soft and pliable with her curly blond hair, big brown eyes and today's floaty hippie-dippy-girl clothing, had Jane firmly in the crosshairs of the dreaded Calloway Evil Eye. "Spill," she commanded.

And like a leaky old oil tanker in a pristine harbor, she did just that. "I think I've gone and fallen face-first in lust."

"Ooh." Poppy plopped down on a nearby chair and wiggled her fingers in a gimme gesture. "Tell sister everything. And don't skimp on the details."

"Me. In lust. That is everything. There are no details, Pop, because there's nothing to tell."

Poppy pursed her lips to blow a skeptical *pffffft*. "Please. We're talking sexual attraction. Pounding hearts. Jingly-jangly nerve endings. Am I right?"

Oh, man. Was she ever. Jane nodded.

"Then of course there's something to tell. When it comes to all things sexy there is *always* something to tell."

"Not this time."

Poppy gave her an indignant look. "Why the hell not?"

"Hey, just because I have certain urges doesn't mean I have to act on them. So I haven't—and I don't intend to." She saved the file she'd been working on and shut down her computer, gazing at her friend over its closing lid. "It's a random case of lust. I plan to get over it."

"Why would you want to?" Poppy blinked, clearly puzzled. "Lust is a good thing, right? I mean, it leads to sex, and sex makes you feel good. Not that I'd know from personal experience," she added virtuously.

"Of course not. You've only been disclaiming personal experience since you first misinformed Ava and me about sex back when we were nine." She gave her friend a lopsided smile. "The only difference being that you really were a total innocent then."

"What do you mean, misinformed? I was always first with the true scoop, and you know it."

"Please. Babies are made when you swap spit with a boy?"

"Oh. Yeah. That. Damn Karen Copelli's sister. I thought for sure she was a reliable source. After all, she was an older woman."

"I know. She must have been all of twelve, which made her a helluva lot nearer to being an honest-to-god teenager than the three of us. I gotta tell you, though, after hearing that spit thing I figured I'd probably never, ever have babies. Because, *ew*."

Poppy grinned. "Yeah, it didn't sound real appealing, did it? Luckily, actual kissing turned out to be so much cooler."

"Not that you'd know from personal experience."

"Of course not," she agreed with a serene smile, then brushed the topic aside with a long-fingered wave of her hand. "But we're not talking about me, Jane. So don't go changing the subject."

"Yes, let's. Let's change it to something else entirely."

"Okay then, how about this? Maybe what you're feeling isn't actually lust at all."

She considered the possibility for, oh, two full seconds before giving a definitive nod. "Trust me. It's lust." A big, fat, flaming-hot case of it. "Or, okay, I suppose it could be heartburn."

Her friend practiced the selective deafness that made her such a formidable meddler-with-a-mission and said with a perfectly straight face, "Maybe it was really a case of love at first sight."

"Uh-huh. Because everyone knows *that's* not a great big fairy tale, or anything."

"Hey, it worked for my parents. And Ava's mom and dad might be sort of benignly neglectful in the parental department, but look how long they've been married."

"I always sort of assumed that was because there was too much money involved to go through the hassle of getting a divorce. But maybe not. They do seem to do a lot of stuff together."

"See? The world is simply lousy with True Love stories. So tell me your guy's name and maybe I can help you figure out how to handle the situation."

"I've figured it out for myself, thank you very much. It's pretty simple, really." She gave Poppy a level look. "I'm handling it by not doing anything at all."

"That's a *horrible* game plan."

"Yet all mine."

"Tell me, Jane-Jane."

"You don't really want to go there with that name— Pop-Pop."

"*Tell* me."

"No."

Poppy treated her to another Calloway Evil Eye. This time, however, Jane wasn't about to budge and she shot the Kaplinski version right back at her.

Her blonde friend studied her for a moment. Then she gave a clipped nod. "Oh, all right. But you know I'll get it out of you sooner or later. I don't know why you don't just save us all some trouble and tell me now."

"I've never minded a little trouble."

"In what universe, pray tell?"

She merely gave the other woman her best inscrutable smile.

"Fine." Poppy heaved a disgruntled sigh. "Be that way. I didn't come here to see you, anyway. Ava told me Dev has some great photos from the Washington State archives. Have you seen him today?"

Jane's heart kicked hard, then commenced to gallop in her chest. Luckily, Poppy was busy glancing around as if she expected her question to make him magically appear and didn't notice her expression. Good thing, because Jane was pretty sure it would render the question about who she was lusting over obsolete.

She managed to compose her features in the moment it took Poppy to turn her attention back to her. "No, I haven't. Considering all the clomping around I've heard from up in the sunroom this afternoon, though, I'm gonna take a wild stab and guess he's upstairs."

Poppy studied her a moment. "Tell me you're not still holding on to that ridiculous grudge because he knocked back a few too many tequilas last week."

"Hey, I'll have you know I'm being incredibly open-minded. Of course, it doesn't hurt that he was sober when I saw him yesterday. Or that those footsteps I mentioned sounded fairly steady." Or the fact she'd already decided she'd been a bit precipitous passing judgment.

"Dammit, Jane! You have got to stop this judgmental shit, because I swear if you louse this up for us—"

"Oh, get a grip, I haven't done anything to upset your

precious arrangement with Kavanagh Construction. As a matter of fact, I was the epitome of professionalism with him yesterday—and if you don't believe me, just ask Ava." Who luckily hadn't been around during her afternoon conversation with Devlin. "Not that I can swear she was actually paying attention, mind you. She was pretty jazzed about those photos."

The mention of which diverted Poppy's attention. "Av said you saw them, too?"

"I did, and they're every bit as great as she's undoubtedly told you."

"Hot damn. I'm gonna go find Devlin and see for myself." She started toward the doorway.

"I'll catch you later, then," Jane said to her friend's retreating back. "I'm going to call it a day and head home." Where she intended to put Devlin out of her mind once and for all and buckle down to finish her report.

Poppy paused to look back over her shoulder. "Hang around for another fifteen minutes. We can go grab some dinner."

She hesitated for a second, not sure she wanted to go another round defending her right to keep a few thoughts to herself. But visualizing her almost empty refrigerator and even sparser cupboards, she nodded. "Sounds like a plan to me."

"Okay, then, I'll be back in a few." She raised her brows. "Unless you wanna come up with me?"

Jane managed not to screech, *"Are you out of your freakin' mind?"* Her face even felt halfway composed when she said coolly, "No, you go ahead. We'll probably get to eat a lot sooner if only one of us is drooling over the pics. And this will give me a chance to get a little more done on my report."

"Okay, then. I won't be long."

"Hey, take your time." She didn't mind waiting. As long as she didn't have to endure any face-to-face time with The Incredible Radiating Pheromone Man, she was perfectly happy to have Poppy take just as long as her little heart desired.

SHORTLY AFTER NOON the following day, Jane left the staff room at the Seattle Metropolitan Museum. She was slightly dazed, yet at the same time completely wired. Her meeting with Marjorie earlier this morning had gone well. She'd expected no less, since she had prepared for it last night with her usual overachiever obsessiveness, working from the time she got home from dinner until a case of scorched-earth eyeballs had forced her to close down her Mac shortly after midnight. Being in her own tidy little Belltown condo had helped her finally shove Mr. Too-hot-for-his-britches Kavanagh out of her mind, which in turn had allowed her to polish up her report until it shone and pore over her notes until she had all the major points in her presentation memorized.

Someone a little more laid-back might have skimped on their report, given that the only condition of Miss Agnes's jewelry and couture-clothing-for-the-ages bequest to the Met was that Jane be the one to catalog the two collections. After all, it wasn't as if Marjorie could yank the job out from under her and pass it along to someone with more seniority. Well, she could, of course. She was the director; she could do whatever she pleased.

But she couldn't do so and have the museum keep the collections.

The notion was moot, anyhow. Jane wasn't laid-back. Preparation was her middle name and she simply could not, in all good conscience, give her superior a half-assed report.

The opportunity that Miss Agnes, bless her heart, had provided her wasn't something Jane took for granted. This was going to make her instantly more visible in the art community. Everyone was going to be taking a closer look at her now, and if she handled this assignment right it would catapult her career beyond anything she might have imagined for this stage of it. She'd have a real shot at Paul Rompaul's position as full-fledged curator when he retired next October. With all her heart she appreciated the boost this bequest had given her and she intended to repay Agnes's faith in her abilities by doing the very best job she could.

So yes, she had been prepared, and therefore the success of her meeting with the director had not come as a major surprise.

What had knocked her socks off was the sheet cake bearing Congratulations, Jane in ruby-colored frosting that had been in the staff room at lunch today. Even more shocking had been the special announcement that Marjorie had given the staff. She'd freely credited Jane with bringing two valuable Wolcott collections to the Seattle Metropolitan Museum. The genuine enthusiasm that the director displayed as she'd shared Jane's newly revised schedule for the next couple of months in order to get them ready for the January exhibit had blown her away.

The last thing she'd been prepared for was public

kudos. In fact, she'd half expected the change in her status to fly under the radar for as long as the powers that be could manage it, given the way it had been forced upon them.

Want these prestigious collections? Then be prepared to take the junior curator along with it was the general theme of Agnes's bequest.

Along with Marjorie's acknowledgment, however, had come her expectations for this exhibit. She'd talked about how much the museum was counting on it to generate needed revenue during the traditionally slow postholiday period in which they'd slated the show. So now Jane was feeling downright twitchy and even more anxious than she'd already been. She had to find the couture clothing, pronto, and get a move on.

"Jane, Jane! Wait up!" a voice commanded from behind her.

She hesitated. Today's events had both rattled and exhilarated her, making her so jittery that simply standing still was very nearly impossible. Still, she forced herself to do exactly that as she waited for her colleague Gordon Ives to catch up.

Gritting her teeth at the delay, she forced a smile for Gordon that probably wouldn't fool a toddler. Hell, she doubtless *looked* like a toddler doing the I-gotta-go dance in front of a closed bathroom door. How embarrassing was that?

Well, too bad. She was fighting the urge to move, move, move as hard as she could. Smiling brilliantly at the same time was simply beyond her.

She tried all the same for a more genuine smile as

Gordon walked up to her. Memories of Marjorie's graciousness helped her produce one.

"I've said it before, girl, but I'll say it again." Gordon greeted her with a big white-veneered smile of his own. "Congratulations! What a huge job you have ahead of you."

"No kidding. The past couple days I've been finding out exactly how immense it's going to be." Which contributed to both her edginess and her elation. "I'm a little concerned about the deadline the director's put me on. I'm going to have to be really focused to get everything done in that time frame."

"Focus is your claim to fame." He waved her worries aside like so many pesky flies. "Obviously Marjorie has no doubt that you can do the job and do it both well and on time. But if there's anything *I* can do—"

She made a noncommittal noise, because the truth be told, if she needed help she'd probably enlist Poppy. Her friend might not be as knowledgeable as Gordon, but they worked well together. Not to mention that with the holidays approaching, Poppy could probably use a little extra cash to round out what she made with her mishmash of jobs.

Besides, as much as she hated to admit it, there was something about Gordon that she didn't quite trust. There was no good reason for it—he'd never done anything to her. It was probably nothing more than his wanna-be-your-best-friend occasional toadying combined with his predilection for narcissistic metrosexual grooming. Because, really, who could take a guy seriously who spent more on manicures and moisturizers in six weeks than she did in a year? She couldn't help it; she preferred men who had a firm grasp on their identity—and were perhaps just the slightest bit rough around the edges.

Like a certain construction foreman...

Whoops. Didn't want to go there. "Thank you for the good wishes. And if I decide I need help I'll definitely keep you in mind." She started edging away.

"Are you on your way over to the Wolcott mansion now?" he asked, taking a step forward for her every step back.

"Yes." She quit trying to be subtle about it and simply started walking down the corridor. The nerves zinging in her arms and legs immediately quieted, but she had to smooth out a frown drawing her eyebrows together when Gordon fell into step beside her. She picked up her pace slightly.

He matched his stride to hers. "If you want, I could stop by after work sometime and give you a hand."

She was a bit startled by the suggestion, but said carefully, "Thank you, Gordon, I appreciate the offer. But I'm still in the sorting phase and kind of want to—" Damn. How did she say this without sounding like little Miss Greedy-guts?

"Stamp your brand all over it before you let anyone else touch it?"

"Yes! Exactly." She looked at him in a new light. And felt a little guilty for her heretofore less-than-flattering opinion of him. Guy grooming products and facials be damned, he obviously had more depth to him than she'd given him credit for. "I will definitely keep your offer in mind, though. Right now there's just so much stuff in the mansion that I haven't even found the Met's collections yet."

"Huh. I'd say poor baby, but the truth is, I'm pea-green with envy." He gave her a crooked smile. "And green is so not my color."

She laughed. "Not exactly a big candidate for sympathy, am I? Man, I still can't believe that I get to be in charge of all this, myself. Speaking of which—" she accelerated her pace to a full-out stride "—if I want to start whittling away at my workload I'd better get to it."

"All right then." He slowed down as she sped up. "Good luck. And don't forget I'm available if you ever need any help."

"I will." She waved a hand, but didn't slow down as she hit the door to the stairs. "Thanks." Feeling kind of warm and fuzzy toward him at the moment, she truly meant it.

By the time she'd pushed through the main museum doors into the blustery fall afternoon a few minutes later, however, her mind was already on other matters. Anticipation began bubbling through her veins.

She could hardly wait to get to work.

CHAPTER FOUR

Holy crap, the Kavanagh family sounds huge. I can't wrap my mind around what it must be like to grow up with a mess of brothers and sisters. Bet it was nice, though.

"DAMN," DEV MUTTERED as he opened the kitchen door to the Wolcott mansion two evenings later and stepped inside to punch the code into the alarm system. "I see *mistake* written all over this in big red letters." Not for the first time he noted the system's advanced age, but shrugged it aside. Its obsolescence was the Estrogen Posse's problem. Right now, he had one of his own.

"Oh, quit your bitching," his problem, in the form of his sister Hannah, ordered. Entering the kitchen hard on his heels, she snapped the back of his head with her fingers.

"Ow! Shit."

"If you'd bothered to stay around for longer than a week at a pop during any of your less-than-frequent visits, you'd know I check out every work site at least once during the project."

Rubbing the spot she'd smacked, he glared at her. "You're just as full of crap as ever, I see. Try to get your facts straight. I come home a minimum of once a year, which is a lot more often than you come to see me. And except for last year when I had to get back to crew a boat to Morocco I always stick around for longer than a week." Before heading back home happy to have seen his family, but feeling vaguely disconnected from them, as well.

"Haven't spent a helluva lot of that time at the work sites, though, have you?" Then she ignored him to look around the kitchen. "Man, I've lost count of the number of times this mansion was discussed around the dinner table. It's kind of like suddenly coming face-to-face with Elvis."

"Except this legend actually has the potential to be brought back to life."

She inspected the worn early-twentieth-century black-and-white harlequin tiles on the floor and the seventies-era avocado appliances. "It's definitely going to need work to revive it, though." She headed for the doorway leading into the rest of the house.

"Hey, wait a minute." He charged after her, only to discover her disappearing into the dining room across the hall. She was already thumbing notes into her Black-Berry as he entered the room behind her.

"Whoever put that scalloping around the windows ought to be shot," she said. "This place has beautiful old bones and they've dressed it up in tacky froufrous."

"The entire house is full of crap like that," he agreed.

"May I help you?" inquired a voice behind them, in a tone that suggested they better have a damn good reason for being here.

Swallowing a curse, Dev slowly turned, already knowing who he'd see.

Sure enough, Jane stood in the doorway, clad in a pair

of black leggings beneath a short, high-necked, black-and-brown tunic. That in turn was layered beneath a skinny black sweater with its sleeves shoved up and its tails looped into a loose knot beneath her round little A cups.

Dark, concealing clothing seemed to be her signature—except on her feet again. This time she wore a pair of yellow velvet slippers sporting extravagant puffs of marabou. They were incongruously cheerful—the frown furrowing her slender brows looked more at home than they did.

"Oh. It's you," she said without enthusiasm when she recognized him. "I heard voices and…"

Cutting herself off, she shook her head. "Never mind." She glanced at Hannah, who hadn't stepped foot outside the door a day in her life since she turned thirteen without her makeup and clothing set on stun, then looked back at him again. Her frown, which had started to lessen, settled firmly back in place. "For heaven's sake. Are you bringing your girlfriends here now?"

"Hell, yeah." Pissed that she always jumped to the worst possible conclusion when it came to him, he crossed the space separating them and didn't stop until they stood toe-to-toe. Without her usual high heels she wasn't nearly as tall as he'd believed her to be.

The observation had squat to do with the topic at hand, however, and he shoved it aside. "Han here is hot for old houses, so I'm just giving her a quick tour of the first floor to warm her up before we go upstairs to pull the shades down and rip off a piece. You got a problem with that, Legs?"

"In my house, on my dollar?" Eyes glowing bluer

than natural-gas-fed flames, she held her ground, not the least bit intimidated by his proximity. "Yes. I guess you could say I have a problem. And that's aside from your date's poor taste in men."

Hannah laughed. "She's got you there, boyo." Stepping forward, she thrust her hand out at Jane, forcing him to back up. "I'm Hannah. Dev's sister."

"Meet Jane Kaplinski, Han," he said sardonically. "Resident conclusion jumper."

"Oh." Hot color flowed beneath Jane's fine-grained skin. "Oh, crap. My apologies."

He noticed her request for forgiveness was directed solely at Hannah, whom Jane checked out thoroughly as they shook hands.

"You don't look anything alike," she said. As if that was a defensible excuse.

"I know," Hannah said cheerfully, tossing back her dark wavy hair. "Finn and Bren and Maureen and I take after Da's side of the family. David and Dev take after Mom's, except David got light brown hair. Kate's a blend. She has Dev's coloring but looks more like… well, no one, really. Da says the postman, but he's just pulling our legs."

"We think," he added.

Jane, as usual, missed the humor entirely. She stared at Hannah unblinkingly. "You have *six* siblings?"

"She can count," he marveled.

Hannah jabbed her elbow into his ribs. "Yep. What can I say? We're both Irish and Catholic. That's pretty well synonymous with big family."

"I'm an only child," Jane replied. "And my two best friends are, as well, so I can't even imagine growing up with that many brothers and sisters. Wow." She glanced back and forth between the two of them. "That must have been…"

When she hesitated as if at a loss for words, Hannah supplied, "Kinda loud, kinda crazy."

"Completely lacking in privacy," he contributed. "Not to mention intrusive as hell." He hadn't dropped out of the UDub and set sail for Europe at the tender age of nineteen for nothing.

"Oh, no." Jane shook her head. "I was going to say nice. It must have been really comforting—you know?—to have all that built-in support."

He snorted. "Boy, you *are* an only child if you believe that." He for one had been tired of all the noise and drama of big-family life, where everyone and his brother knew his business. He'd just wanted to go somewhere where he would be judged strictly on his own merits and not compared for once in his life to his brothers or to his family as a whole.

"Shut up, Dev." Hannah narrowed her eyes at him. "You might wanna note you're the only one who ran away from home. The rest of us actually do find family support comforting."

"Ran away, Han? *You* might want to dial down the melodrama a notch." He hadn't *run;* he'd judiciously removed himself from a situation that had a bad habit of making him feel constantly at odds with his family.

Hannah made a derisive you-are-so-full-of-it-I'm-amazed-your-eyes-aren't-brown noise in her throat.

Refusing to get into this with her again, he shrugged and leveled his attention on Jane. Hell, she'd brought the subject up in the first place and was probably just jerk-

ing their chain with that whole *must be nice* bullshit—
no doubt just to piss him off.

Except…

She appeared totally sincere. In fact she looked all
sort of soft and wistful-eyed, as if they lived some sort
of perfect existence. And he didn't like it one damn bit.

The funny tug it caused deep down in his gut bugged
the hell out of him.

"What are you looking at?" she demanded.

Her irritated tone chopped the funny feeling in two
and, with a mental *Thank you, sweetheart,* he shot her
his best Son of Satan grin. "You, short stuff. I was just
thinking you look like a little girl with her nose pressed
up against the candy-store window."

"I look nothing of the sort!" She took an incensed
step toward him, her chin shooting up into what he was
starting to consider her default mode. As usual, the sudden movement caused a hank of shiny hair to slide free
of her bun and slither down her throat.

And another of those odd feelings hit him, this time
making his palms itch.

His innate common sense blown to hell, he took a
Mother-May-I-worthy giant step closer, bringing them
once more mere inches from each other. Whipping a
hand out, he liberated the two combs still holding together the remainder of her crooked topknot.

"Hey!" She made a grab for them as her hair tumbled
free. "Give those back!"

Dev tossed the combs into the largest of a group of
leather bowls sitting on a nearby sideboard, then grasped
her forearm to prevent her from going after them when
she started to muscle her way past him. Why, he couldn't

say, considering he already regretted the impulse that had caused him to muss her up. The dark waterfall of hair slinking over one eye and draping her shoulders gave her an entirely different look.

One he had a feeling he'd be better off not seeing.

"Why the hell do you even bother putting your hair up?" he demanded. "It's not like it ever stays there—every damn time I've seen it, it's been half-down."

"What are you, a closet hairdresser?" She tugged against his light grasp. "Let go of me."

His fingers tightened. "Make m—"

"O-kay," Hannah said. "I think it's time you and I took off, Dev. Jane, it was nice meeting you. Love your yellow slippers, by the way. They're *très* sexy."

Jane blinked as if she'd forgotten Hannah was even there, then glanced down at her feet. "Oh, no, they're just—" Chopping off her protest, she cleared her throat. "That is, thank you. They're more comfortable than my heels for all the backing and forthing I do here."

"Not to mention gorgeous. Well, listen, I hope to see you again. I'd also like to come back another time to inspect the property. I try to do that with every Kavanagh job in order to get an idea of the scope of the work for scheduling, and also to add the female perspective. *Most* of my brothers," she said, shooting him a look, "seem to appreciate that. Next time, however, I'll make an appointment for a time when I won't be inconveniencing you."

Which is exactly what I tried to tell you to do in the first place. Dev turned Jane loose, wondering what the hell had just happened. Jesus. He didn't go around grabbing women. And had he really said *make me?* He rubbed his palm down the outer seam of his jeans, trying to erase the sensation of her soft skin imprinted on it. "Maybe during one of the mornings," he muttered. "She's not around then."

Jane didn't so much as glance in his direction. "*You're* welcome anytime," she told his sister. "Just don't bring him with you."

"Listen, lady—" He took a hot step forward, self-recrimination suddenly nothing but a mushroom cloud on the horizon. Don't bring him, his ass. He *worked* here.

Hannah wrapped both hands around his left biceps and tugged him toward the door. "See you around, Jane."

A damp gust of wind slapped him in the face as his sister hauled him through the kitchen door into the blustery evening. He pulled free of her grasp, looking at her warily. "I'm good. I'm not going to pop her or anything."

"You hitting her never even entered my mind." Stabbing the remote keyless entry button to unlock her car, Hannah stalked around its hood. "Man, I have seen some crazy excuses for foreplay in my life, but you two take the cake."

He froze in the midst of reaching for the passenger door handle to stare at her across the roof. *"What?"*

"Oh, that's good. You oughtta be an actor." She shook her head at him. "Please. I almost called 911. If there'd been any more heat pumping off the two of you the house would have burned to the ground."

A short, sharp laugh escaped him. "And you're supposed to be the smart one in the family."

"No, that would be Kate."

Ignoring her reply, he yanked the door open and climbed in, then glared at his sister across the console when she followed suit. "Don't confuse heat with irritation, sis. Jane Kaplinski is a cranky little crow who hasn't hesitated to think the worst of me from the instant we first clapped eyes on each other." Well, not from the *very* first instant, he admitted to himself, recalling the look in her eyes when their gazes had originally connected.

Now *that* had been heat.

"Yeah, I heard you got clumsy drunk." She started the engine and pulled out of the driveway.

"Of course you did. No such thing as a secret in the Clan Kavanagh."

"Never has been, never will be," she agreed cheerfully.

He had given up defending his actions years ago, yet he found himself twisting in his seat now to face his sister. He'd always been closest to her and Finn, both in age and interests. "I was seriously jet-lagged that night, Han. Then Da poured me a couple of strong ones at my homecoming, and the drinks I had on top of them at the bar with Bren and David and Finn hit me harder than usual."

"That seems to be the general consensus, all right."

He laughed without humor. "And you wonder why I've spent my adult life on the other side of the world. Don't you ever get tired of everyone in the family knowing every move you make, practically every thought you think?"

"No." Braking at the stop sign to Queen Anne Avenue, she reached over to pinch his cheek. "Ach, but then I'm a tough little hazelnut. Our Devlin, now, he's a sensitive boyo."

He couldn't help it, he grinned. "You ever let Aunt Eileen catch you imitating her?"

"Do I strike you as the suicidal type?" She looked both ways before turning left down the steep hill. Then she shot him a glance that was wiped free of humor. "This is a huge opportunity for us, Dev. Don't screw it up."

"There's nothing between me and Kaplinski to screw it up with!"

She shot him a disbelieving look.

"There isn't," he insisted. "But even if there were, I wouldn't do anything to mess up your business opportunity, okay?"

"It's your business too, you know."

No, it wasn't. The minute Bren's cancer went into remission and he was strong enough to return to work Dev had every intention of heading back to the Continent. He'd made a life for himself there crewing sailboats and picking up construction work in his downtime—which was increasingly rare these days.

"Anyhow," she added when he didn't comment aloud, "I guess deep down I already know you'd never jeopardize our livelihood."

He pulled a face. "Sure you do."

"No, really. I may no longer know you the way I used to, but the Dev I got into trouble with back in the day would never deliberately do anything to mess up his family—no matter how crazy they drive him."

They crossed Denny Way a while later, leaving the Queen Anne district behind and entering Belltown. She let him out on Second and he crossed the street to the Noodle Ranch, where he ordered Spicy Basil stir-fry to go and a beer to stay. Taking his drink to a nearby table, he sipped from the bottle and thumbed through a copy of *The Stranger* while he waited for his order. The personals in the alternative weekly newspaper were always good for killing some time.

His mind, however, was apparently more interested in wandering back to what Hannah had said about him and Jane than reading about nerdy punk girls searching for passionate dominates. She saw their constant clashing as foreplay? That was just plain nuts, right? Maybe his sister had taken to snorting illegal substances in his absence.

Yeah, right. He took a deep pull on his beer. That being such a likely possibility and all.

Still. It was no more absurd than her theory.

"One order of Spicy Basil to go," the counterman called out.

He rose to his feet with alacrity, more than happy to shitcan the entire line of thinking. He reached the counter just as a woman wearing a black coat, leggings and high-heeled boots did, and they both reached for the to-go bag at the same time. His hand slid across hers. And he felt...

Warm skin.

Smelled...

Scented hair.

Aw, shit. The scent might not have implanted itself already in his mind, but he knew that skin.

Jane looked over her shoulder at him, and if he hadn't felt so blindsided himself he might have smiled at the perfectly round *O* her lips formed when she saw who was wrestling her for the Spicy Basil. Then she narrowed her eyes, giving him her Psycho Bitch From Hell look.

"Oh, for God's sake." She slowly pivoted to face him head-on and her hair, which she still wore down, gleamed beneath the restaurant's lights as it spilled over her coat collar. "Are you *following* me now?" She tugged on the take-out bag beneath their hands.

"Don't flatter yourself, babe." He didn't relinquish his hold on her or the sack. "I was here first, and those are my noodles you've got your greedy little fingers all over."

"You wish. I live in this area—it makes sense for *me* to be here."

"Yeah? Well, so do I. So I guess you must be following me."

His thumb stroked her hand. *Damn,* she was touchable.

He grimaced. Where the hell did this shit keep coming from? She was bad-tempered and judgmental and except for unexpectedly hot taste in shoes she didn't know jack about dressing to entice. So there was no way in hell she should be getting him all steamed under the collar.

Yet he couldn't keep pretending that she wasn't doing exactly that. Lie to the Feds, lie to your sister if you had to, but don't lie to yourself. Truth was truth, and the big reality here was he would do silky-skinned Ms. Kaplinski in a heartbeat. She wasn't even close to his usual type and he didn't understand the attraction, but there it was.

Hell, maybe it was nothing more than the fact he was a guy. Men were a species who saw an opportunity for sex everyplace they looked. So shoot 'em.

She shivered and her hand clenched beneath his. "They aren't your noodles, but take—"

"Uh, actually, ma'am," the counter clerk interjected, "they are his. Yours will be up in a minute."

"Oh." Embarrassment scudded across her blue eyes, but she promptly hid it behind a bland expression as she let go of the bag. "Then I apologize." Hot color scorching her cheeks, she said in a voice so low, he had to bend his head closer to hear, "I seem to keep putting myself in positions that make it necessary to say that." Shaking her head, she about-faced on a three-inch heel and strode away.

Okay, he thought as he dug out his wallet. The big problem here wasn't that he was attracted to her despite the fact she had no discernible sense of humor and apparently didn't believe in dressing to display the goods. It was that he had just finished making his sister a promise not to screw up the sweet deal Kavanagh had made with Jane and her friends. Hannah *would* shoot him, and he had a feeling his Guy Chromosome defense wouldn't carry much weight with her.

Not to mention his word was gold. That was probably the first lesson his father had ever taught him, and it had stuck like gorilla glue. *A man's only as good as his word, Dev.* It was practically the Kavanagh credo.

He paid for his noodles, hesitated a second, then walked over to where Jane had buried her nose in a copy of the *Seattle Weekly.* "Can we talk a minute?" he asked and seated himself at her table when she ignored him.

She rattled the paper, the *go away* subtext clear.

He sat without speaking and waited.

Heaving a big sigh, she lowered the weekly. Pink

still tinged her cheekbones as she met his gaze. Then she sighed again, only this time it was little more than a soft exhalation.

"Okay, here goes," she said. "I truly am sorry. For a lot of things. I've been throwing around wild accusations like confetti and making way too many half-assed comments. I know you'll find this hard to believe, but I'm not usually like this. And I'm going to stop it. Starting now."

Oh, low blow. If he didn't get to see her naked he'd really prefer to hang on to the illusion that she was an unlikeable bitch. But since he'd come over here in the first place to show her he could be professional, he squared his shoulders.

"I've heard stuff coming out of my mouth that's not familiar to me, either. Things my mother would've had me by the ear to wash my mouth out with soap if she'd heard. So here's the deal. I propose a truce."

She studied him for a moment, then nodded. "I'm for that. We've got to work together—are going to *be* working together for the next several months. And being angry all the time is exhausting." She thrust her hand across the table at him.

Reluctantly, he met it halfway, knowing damn well that touching her would only fuel his awareness. She kept their handshake mercifully brief, however, and he discovered that she had a good, strong grip.

Discovered, too, that instead of swamping him with the undercurrent of sexuality that seemed to run like a 220 volt between them, this actually felt more like what it was intended to be: the sealing of a pact. He sat back in his chair. "So you like Spicy Basil stir-fry, too, huh? I was going to take mine home, but you want to eat here? We can get to know each other a little better."

She appeared a little less than certain, but said, "I guess."

What the hell. Maybe this wouldn't turn out so awkward after all.

CHAPTER FIVE

Turns out Devlin isn't a complete ass after all.
Why does that seem worse somehow?

OKAY, THIS IS AWKWARD. Jane didn't know about Devlin, but the laden silence as they removed their cartons from the take-home sacks and peeled wooden chopsticks out of their paper wrappings was uncomfortable as all get-out to her. She snapped the joint connecting the two sticks and opened her container, taking a peek at him. God knew she didn't know what to say and he either suffered from the same problem or felt no need to fill the void, because several long, prickly minutes passed without either of them uttering a word.

She ate a few bites to give herself a reason for not talking. But the weighted silence gnawed at her. "Great dish, huh?"

Oh, brilliant, Kaplinski. She wanted to smack herself. Could she *be* more inane?

Devlin surprised her with a grin, however. "Yeah," he agreed. "I love this stuff. I could eat it three times a day, four days running." Shifting in his chair, he was all muscle in motion, his wide shoulders straining the seams of his black tee and the unbuttoned green-and-black flannel shirt he wore over it, the sinews of his forearms beneath his rolled-up sleeves bunching and releasing with the subtlest movement of his wrists. He settled in his seat and scooped up a couple more bites of his dinner.

A moment later he planted his chopsticks in his still half-full container and dabbed his mouth with a paper napkin. Then he caught her in the crosshairs of a seriously intense hazel-eyed gaze. "It must be pretty cool working in a museum. I'm sort of a museum junkie myself."

A snort escaped her. "Sure you are." Immediately, she wished the words unspoken. *Oh, nicely done, Jane. Way to keep the truce going.* But, c'mon. One look at that build, those reckless eyes, and she was pretty sure most people would excuse her for doubting museums were the kind of entertainment to draw a guy like this.

Particularly if they were the female half of the human race.

"No, I'm serious. It started years ago when I went to the Viking Ship Museum in Oslo." Sliding his carton to one side and the salt and pepper shakers to the other, he leaned on his forearms, his long fingers splayed out on the tabletop and his eyes alight. "Have you ever been there? Seen the Gokstad and Oseberg ships?"

She shook her head, fascinated by the enthusiasm in his voice and the way his dark eyes lit up with it.

"They're clinker-built oak Viking boats that were found in burial mounds on farms in Norway in the late eighteen and early nineteen hundreds. Both were built in the ninth century. Eight hundred thirty-something and eight-ninety I think it was, which just blows me away. If I could have, I'd have crawled over those babies from stem to stern to check out their construction up close.

Because they may be more than eleven hundred years old, Jane, but the craftsmanship still rocks."

He pushed back, shooting her a lightning-quick self-deprecating smile. "Anyhow, for a while after I discovered them, it was all boat museums all the time. Then I started branching out. I admit the kind of museums that mostly host paintings aren't my thing." The brawny shoulders she couldn't seem to peel her gaze away from lifted in a careless shrug beneath worn flannel. "But show me stuff made by some highly skilled craftsman, and I'm all over it. Those ancient boats? Most of them were built by guys who had to make their own tools first. And the end product is a ship that's still standing today. How cool is that?"

"Very cool."

"Yeah. Now *that's* an artist." Pulling his container back in front of him, he scooped up another bite, chowed it down, then gave her a sheepish smile. "Sorry. I didn't mean to go on. So, how about you? I'm guessing those painting-type museums are right up your alley, huh?"

"Oh, I like paintings well enough, especially if it's a Renoir or something by one of the Pre-Raphaelite artists. But my true love will always be iconic *objets d'art.*" Seeing his eyes go blank, she laughed. "Stuff," she clarified. "Along the lines of what I'm cataloging now. Like you, I get off on the artistry of the craftsmen. Even the mass-produced items were made better back in the day."

He was staring at her mouth with a sudden intentness, the chopsticks he'd been bringing to his lips suspended midair, and she faltered for a moment, wondering if a piece of bok choy had lodged between her teeth. Then she gave herself a mental shake. Short of fleeing to the restroom to check, there wasn't a lot she could do about it if it had. So, drawing a quiet breath, she soldiered on.

"That's how I ended up at the Met," she said, and was relieved when he lifted his gaze and resumed eating. "It's definitely my kind of museum. We host our share of shows featuring paintings, but most of our permanent collection falls under the history and culture umbrella, which tends to reflect areas of the human experience. Of our eleven permanent exhibits, only two are paintings. And if I ever get my act together and sort out all Miss Agnes's stuff I'll be adding exhibits twelve and thirteen to the nonpainting side."

"I've never been to the Metropolitan. But it sounds more like a Smithsonian-type museum or something?"

"We definitely lean more in that direction than we do, say, toward the Louvre." She grinned again. "Which, I gotta be honest, I'd kill to see in person."

He shoved back from the table suddenly, his chair screeching across the linoleum as he surged to his feet. "I'm gonna go get a glass of water. You want a refill on your Diet Coke?"

Smile fading, she blinked up at him, thrown by the abruptness of his action. "Um, okay. Sure." She handed him her glass but her brows knit over her nose as she watched him weave through the crowded tables and chairs. *Am I boring you, bub?*

Okay, so that wouldn't be the worst thing in the world. Not that anybody wanted to be considered boring, but, really, the guy was turning out to be not nearly the ass she'd expected him to be—and, face it, when she'd agreed to let him join her for dinner she had sort of been counting on that aspect of his personality to help keep him at arm's length. Because she couldn't lie; he seriously lit her fire.

She sure didn't need that. It was atypical as hell, and she didn't get it. But she was nobody's fool—and while having the hots for a man might be a rare phenomenon for her, she couldn't ignore how she felt.

She merely needed to find a way to work around it.

Past it.

Through it.

Whatever it took to put it behind her. It was just…

She hadn't been prepared for him to be so likeable, hadn't anticipated they might actually have anything in common. And learning differently was sure not helping to tamp down this fire.

She snapped erect. *So, what the hey—all the more reason to embrace your blandness in his eyes.* Hey, it wouldn't be the first time she'd used her ability to blend into the woodwork to her advantage. It wouldn't even be the tenth. Growing up all but invisible in her own home and lacking the curb appeal of her best friends, she had learned young to employ her over-lookability—particularly when it came to the opposite sex.

And if she'd sometimes gone beyond merely making use of it, and had, in fact, actively courted it? Well, big deal. Because except for that brief romance with Eric Lestat during her junior year in college, her chameleon-blending-into-its-environment factor had stood her in good stead. If she'd been half as smart at the time as she'd thought she was, in fact, she would have clung to it then, too. But she'd been enamored of Eric's pale poet's hands, dazzled by his high, intelligent forehead.

It was an established fact in her family that the passion gene had passed her by—and in truth she gave thanks for it. As the unwilling observer of her parents' near-daily passion play, she'd known young that it was a dangerous, twisted emotion she would do well to eschew. So her relationship with Eric had been longer on the cerebral than it'd been on the sexual. And for a short while she'd been happy.

Until Eric had gone and changed the rules on her.

But that was all water over the dam and irrelevant to today. Except perhaps to note that she didn't give a good G-D what Devlin thought of her.

She picked up her purse. It was time to call it a night.

But before she could close the take-home carton containing her remaining dinner, Devlin returned. And if he did find her boring, he sure had a funny way of showing it. Because the first thing he said as he handed her the refilled glass was, "So, how did you get interested in the curator business?" Setting his water glass down, he hooked his chair with his foot and scooted it back up to the table. Then he seated himself and gazed at her with bright interest.

She studied him for a second, trying to judge his sincerity and wondering in a fit of unwelcome honesty how, if she lacked the lust gene, he was able to make her feel so damn…warm.

So edgy.

Itchy.

Then, shrugging the question aside, she said slowly,

"I was twelve when I started spending time with Miss Agnes. She was different from any other adult I'd ever met."

The corner of Devlin's mouth ticked up in a slightly cynical half smile. "How's that?" he asked dryly. "Did she call you Grasshopper and pepper you with wise advice? Give you long, profound pep talks?"

Her own lips curled up at the memory of the woman she'd come to love so dearly. "No, that wasn't her style— her influence was a more subtle thing. I think it was the way she turned up at all the events that were important to us and how she made her faith in us clear. Poppy was the only one used to that sort of attention from a grownup. It's funny that she and Ava and I have never really discussed this—" since they talked about everything else under the sun "—but I think we each got something different from her. Something that was geared to our individual needs."

Planting his chin in his palm, he looked at her. "And what was it for you?"

"The fact that she really listened when I had something to say. That she looked at me and saw *me*. She was a refuge from my home life. I could *breathe* around her."

He gazed at her thoughtfully and she went very still. Had she said too much? Revealed something she shouldn't? She didn't usually mention that refuge thing, not being a spill-your-guts kinda woman. Well, she talked to Ava and Poppy, of course. But she wasn't exactly known for telling all to a man she hardly knew and wasn't even sure she liked, and she scrambled to cover her tracks.

"Agnes taught me an appreciation for her treasures.

And the fact that she never minded me messing around with them was just the mustard on my bologna. She encouraged me to lose myself for hours on end, simply enjoying their beauty and the skill with which they were constructed."

Of course he had to home right in on the part she'd just as soon he ignore. "Babe," he said, giving her a single nod. "Trust me, I get the need to escape from home."

"You do?" She braced herself.

"Sure. You've met some of my family. Multiply that by about twenty, because the little you've seen so far is just the tip of the iceberg. There's an entire platoon of Kavanaghs, and growing up everyone from the checkers at the local Safeway to every teacher I ever had knew them. They knew my brothers and sisters, both those who had come before me and those who came after. They knew my parents—knew my aunts, my uncles and my cousins. You couldn't get away with a damn thing in the neighborhood because everyone saw you coming, they saw you going and they knew exactly who to report you to. There wasn't a lick of privacy to be had."

She stared at him. "And that was a bad thing?" It sounded comforting to her, all those people concerned about your welfare, interested in what was going on in *your* day.

"Hell, yeah. I was *smothered.* You must have suffered something similar yourself."

"Huh?"

"Being an only child. Tell me that wasn't constant attention of another sort."

She stopped herself from laughing in his face, but just barely. Aside from when her folks had felt the need of an audience for their theatrics, parental attention had been in short supply in her house. Mike and Dorrie had a passion for each other that was always front and center. They fought hugely and made up extravagantly. Rarely, however, had that ardor spilled over onto her. Devlin had felt smothered by all the attention he'd received? She'd been so lonesome sometimes she'd just wanted to curl up and cry.

Luckily, she'd had Poppy and Ava to keep her from diving head-first into the pity pool. Over and over again they'd saved her from her parents' lunacy, from being the odd one out in her own home, and Jane considered them her true family. So had Miss Agnes been.

"So am I right?" he inquired, cutting into her thoughts.

She gazed at him across the table. His bright hair glinted with exotic fire beneath the lights and his eyes were narrowed with amusement as he looked back at her.

"I'm right, aren't I?" he demanded. "Your folks probably saw your potential early and hounded you to death to live up to their idea of it."

Not. Oh, man, *so* not. But she wasn't about to admit the way it really was—not to someone who'd had an army of people doting on his every move.

Instead she gave him a small smile.

"Wow. That's downright uncanny. You're obviously a student of human nature. But hey, you don't need me to tell you that. I bet you hear it all the time." She looked at her watch. "Oh, man, look at the time. I'm sorry, I've gotta run." She had to get out of here, had to get out of here, had to—

She closed up her carton and stuffed it in its sack. Pulled on her coat.

Then met his gaze once more. "Well. This has been, um, nice. We'll have to do it again sometime."

Like when hell froze over.

CHAPTER SIX

I woke up in a cold sweat this morning, my heart pounding and my mouth dry. What have we been thinking?

MAN. JANE WATCHED Devlin walk away. She really, really needed a break from that man. Not that they were arguing any longer. In fact ever since their chance meeting at the noodle shop several days ago, the two of them had been acting superpolite with each other. Very grown-up.

"That man has a seriously nice butt," Ava observed from her spot in the living room window seat, a rain-lashed view of the Space Needle and Lake Union glowing in night-lit splendor behind her.

"No foolin'." Poppy turned her head sideways, checking out the flex of his muscular rear from a different angle as he headed for the open staircase across the hall. "It looks good no matter which way you look at it. Yum-my."

"Very biteable," Jane contributed. And that was her problem in a nutshell. For all that they were being so civilized and professional and all, she just couldn't seem to drag her libido out of the equation.

Realizing the room had gone silent and her friends were staring at her, she blinked her way back to the matter at hand. "What?"

"You said it was biteable," Ava said wonderingly.

"Well, it is. I mean, isn't that basically the same thing you two were just saying?"

"Sure, but that's Ava and me," Poppy said. "You never notice that kind of stuff."

She huffed a laugh. "Of course I do. Just because I don't act on my observations or yak it to death doesn't mean I'm blind. *C'mon.* There's probably not a woman alive wouldn't notice buns that fine." Which was perhaps a mistake to mention, considering the sudden speculation on Poppy's face.

She changed the subject. "Listen, I asked you guys to meet me here this evening for a reason."

"Aside from a yen to see our pretty faces and wallow in our sweet dispositions, you mean?" Ava fluttered her eyelashes.

"Goes without saying. In addition to that, though, I've got a concern I need to talk to you about."

In the manner that made them such steadfast friends, they gave her their immediate, undivided attention.

"Last night I awoke from a sound sleep to practically a full-blown panic attack." Her hands got clammy just thinking about it. "Do you guys have any idea how *valuable* all the stuff in this house is?"

"Well…duh," Poppy said at the same time Ava said, "It's kind of hard not to, Janie."

"You're both looking at me like I've grown a second head, but I've got a valid concern here. We're in agreement that Miss Agnes's collections constitute a small fortune, right?"

Both women nodded.

"So you must know that we need to do everything

we can to protect them. I don't know why it didn't occur to me right away, but I doubt the burglar alarms in this place have been upgraded since Miss A. did it back in '85. And can you imagine how much the technology has changed since we were seven?" She looked from one friend to the other. "It's way beyond time it was upgraded—and the sooner the better, if my nervous system has any say in the matter."

"Sounds like a huge expense," Poppy commented mildly.

"But a necessary one."

"With this remodel we've got a shitload of other expenditures coming up, as well."

"Yes, we do. But we also have a shitload to lose if we're ever robbed—and most of it potential income that can be used to finance the work we're having done." She touched Poppy's arm. "Look, I freely admit I'm already starting to obsess over my responsibilities to the Met and, by extension, to the faith Miss Agnes put in me to do a good job for them. It's just—when the will was first read it seemed like there was plenty of time to get the collections in order for the winter exhibit. But probate took longer than I expected and suddenly it doesn't seem all that long after all, and it's not like the collections are all in one place just waiting for me to start cataloging them.

"I know I'm probably borrowing trouble, worrying about what would happen to them if we experienced a break-in, but at the same time… Oh, shit, I'm babbling, aren't I?" She drew a deep breath and blew it out. Then she gave both her friends a level look. "Sorry. Still, if something *should* happen, it will affect all three of us, not just me."

"We're insured, right?" Poppy asked.

"Yes. But that's kind of a catch-22 because I doubt it covers everything, considering no one has ever cataloged the contents of this place."

"I wonder why Miss A. never had that done?"

"Probably for the same reason she didn't upgrade her alarm system beyond that one time. I think she was more into finding and acquiring stuff she loved than she was into being the owner of anything so formal as a 'collection,'" Ava said. "But Jane's got a valid point. The insurance policy probably put a standard blanket value on the contents of the house."

"And unless Miss Agnes made special provisions for her collections," Jane added, "that would only cover a fraction of what she accumulated over the years. In fact, that's something else we need to look into—checking out the current policy and setting up our own. I don't even know if we're covered at this point."

Poppy pulled a small tablet out of her voluminous shoulder bag, rooted around until she located a pen, then scribbled herself a note. "I'll look into it."

"Thanks. What really scares me is the thought of having the stuff she spent years acquiring just disappear into the ether so some drug addict can feed his habit."

"Lot of responsibility being a home owner," Poppy observed.

"Along with the good stuff comes the not so much," Ava agreed. "Still, we walked into this, if not fully prepared, at least with our eyes wide-open. So I vote we bite the bullet and get the alarm system replaced."

"Me, too." Jane looked over at their blonde friend. "Poppy?"

The first thing they had done when they discovered Miss Agnes had left the bulk of her worldly possessions to them was agree that they didn't want to abide by majority rules. Unless they could unanimously agree on an acquisition, they'd decided, it would remain unpurchased.

"Okay." Poppy gave a decisive nod. "I'm in. But I don't know jack about burglar alarms and neither do you two. So how will we know what's a good one and what's just flushing our money down the loo?"

The attenuated screech of a board being ripped from its mooring, then the thud of it hitting the floor, sounded overhead and they all glanced up at the ceiling. Then they looked at one another.

And laughed. "So speak the gods," Poppy said. Sticking her head out the salon door, she hollered Devlin's name.

"That's one of the things we like best about you, Pop," Ava murmured dryly as she rose from the window seat to join her. "Your unremitting refinement."

"Oh, screw refinement," Poppy said as Dev responded from upstairs. She yelled a request for him to come down for a minute, then turned back to her friend. "He's a carpenter. I'm guessing the big R's not as important to him as it is to, oh, say…you."

Jane would have preferred not to involve Devlin at all, but she knew Poppy was right—they didn't know the first thing about what constituted a decent alarm system. A contractor was much more likely to.

He strolled into the room a few moments later. "Just can't get enough of me, can you, ladies?"

"It must be your biteable butt," Poppy said.

His black brows rose toward his Irish-setter-red hairline. "Say what?"

"Jane didn't mention that's what she thinks your butt is— OW! Jesus, Ava." Sinking down on the love seat behind her, the lissome blonde propped her left foot on her right knee and gingerly massaged her instep where her friend had trod.

"Oops, sorry," Ava said serenely. "That was very clumsy of me."

Jane barely heard. Scorching currents sparked through her veins like a downed power line when Devlin's gaze locked with hers.

It was awfully stuffy in here all of a sudden, wasn't it?

Oh, get a grip, Kaplinski. She squared her shoulders and tilted up her chin, for she knew exactly what her problem was—and it didn't have a thing to do with the number of degrees on the thermostat. Dammit, this was the very reason she'd been trying to keep her distance. It was this precise chemistry that scared her spitless.

Blowing out a breath, she deliberately broke their gaze and took a large mental step back. "You'll have to excuse Poppy's babbling," she said and—hallelujah!— actually sounded composed. "She's easily sidetracked. The reason she called you down here is so we can pick your brain about alarm systems."

He took a step in her direction, all hot eyes and masculine cool in his worn jeans, black tee and heavy work boots. "You think I have a biteable butt?"

Oh, daddy. But she wasn't even going there, and in the same collected tones she said, "Absolutely. Now about our burglar alarm—"

He stuffed his hands in his pockets. Stepped back and propped his shoulder against the doorjamb. "If you're talking about the security system in this house, it blows. You need a new one."

"Yes, we pretty much came to that conclusion on our own. Unfortunately, we don't have the first idea what we should replace it with."

"Since I've been out of the country for several years, I'm not exactly sure what's considered best these days, either. Technology changes on a dime with this sort of thing. But let me check with Bren. He'll know."

He'd been out of the country? Where? Well, Oslo of course—he'd told her that much, but she'd assumed he'd been on vacation. "Several years" sounded like a whole different lifestyle, however, and she wanted to know what and why and where else. Determined, however, to maintain her professionalism, she bit back the questions crowding her tongue.

"You've been out of the country?" Poppy said. "Where? Why?"

It wasn't for nothing that girl was one of her best buds.

"Everywhere, really," he said. "Well, everywhere connected to an ocean. I'm a sailor."

Which explained his fascination for boat museums.

"In the navy?" Ava asked.

"No. I sail yachts—mostly for private parties. I take their boats from point A where they left them to point B where they want to pick them up, or simply do the sailing for them so they won't have to." He shook his head. "You'd be amazed how many people buy the most gorgeous boats in the world—then don't have the slightest interest in sailing them."

She could picture him at the helm of a big sailboat. Far too easily, she could picture that, and her brow knitted. "So if you're a sailor, what are you doing heading our construction project?"

"Babe." He gave her a crooked smile that did dangerous things to her equilibrium. "I was born in this business and still pick up jobs between sailing gigs. I can money-back-guarantee you I won't screw up your job. I know my way around a construction site maybe even better than I do an IACC yacht." He met her gaze. "And that's saying something."

"He said modestly."

"Yeah." He pulled out his cell phone and called his brother. By the time he'd hung up a second time, not only had he gotten the name of Bren's top pick for the job but had called the company for them and bargained until the firm agreed to install a top-of-the-line security system for fifteen hundred dollars below the original quote.

Ava and Poppy made a big fuss over him and it was all Jane could do not to join in. She knew just how she'd like to thank him, too, and the fact that her mind kept drifting in that direction shook her right down to the ground. Consequently, her thanks came out sounding all stiff and insincere. Well, she regretted that, but the last thing she needed right now was a case of run-amok hormones.

Like Devlin cared, anyway. He merely looked her

over from head to toe, licked his lips, then bid them a good day.

The minute he left to go back to his teardown of the poorly added-on sunroom, Poppy rounded on her. "Jane Kaplinski, you slutty little she-devil. *He's* your object de lust!"

"What?" Ava demanded, looking at their blonde friend as if she'd lost her mind. "Don't be ridiculous. Jane isn't lusting after Devl—"

But something in her expression must have given her away, because Ava quit speaking midprotest and studied her closely. "Jane?"

"Fine, all right." She threw herself down on the love seat. "I admit it, I've got the hots for Devlin Kavanagh. How awkward is that?"

"It's surprising, considering I can't remember the last time you had the hots for anyone," Poppy said, sitting down beside her. "But I don't see why it should be awkward at all. He's obviously hot right back atcha."

She snorted.

"No, Poppy's right," Ava said. "At first, when he moved in on you after Big Mouth here told him what you thought of his butt, I assumed he was just one of those guys who has to strike sparks off every woman he meets."

"Which is probably the case." She dug her shoulder into Poppy's. "And thanks a heap, by the way."

Ava ignored the byplay to shake her head. "I don't think it is. Because when I think about it, I realize he's never displayed a hint of that with either Poppy or me. He teases in a generic sort of way, but there's no real heat to it."

"There was definite heat with you," Poppy agreed.

Her stomach clenched at the thought, but she shrugged it aside. "Doesn't matter. I don't have time for this."

"Make the time," Poppy said. "Sex is good for you—it releases endorphins and—"

"Will you give it a rest?" Jane interrupted, trying to nip Poppy's let's-get-Jane-laid campaign in the bud. "I wasn't kidding when I said I'm nervous about getting the Met's collections ready on time."

"All the more reason to seek those all-comforting endorphins." Poppy drew her knee up onto the love seat next to Jane and shifted to look her in the eye. "I'm telling you, that would do more to help relax you and make your work go easier than three assistants and a week at the spa."

"My work would go easier if my good friend would quit trying to improve my sex life and lend me a hand instead."

Poppy studied her a moment, then swept her cloud of curly hair behind her shoulders. "You're going to ignore my brilliant advice, aren't you?"

"Yes."

She blew out a disgusted breath, but merely said, "Fine. I'll help with whatever you need."

"If it's any consolation, I'll put in a voucher with the Met and you'll draw a paycheck for your work."

Poppy brightened. "Great. You know me—I can always use extra cash this time of year. I haven't received the grant money yet for my new program with the kids and it will be a while before I see the advance for the card design I sold."

"In that case," Ava said, "I'll take over researching our insurance situation."

"Thanks, both of you. I'll talk to Gordon Ives at work tomorrow, too. Maybe if I can clear the decks a little there, I'll start making some headway here."

AT THE MUSEUM the following day, she freed up some time from her schedule and went looking for Gordon.

When she failed to track him down in the exhibit rooms, the storage area or the staff room, she went up to the sixth floor where their offices were located. Approaching his at the far end of the hall, she saw through the slightly opened door that he was on the phone. She knocked softly on his doorjamb and leaned into his office, a room that was even smaller and more crowded than her own. Who would have thought that was possible?

His head jerked up and the quick glimpse she caught of his expression had her murmuring, "Sorry," and straightening back into the hall. She got the impression of annoyance, yet the hunched shoulder he immediately put between her and the receiver looked closer to guilty.

Either way, it was clearly not a good time to be interrupting him.

After tossing the receiver into its cradle a moment later, however, he leaned back in his chair and waved her in with a big smile that belied both emotions. "Sorry to keep you waiting," he said. "What can I do for you?"

"I have a favor to ask. Were you serious about lending me a hand?"

He slowly straightened in his seat. "Absolutely. I wouldn't have made the offer otherwise."

"You're a prince among men." She moved a stack of brochures for the upcoming Anselm Kiefer: Heaven and Earth exhibit from the visitor's chair to the floor and sank down upon the now-cleared space. "I'm starting to feel a little overwhelmed about the Wolcott collections and I know if I can get even one solid week of uninterrupted work under my belt, things will start falling into place. So if you'd be willing to take over my duties on the Art in the Age of Exploration exhibit next week, I would be so grateful."

"Art in the—" He blinked. "The Spanish exhibit?"

"Yes. I've got it pretty well organized, but the pieces need to be checked in as they arrive, which is looking to be early next week. And my plan-o-gram needs to be double-checked against the exhibit to make sure I have the true sizes. You know how that goes sometimes."

"Yes," he agreed. "The minute you trust the reliability of the specs that come with the exhibits, everything goes to hell."

She couldn't put her finger on why, but something made her wonder just how happy he actually was to be asked to fill in, and never mind the lip service he paid to the contrary. "Look, I know it's a lot to ask, Gordon. So if you'd rather not—"

"No, of course I don't mind."

He gave her a big smile and the whatever-it-had-been was no longer, so she relaxed. "Thank you. You have no idea how much I appreciate this. You'll be named co-curator in the brochure, of course, and receive an invitation to the banquet for the King and Queen of Spain." She rose to her feet. "Thank you so much."

"You're more than welcome." Gordon rose to his feet,

as well. "I told you before and I meant it—whatever I can do to help."

Just knowing she had freed up several blocks of time made her feel considerably lighter as she headed for the door. Pausing at the threshold, she shot him a brilliant smile. "I'll go get you the paperwork you'll need. You're a lifesaver, you know that?"

Gordon returned her smile. "No problem."

Laughing, she whirled away and headed back to her own office.

And missed seeing his eyes narrow.

CHAPTER SEVEN

Why do things always have to get so flippin' crazy?
I seriously need some shoe-shopping therapy.

GORDON'S SMILE FADED about the same time Jane cleared the door. The Spain exhibit? She'd given him the fucking *Spain* exhibit? That *bitch!* Had he offered to do her fucking museum work for her?

No, he had not.

Okay, so he'd said he'd do whatever she needed. What he'd meant was at the Wolcott mansion, where there were bound to be lots and lots of portable treasures just waiting to be donated to his cause.

He had debts to pay off. Beatings to avoid. Which was too frigging unfair. He never should have found himself in this predicament.

It wasn't his fault. He was a brilliant gambler—just look at all the loot he'd won over the years—and any day now he was going to hit the big time. Then he'd quit this picayune museum gig where they didn't have the sense to see his brilliance, which far outshone Kaplinski's. Yes, sir, he'd join the professional poker circuit and retire young, with money to burn. And considering the exquisite care he took with his grooming, he knew that announcers would probably be tripping all over themselves trying to tag him with a fitting nickname—

something along the lines of Dapper Dan, no doubt. Or maybe Impeccable Ives. But not this year.

He found himself clenching his fists and breathing hard, nearly panting. Gulping in air, he restored some calm.

Well, BFD—so he'd had a little run of bad luck. It happened to the best of players. Trouble was, he'd blown through his winnings, a small fortune that he'd been saving toward his entry into the Vegas Challenge. Then instead of giving the Challenge a pass this year—even if the competition *was* the goal he'd been building toward for nearly eighteen months and the springboard that would launch his career—he'd borrowed the ten grand he'd needed for the entry fee from Fast Eddy Powell, a loan shark from his old neighborhood.

Only to have his losing streak continue. He'd drawn a crappy table and even crappier cards, and he hadn't even made it past the first day.

He'd been robbed, pure and simple. Hell, the frigging competition was probably rigged.

But did Powell give a flying fuck about any of that? No, sir. The man was a shark in more ways than one and all he cared about was seeing a return on his investment—preferably yesterday, if not sooner. He wasn't exactly known for his patience.

Gordon had been on the phone buying himself more time by swearing to Fast Eddy that he'd sell his Lexus when Her Royal Highness had thrust her pointy little nose through his doorway.

God, she annoyed him. It wasn't bad enough that she had a prep-school finish and a degree from a Seven Sisters college, as well as quiet good breeding—she had to receive a whopping big inheritance on top of it? It wasn't like she'd done anything to deserve it. Yeah, yeah, she'd acted friendly toward a whacked-out old lady known for her eccentricity. For *that* the entire Wolcott fortune had just fallen into her lap?

It just went to show you, didn't it? The rich got richer and guys like him who'd had to claw their way out of the Terrace, one of the roughest housing projects in Seattle, got squat.

Zip.

Fucking nada.

The Met powers that be already loved Kaplinski's ass, but was that enough for little Miss Overachiever? Hell, no. She'd had to bring them not one but two prestigious collections—making her the effin' Metropolitan Museum It Girl. Like the bitch *needed* any additional diamonds on her tiara.

And when he'd tried to get himself just one tiny slice of the pie—strictly in the interest of saving his ass from annihilation—what did he have to show for it?

The fucking Spain exhibit. Which he'd all but begged Marjorie for when he'd first learned the Met would be one of the museums on its traveling tour. But had she given it to him? Hell, no. She'd said she wanted Jane to handle it. Now, however, he was suddenly good enough to hand it off to. Now that little Miss Correct-schools-and-connections had something *better*.

Well, he'd do the stupid job for her—God knew he could handle it in his sleep. But that was merely Plan B.

And you could bet the frigging bank he wasn't giving up on Plan A.

JANE WAS WORN to the bone by the time she fumbled for her key outside her condo the following evening. It had been a long couple of days.

She'd been so excited yesterday morning about freeing up some extra time to work on the Met collections, and the good news was she'd made a little progress.

The bad news was it wasn't nearly as much as she had hoped.

A problem she hadn't anticipated was that Miss Agnes might not have kept all her treasures in nice, orderly, *complete,* exhibit-ready collections. Various pieces of the Haute Couture for the Ages collection seemed to be stored all over the mansion. Which, if Jane had been thinking straight, she would have anticipated. Because, face it, Miss Agnes hadn't bought decades' worth of glamorous designer clothing with its eventual "exhibit" value in mind. She'd bought it because she'd loved and lived in beautiful clothes.

Which, of course, was as it should be. It just made matters more difficult for Jane when it came to locating everything—especially the late-fifties-era Christian Dior glass-beaded crepe gown and its accompanying ermine evening cape. Ever since she'd come across a photograph of Miss A. emerging from a limousine wearing those, she'd known they would make the perfect centerpiece for the exhibit—if only she could find them.

She remembered coming across the same picture as a teenager and Miss A. telling her about the night she'd worn that outfit. She had been in her twenties at the time, and she'd said her father had been furious with her that night because she'd turned down a now-or-never proposal from a well-connected young man who hadn't been willing to wait for her to come back from a trip she'd planned to South America.

Excitement jittered along her nerve endings. Agnes Wolcott might not be a nationally recognized name, but her eccentricities, adventuresome travels, philanthropic tendencies and stunning clothing made for a marketable commodity. Jane intended to include some of the more fascinating snippets of Agnes's history along with the centerpiece photograph and a selection of others featuring her wearing the pieces that would be on display in the exhibit catalog. And she just knew deep down that this show had the potential to rocket right to the top, second of its kind in prestige only to the Jacqueline Kennedy collection.

She snorted. *Pretty lofty goal when you can't even locate half your exhibit.* Maybe she had more of her parents' flair for the theatrical in her than she'd imagined. Scary thought, since she'd always considered the productions for the museum's exhibits a giant step up from Mike and Dorrie Kaplinski's funded-on-a-shoestring little playhouse theater. But sometimes a show was simply a show, no matter what the budget or where it was staged.

At least this afternoon she had made a breakthrough of sorts on hers. She'd discovered that Agnes had boxed up most of her personal belongings by era. Since both the clothing and jewelry collections Miss A. had bequeathed to the Met spanned several of those, Jane still had a load of work in front of her just locating everything. But at least she was on the right track now, and from this point forward she hoped to start seeing more progress.

But that was tomorrow's problem. Tonight all she wanted was a long soak in a hot bubble bath and maybe a bite of whatever she had in the fridge. Applying key to lock, she opened her front door.

The scent greeted her first, a lingering waft of Obsession. Then she nearly tripped over the suitcase sitting in the middle of her narrow hall. "Aw, crap."

"Darling! I thought you'd never get home." Dorrie Kaplinski appeared at the far end of the narrow hallway, a lowball glass clutched in one hand. Two ice cubes and a splash of dark amber liquid sloshed gently from side to side as she waved Jane into the kitchen area. "Come in. You look tired. I'll make you a sandwich or something." Taking a sip of her drink, she looked around as if expecting the makings to magically materialize.

"How did you get in here, Mom?" Jane tossed her purse next to her mother's flask on the L-shaped breakfast bar that separated the kitchen from the rest of the living space. She'd made a point of not giving either of her parents a key to her place.

"Oh, that nice young woman at the desk let me in. She knows I'm your mother, of course, and she took pity on me when it became clear you were going to be late and it started looking like I might have to wait down in the lobby all night. You work too much, you know."

"Why do you assume I was working? Maybe I was out on a hot date."

Her mother merely looked at her, and Jane shrugged. "Okay, you're right, I wasn't. But Miss Agnes's bequest to the Met is the most important exhibit I've ever headed and I'm on a pretty tight schedule."

"I still don't see why you couldn't donate some of the

dresses and jewelry to our theater. They'd make wonderful costumes and frankly, we need them more than your precious Met does."

I will not yell, I will not yell. "As I've told you—more than once, Mom—they weren't mine to give. They were willed directly to the Metropolitan and I'm just in charge of the exhibit. Which means putting in long hours is going to be a fact of my life for a while." She toed off her heels and sighed in relief as she curled her overheated toes against the cool hardwood floor. "And not that it isn't always lovely to see you, of course, but what are you doing here?" *With your suitcase?*

"I've left your father." High color flew in Dorrie's cheeks, a match for the scarlet highlights in her hair, her formfitting scoop-necked sweater and the aura of high dudgeon that all but pulsated off her.

"Again?"

Dorrie blinked. "Well…yes. He's nothing but a cold, heartless—"

"—philandering son of a bitch. Yeah, yeah. Heard it a hundred times. And I've been telling you since I turned eighteen that I won't be dragged into the middle of your and Dad's dramas anymore."

"But—"

"You can't stay here, Mom. If you insist on mounting an overwrought production, at least be willing to finance it yourself."

"Jane Elise!"

The doorbell rang and she sighed. Great. Knowing who to expect on the other side of the door, she stalked back down the hallway as her mother, clearly sharing her suspicions, yelled, "If that's your father, you can just tell him for me that—"

She yanked open the door without bothering to check the peephole. "Come on in, Dad."

"I'm not your father," Poppy said, sauntering into the apartment, "but I'll come in anyway." Spotting Dorrie's suitcase, she shot Jane a sympathetic glance and stepped in front of her to half block Jane from her mother's sight. "Hey there, Mrs. Kaplinski."

"Hello, dear." Dorrie blinked, patently struggling to readjust her expectations. "Um…how are you?"

"Just dandy, thanks." Turning back to Jane, Poppy thrust a bag into her hands. "Here. I had dinner at Mom and Dad's tonight and they sent along a doggy bag for you."

"Oh, wow." She hadn't realized until that moment how hungry she was and she headed for the kitchen and its microwave, pulling a disposable container from the brown paper bag. "That was so sweet of them. How come you got all the luck in the gene pool?"

"I heard that, little Miss Smart Mouth." Dorrie flushed, and, killing off her bourbon and water, she glared at Jane. "It's just all so easy for you, isn't it, with your fancy job and your fancy condo? But what does a cold fish like you know about the intensity of a lover's feelings? You don't even date—and you wouldn't understand passion if it walked up and kissed you on the lips!"

"You might be surprised how much I know about it, Mom," she retorted without inflection, even as her intestines tied themselves into one big hot knot. "You and Dad were excellent teachers—and I learned a valuable lesson simply from watching you."

"And what would that be?"

"To hightail it in the opposite direction just as fast as my legs will carry me the minute I see even a hint of passion headed my way."

Dorrie gave her a sour smile. "Hardy har har."

Jane glanced down at the container she'd uncovered and broke into her first genuine smile since walking into her apartment. "Oh, man," she breathed, looking over at Poppy. "Your mother's stroganoff! Please, please, please thank her for me, okay?"

"Like your thank-you note won't be winging its way to her first thing in the morning. But hey—" Poppy gave her a friendly nudge with her shoulder "—she'll adore the double dose of appreciation."

Jane popped the container into the microwave and began pushing buttons to set the time. The doorbell rang again. Figuring that this time it was bound to be her father, she took a second to begin heating her leftovers before she headed for the door once more.

"Don't you let that bastard in!" her mother commanded in a voice that had gone so shrill and high-pitched Jane was amazed her rarely used wineglasses didn't shatter in the hanging rack.

"Would you chill?" She sighed and pulled the door open. "Hello, D—"

Her father burst into her apartment. His complexion was florid and his waistline seemed to expand more with each passing year, but his hair was as thick and dark and shiny as ever. "Is she here?" he demanded. "Where is she? Where's your mother?"

"And hello to you, too, my lovely daughter," she murmured. "How's life been treating you?"

He barely paused long enough to peck an absent-minded kiss on her forehead, and the scent of gin wafted on his breath as he murmured, "Hello, Jane." Then he stiffened as Dorrie stormed out of the kitchen, and Jane knew she was already forgotten.

Sweeping up his wife's suitcase, he pinned her in his sights. "Get your coat, Dorrie. We're going home."

Her mother's nose tipped ceilingward. "I'm not going anywhere with you."

Jane sighed and went into the kitchen to pull her heated stroganoff from the microwave. Grabbing a fork from the drawer, she leaned back against the counter to keep a jaundiced eye on the Dorrie and Mike Show as she scooped up noodles and beef straight from the container.

Poppy joined her. "What, no plate? No place mat? Ava would be so disappointed in you."

"Then she oughtta be here setting my table." Glancing over at her blonde friend, she tipped her head toward the refrigerator. "Can I get you a can of pop? Or whatever's left in that bottle of wine you guys brought last week?"

"Nah, I'm good." Bracing the heels of her hands on the edge of the counter behind her, Poppy hoisted herself to sit atop it. Gazing at its pristine surface, she grinned. "I love the way you're so tidy. If I did this in my kitchen I'd end up with cranberry juice rings on my butt."

"You're such a bastard, Mike!" Dorrie's voice, which had momentarily dropped in pitch and volume, rose again with every syllable she uttered and, sighing, Jane directed her attention back to her parents.

They stood toe-to-toe, glowering at each other. "Go

home," her mother commanded, thrusting out her arm to point the way to the exit. "There's nothing for you here."

"There's you."

"No, there is not. So just go away!"

Her father didn't budge. "I'm not leaving here without you, D."

"Then I guess we're at a standstill, aren't we? Because I already told you I'm not leaving with you." The blue eyes that Jane had inherited shot fire as Dorrie glared up at Mike. "I know you're having an affair with that skanky little box-office slut."

"Oh, boy, here we go again," Jane muttered.

"I'm not having a goddamn affair with anyone!" Mike roared, crowding even closer to his wife. "And if I ever did consider the idea, what the hell would you care? You've got your hunky little yard boy to keep you warm."

"Oh, *ick*." Jane's lip curled in disgust even as sickness settled low in her stomach, and without conscious thought she reached out and clutched Poppy's hand for comfort. "This is scraping bottom, even for them."

For once, her mother seemed to agree, for she stared up at Mike with the same sort of stunned horror that Jane felt. "That *teenager?* My God, Mike! What would I want with a boy-child when I have you?" But of course she couldn't simply stick with honest emotion when the opportunity for melodramatic embellishment presented itself. "This is the final straw, Michael Kaplinski!" she vowed, thumping a fist to her breast with theatrical fervor. "This is the end! You are clearly never going to accept what everyone else knows—that you own me heart and soul!"

And she burst into tears.

"Oh, for God's sake," Jane said in disgust. "And they wonder why the theater is always on the verge of bankruptcy."

"Don't *cry!*" Mike's voice went panicky and he reached out to yank her into his arms. "Oh God, Dorrie, please, I can't bear it when you cry."

Within minutes they'd gone from all-out war to billing and cooing at each other, and Jane abruptly reached her flash point. Dropping Poppy's hand, she pushed away from the counter. "I want you both out of here," she said hoarsely. When they turned their heads to stare at her with blank surprise, she snapped, "Now!"

"For heaven's sake, Jane," her mother said. "Relax. Your father and I are back together again."

"You were never apart, Mom!"

"Of course we were. Weren't you paying the least bit of attention? Where's your sense of romance?"

"It went down the toilet when I was seven years old," she said wearily. "This is not exactly new theater, Mom. In fact, it's the longest-running production of my life, and there's nothing romantic about it."

"Don't you speak to your mother in that tone," Mike commanded sternly, his arm tightening protectively around Dorrie's shoulders.

"Fine. How about I speak to you instead? For as long as I can remember one or the other of you has been slamming into or out of our lives. Do you have any idea how insecure that makes a kid feel, Dad?"

"I'm sorry for that." And for a millisecond he looked sincerely chagrined. Then he shook his head. "But you're not a kid any longer. It's time to get over it."

She straightened her shoulders. "You're right, I'm not a kid. Which is all the more reason I don't have to suffer through your crap in my own home. Do you remember a show called *Name That Tune* that used to be on when I was really little?"

"Sure." Mike sent a fond glance at Dorrie. "Your mother loved that show."

"I could name most of those tunes in just a few notes," Dorrie said proudly.

"Well, guess what, Mom?" Grabbing up her mother's suitcase, Jane wheeled it down the hallway, casting her parents a glance over her shoulder. "I must be more like you than either of us suspected, because I can name the tune of your battles in three words. Sometimes in two. And I'm so tired of it I could spit. So the next time you two want to stage the same old fight yet again, do it in front of someone who's not worn to a nub from thirty years' worth of front-and-center seats at your histrionics."

Yanking open the front door, she shoved Dorrie's suitcase into the hallway. "Go home," she said wearily. "I'm not interested in being your audience any longer."

They stalked out, stiffly indignant, and, closing the door behind them, she rubbed her fingers over the throbbing ache that had taken up residence between her brows. Then she drew a few deep, calming breaths and joined Poppy in the living room. Dropping down on the couch in front of the window overlooking both the dark Sound and the lights of downtown Seattle, she said, "I'm sorry. You've been exposed to the Battling Bickertons' Always Amazing Traveling Road Show more than any friend should ever have to be."

Poppy shrugged. "Big deal," she said without senti-
ment. "You've eaten more tofu at my folks' house than
any friend *or* enemy should have to. Parents can be…
difficult."

A bleak laugh escaped her. "Ya think?"

"It's probably a rule or something." A wry smile
tipped up the corner of Poppy's lips. But her brown eyes
were serious as she said, "Maybe tonight your folks actually took your words to heart. Your dad looked pretty
contrite when you mentioned how insecure all their theatrics made you feel as a kid."

"Oh, don't I wish." Resting her head against the back
of the couch, she turned it to look at her blonde friend.
"But we've had this conversation literally *dozens* of
times. It's like a bad show that never closes, and until
they cut way back on their booze consumption or—
here's a thought—give it up entirely, nothing is going
to change.

"But you know what?" She straightened. "It doesn't
matter. I've got you and Ava. Plus, I'm a woman on
a mission. I've got an exhibit to mount. And no one,
least of all my parents, is going to stop me from carrying it out."

CHAPTER EIGHT

I wonder what a guy like Devlin would write in a diary. Bet he'd refer to it as a journal, for starters. (Sounds more manly-man.) And it would probably be all about his sex life. I suppose I could write about my sex life. If I had one.

DEVLIN KNEW the exact moment Jane arrived at the mansion. He didn't need to hear the kitchen door opening over the screech of the baseboards he was prying from the wall in the sunroom; he just…knew. It was crazy how attuned to her he'd become, considering they hadn't had a meaningful conversation since that night at the Noodle Ranch more than a week ago.

But he was tired of revisiting that evening. Impatient with the subject, he set down his crowbar and surged to his feet. Fists on the small of his back, he twisted his torso from side to side, then arched over his hands to stretch the kinks out.

He didn't want to think about that night or her. It was kind of hard not to, though, given that their encounter had been preying on him ever since he'd watched her erect, black, wool-covered back disappear out the restaurant door.

He'd obviously put his foot in his mouth, because she'd gone from being as engaged as he in their conversation to a phony show of politeness. Then she'd practically burned rubber getting the hell away from him.

Her chilly civility since then had threatened to give him frostbite. It didn't take a whiz kid to understand his assumptions of her relationship with her parents had been way off base. If he had more than a two-minute memory for this kind of shit, in fact, he might have kept in mind her earlier behavior with him and Hannah. The girl had, after all, gone all wistful-eyed over the thought of their numerous brothers and sisters. What he considered a pain in the ass, she obviously saw as some sort of golden family circle.

But of course by the time any of this had occurred to him, she'd already manned the barricades. How the hell was he supposed to climb over the wall she'd erected when she refused to even let him near enough to make an overture?

Hell, he didn't know why he felt the need to scale her frigging walls anyhow. He'd never met a woman who bristled with so many warning signs—and who needed that hassle? She was bound to be way more work than she was worth.

Yet he had this crazy urge to see her smile again.

Jane had a killer smile. Maybe it was because her teeth were extremely white and under ordinary circumstances you only caught glimpses of them, so they about blinded you when she smiled wide. Or maybe it had to do with her lips, which looked break-your-heart soft. More likely, though, it was because her default expression was melancholy, and her smiles, although rare, lit her up from the inside out.

Whatever the reason, he registered each one in his gut.

Things wouldn't be so bad if they'd just stay there. But that was a mere pit stop—and no sooner did her smiles hit him than there was a ricochet effect that shot faster than a speeding bullet straight to his dick.

Which was probably a metaphor he should keep in mind when it came to Jane. Not many men were looking to see a bullet headed anywhere near their jewels.

The problem was, when she smiled he quit thinking and simply reacted. Look at the other night when she'd grinned that second time. Only pushing away from the table to fetch water he didn't need had kept him from climbing over the table to get to her.

Because one of her smiles was rarity enough. Two... well, that second one had spoken directly to him.

And it'd said, *C'mon and get me, big boy.*

There was clearly more to Jane than met the eye. He'd gotten an inkling of it the evening he'd caught her all decked out in the Wolcott jewels, laughing that dirty-girl laugh with Ava. He'd seen more than an inkling at the Noodle Ranch before the evening had gone south.

Didn't mean he was going anywhere near her today, however. Squatting, he picked up his crowbar again, wedged the flattened points beneath the top edge of the baseboard and pushed the curved end of the bar toward the wall, popping a space between the two. No, sir. He was going to stay on target here, concentrate on the job and accomplish as much as he could before quitting time.

He plugged his iPod into his ears, cranked up Wolf Mother and got down to it. Twenty minutes later, he'd worked up a sweat and had to stop to strip off his flannel shirt. But he went right back to work the minute it hit the floor. Ten minutes after that someone tapped him on the shoulder.

"Jesus!" Heart slamming against the wall of his chest, he leaped to his feet, ripping the earphones from his ears.

The tip of his shoulder drove into something soft on his way up, and he heard breath explode out of a set of lungs. Whirling, he was in time to see Jane go stumbling backward. He lunged, but even as he reached out to catch her, she tripped over the stack of discarded baseboards behind her, and his fingertips, which had just connected with hers, slid away without finding purchase.

She landed on her back.

"Aw, hell." So much for his sixth sense where she was concerned. Not only had he not sensed her in the room with him, he'd knocked her on her ass when she had made her presence known. Smooth. Very smooth. The only saving grace here was that he'd removed the damn nails from the boards, or he'd be carting her to the E.R. for a tetanus shot. "Are you okay?"

Hand splayed over her diaphragm, she blinked up at him, gasping for air. "Can't…seem…catch…breath," she wheezed.

He cursed. "Oh, man, I am so sorry. I didn't hear you over the music and—" Cutting himself off, he shook his head. Explanations wouldn't get her wind back. "Try to relax. I know that's easier said than done, but it will help the nerves in your solar plexus also relax, which will kick your breathing reflex back in. Here, let me get you on your feet." He bent to offer her a hand.

She'd landed mostly on the far side of the baseboard pile, but her feet were planted pigeon-toed on his side.

The position left her knees raised and her legs in an awkward sprawl, and involuntarily he tracked his gaze up their long, coltish length. Until he reached the hem of her navy skirt, which was rucked up around the tops of her thighs, exposing—

Ho-ly shit. He stared. Miss Black-and-Tan Kaplinski was wearing red panties.

Red. Panties.

On Jane.

Feeling her fingers clasp his proffered hand, he shook his head and ripped his gaze away from the little slice of brightly colored satin between her pale thighs. He kept his eyes on her face with steadfast resolve and hauled her to her feet.

"I...still...can't get...a decent—"

Her jaw felt delicate as he framed her face with his hands. Her skin was every bit as silky as it looked.

Leaning down, he blew hard in her face.

"What the—" She slapped at his hands. "Stop that! What do you think you're do—oh!" She inhaled deeply. "I can *breathe!* My lungs are working again." She grinned up at him. "How did you know that would work?"

He dropped his hands. Stepped back. *Dammit, girl, you don't want to smile at me. Not if you know what's good for you.* "When I was about ten, Bren used that trick on our dog Roxie when the stupid mutt tried to follow us up a ladder and landed tits-up on her back. Something about the surprise factor makes you automatically inhale." He shrugged and checked her over. "Are you all right? Did I hurt you?"

"I'm fine." She brushed it aside as if she got knocked

on her butt every day of the week. "So you had a *dog?* What kind was she? Was she big? Little? I always wanted a dog when I was a kid."

He wasn't getting sucked in by that wistful crap again. "Rox was a medium-size, medium-colored fifty-seven variety American mutt," he said evenly. "Her lineage came from a little of this and a little of that. She wasn't particularly attractive, but not real ugly, either." Jane was looking way too enthralled and he realized he had unconsciously leaned closer. Straightening smartly, he cleared his throat. "So, do you have one now?"

"Huh?"

"A dog." Snapping his fingers in her face, he gave her the insolent look he'd perfected on his sisters. "Try to stay on track here, babe."

She narrowed her eyes at him. "You'll have to excuse me if I'm a little off my game. It's not every day a girl comes to ask a favor and gets knocked on her butt for her efforts."

Yes! He had to stop himself from pumping his fist in the air. But this was more like it. Feisty, irritable Jane he could deal with, no sweat. Friendly Jane was armed, dangerous and likely to shoot his legs out from under him with no more than a smile. "You're a pretty high-maintenance chick, aren't you?"

"I am *so* not!" Her blue eyes shot fire. "I'm not even low maintenance. Hell, I'm like *no* mainten—"

He cut her off with a rude noise. Gave her the look again. "Did I or did I not apologize to you?"

"Well…yes."

"Damn straight. So don't try to change the subject."

She rubbed long, pale fingers across her forehead. "At this point I'm not even sure what the subject was."

"You were whining about not having a dog as a kid."

"I do not whine, Slick!"

"Fine. You were stating. So tell me this—you're a grown woman with a place of your own, I assume. How many pets do you have now?"

She thrust her chin up. "None. I had the time to take care of one when I was a kid. I rarely seem to be home these days, so any pet I owned would spend way too much time by itself. And animals should have an owner who'll be around to give them the attention they deserve. Or that's my story, anyhow." Her chin lowered and her lips curled up once more. "And I'm sticking to it."

"No smiling!" he snapped, only to feel like a fool when she blinked at him in confusion. "What are you doing up here, Jane? You said you wanted to ask a favor?"

"What? Oh! Yes." Much to his relief she became all business. "The security system people called. They want to install our new alarm tomorrow around one-fifteen. But the thing is, I requested money from the Met to hire Poppy part-time to give me a hand cataloging the Wolcott collections."

"And this has what to do with me?" Crap. What was it about her that commanded his attention so, even when she was both all pokered up and a little rattled the way she appeared right now?

"Well, I'm guessing because of my request, out of the blue the director invited me to the monthly budget meeting. This is unprecedented." Peering into his face, she waved that aside. "Okay, you don't care. But, honestly, it should be over before then—by one-fifteen, that is—so I could very well make it back here in time. But this kind of meeting can run over sometimes and you never know what traffic will be like, so I wouldn't put money on it. Which brings me to you." She looked up at him, all earnest blue eyes, flushed cheeks and a prim navy dress.

With red panties underneath.

"What?" Realizing she'd said something and he hadn't caught a word, he snapped his focus back on her request. "Sorry," he said gruffly to cover the fact he'd been jonesing on her underwear. "I didn't catch that."

"I said I wondered if you could let the installer in tomorrow if I don't get back in time."

"Sure. No prob— No, wait! I'm sorry. Tomorrow afternoon is my day to take Bren to Swedish for his chemo."

She clutched his wrist. "Your brother has *cancer?*"

Damn. Bren might not have wanted that known. Well, the cat was out of the bag now, and he didn't see where it would hurt anything for her to know. "That's what brought me back to Seattle—he needed me to fill in for him while he went through his treatments."

Now, if they could just get him to stop showing up for work despite those treatments, Dev would be a lot happier. He worried about his brother, certain Bren's recovery would be much faster if he would just for once actually rest for more than the day he went in for chemo.

"Oh, Devlin, I am so sorry. That must be terribly scary for your entire family. Does he have other family, as well? His own, I mean, aside from you and your brothers and sisters?"

"Yeah, he has a wife and three sons. And Mom and Da, of course—plus a raft of other relatives."

"I can't even imagine the worry you all must be feeling. Do you mind me asking what his prognosis is?"

"It's not terminal—that's the good news. The treatments are going well, and the doctors are optimistic."

"Still, the bad news must be actually going through those treatments. If he's anything like the rest of his brothers, I'm sure he was accustomed to feeling strong and now feels way less than his best."

She gave his wrist a comforting pat then dropped her hand to her side. "Don't you give my problem a second thought. Poppy has a pretty flexible schedule. I'll call her and see if she can come over." Her lips curled up in a little one-sided no-grass-growing-under-*this*-girl's-feet smile. "Neither of us is the least bit knowledgeable when it comes to this handyman stuff, but she's a better bet than I am to deal with the installers. When in doubt Poppy will charm their pants off."

Jane's smile grew even more wry, and she hunched her shoulders up around her ears for a second before letting them drop. "I'm more likely to end up pissing them off. The end result being that what was only a small problem to begin with turns out huge."

Aw, dammit, she had a sense of humor after all. Not only that, but a self-deprecating one, to boot, which was his all-time favorite kind. Why'd she have to go and have one of those when he'd been so certain her humor gene had been surgically removed at birth?

His good intentions going up in smoke, he stepped closer. "You shouldn't have done that, Jane."

"What?" Tilting her head back, she looked up at him suspiciously, her smile fading. "What'd I do?"

"Smiled. You shouldn't have done that, because you've got a seriously…hot…smile."

She gave him a straight shot to the chest with the heel of her hand. "Get out!" she said with a muffled snort.

"You get out. I'm serious. And now that you've carelessly unleashed it, I think I'm gonna have to kiss you." He waited for her to bolt for the door.

"Trust me, Kavanagh," she said dryly. "You don't have to do any such thing." Her lips retained that wry twist as she stared up at him. She looked half-amused. Half-irritated.

But she didn't run for the hills like a smart woman would do.

Laugh and walk away, boyo, his better sense barked. *Now!* Instead he stepped nearer yet. Smelled the hint of pear and sandalwood that emanated from—he didn't know where. Her throat maybe. Or maybe her shampoo.

Wherever it came from, he was lost. "Oh, yeah. I think I have to." And, clasping her head in his hands, he tilted it back. His fingers dislodged her already precariously piled updo and cool strands of sleek hair unfurled over them. He lowered his mouth. Slowly. Waited for her to shove him away and save them both.

Only she didn't. So he bent his head that final fraction of an inch and touched his lips to hers. They were every bit as soft as he'd imagined they would be and he sipped at them. Gently. Carefully.

When an appreciative sound vibrated in her throat, his gentleness took a hit. He tried to hang on to it, but the suction he exerted grew the slightest bit harder. He opened his lips a little wider over hers before dragging them closed again. Then, opening them once more, he bit her bottom lip before tickling the seam where it met her top lip with the tip of his tongue.

Willing her to open her mouth.

With another of those sexy, throaty sounds, she grasped his shoulders and stood on her toes to get closer. Her breasts grazed his chest as she returned his kiss pressure for pressure.

Dev's fingers tightened in her hair and he raised his mouth until they were connected only by his tongue as it continued to meddle with the lightly sealed seam. "Open up, Jane," he murmured, half hoping for a reprieve, but dreading it, as well. "Let me in."

Her lips slowly parted.

A wordless sound of satisfaction rumbled in his chest. He eased his body closer to hers while his tongue stole over the slick inner lining of her bottom lip. The serrated edges of her teeth scraped his tongue's underside as he slipped it farther into the damp cavern of her mouth. Her flavors burst upon his taste buds. And she was searing where he'd expected lukewarm.

Richer than a Starbucks double-shot latte.

Sweeter than he ever could have imagined, given the acerbic nature of most of their exchanges. He lifted his head to come at her from another angle, his mouth turning fierce against the soft lips cushioning his.

With a little moan of her own, Jane released his shoulders and slid her arms around his neck. Still on tiptoe, she plastered herself against him and clung, her breasts flattening against the plane of his chest. Without so much as a hint of hesitation, her tongue surged off the floor of her mouth to engage his in a lusty duel.

His last kernel of common sense disintegrating, he whirled them around and pushed her up against the wall he'd been denuding of its baseboards. His mouth ground against hers with testosterone-fueled aggression.

And far from shrinking from it, Jane fisted her hands in his hair and begged for more. This was no repressed little black crow of a female. This was the woman he'd caught a glimpse of the first night they met, a firecracker who kissed him back like someone who habitually strutted her stuff in leopard-skin heels.

In red satin panties.

Slowly, he stroked his hands down her back until he reached the curve of her ass. Cupping its round weight in his hands, he started drawing up her skirt, accordion-pleating the fabric between his splayed fingers.

Reluctantly lifting his mouth free, he kissed his way down her neck. "Damn," he breathed. "I need to get my hands on those red panties." He knew it was too soon—that he was going from zero to ninety like a high school jock in the backseat of his daddy's car—but he didn't care.

She blinked sleepy-looking eyes. "What?"

"Your panties. You're not at all who you appear to be, are you, Jane?" He inched the back of her skirt a little higher. Pressed his open mouth against the side of her neck. God, her skin was smoother than whipped cream. "I have a feeling you're hiding your light under a bushel. Or at least red satin under a prim little skirt."

"Oh my God." She went very still for a moment.

Then she burst into a flurry of activity, shoving at his shoulders.

He stumbled back, befuddled. "Jane?"

"I'm sorry. God, I'm so sorry." Stepping around him cautiously, she put a sizable distance between them. "I can't do this!"

"Huh?" It was his turn to blink as he slowly turned to keep her in view. "Sure you can. You excel at it, in fact."

She moaned, but it bore little relation to the satisfied sexual sound that had purled out of her throat just a moment ago. "Trust me, I don't. That woman against the wall with you?" She gestured jerkily at the wall now behind him. "That's not me."

He had a hard-on he could drive nails with, and the realization he'd be taking care of it without any help from her made him feel seriously misused. He tried to step away from it, because that sort of me-my-I type thinking really did belong more to an eighteen-year-old stud-wannabe than the man he was. But taking his high school correlation a step further, shouldn't she be long past this cock-tease shtick by now?

As if he'd said the words out loud, she stopped her backward inch toward the door and looked him in the eye. Her own eyes were still heavy-lidded and a deeper, more crystalline blue than usual—as if lit by some unseen fire within. Her cheeks were flushed and her lips swollen and reddened from his kisses.

And he wanted to grab her back into his arms.

"I truly am sorry, Devlin. I didn't set out to tease. I just got…carried away for a minute."

"Hell." He rubbed his fingers over his face, stretching the skin as if it were made of rubber. Then he raked both hands through his hair and let them drop, returning her steady look with a surly one of his own. "Yeah. Well. Whatever." Okay, now he truly did sound like some callow high school kid.

Well, sue him if a raging case of blue balls didn't showcase him at his best.

He stared at the floor, waiting for his erection to subside and refusing to look at her again, even when he heard the unamused little laugh she uttered.

"Right," she agreed softly. "Whatever."

The unhappy tightness in her voice made him finally look up, but it was too late, for by then she was just the sound of footsteps racing down the stairs.

He took a step after her, but then stopped. What was the point? He didn't get what had just gone down. Okay, so maybe he'd started it. But she was the one who'd run with it. She'd led him on just to drop him flat. Had teased him into a frenzy, then walked away.

So why did he have the feeling he was the one in the wrong?

CHAPTER NINE

Shit shit shit shit SHIT. I am not a passionate per-son. I refuse to be a passionate person. Please tell me I am nothing like my parents.

WHAT HAVE I DONE?

Jane stumbled back to the parlor without any recollec-tion of how she had gotten there. For the first time since beginning the Wolcott project, she rolled the pocket door closed behind her.

Then she leaned back against its ornately detailed panels, her fingertips pressed to her lips. They felt bee-stung—*hot*—and seemed to have developed a heart-beat of their own.

It matched the one beating between her legs.

Holy crap. All this time she had imagined herself immune to passion. Or if perhaps not entirely impervi-ous, at least smart enough to prevent what little she had experienced from ruling her.

She'd felt a bit smug about it, actually, often reflect-ing that the world would be a far more manageable place if everyone would exercise their willpower a bit more often.

An unhappy laugh escaped her. Because it turned out she didn't have supersized willpower at all, did she? She'd simply been fortunate enough never to have run up against a man who could tap into her inner wild woman—that sybaritic creature within that she rarely let loose…and then only long enough to indulge her love of sexy shoes and sensuous undies before slapping her into restraints once more.

Her college lover Eric had certainly never managed to access that inner siren. That very inability had been part of his attraction for her. A sizable part, if she were to be honest. Because while they'd had perfectly agreeable sex, it hadn't been the be-all and end-all for them that it seemed to be for so many others. Their cerebral connection, on the other hand—now *that* had been amazing. The sex simply hadn't been that important.

Or so she had thought, anyway. Pushing away from the door, she crossed to the Edwardian-era twin-pedestal desk she'd recruited into use as her command center. She opened up her laptop, but merely stared blankly at its desktop icons.

She'd naively believed it wasn't that important to either of them. Until the day Eric had accused her of always holding back—and told her he was tired of waiting for her to trust him enough to cut loose with him.

Well, she'd sure as hell cut loose today. Just the memory of plastering herself against Devlin's body made her cheeks throb with unrelenting heat, and she rammed her fingers through her hair, raking it off her temples. The last remaining comb still securing her updo fell to the ground, and with a pang she realized the rest of them were probably scattered on the sunroom floor upstairs.

She gave her shoulders an impatient twitch. Because, big deal. Devlin was right about one thing—it was not as if her hair ever stayed up, anyway.

"Yeah, like *that's* your biggest problem," she muttered to the empty room. Damn. How could one kiss spin so far out of control so fast? How could it come to feel so…necessary between one breath and the next? It was only a *kiss,* for God's sake! She'd been kissed lots of times. Well, a respectable number of times, at least.

She snarled a curse. How often she'd been kissed wasn't the point. The way they had made her feel—all warm and fuzzy or comforted or admired or a host of other emotions along those lines—was. And the truth of the matter was, they'd been…nice.

She nearly choked on the harsh laugh that erupted in her throat. There hadn't been a damn thing *nice* about Devlin's kiss. It had been hot and wet and hard and—good God, so many things that had reduced her to near-animalistic behavior in the blink of an eye. How was that possible? How was he able to *do* that to her? To make her want to rub herself all over him, to lick him up and feel his hands slide beneath the elastic of her undies?

The man was dangerous and she was staying the hell away from him—that was all there was to it. The I-don't-do-hot consideration aside, she couldn't afford to have her attention drawn away from her work. She'd been handed the biggest opportunity of her life and instead of running with it with all the efficiency she knew herself capable of, she instead seemed to be spending all her time just searching for the pieces to her couture exhibit. She was falling farther and farther behind, and she wasn't about to let Devlin add to the problem. No man was worth that.

Blowing out a breath, she sat down at her desk and focused on wrapping her mind around everything she'd planned to accomplish today. And if the episode upstairs with Devlin kept trying to fracture her attention? Well, she was damned if she'd let it throw her off track. She would simply begin with the easiest task on her list, then work her way up from there. It was merely a matter of picking something and starting. Of getting her butt in gear. Once she'd done that her concentration was sure to improve.

Please let it improve!

No negative thinking! Sitting ramrod-straight, she reached for her cell phone. *You haven't been busting your hump since you were ten years old to fall on your face now.*

Flipping open her phone, she speed-dialed Poppy's number.

WELL, WHATAYA KNOW? Gordon Ives marveled the following afternoon. Occasionally he did catch a break.

Stopping outside Jane's office, he reveled in the faint rush of triumph that coursed through his veins. God knew that lately there had been too many days when the only thing he'd felt likely to catch was a cold. But at this particular moment he felt like one lucky bastard. Clearly his fortune was about to change back to what it was meant to be. To the way it had been before his loss in the fucking Challenge had knocked his agenda—hell, his freaking world!—on its ass. What else explained showing up just in time to hear Jane talking on the phone?

To an obvious friend.

About the security system for the Wolcott mansion. He'd been wondering how the hell he was going to get into the place ever since Kaplinski had mentioned getting a brand-new state-of-the-art alarm system. He'd assumed it was already a done deal, but apparently that wasn't the case.

Yes, sir. The Ives luck was back.

Staying carefully out of sight to one side of the door, he listened to Jane's side of the conversation. And smiled to himself.

"I really appreciate this, Poppy," she was saying. "Yeah, yeah, I know. And yes, I hope I would do the same for you. Doesn't change the fact that I appreciate it. So, the installation went smoothly?"

Silence beat against his eardrums while the party on the other end of the line prattled on forever. His eyes were growing heavy and it was all he could do not to jerk in reaction when he suddenly heard Jane ask, "So what's the security code? Wouldn't it be just like us to forget that part and have me set off the alarm when I let myself in this afternoon?"

Yes! All his senses strained toward the telephone receiver in her hand. *Now we're getting somewhere!* In an ideal world, she would repeat the code out loud.

He wasn't exactly bowled over with surprise when that didn't happen. If experience had taught him anything, it was that the world was seldom ideal.

Instead he heard her say, "Uh-huh, uh-huh. Okay, good. You are a queen among women, high priestess of the Sisterhood. I'm so relieved to have this finally taken care of—it's one more thing that I can cross off my lying-awake-all-night-worrying list. What? No, I've got a little paperwork to clean up here before I can head over. But I'm looking forward to being the second one to give the new system a try. Oh, he did? Well, third then, I guess. Will you still be there in an hour? Rats. In that case, I'll try to catch up with you later. Maybe we can grab dinner somewhere or something. You and I have reason to celebrate—I got the go-ahead to hire you."

What the hell did that mean? It better not have anything to do with the Wolcott exhibit! But Gordon knew this was not the time or the place to worry about it. To risk being caught skulking out in the hallway was a poor-odds gamble. The last thing he needed was for Jane to remember somewhere down the road that she had seen him near her office mere moments after receiving news of the mansion's new system installation—not to mention its code. So he forced himself to walk away.

For fifteen long minutes, he sat in the café down on the first floor sipping at a cup of coffee he couldn't recall actually tasting and staring at museum-goers that he couldn't identify if someone offered him a million bucks to do so. Instead he stewed over Jane's last comment to her friend. She was going to hire some bimbo off the street to work on the collection when she could have had him? That bitch!

One way or another, he was getting his hands on the code to that security system.

He saw no reason to stay away any longer. Judging that enough time had passed not to have her connect his appearance with the conversation she'd had about the security installation, he drained the last of his by-now-lukewarm coffee, stood and headed back up to the sixth floor.

She wasn't in her office—another piece of luck. With a quick look up and down the hallway, he stepped inside. Unfortunately, no scrap of paper with the code scrawled upon it lay conveniently atop her desk. He felt a moment's worry, since for all he knew the code could be a number that had some esoteric significance for Jane and her friends. Something she had no need to write down at all.

But as he looked closely at the blank notepad arranged just so upon her desktop, he discerned a line of faint impressions in the middle of its pristine surface. Picking a Number 2 pencil out of the Murano glass container aligned adjacent to the tablet, he swiped the side of its sharpened lead back and forth across the indentations. A zero appeared white within the graphite wash. Then a five. And a one. And a six.

Adrenaline rolling through his veins, he swept the pencil lead over what appeared to be the final number.

"Is there something I can help you with, Gordon?" a voice behind him inquired.

Fuck!

With his back blocking her line of vision from the pad he was decoding, he silently slipped off its top sheet and scribbled her name across the top of the sheet below it before straightening. Sliding the one that interested him under his waistband, he slowly turned, crumpling the second sheet while being careful to leave her name visible.

"Hey, I'm glad I caught you." He gave her the *Trust-me* smile he'd perfected at a tender age. "I was afraid you'd already left for the day and was just leaving you a note. I gotta admit, though, I'd much rather get my question answered today rather than wait until tomorrow. It's another chance to whittle down my list before I call it a day." He essayed a good-natured shrug. "Some of us don't get to leave right after lunch."

She grimaced, obviously diverted. "Trust me, this is not my idea of downtime."

"I know." She was so predictable. He, on the other hand, knew a little something about playing a role, and, keeping his expression sympathetic, he reached out to brush his fingertips lightly, briefly, across the back of her hand. "I don't doubt for a minute that you're up to your eyeballs with the Wolcott project. So I won't take up too much of your time. Catering is already agitating to know about any dietary restrictions there might be for the king and queen's banquet, though, and I didn't know what to tell them. They want to get a jump on planning the menu."

"I'm pretty sure there aren't any restrictions, but let me pull the folder." She crossed to the utilitarian filing cabinet in the corner of her office. Tossing atop it a manila envelope she'd had in her hand, she stooped to slide open the second drawer from the bottom. "I'm sorry," she said as she bent her head to rummage thorough the files. "I thought I'd copied you everything I had."

"Sometimes things fall through the cracks," he said as if it were no big deal, discreetly craning his neck in an attempt to read, while she was otherwise occupied, what she'd written on the sheet of notepad stationery she'd paper-clipped to the envelope's flap. "It's not a problem and it's hardly urgent, but it'll make my day a little easier to have the information now."

He identified a set of numbers that he couldn't quite make out on the notepaper. Just as his heart rate started to jack up at the discovery, however, she uttered a soft, "aha"-type noise and pulled a file folder from the drawer. Rising, she bumped the drawer closed with an outer calf that he noticed was surprisingly shapely.

He swallowed the derisive sound that rose in his throat. Like he was interested. He simply wasn't accustomed to thinking of her as a person, let alone a woman. Jane was just someone who was in his way on his climb up the ladder. After all, this job helped maintain his lifestyle until the day he hit it big on the poker circuit.

Then she brought the folder over and dropped it in front of him on her desk, and he shoved every other consideration aside.

Flipping open the buff-colored card-stock cover, Jane bent over it. "Okay, let's see what we've got." Pulling out the information document that had been filled out by the Patrimonio Nacional, the Spanish national heritage agency who had organized the loan of most of the exhibit, she ran a slender finger down the first page. Obviously not finding what she sought, she turned it facedown on the desk and repeated the action on the second page.

It stopped halfway down the latter piece of paper. "Here we go, food. Nope. No dietary restrictions." She nudged the entire folder an inch closer to him. "Why don't you take a quick look through this and see if I missed anything else. I'll make copies in the morning and get them to you asap."

He found one additional document that hadn't been included in his original packet and handed it over. Then he glanced over at her. "Is there any way you could make those copies now? Or that I could? I hate to be a pain but it would be nice to take this home tonight to study up."

She hesitated, but then as he'd suspected she would, said, "Sure. I'll make them."

He sternly prevented himself from indulging the smug smile he felt tickling the corners of his lips. But, really, the woman had no mystery at all. She behaved exactly as he expected her to, time after time after time.

"I'll just slip across the hall and use the copier in Marjorie's office," she said.

Well, shit. Not every time, it turned out. He'd expected to have plenty of wiggle room in which to finish his pencil trick with the last number on the notepad while she went down to the copy room on the fifth floor. He smiled gamely, however, and reached over to pick the pad up off her desk. "Great. Mind if I jot a few notes down while you're doing that?" Now if she'd just save him the trouble by leaving her envelope with the note attached on the file cabinet where she'd put it a moment ago, he could call it a day.

"Help yourself," she said agreeably.

Then the bitch proved that while she might be neither terribly exciting nor the least bit capricious, she was no fool. Detouring to the cabinet, she retrieved the manila envelope and took it with her when she strode out of the office.

With no time to waste, he smoothed out the paper he'd crumpled, lined it up beneath a fresh sheet and got busy laying down a graphite wash, starting on the right side of the paper this time. Two numbers popped up, but he didn't have time to decipher their impression, which was a good deal fainter from being manhandled so much. He shoved the paper into his back pocket and started scribbling a to-do list as he heard the copier in Marjorie's office whine into silence. Looking up when Jane walked back into the room, he blinked as if he'd been so involved he had forgotten where he was. He buried the pencil he'd been using in the middle of the dozen or so other pencils and pens in the cup, unwilling for her to notice how pointy its lead had suddenly become. God knew the devil was in the details.

He smiled faintly.

Because he was nothing if not a detail man.

CHAPTER TEN

Guys are an entirely different species. Swear to God.

WHEN JANE ARRIVED at the mansion the already undersize Wolcott driveway didn't have room to park a tricycle, it was so packed with vehicles. Grateful she'd been paying attention when she'd swung into it, she backed out onto the street again and drove another six and a half blocks before she found a spot big enough to squeeze her car into. She hiked back, wishing she'd changed out of her high-heeled boots at the Met rather than following her usual custom of waiting to exchange her shoes du jour for the comfy yellow slippers she left here for that purpose. Who on earth was at the house?

Even before she put her key into the back door lock, she heard the sound of men's voices. Loud and boisterous, they didn't merely come from the other side of the door, but rolled down the stairs of the mansion and seeped into the yard through single-paned windows and various crannies. Jane caught glimpses of two, maybe three, men in the kitchen. She couldn't say how many for sure, since they were moving and she could only see a bit here and a bit there through an awry Venetian blind so old it was back in style again.

She wiggled the key in the dead bolt. Its teeth suddenly felt too large to fit the slot and the part she grasped too small.

Then the knob turned beneath her hand and the door was yanked open. She staggered into the room.

If she thought the commotion sounded rowdy from outdoors, it was nothing compared to the noise that assaulted her once inside that kitchen. The screech of nails being rent from old timbers sounded from upstairs, and men's voices yelled, swore and laughed on both floors.

"Good going there, David," said a deep voice close to her, and hands that felt warm even through her woolen coat closed over her shoulders, stopping her headlong stumble. "You all but knocked her flat on her face. You never did know squat about how to treat a lady." The big hands gave her shoulders a gentle squeeze. "You okay there, darlin'?"

She looked up into a man's long, narrow face. Brown hair flopped in his eyes, which were deep-set and the color of bittersweet chocolate. His nose was bony and long, his cheekbones sharp, and he had the austere look of a Trappist monk—except for that dark-eyed gaze, which was busy giving her the once-over.

He looked up to see that she'd caught him at it and didn't even have the grace to look embarrassed. "You must be Legs," he said easily, setting her loose. "I'm Finn Kavanagh. The clumsy oaf over there is my brother David."

Another brunette, this one beefier, several years younger and perhaps a smidgen less self-assured, tipped his head at her. "Hey. Sorry about that business with the door. I meant to help you, not jerk you off your feet."

"Don't worry about it—I just wasn't expecting anyone but Devlin to be here. And my name is *Jane,*" she said pointedly to Finn, then gasped, noticing the new security pad for the first time, blinking red just to the right of Finn's wide, bony shoulder. "Omigawd! The new alarm!" She lunged past him to get to it, but once she reached it she simply stood there, her mind a blank. What was the code? *What was the freakin' code!*

Finn pressed his hand on the wall next to the number pad, his body close behind her, giving her the impression of being surrounded even though he didn't actually touch her. He bent his head until his lips were next to her ear. "Dev turned it off, darlin'." Then he pushed away. Took a step back.

She should have been relieved to know it. Instead, as she turned slowly to face him, she felt strangely unnerved—and it had damn little to do with the alarm. While Finn's every move didn't make her hyperaware the way she seemed to be of Devlin's, she was very much aware that he, and his younger brother, too, were men.

What was it about the Kavanagh males, anyway? Had they been dealt more than their fair share of pheromones at birth or something?

Not about to behave like a scared little rabbit hanging with the wolves—even if that was pretty much the way she felt at the moment—she looked him in the eye. Elevated her chin. "And this was his call to make... why?"

"He's a pushy guy, our Dev," David said with a grin and hooked the leg of a chair with his work boot toe to draw it away from the long parson-style table. Swinging a long leg over its seat, he lowered himself to sit in front of a lunch cooler that Jane just that instant noticed was on the table. There were two others there, as well, along with three tall thermoses.

"He can be when the mood is on him," Finn agreed. "But this was strictly a business decision." He gave her a direct look, his former me-man-you-woman sexuality nowhere in sight. "We've been coming and going through this door all morning long, lugging tools in and the scrap we're tearing off the walls upstairs out. We don't have time to be messing with alarm codes."

It had been a dumb question in the first place and she acknowledged the fact with a slight smile. "I don't suppose there are too many burglars stupid enough to risk breaking in where three big, highly visible men are working, anyway. Especially given all the noise you guys make."

"Four," David said, looking up from emptying the food from his padded cooler and arranging it on the table. She apparently appeared as puzzled as she felt, for he added, "There are four of—what'd you call us?"

"Big, highly visible men," Finn supplied and gave her a smile. "You got that right, darlin'. David, give the lady a demonstration."

David barely took his eyes off his lunch long enough to flex his arm. Even beneath his loose thermal henley, however, it was easy to see a sizeable bicep press against the fabric. He glanced up at her and said, "Anyhow, there are four of us big manly men here today."

"Highly visible men, idiot." Finn flicked the back of his brother's head with his fingertips.

David shrugged, opened his thermos and poured a cup of coffee into its top. "Whatever. Bren's upstairs with Dev. And the noise factor was just while you were gone. We're under strict orders to hold it down once you get here."

"Yet here you are jawing away," Devlin said from the doorway to the hall.

Jane's heartbeat immediately kicked up a notch and heat suffused her chest, her throat, her cheeks. She envied David, who didn't so much as glance around.

"Yeah, well, it's lunch hour and she's not working yet. I'm gearin' up."

"Down." Bren, who looked thinner than the night Jane had seen him at Matador's, crossed the room and eased himself into the chair in front of the third lunchbox. "You'd be gearing down."

"One or the other," David agreed good-naturedly and took a huge bite out of the large, sloppy sandwich he'd unwrapped. He tore open a bag of chips while he chewed.

Jane watched, fascinated, as Bren opened his cooler and pulled out a large disposable container, which he passed to Devlin, who gave her a cool-eyed appraisal before taking it over to the microwave. Finn arranged his own lunch, and the three brothers at the table passed or accepted offerings from each other. David and Finn dug in. The fluidity and familiarity of all four men was sort of like a rough-edged, no-words-needed ballet.

"You show Jane how to use the alarm system?" Dev asked Finn.

"No, hell, I forgot." He rose from the table. "C'mere, darlin'." He led her over to the system. "You already know to punch in the code to disarm the alarm when you let yourself in. But because Dev said you work here by yourself some nights and this is such a huge place, we set it up to automatically rearm. That means you'll also have to enter the code to let yourself out again. If, like us today, you're going to be constantly in and out, you can just turn the alarm off."

"Okay. That seems simple enough."

"Yeah." He chucked her under the chin. "I have a feeling you can handle it just fine." He strolled back to the table.

Holy smokes.

While Dev was heating his lunch, Bren pulled an entire bag full of pills from the tote. He looked up to find her watching, and she realized she'd been simply standing there, gawking.

"I'm sorry. I'll get out of your way and let you eat your lunch in peace."

The microwave timer dinged, but Devlin ignored it to look over his shoulder at her. "From what I overheard of the conversation, you've seen our version of peace," he said with a crooked smile. "It's rarely likened to anyone else's."

Oh God, don't smile at me like that! She suddenly understood his command yesterday not to smile. If hers had affected him half as much as his was affecting her…

Bren studied her with concern. "Have you eaten lunch already?"

"No, but I've got it in here." Pulling herself together, she patted the oversize tote that she used to schlep her stuff between home, work and here. "I'll eat at my desk."

All four of them stared at her, and David shook his head. "Good thing Mom's not around to hear you speak such heresy. She'd wash your mouth out with soap."

"Why? It's not like I damned God to hell or anything." Something she'd heard at least one of them do at the top of his voice when she was still outside.

"We Kavanaghs take our meals seriously," Bren said. "And working while you eat is no way to digest food."

"Yet I'm not the one with the bag full of pills." The words left her mouth before she could corral her brain and she stared at him in horror, stunned and appalled at herself.

There was a second of silence while all four men held her captive in the cynosure of their regard. Then Finn said, "Girl's got a mouth on her."

"I am *so* sor—"

"Not to mention a mean streak, picking on a man with cancer," Devlin agreed.

"Yeah," Bren said. He looked at her for one, two, three heartbeats. "I like that in a woman. Hell, if I wasn't such a happily married man it would make me seriously hot." He kicked out the chair across the table from him and looked up at her. "Take a seat, Legs."

She took a seat.

"She prefers to be called Jane." Devlin brought Bren's container over to the table, now lidless, steaming and smelling divine, then headed over to the fridge. Opening it, he looked at her over its door. "You want something while I'm up?"

"A Diet Coke?" The heat was finally fading from her cheeks and maybe—just maybe—they were no longer as red as they had to have been a moment ago.

"I don't suppose you can drink it like a man."

"Well, I don't know." She met his gaze squarely. "Does that involve crushing the can above my open

mouth and hoping to catch the stream from any holes
I might pop?"

"Nah. Just talking about drinking from the can." He
sighed. "But I can tell just by looking at you that you're
one of those girly-girls who always drink their pop diet
and want it poured in a glass."

She almost said that the can would be fine. Her
friends were all women; she wasn't accustomed to
men who teased—that being a species she'd never been
around. But she remembered his sister Hannah and her
don't-mess-with-me attitude. She also reflected that for
all she had just embarrassed herself, the four brothers had taken the rude repartee that passed for wit between her, Ava and Poppy in stride. Not one of them had
acted nearly as horrified at her bringing up Bren's ill-
ness as she had been. She raised her chin slightly. "But
of course," she told him as if she were a princess who
would tolerate no less. "With ice."

She pulled the little side salad she'd grabbed from
the Met café out of her tote and set it on the table, then
delved back into her bag, looking for the plastic fork,
dressing packet and napkin that had all started out attached by a rubber band atop the plastic container.

Just as she finally located everything, a glass was
thumped down next to her and she straightened in her
seat. A tall, frosty tumbler of cola, loaded with ice cubes,
sat next to her salad and she smiled. "Thanks."

But the microwave had just dinged and Devlin was
already walking away from the table once again to fetch
whatever was in it. Faced with his back, she smiled at
his brothers instead.

Only to find all three of them gawking at her, looking appalled.

"What?" She loosely cupped her hand over her mouth. "Do I have something in my teeth?" But that didn't make sense. She hadn't even taken a bite yet.

"*That's* your lunch?" David asked, staring at the little black plastic container of salad.

She looked down at it, as well, wondering what it was about it that made all three men regard it with such horror. "Um, yes."

"That's not a meal, girl," Finn said, shaking his head in disgust. "That's rabbit food—and barely even enough of that to keep a body alive."

"Dev," Bren said. "Grab Jane a bowl. She can have some of my corned beef and cabbage."

"I'm not taking food out of your mouth!" she protested, scandalized. "You guys do hard, physical work. Me, not so much."

"You're not taking a thing out of my mouth," Bren assured her, tipping his container over the bowl Dev handed him and using his spoon to direct some chunks of meat and vegetables into it along with the fragrant, steaming broth. "Jody packs me way too much food and she just worries if I bring any home with me. She's trying to fatten me back up, but I can only eat so much these days. You'll be saving me from having to toss out what I can't finish."

"Here's some milk, Bren." Devlin set a tall glass on the table. "Take your pills." He set his own meal on the table, took the seat next to Jane and turned his head to look at her. "Eat your soup." The look in his eyes warned her not to argue.

She picked up the spoon he'd put in front of her and took a sip. All four men watched and she could only pray she didn't look as self-conscious as she felt. She mustered a smile for Bren, however, and told the truth. "It's great."

They all nodded, and he said, "Damn straight. My Jody's one helluva cook." He spooned up a bite of his own.

And the tension dissipated.

"Should you even be working?" she asked Bren.

The other Kavanagh brothers turned as one to look at him, and he rolled his eyes. "Aw, man, don't you start, too. Trust me, they've got me on such light duty a baby could do it, and I feel better doing anything that's not hanging around the house playing invalid."

She bit her tongue to keep from saying she doubted there was anything "playing" about it. Instead she ate her salad and her soup and sipped her diet cola while listening to the men talk. They insulted each other with impunity, but it was plain to see that they cared for one another and that they were all easy in their skin, whether it came to dealing with her or each other.

David was clearly the youngest, but he was by no means a kid. And listening to their conversation, she learned that he was married and already had two kids, a boy and a girl, the latter of whom was home from school today with an earache. Bren was the father of three boys. Finn was single.

Determinedly so, if their spirited teasing was anything to go by. Planting her chin in the palm of her hand, Jane listened to the fascinating give-and-take between the brothers. It seemed to be composed of equal parts verbal abuse and affection.

Devlin covertly watched her watching them. Walking in and finding her in the kitchen with his brothers had been a jolt. It was the first he'd seen of her since she'd taken off after their little make-out session against the wall yesterday. Given his own behavior during that episode, he'd planned on keeping his distance. Because once his hard-on had subsided, he'd had no choice but to acknowledge he'd acted like a Grade-A jerk.

He didn't know what the hell it was about Jane, but he was through pretending they didn't have some serious chemistry sparking between them. Sitting next to her, catching the occasional whiff of her pear-and-sandalwood scent and wondering what sexy underwear she wore today beneath her dark—big surprise—dress-for-success suit and prim cocoa-colored blouse made it tough to sell himself any other bill of goods.

He was leaning back in his chair to check out her legs and today's hot shoes, which were a pair of stiletto-heeled ankle boots with enough straps to do a dominatrix proud, when he heard David say, "Then there's Dev."

"Huh?" Tearing his gaze away, he looked across the table to see David finishing off his sandwich and pouring the last of his chips into his palm.

Tossing them into his mouth, his brother then pointed his fingers at him, cocked like a pistol primed to fire. A few crumbs drifted to the tabletop. "Good to see something can get your eyes off Jane's legs." Shifting his attention to her, he gave her the sad smile of a snake-oil salesman, just brimful of faux concern. "You want to

be careful of this one, Jane," he warned her solemnly.
"Our Dev's got a girl in every port."

Shit. He'd always been pretty good with the ladies
and usually he got a charge out of the way his brothers
regarded him as some sort of globe-trotting stud. But
for reasons he couldn't fathom he didn't want Jane getting the wrong impression.

She merely swiveled her chin in her palm to look at
him. *"Really."* Her gun-smoke blue eyes surveyed him
from top to bottom and up again.

Okay, so she had no reason to buy into his brothers'
image of him. He swallowed a self-deprecating snort.
God knew he'd been far from suave or polished with her.

"I'm tellin' ya," David said. "Love-'em-and-leave-
'em Kavanagh, they call him."

"Huh," Finn said. "And here I thought it was The
Heartbreaker." He looked at Jane. "You should know
up front that the guy never stays in one place for long."

"Yep," Bren agreed. "Soon as I'm well he'll be heading back to Europe so fast, he'll be nothing but a cloud
of smoke from the patch of burned rubber he leaves in
his wake."

She studied him with a slow, thoughtful gaze. "Well,
you just sound like a real good catch."

"You bet. Chicks line up for the sheer excitement of
my company. Many have been known to throw themselves into the Mediterranean at the mere thought of
losing me."

She cocked her head. "You sure it's not to wash off
that fog of conceit clinging to you? I'm guessing it's
probably like slug slime—once brushed up against, you
need something salty to get rid of it."

He couldn't help it; he laughed, tickled with her. She might look prim and proper, but Finn was right, she had a mouth on her and, more often than not, it struck right to the heart of Dev's funny bone.

A small smile curved up the corners of her own lips before she turned away. "So what brings you all here today?"

He only half listened to Bren's explanation of having a couple of days to help out while they waited for a delayed shipment of epoxy-based grout for their other job. He simply appreciated having Jane's attention diverted. Because it was occurring to him that he liked her, from her sense of humor to the way blood ebbed and flowed beneath that baby-fine skin. And that wasn't on his agenda. Liking little Jane Kaplinski could too easily turn into a complication he didn't need.

That sat him straighter in his chair. *What the hell are you talking about?* If they did get together—and he for one was sure as hell leaning in that direction—then she would be nothing of the sort. He'd make sure that she went into it knowing exactly what to expect from him—a mutually lust-filled fling that would be fun while it lasted and over and done when he headed back to Europe.

Or it could be that you're just as conceited as she claimed, he thought ruefully. Because Jane struck him as a by-the-book kinda woman. And that type generally wasn't big on rushing into rash, dead-end relationships. So when it came to the idea of her slipping into bed with him?

He'd be wise not to hold his breath.

CHAPTER ELEVEN

Poppy went and planted an idea in my head—and now I can't get the damn thing out.

THERE WAS SOMETHING almost narcotic about watching the Kavanagh brothers interact with each other, and by the time Jane left them and headed up to the attic she felt downright laid-back.

The mood didn't last.

Well, how could it? She had a timetable to keep, and only so much of it was allotted to assembling the two exhibits for the Met and logging them into her database. Under ordinary circumstances, timelines and goal-setting were the lubricant that kept her schedules running smoothly. But day by day on this, the most important agenda of her career, she was falling behind.

So she had to get off the dime *tout suite*. Because the last thing she could afford was to be crowded for time when she planned the actual floor diagram for her exhibits and put together the programs that would accompany the collections. That was a process you didn't want to rush, as the flow of the exhibit and an exceptional catalog could take an already great show and bump it right up into the spectacular zone.

The jewelry collection wasn't a problem, as most of the funky costume pieces had been in Miss Agnes's jewelry armoire in her bedroom, and the good stuff in the safe. And while Jane still had some research to do on several of the pieces and needed to have a good portion of it professionally cleaned, she'd at least finished logging it into her database and had a good start on the catalog copy.

The haute couture collection, on the other hand, was giving her fits. If she could just locate a fraction of what she remembered seeing either on Miss Agnes or in photographs of her, she knew she'd have one knock-your-socks-off show on her hands, and her reputation in the industry would be made. The only problem was, a fraction was precisely what she had found so far, and none of it was the stuff she remembered. Not one piece she'd located had the potential to pop on a museum floor.

The attic was musty and cold, but she ignored both conditions and applied herself to the project at hand. She located a couple of suits in one closet, a few dresses, gowns, coats and hats in another. But like the items she had already assembled, they weren't the cream of Miss A.'s collection. Where were the rest of the pieces—particularly the Christian Dior beaded gown she hoped to use for the focal point?

Dammit, where was the freaking *bulk* of it?

She moved old pieces of furniture out of her way, opened trunks, looked under the ancient iron bedstead and even felt around the insides of closets hoping to find a latch that would release a secret space behind or beside it. All she got for her efforts were layers of grime on her hands and clothes and dust-laden cobwebs in her hair.

After exhausting every possible inch of space she could think to search on the third floor, she came back

down to the second. The men had returned to work, and
laughter and swearing accompanied the crashes and
screeches of a room being torn apart. She found herself no longer charmed as she picked the worst of the
cobwebs out of her hair and washed up in Agnes's bathroom. Instead a headache began to throb in her temples.

It intensified as she went over the suite's bedroom
closets for a second time, this time giving them the same
careful inspection she'd given the ones upstairs in hopes
of finding a hidden section. But she found nothing.

Nothing, nothing, *nothing.*

Her mood growing blacker by the minute, she moved
on to the adjoining sitting room. She knew darn well
Miss Agnes had wanted her to succeed. The old lady
had been very specific about which collection the Metropolitan would receive as a bequest—so why hadn't
she left Jane some sort of instruction as to where those
items might be found? Even the most rudimentary direction would have been helpful. Hell, at this point a child-
drawn treasure map sounded good, if it would help her
locate the items she needed to do her job.

There was a box under the settee but it merely held
two throw blankets. The room's only closet held more
linens than clothing and what little clothing there was
wasn't haute couture. And perhaps it was anxiety over
how poorly she was doing, or how long everything was
taking, or maybe it was the incessant racket that came
from the room down the hall.

Whatever the reason, something inside her snapped.

"Shit. Shit shit, shitshitSHIT!" Her usual iron-clad
control shot to hell, she hammered the side of her fist
against the ornate molding that comprised the jambs

and lintel of the closet door. Then she kicked the jamb for good measure.

"Ow! *Fuck!*" Breathing hard, she limped in a circle as her toe in its soft, now slightly grubby yellow slipper throbbed a protest over her idiocy. Not only did it smart, but she felt like an utter fool. What the hell was she doing?

Jane Kaplinski didn't lose her temper. She stuck to her agendas and procedures, she never gave up and she remained calm. *Always,* she remained calm. She did…not…lose…her…temper.

Just as she never, ever locked lips with men the ilk of Devlin Kavanagh.

Like a mugger leaping out of a dark alley, the thought made her jerk as if she'd been shoved up against a dirty wall and had a pistol thrust in her face. But even as she wondered where *that* had come from, she completed her hobbled circuit.

She stopped dead, the kiss and her abused toe forgotten as she gawked at the fir-paneled wall adjacent to the closet. Or rather what was left of it, since it was…gone.

"Oh my God." A choked laugh escaped her as she gaped into the cedar-lined space that stood in its place. All that pounding and kicking had obviously triggered a mechanism somewhere in the jamb, although she couldn't for the life of her tell how.

It didn't matter. Because there before her was…

"Hello, my beauties." This time her laughter was full of delight and she stepped into the tall, long and narrow area—and ran her hands lovingly over the shoulders of her missing collection.

Designer dresses, gracious suits and formal gowns

from a bygone era hung from padded hangers. The Dior, every bit as lovely as she'd anticipated, was included among them. She opened the acid-free boxes stored on the shelves above the hanging rod and found shoes and scarves and hats and gloves. Opened tubes and found shawls and scarves rolled in white cotton.

Of *course* she hadn't found any of this stuff in the attic. The fluctuating temperatures and humidity would have been the kiss of death for delicate textiles. Not to mention that she had lost track for a while of her mentor's stunning attention to detail.

She should have remembered Miss A.'s single-mindedness, her sheer focus when it came to her collections. Agnes might not have noticed her home slowly deteriorating around her, but she had known down to the last element what needed to be done to preserve anything she considered exhibit-worthy.

Jane whirled out of the closet. She had to call Ava and Poppy! Laughing aloud, she raced from the room and down the stairs to the first-floor parlor, where she retrieved her cell phone from her purse. Since Ava was Speed One in her phone system, she called her first.

"Hi, you have reached Ava Spencer. I'm tied up at the moment, so lea—"

Damn. She wanted to talk to Ava in person, not leave a message, so she simply requested a call back. She was punching up Speed Two when she abruptly hit the end button.

Poppy was due to give her a hand here in—Jane looked at her watch—less than twenty minutes. It killed her to have to keep her discovery to herself, but Poppy was the most right-brained person she knew, and you did not want to call her on her cell phone if she was behind the wheel. Besides, just think how much more bang for her buck she'd get *showing* her friend. She could wait.

Except she should have known that Poppy would be late. When she entered the parlor to see the blonde had finally arrived and was tossing a laptop onto the settee, she all but danced in place. This was her fifth trip downstairs since unearthing the secret closet and she didn't even wince at the lack of respect her friend showed for a valuable piece of electronics. "I thought you'd never get here!"

Twisting about to face her, Poppy paused in unwinding a colorful scarf from around her neck. One expertly darkened eyebrow shot up. "Did I get the times wrong?"

"No, no, you're actually pretty close to being on time, for you. But I've made a fabulous discovery that I've been dying to show you, and it's made the minutes drag by in dog years." She waved that aside. "But you're here now and bless you, too, for remembering your computer."

"You told me to bring it."

"Uh-huh." She shot Poppy's paint-splotched hands a wry look. "And you've never been known to forget your own name when you're in the middle of an art project with your teen group."

"Which is why I set two alarm clocks in the classroom." But Poppy flashed her a wry, okay-so-you-know-me-well twist of her lips.

"Anyhow, forget all that. Come upstairs with me—you have got to see this." Grabbing her friend by the hand, Jane towed her through the door and up the main staircase.

Minutes later, they stopped inside the sitting room. She indicated the wide gap in the wall. "Huh?" she demanded, gesturing like Vanna White exhibiting the day's Grand Prize. *"Huh?"*

"Ho-ly shitskis." Poppy walked over to inspect the cedar-lined rectangle in the wall. "It's a freaking closet. A *hidden* freaking closet." She turned a stunned face on Jane. "How did you find this?" But she didn't await an answer before turning her attention back to the newly revealed storage area.

"Pure, blind luck," she admitted. "Well, that and a display of bad temper on my part."

That tore Poppy's attention away from her inspection. *"You* lost control? That's very un-Jane-like."

"I know." She laughed. "And I've never been so glad to lose my cool in my life. I've been searching high and low for Miss A.'s designer duds ever since probate ended."

"Yeah, I wonder why she didn't tell you where they were." But Poppy shrugged as she bent to look at something on the floor of the closet. "What do you bet there's a note for you stuck in a book or a desk somewhere? Or maybe in one of her diaries. What the hell are these things along the baseboards?" She squatted down to get a closer look, stuck her finger in one and wrinkled her nose. "Ugh. They're tacky."

"They're moth traps."

She snatched her hand away. "Ew."

"The fact that they don't have anything in them is a good sign, since it indicates the closet was sealed tight enough to keep critters out. Miss A. knew her stuff. This baby is climate controlled, situated so it's never touched by direct sunlight, and the only light bulbs in the entire closet are low-watt nonfluorescents. Which reminds me, I need to check at work to see how many ultraviolet-light filtering glass cases I'll have to work with." She patted her empty pockets. "If I had a pencil, I'd write myself a note."

Then, shrugging, she dropped down on her haunches next to Poppy. "I also need to figure out how I got this thing open in the first place, so I can continue using it for storage until I transfer everything to the Met." She ran her hands over the molding but couldn't find an obvious trigger.

She was beginning to lose her euphoric high at the thought of how much time it might take her to figure the damn thing out. Then a loud crash reverberated down the hall, followed by rude remarks from several male throats. She turned her head to look at Poppy.

"Men," she murmured. "Now there's a different species. They're loud and uncouth and I don't mind admitting I don't always understand what makes them tick. Still, they know things—handy stuff that I'm clueless about. And that can be very…"

"Appealing?" her friend suggested. "Accommodating? *Useful?*"

"You bet."

"Seems to be a universal truth, too, that they love it to pieces when women admire their talents." Poppy raised that perfect eyebrow at her again. "Seems a shame to disappoint them by *not* showing our appreciation."

She nodded in sage agreement. "Allowing all that raw skill to go untapped would be just plain wasteful."

They rose to their feet in unison and made their way down the hallway to the sunroom.

But once in the doorway, they stopped short and simply stared. For bedlam and disorder ruled inside the room, an unfamiliar universe in which testosterone triumphed. The last time she'd been in here Devlin had just been getting started tearing the room down. Now, with the four men working together, it was more than half gutted. Each guy performed a different job, but every action seemed to involve loud tools and creative cussing.

And sweat. Flannel shirts had come off and T-shirts clung to damp muscles.

Demonstrating that, to a man, the Kavanagh brothers were very, very fit indeed.

Okay, Jane admitted it—it took her a moment or three to drag her attention beyond that. But once she pried her gaze from the wide shoulders, elongated muscles and long, supple groove that comprised Devlin's back, once she looked past his truly fine butt straining the seat of his jeans as he half squatted, half knelt in front of whatever it was he was doing on the floor, she realized that what she'd first perceived as disorder was actually controlled chaos. He and his brothers functioned together as one well-oiled, multicogged machine.

David noticed them first. He'd set down his drill, risen to his feet and climbed over a stack of wood to where a lunch cooler like the ones Jane had seen earlier in the kitchen rested. Pulling a bottle of Gatorade from it, he surged upright and spotted them when he turned. "Hey," he greeted them easily, then crossed over to Bren and nudged him, nodding in their direction as he handed his brother the drink.

Bren glanced over as he chugged half the drink in one swallow. He looked a little pale, but, lowering the bottle, he wiped the back of his hand across his mouth and flashed them a smile. "Well, hello there, ladies."

That got Finn's attention and he craned his neck to look at them over his shoulder. Reaching out, he used his crowbar to poke Devlin in the side.

Looking over at his brother, Devlin removed his iPod earbuds. "What?"

"Skirts in the hole."

"Is that anything like fire in the hole?" Poppy wondered aloud as Devlin's head whipped in their direction.

"I'm guessing the skirts would be us," Jane murmured. "Even though *you're* not wearing one and *I'm* not wearing one."

Her blonde friend shrugged good-naturedly. "We've been called worse, I suppose."

Ignoring their admittedly juvenile byplay, Devlin climbed to his feet in an easy, fluid motion. Wiping his forearm across his forehead, he crossed the room to them. "Something I can help you with, ladies?"

"I have a favor to ask." He'd stopped so close to her that she had to tip her head back. "It's nothing urgent, but if any of you have a minute, could you check out something for me?"

"Sure. What is it?"

"I found a secret closet in the sitting room part of Miss A.'s suite and I can't figure out how to—"

She found herself talking to an empty room. Every last one of the Kavanagh men had deserted the place.

She found them in the sitting room, either squatting in front of or crawling around inside of the hidden closet, inspecting it with the intensity of scientists discovering a hot prospect for the cure for the common cold.

She glanced at Poppy, who gave her a crooked smile that said, *Men. Bless their pointy little heads.*

"How did you open it?" Bren demanded.

"Well, see, that's the thing. I, uh, sort of lost my temper for a minute and started banging on the jamb thing there. And it's possible I might have kicked it, too." She swallowed a snort. As if there were any question. "Anyhow, the wall opened, but I'm not sure *how* I did it. I was hoping you could tell me." She looked beyond him to Devlin, who was inside the closet, shining a flashlight up at the woodwork surrounding the opening. Leaving the beam trained there, he backed up.

She took a step forward in instinctive protest. "Devlin, please. You're about to brush up against my collection and you're a tad bit…sweaty." But she couldn't help but grin at him. Because, *her collection,* she'd said. Which was right there in front of her. Funny how matters could turn on a dime. An hour ago she'd visualized her shiny new prospects at the Met spiraling down the loo.

Now, in the wake of one stupid, impulsive temper tantrum, her future was looking bright.

Devlin paused in what he was doing to stare at her, his gaze like liquid silk as it poured over her. Shifting her shoulders, she turned to Poppy. Cleared her throat.

"We should probably move the contents down to the parlor to catalog them." Okay, good. Her voice hadn't cracked. But what *was* it about that man? "Once these guys go back to work we won't be able to hear ourselves think if we stay up here."

"Hey, I resent that remark," David said cheerfully,

running his hands over the ornate molding around the closet.

"Gotcha, you bastard," Dev muttered from within it. Then, raising his voice, said, "Found the latch."

Everybody turned to look at him.

He shot them all a cocky smile. "Here, I'll press it down. You see any corresponding parts moving out there, little bro?"

"Yes! Here we go," David replied. "It's in this bit of fancywork on the outer molding."

The Kavanagh brothers played with the mechanism for another ten or fifteen minutes, opening and closing the closet. They tested it with Devlin still in it to see if he could get out from the inside, then tested it again empty of all save the clothing. There was a lot of laughter and the same good-natured bad-mouthing and ribbing that they'd treated each other to down in the kitchen.

Eventually they tore themselves away and went back to their teardown. Jane and Poppy paused in the newly revealed closet, where they were each grabbing an armful of clothing, to watch the men exit the room.

"My God," Poppy breathed as they headed downstairs to their own project. "That is one hunky group of guys. I don't usually go for men a decade older than me, but there's something about that bald guy…"

"Maybe the fact that he's married," Jane said dryly. "And before you get fixated on David, so is he." At Poppy's questioning glance she added, "The one with the light brown hair. He's the youngest brother."

"And you've become a sudden font of knowledge of all things Kavanagh, how?"

She shrugged. "I ate lunch with them."

Poppy stopped dead halfway down the staircase. When her armload of couture clothing threatened to slip, she tightened her grip and got moving again. But not before shooting Jane an admonishing look. "You lie like a rug, girl!"

"Uh-uh. Scout's honor." Carefully laying her treasures upon the couch in the parlor, she explained how she'd come to be at the kitchen table with a rowdy pack of construction workers.

Poppy set her armful down, as well. "Four brawny men and you, huh?" Straightening, she pitty-patted her fingertips over her chest. "Be still my heart. Why, I'm getting all excited merely hearing about it."

"Down, girl. Don't make me get out the hose."

Her friend grinned at her. "So how about the sexy monk? Is he married, too?"

The description delighted Jane. "That's what *I* thought Finn looked like, too! At least until I caught him giving me the once-over, anyhow. And no, he's single. Determined to stay that way, too, if the conversation they had over lunch is anything to go by."

"Not a problem. I'm not looking to marry the man—maybe just fool around with him a little."

Jane made yapping motions with her hand. "Talk, talk, talk, talk, talk."

A small smile curled up the corners of Poppy's lips. "Maybe. Maybe not. Admit it, he looks like he'd know his way around a girl's erogenous zones." Her smile developed a wry edge. "Not to mention that whole naughty priest thing he's got going." Then she turned brisk. "But let's talk about you, Janie. When are *you* going to have yourself a red-hot affair with the oh-so-studly Dev?"

Her heart gave a solid thump against the wall of her chest. "Uh, never?" she said dryly, giving her friend a What, are you kidding me? look.

And tried to ignore the fact that, as ideas went, this one suddenly seemed almost workable.

"Jane, Jane, Jane." Poppy shook her head sadly, her wild ponytail shifting with the movement. "What are we going to do with you? Because you really are missing the boat here, you know."

Jane tried to keep her mouth shut. She really did.

Yet still she heard herself say slowly, "Funny you should mention boats. Because it appears that Devlin plans to stay in Seattle only long enough to see his brother well again. Then he's going back to his sailing gigs in Europe."

"*Really.*" Poppy studied her. "Now, that's interesting. So if you ever *did* consider having a brief fling with the man, that would sort of give you the best of both worlds, wouldn't it? Given your own personal criteria and all? You could have the fun of some down-and-dirty sex with a guy I'm betting knows his stuff when it comes to women—and escape the messy relationship part you're so afraid of."

Her chin rose. "I'm not afraid of anything. And anyway, you know that red-hot passion stuff is so not my sty—"

She cut herself off as she remembered her response to Devlin's kiss.

Glanced at her friend.

Studied her fingernails closely for a moment. Why *not* have a brief affair? What could it hurt? Surely passion wasn't necessarily a bad thing if it had a finite run, with understood rules and a beginning and an end. Right? Why, it would probably make her a better curator. She'd gain firsthand experience with sexuality and all the emotional grizz that went with it. That was bound to be quite useful when it came to understanding the various artists one dealt with in this business.

And face it, Devlin affected her like no other man ever had. He was intelligent, he had a level of sophistication and God knew he was sexy. And he was *leaving*.

Hard to beat that combination.

She looked up at Poppy again.

And slowly said, "Okay, not committing to anything here, mind you.

"But I could maybe handle a little fling."

CHAPTER TWELVE

*I wonder why Miss A. never told me about the se-
cret closet? Ava thinks she probably thought she
had. In any case, thank God for my temper tantrum. Imagine trying to explain to Marjorie not
being able to find the collection! I would have
been* so *up the creek.*

GORDON WAS READY to chew nails by the time everyone
left the Wolcott mansion that evening. He'd prepared
himself for the possibility of having to wait for Jane to
vacate the house. What he hadn't expected was to find
the place crawling with construction workers, as well.

It had just turned six o'clock, though, so how much
longer could they stay? Afraid a nosy neighbor would
become curious if he circled the block one more time,
he took to slowly driving down the street below instead.
The mansion was easily visible from the new vantage
point, and when he lowered his windows he could hear
the sounds of construction coming from one of its upper
floors.

He was only catching glimpses of it during the brief
seconds he managed to tear his attention away from
navigating the narrow, parked-up street, however, and
that just wasn't cutting it. So he pulled the car over at
the end of the block. What the hell. No one seemed to be

paying him the least bit of attention anyhow, so he took a moment to subject the building to a rigorous study.

Holy fuck. The place was mammoth. Squatting on the east side of Queen Anne hill, it commanded a sweeping view of Lake Union, the 1962 World's Fair-built Center with its Seattlecentric trademark Space Needle, and the north end of downtown. The mansion itself appeared surprisingly run-down, especially compared to some of its neighboring steroid-fed houses. Still, the property alone had to be worth a fortune.

And a full third of it belonged to Jane.

Not that he'd heard that from her. Neither had anyone else at the museum, so far as he could tell. Bragging about an inheritance of that magnitude probably wasn't "done" in her circles. And little Miss Perfect was nothing if not well bred. Hell, she had that breeding shit down cold.

Tight-assed bitch.

Well, *he* was nothing if not efficient. And coming up rough in a low-rent housing project had taught him that it always paid to have information on one's opponent. So he'd done some digging. Not that it had taken all that much effort, because, face it, a curator who didn't understand the value of research was in the wrong business.

Gordon Ives didn't deal in being wrong—in business or otherwise. Sure, he might be preparing to jump from museum curator to hotshot poker player. That didn't negate the fact that he was damn good at what he did. In fact, he probably possessed more esoteric knowledge about art and objets d'art than most.

And he'd discovered that the collections Agnes Wolcott had bequeathed to the Metropolitan Museum with the caveat that Jane be the curator of record weren't Kaplinski's only lucky break.

No, sir.

She and her glitzy gal pals had inherited the whole freakin' enchilada.

Fucking overkill was what that was. Once again the old axiom the rich get richer was right on the money. Hell, the rich not only got richer, they got promotions. They got special treatment.

While saps like him got jack shit.

He felt himself tensing up all over and made a conscious effort to relax his jaw, his neck, his shoulders, his gut. He took a few calming breaths and blew them out. Rolled his head from side to side. Shook out his hands. He couldn't afford to get all bent out of shape, at least not right this minute. He was cool; he was in command, and he planned to stay that way until his job here was done. He could blow off steam when he was finished. Until then he had to keep things loose.

Play it smart.

Speaking of which, he really should move before the neighbors down here noticed him. Who knew what kind of networking went on in a 'hood this fine? They probably instructed their South American maids to keep their big brown eyes peeled 24/7 for strangers on their streets.

He found a parking spot not too many blocks away. Grabbing his Burberry raincoat in case the skies opened up as they were more likely to do this time of year than not, he folded it neatly and placed it in the backpack he'd brought along to tote his finds home. Then he locked the rattletrap Chevy he'd gotten to replace his beautiful Lexus—a much-mourned but necessary sacrifice to stave off Fast Eddy's goons—and hoofed it back to the street where the Wolcott mansion resided. Stopping in the shadow of an ancient cherry tree on the corner, he scoped the place out.

And found himself just in time to see three cars backing out of the short drive.

Yes! About damn time. He watched them disappear around the corner, then strolled down the block.

The mansion's driveway was now empty. Exerting care not to demonstrate any suspicious behavior like shooting furtive glances to see if anyone was watching, he strode up the drive as if he owned the joint.

Moments later he was at the kitchen door and then he did allow himself a quick look around. The secluded yard was small and overgrown and the house could stand, at minimum, a new coat of paint. But that wasn't his problem. He wasn't here as a buyer; he was more of a…borrower. Smiling at his own cleverness, he fished a loose key from his pocket.

And shook his head in mock sympathy. Poor Jane. She was so fricking predictable. It must be a drag to go through life lacking imagination. God knew he had more in his little finger than she had in her entire anorexic body.

Because where did women store their purses at work? Why, in their desk drawers, of course—which was exactly where he had found hers, in a deep bottom drawer that she'd left unlocked and unattended. And as a man with a sharp eye for detail, it had taken him less than two seconds to cull the key to the mansion from the other three on her ring.

Not that he'd needed to be particularly observant to

distinguish one shiny new key from a few duller, well-used models—especially when one of those was a combination keyless remote and car key unit.

There'd been none of that fancy-ass Agent Double-O Seven shit for him, either. He hadn't made a quick impression in a tin full of putty because one, he didn't know anyone who knew how to actually make a key from an impression and two, he was a thrill-seeker at heart.

But a thrill-seeker who utilized his generously endowed intelligence. He'd simply picked a day when Jane had been invited (a euphemism for commanded) to discuss the progress she was making on her exhibits. The minute he'd seen her go into Marjorie's office and close the door, he'd liberated her key from the ring and hoofed it over a couple of blocks to the locksmith kiosk in the Comstock Building. He'd had the copy made and the original returned to her key ring with time to spare.

And here he was, ready to reverse his fortunes.

He let himself in through the kitchen door and deactivated the security alarm. Drawing even breaths to center himself, he looked around.

There wasn't a lot to see—it was simply a kitchen, neither beautifully remodeled nor completely butt-ugly. There sure as hell weren't any bars of gold bullion lying around just waiting to be picked up and hauled away. And that being the case, he couldn't give a crap what the room looked like. He stepped out into the hallway.

"I'm starving," a female voice said from the room with the square archway down the hall. "I'm gonna go see if there's anything in the fridge."

Gordon plastered himself against the wall, his heart

jackhammering so fast and furiously he was surprised it hadn't set off the neighbors' car alarms.

Fuck! Fuck, fuck, fuck! When the cars had left he'd thought everyone had gone with them. Well, that clearly wasn't the case, which made that old saw about what assume made of you and me a little too close for comfort. And every word the woman's voice spoke made it clear she was coming nearer the hallway where he stood like a fucking moose caught in the headlights.

He was screwed. Looking around frantically, he confirmed what he already knew—that there was no place to hide. Not without crossing the hall again—and who knew what the line of sight might be for anyone approaching the wide archway to the corridor?

These thoughts raced through his mind at the speed of light as he inched along the wall away from the occupied room.

"You and your appetite," Jane's voice said. "If you can hang on for ten minutes, I'll take you out to dinner."

"You're actually considering quitting for the night?" The other woman's voice sounded surprised, but thank God it was lower in volume, as if she'd turned back into the room. "I thought for sure you'd be sleeping with your couture collection to celebrate its discovery."

"You're such a card, Poppy."

Sagging relief at his reprieve immediately morphed into anger at the two women who had put him in this position. What kind of name was Poppy for a grown woman, anyway? What the hell was Jane's other friend's name, *Muffy?* And did she date men called Biff? Shaking his head, he judged the risk of crossing the hall was now negligible and slipped back into the kitchen.

"Anyhow," he heard Jane continue more faintly, "we got a great start this afternoon. I can't tell you how relieved I am to have finally found all this stuff. I'm not quite prepared to camp out with them, but no doubt about it, I'm definitely relieved. Let's grab the items we cataloged today and put 'em back in the closet. Not that, though!"

"Did I not just hear you say the items we cataloged today?" her friend demanded dryly.

"I know, I know." Jane's sheepishness was evident even from where Gordon stood. "What I meant was everything except the Dior. That's my talisman, and I want to leave it down here to admire while we log in the rest of the exhibit. I should be finished with this project long before the guys start in on this floor, so I don't have to worry about construction dust."

"The gown is definitely gorgeous," the woman with the stupid name agreed. "It's gonna rock as the exhibit's signature piece."

"Oh, God, isn't it? I am so psyched. Anyhow, help me put away the stuff on this rack and I'll buy you the biggest combination plate Mama's Kitchen sells."

As the females talked, Gordon eased open the kitchen's broom closet. Doing a quick calculation, he figured he was probably slight enough to squeeze inside. What he was less certain of was whether he could do so without disturbing the broom and mop already in there. Hearing the women shuffling into the hallway, then climbing the stairs, he quietly crossed the room to another door. This one didn't lead out into the hallway and it didn't appear to go out to the backyard, either. Twisting the knob, he opened it a hair. The hinges squealed.

Except for his head, which whipped to stare over his shoulder at the doorway, he froze. No exclamations erupted from Jane or her friend and no footsteps came pounding on the double. Exhaling the breath he hadn't even realized he'd been holding, he decided what had sounded as loud and startling as the crack of the whip to him probably hadn't even registered past the kitchen door, let alone upstairs. Turning back to the door, he peeked through the space he'd opened.

Huh. It led to a laundry room and he eased the door wide enough to slide through. Once inside, he closed it behind him.

There was a large floor-to-ceiling closet next to the washer and dryer, and when he opened it he discovered plenty of room to host a medium-size man, if he didn't mind folding up a bit. Gordon climbed in, sat on the floor with his knees pulled up to his chest and tugged the door shut.

Then he waited....

And waited...

And waited some more.

It seemed to take a good deal longer than the ten minutes he timed, but eventually he heard the two women entering the kitchen. Through the two sturdy doors separating them, he could only make out a word here and a word there of their conversation. He caught enough of it, however, to know they were getting ready to leave.

Then finally—*finally!*—he heard the back door slam.

He waited an additional five minutes, which crawled by in a manner more befitting thirty-five, before climbing out of the closet. Sitting semicurled had stiffened every muscle and joint in his body and they screamed a protest as he slowly straightened. He hobbled over to the door—then simply stood there with his hand on the knob.

This was the moment of truth. The door was solid and dense, so there was no way of telling if the room on the other side truly was empty. But not only was Lady Luck generally on his side, his mama hadn't raised no chickenshit.

He turned the knob. Slowly inched the door open.

And found no one in the kitchen.

He breathed a sigh of relief because, while Luck was usually his lady, sometimes you just couldn't trump the fucking rich. They had all the advantage of education, connections and trust funds, but were they content with that? Hell, no. They had to plant their feet on the necks of the poor on top of it. Moving cautiously, he exited the kitchen for the second time to creep down the hallway to the area where he'd heard the women. He peeked around the doorjamb.

Then stepped fully into the archway and stared, slack-jawed. "Holy shit."

The place was Aladdin's cave, with treasure trove after treasure trove displayed upon the shelves, on the floor, on bookcases, on…well, every available flat surface. There was so much stuff, he was stymied as to what he should examine first.

Hot damn. Every article he'd ever read about old lady Wolcott had obviously been right on the money. The woman had been a Grade-A collector.

He barely even spared Jane's exhibit pieces a glance,

other than to note that there were two rolling racks, one of which was packed with couture clothing that appeared to be in prime condition. Any other day he would have inspected every single garment and accessory inch by inch, thread by thread.

Today he only had eyes for the amazing array of portable swag. As a curator he was fascinated by the sheer number of collections, not to mention their quality and completeness. As a man with an ax hanging over his neck he saw salvation.

Yes, sir. He smiled widely. He was one lucky son of a bitch.

He would have loved nothing more than to scoop up an entire collection. He could get a fortune for those Cairo Regency snuff boxes, for instance.

But his aim here was to avoid drawing attention to the fact that things had been taken. The only way to do that was to appropriate one item from this collection and one item from that one. Once he was out from under Fast Eddy's thumb there would be time enough to do a little judicious planning on what additional booty he could help himself to. He saw more than one piece that single-handedly would fund his next poker tournament.

For a while, however, he merely wandered around and looked at everything. He didn't touch and he didn't even particularly covet. He merely admired it all for a bit.

He could almost give up his dream of being a big-time poker player and be happy as an underpaid curator if he were ever given charge of objects like these. The old lady had known what she was doing when she'd collected this stuff.

But he was a realist. And realistically, exhibits of this

caliber would always go to the Jane Kaplinskis of the world: people with the right education and the right connections. Guys with state educations who hailed from places like Yesler Terrace would forever come in a distant second in the eyes of the museum muckety-mucks.

Recalling himself to the job at hand, he made a mental note regarding a couple of possibilities, then left the room to explore some other options.

The whole house was one huge pot of gold, he decided forty-five minutes later. There were incredible objects in nearly every room in the joint.

He helped himself to several that he found in rooms on the second floor, rolling them in the kitchen towels he'd brought, tucked into his pack, for that express purpose. He knew, however, that what he'd liberated so far wouldn't buy him free from debt. As much as he'd like to avoid disrupting any of the collections down in the room where Jane was apparently spending the bulk of her time and was therefore more likely to notice if something went missing, that was where the cream of Agnes Wolcott's collections was kept.

He went back downstairs.

It was dark in the study, or whatever the hell the swells called this space. Luckily, it was located at the back side of the house, so he tugged closed its huge rolling pocket door and risked turning on a desk lamp. Then he pulled out his high-powered flashlight to more closely inspect those items out of reach of the lamp's weak illumination. He purposefully started his organized inspection within the groupings farthest away from her work space.

He was discriminatory about what he took and very

careful to rearrange the collections in order to fill in any gaps left by the objects he selected. And an hour and a half later, he thought he had enough to get Fast Eddy off his back once and for all.

He'd turned off the lamp and was on his way out when the shadowy rack of couture clothing caught his eye once more. Flipping his flashlight back on, he took a moment to subject the collection to a closer scrutiny.

Depending on how Jane handled the exhibit, this had the potential to be important. *Hugely* important, he acknowledged, and resentment spread bitter poison throughout his system.

For just a moment he thought of the concealed dagger in the nineteenth-century Chinese hand-tooled opium pipe he'd liberated. Bearing in mind its honed narrow blade, he thought longingly about how much damage he could do to this collection in a brief but satisfying minute or two.

It would serve her right. He was the superior curator, but she was stealing his career right out from under him. The fact that he didn't intend to work the rest of his life for a museum that didn't appreciate him didn't excuse her from climbing over his back on her way up the Metropolitan career ladder. Just a slash here and a slash there and they'd be back on equal footing once again.

Then he blew out a resigned breath, clicked off his flashlight and crossed to the ornate pocket door once again. That would hardly serve his determination to keep this mission clandestine, he admitted, rolling the door back into the wall. It wouldn't advance his chances for further forays into the wonderful world of old lady Wolcott's collections.

So he'd walk away. Leave the clothing in the same pristine condition in which he had found it. But when he was done here once and for all?

He was going to stick it to Kaplinski. Stick it to her where the bitch would bleed the most.

Right in her oh-so-big-deal career.

CHAPTER THIRTEEN

Omigawd. Omigawd. OH. MY. GOD! Who knew?

EVER SINCE Jane had admitted she thought she could handle a fling, she hadn't been able to get the notion out of her head. She could barely think about anything else.

Maybe that was why, when she came into the mansion kitchen a few days later to grab something to drink and found the refrigerator door already wide-open with Devlin checking out the beverages inside, she blurted, "Do you wanna have no-strings sex with me?"

She promptly went hot, then cold, then hot again. Every self-protective instinct she possessed—and there were a ton of them—screamed a protest along the lines of *What the hell are you doing?* Holy crap, what had become of her ability to bite her tongue while she deliberated over any inappropriate words agitating to leave her mouth? Except when she was with Ava and Poppy, she never just verbalized the first thought that popped to mind. No, sir, she very carefully considered the ramifications. Weighed the consequences. Measured the—

Devlin released the water bottle he'd just reached for and slowly straightened, derailing her train of thought. Heart slamming, Jane wanted badly to run as he turned to look at her, but pride nailed her Beverly Feldman platform peep-toed heels to the floor.

He slammed the refrigerator door shut and it was as if a moment that had been dragging through molasses suddenly shot into hyperspeed. He looked at her, his face impassive, his eyes hot. "Get your coat."

"What? Oh." She stacked one cork-soled shoe atop the toe of the other and entwined her fingers behind her back. "I didn't mean right this minute."

"I do. I've been thinking about this ever since you gave me The Look the night we met. The one before you froze me out."

She would have loved to demand *what look?* Except she knew. It had been the one a woman gives a man when she's interested, and she couldn't deny it. There had been a spark, a combustible chemistry from the first moment she'd set eyes on him. She'd tried to bury it when she'd realized he was drunk, but she could not refute the fact that it had existed. All the same she said weakly, "No, you haven't."

"Oh, yeah, I have, and now that I've been invited to do all the things that I've imagined doing to you, I'm not taking the chance you'll change your mind." Reaching her in two ground-eating giant strides, he encircled her wrist with callused fingers rendered cool by the bottle he'd touched. "Let's go."

She stuttered a protest, but found herself following a willing arm's length behind as he walked with long-legged strides out into the hallway.

He stopped at the foot of the stairway. "Finn!"

A saw whined into silence. "Yo."

"I'm taking off for a while."

"The hell you say!" There was a thud, then the stomp of footsteps striding out into the upstairs hall. "The grout we've been waiting on's coming in tomorrow, which means David and Bren and I gotta get back to the Morris job. We've still got a shitload of work to finish here, bro, and—"

His voice had been growing closer and more irate with each heavy-booted step, but it abruptly cut off as Finn stopped at the top of the stairs and looked down at them. His posture, which had been aggressively tense, went loose as he perused Dev's grip on Jane's wrist. Then his gaze rose to her face, where he no doubt saw the blush scalding her skin from throat to forehead.

"Huh." A slight smile tipped up one corner of Finn's mouth. "Alrighty, then. See you later." A storm of protest came from within the sunroom, but Finn merely said, "Deal with it," as he strode back down the hall. "Dev's gotta give Legs a ride." He disappeared from sight, but laughter at his own double entendre floated behind him.

"Oh God." She tugged at the fingers lightly grasping her wrist. "This is *so* not a good idea."

"Yes, it is." His clasp didn't tighten, but neither did he set her loose. "It's probably one of your more excellent ideas." He headed for the parlor.

She trotted along in his wake. "Not if your brothers are going to be snickering about it, it's not."

Inside the room he freed her and looked around. "Finn's not the kind to kiss and tell," he said absentmindedly as he strode a few steps first in one direction, then in another. "And his give-you-a-ride crack was just a shot to let me know that *he* knows the score. But I can guarantee he won't be sharing his knowledge with Bren and David. Here." He snatched her coat off the rolling rack that she'd only half filled with today's inventoried stock and thrust it into her arms. Then he bent his head and, touching her with nothing more than slightly chapped lips, he kissed her.

White noise filled her brain and she forgot all about the resurrected sense of responsibility that seeing the not-nearly-full-enough rack had raised in her. Sighing, her own lips softened, opening beneath his.

Devlin rewarded her by slicking his tongue over her bottom lip for a single, finished-much-too-soon taste. Then he slowly raised his head. Stepped back. And looked at her through heavy-lidded eyes.

Their gazes locked for one heartbeat. Two. Then simultaneously, they made twin yearning sounds deep in their throats, and his hands reached out to frame her face. They each took a step forward and Jane abandoned the coat in her arms to reach for him. Their bodies slapped together before the garment could drop to the floor.

Dev's mouth slammed down on hers.

This kiss was all speed and moisture and hard, urgent pressure, and it made Jane mindless with lust and need. She was only vaguely conscious of being danced backward until her shoulder blades pressed up against the wall, only peripherally aware that her right leg immediately rubbed up his outer thigh to hook around his hip. The bulk of her coat was a barrier that kept him from rocking against her as intimately as she'd like, and her restless plucking at its dangling sleeve had no impact. But there wasn't much she could do to rectify the matter. Not when she couldn't bear the thought of putting the necessary distance between them that would allow the damn thing to drop to the floor.

He ripped his mouth free. "It's either right here, right now, with my brothers upstairs," he panted, "or privacy at my place, which, thank you, Jesus, isn't too far away." Pulling back, he grabbed her coat when it began its slide toward the floor, then shook it out and held it open, an invitation for her to slip into it. "What's it gonna be, Jane? My control is fraying fast."

She slid her arms into the sleeves, pulled her hair out of the collar and snatched up her purse.

When they reached the driveway a moment later, however, Devlin stopped dead. "Son of a bitch!" he snarled.

"What?" She blinked, confused by his sudden anger. Then a wisp of unease wafted through her stomach as the damp fall air started blowing some of the lust vapors from her head. What was she doing?

"I didn't drive today—Finn picked me up on his way in." Thrusting his fingers through his hair, he stared at the three vehicles in the driveway. "Who the hell does this CR-V belong to?"

"Me. And pretty darn pumped I was, too, to get a spot in the drive, lemme tell you. Usually by the time I get here you and your brothers have hogged all the parking space."

"Babe. This is yours?" A slow, crooked smile curved his lips and his eyes lightened from a dark amber-flecked brownish-green to a mossier hue. "How brilliant of you to have parked right at the end where we can pull out without having to wait for anyone to move their car. Fork over the keys."

"Forget it. My car, my keys. I drive."

He hooked a hand behind her neck and hauled her

in for another kiss. By the time he raised his mouth off hers once again, she'd wound her arms around his neck and plastered herself against him from chest to knees.

"I know all the shortcuts to my place," he murmured, using his thumb to rub the moisture left behind from her bottom lip. "I can get us there faster."

She flipped him the key ring but narrowed her eyes at him. "Don't even start thinking that every time I disagree with you, you can kiss away my objections."

"No, ma'am. Wouldn't dream of it." He opened her door for her.

She climbed in, but turned her head to look at him before he could close the door. "Because two can play that game, you know."

He scooped a strand of her hair away from her face. "I'm not trying to manipulate you, Jane. I'm just trying to get you into my bed by the quickest route possible."

"Just so you know."

"Duly warned." He closed her door and loped around the front of the SUV.

They didn't say much as he drove out of the Queen Anne district and headed into Belltown, but the atmosphere inside her vehicle was thick with sexual awareness. At one point he reached over the console and stroked her leg.

"You do understand that I'm going back to Europe once Bren is back on his feet, right?"

"Yes." She cleared her throat, then a laugh tinged with hysteria escaped her. "I'm counting on it."

His fingers dug into her thigh for a second as he took his eyes off the road to glance over at her. "Ouch."

She doubted he wanted to hear about the befuddled

mixture of curiosity and fear she was experiencing over this terrifying, exciting passion he aroused in her. "Would you rather I got all clingy and demanding?"

His quick grimace elicited another laugh, this one wry. "I didn't think so."

They arrived at Devlin's place on the north end of Belltown moments later. He escorted her from the car to the garage elevator and from it to his apartment on the third floor.

He helped her out of her coat and turned to hang it in the hallway closet. Jane walked into the living room and looked around, trying to quell her nerves. The room was pretty bare, just a chair and a couch that looked as if it had been culled from somebody's basement. Next to the couch sat a narrow end table holding a lamp. A small television set with old-fashioned rabbit ears sat on a bookshelf composed of four decorative cinder blocks set on end to support two inexpensive shelves.

Devlin joined her and she looked up from the stack of Sudoku puzzle books on the end table. "Your decorating style is very…spare."

He laughed. "When I found out about Bren I was taking a yacht from Marseille to Athens. I was still almost two days out and couldn't jump ship, so by the time I brought it into port and turned it over to its owner I didn't want to take the time to go back to my home base in Palermo for my stuff. I came here with the duffel I had with me on the boat." He shrugged. "Not that I would've brought much in the way of knickknacks anyhow. I share a house with a guy who does the same thing I do, and since neither of us is there very often, it, too, is pretty spare. It's an improvement on this, but not by much."

"It's a far cry from my nesting style," she admitted. "I've got stuff in my place. Lots and lots of stuff." The majority of which held meaning for her or had memories attached. "I don't see anything personal here."

"I've never collected a lot in the way of material things—my lifestyle is too nomadic to carry around much more than the basics. But come with me and I'll show you something personal." He wagged his dark eyebrows at her. "Something I know you'll like." Taking her hand, he led her toward what could only be a bedroom.

"And would this something be an item that accompanies you everywhere you go?" she asked dryly. She was surprised, because she'd expected his approach to be smoother, more sophisticated. Still, she was grateful to be moving, to have his hands on her again because she didn't *think* so damn much when he was touching her.

"What?" He stopped and stared at her. "Oh, shit, you thought I meant—" Throwing his head back, he roared with laughter. Then he hauled her in and gave her a rib-creaking hug that lifted her high heels clear off the ground. Controlling himself, he set her on her feet again and stepped back. But he held her shoulders and grinned at her. "You thought I was talking about my dick?"

She tried not to squirm, but she knew there wasn't a hope in hell that her face wasn't red. She could feel it flaming.

His lips quirked again, but, firming them up, he gave her a solemn look. "I like to think I have a little more style than that." Slinging his arm around her shoulders, he ushered her into his bedroom, which was as sparsely furnished as the rest of the apartment. Leading her over to a headboard-free bed, he stopped next to the nightstand and picked up a framed photograph.

"I know how much you like the idea of big families," he said, handing it to her. "This was taken the night I got home. My aunt Eileen took it and my mom and Hannah matted and framed it for me."

"Oh my God." She looked down at a group shot that must have contained twenty-five people. "You're related to *all* these people?"

"Babe. These are just the ones who didn't already have plans." Snuggling up behind her, he reached around to point out a couple who appeared to be in their midsixties. His breath was warm against her ear when he said, "That's my mom and da. The short lady next to Mom is my Grandma Hester and this is Grandma Katherine—who my sister Kate is named after—and Grandpa Darragh. That's Kate there. You already know Hannah and this is my sister Maureen and her husband, Jim."

He turned his head to press an openmouthed kiss against the side of her throat. "The redhead next to her is Aunt Eileen—"

"Who took the photograph," she said breathlessly, to show she was paying attention. But she could feel her bones dissolving, and shivers raced up and down her spine.

"Who took the photo," he agreed and, as if in reward, kissed another spot lower on her neck.

"Wait a minute. How can she be in the picture if she took it?" See? She had her wits about her.

"By putting a camera with a shutter timer on a sturdy

bookcase. That couple next to her is my auntie Mag and uncle Clem."

Somehow she hung on to the framed photo, but he kept punctuating each new identity he revealed with a kiss to her neck, to her nape or her earlobe, and she lost track of who several of his aunts and cousins and his various nieces and nephews were. She also gave up trying to stay upright and slumped back against him. With her in heels, only a few inches separated them in height and his erection pressed against her bottom. She began to move her hips in subtle oscillations, grinding her rear against the solid length of his sex.

He sucked in a breath and his teeth closed over her earlobe. "Did I mention I think your shoes are sexy?" he murmured. "For someone who dresses like a librarian most of the time—"

"I do not!" She pulled away slightly, craning her head around to look at him over her shoulder. "And stereotyping merely shows your ignorance, Kavanagh. Have you even been in a library lately?" She infused her voice with faux concern. "You can read, can't you?"

He snugged her back against him and tightened his arms around her waist to keep her there. "I'll have you know I've graduated to Dick and Jane primers—and wicked proud it makes me, too." He gave her a smile that loosened the muscles in her thighs, then bent his head to her neck again. "But, okay, no more comparing your style to old-maid librarians." His lips traveled the side of her throat to the underside of her jaw, then returned to her ear. "Still, you gotta admit no one's ever going to mistake you for a stripper."

"Aw, gee, and here I always hoped that someday someone would."

"Well, all right, it could happen—if they got past all the black and brown and the occasional tan to take a good look at your feet. Your shoes are hot. And your panties are incendiary. What color are they today, my not-so-repressed Jane? I'm partial to those red ones."

"White," she promptly lied. "Made of cotton. Granny-size."

She felt the huff of his laughter insinuate itself down the whorls of her ear.

"Bet you a hundred bucks they're not."

She set the framed photo back in its spot and turned in his arms. "You'd win," she whispered. Then, winding her arms around his strong neck, she kissed him with all the pent-up desire he'd spent the last five minutes building in her.

The minute their lips made contact, it was like history repeating. In the vein of every other time they'd touched, Jane's mind shut down and her libido rose up onto its hind legs to roar like a wildcat. With an easy hop, she wrapped her legs around Dev's hips and crossed her ankles behind his back, her heels pressed against the hard swell of his butt.

The room whirled and suddenly she was lying on the bed with a hundred and eighty-five pounds of aroused male propped over her. Dark hazel eyes burned into her own.

"One more kiss, and then I'm peeling you out of all this black," he said in a raspy voice, and she wasn't sure if he was threatening her or making a promise. Before she could decide, Devlin sank down to cage her against

YOUR PARTICIPATION IS REQUESTED!

Dear Reader,

Since you are a lover of romance fiction – we would like to get to know you!

Inside you will find a short Reader's Survey. Sharing your answers with us will help our editorial staff understand who you are and what activities you enjoy.

To thank you for your participation, we would like to send you 2 books and 2 gifts – **ABSOLUTELY FREE!**

Enjoy your gifts with our appreciation,

Pam Powers

SEE INSIDE FOR READER'S SURVEY

For Your Romance Reading Pleasure...

Get 2 FREE BOOKS that will fuel
your imagination with intensely moving
stories about life, love and relationships.

We'll send you 2 books and 2 gifts
ABSOLUTELY FREE
just for completing our Reader's Survey!

YOUR READER'S SURVEY
"THANK YOU" FREE GIFTS INCLUDE:
▶ **2 Romance books**
▶ **2 lovely surprise gifts**

PLEASE FILL IN THE CIRCLES COMPLETELY TO RESPOND

1) What type of fiction books do you enjoy reading? (Check all that apply)
- ○ Suspense/Thrillers
- ○ Action/Adventure
- ○ Modern-day Romances
- ○ Historical Romance
- ○ Humour
- ○ Paranormal Romance

2) What attracted you most to the last fiction book you purchased on impulse?
- ○ The Title
- ○ The Cover
- ○ The Author
- ○ The Story

3) What is usually the greatest influencer when you <u>plan</u> to buy a book?
- ○ Advertising
- ○ Referral
- ○ Book Review

4) How often do you access the internet?
- ○ Daily
- ○ Weekly
- ○ Monthly
- ○ Rarely or never.

5) How many NEW paperback fiction novels have you purchased in the past 3 months?
- ○ 0 - 2
- ○ 3 - 6
- ○ 7 or more

YES! I have completed the Reader's Survey. Please send me the 2 FREE books and 2 FREE gifts (gifts are worth about $10) for which I qualify. I understand that I am under no obligation to purchase any books, as explained on the back of this card.

194/394 MDL FVVW

FIRST NAME	LAST NAME

ADDRESS

APT.#	CITY

STATE/PROV.	ZIP/POSTAL CODE

HARLEQUIN® READER SERVICE — Here's How It Works:

BUSINESS REPLY MAIL
FIRST-CLASS MAIL   PERMIT NO. 717   BUFFALO, NY

POSTAGE WILL BE PAID BY ADDRESSEE

HARLEQUIN READER SERVICE
PO BOX 1341
BUFFALO NY 14240-8571

NO POSTAGE
NECESSARY
IF MAILED
IN THE
UNITED STATES

the coverlet with his arms and legs. Lowering his head, he rocked his mouth over hers.

This kiss was slow and deep, and she sank into a hot, rich world brimming with his flavors. At one point she caught his lower lip between her teeth, and it was firm and full when she scraped her teeth over it, flexible when she sank them in to catch it in a firmer grip and give it an experimental tug. The membrane stretched as he slowly lifted his head, and when he smiled she felt it change shape. The next second his lip slid free.

Scooting down a few inches, he applied that wicked, knowledgeable mouth to her neck once again. Only this time he burned a path down the front of her throat. Her hands threaded through the cool strands of his warm-colored hair, and he paused at the hollow of her throat to look up at her. Pushing up onto his elbows, he slipped his fingers beneath the opening of her little black cashmere sweater.

"This has gotta go." He eased it off her shoulders, then wrestled her around until he had her out of the garment.

Pushing up to kneel astride her, he made a production out of swiping his forearm across his forehead. "Man, this is hard work. I've never met a woman who goes to so much trouble to hide her light under a bushel the way you do." Dropping his arm, he reached out to trace the high, collarless neckline of her silk organza blouse. His face set in lines of concentration, he slipped a small self-fabric button through the buttonhole, unveiling a tiny triangle of flesh.

"You've got the prettiest skin," he said, tracing the uncovered spot with the tip of his forefinger. "Why do you cover it all up?" Applying himself once more to his task, he slipped another button free. Then another.

"To avoid situations like this," she admitted, then marveled at herself. Only with Ava and Poppy did she usually speak without first measuring her words. But from the moment she'd met Devlin, she'd had a tough time censoring herself with him.

"I'd like to hear the reason for that someday, but not right this min—" Finishing with her button placket, he peeled the sides apart. *"Blue,"* he breathed, stroking reverent fingers across the little embroidered butterflies on her bra.

"Aqua."

"I'm a guy, honey—we don't know from fancy colors." He slid his palm over her breast and gently squeezed. "But, *damn,* I like your underwear!"

One touch of his hard-skinned hand on her breast—even with the padded fabric separating them—and conversation was beyond her. She arched into his touch. Her boobs might be small—okay, there was no might about it, they were small. Still, there was nothing diminutive about their sensitivity. That was huge.

Killer huge.

Double D huge. And Devlin appeared to be a man who knew how to cater to that sensitivity.

She wasn't sure how she felt about that, since the only person who'd touched the girls in a long, long time was her. And generally she liked it that way—it meant that everything was under control. But he raised her off the mattress to unfasten her bra and peeled her out of it and her nipples promptly leaped out at him like eager puppies begging for attention.

He didn't hesitate to give it to them, either. Grasping the spiked peaks between his thumbs and index fingers, he gently squeezed.

She didn't recognize the desperate sound that rolled from her throat and under ordinary circumstances it would have embarrassed the hell out of her. Now, she couldn't bring herself to care. Not when sensation shot from her nipples to deep between her legs, arching her back off the coverlet and making her legs shift restlessly apart.

He swore beneath his breath, gave her nipples another tug, then set her loose to rear up on his knees. Devlin dragged his shirt off over his head, tossed it aside, then came down on top of her, all warm skin and hard muscle as he drove her deeper into the mattress.

He slithered down her body, his chest dragging against her sensitized nipples, before coming to rest against her stomach. Cupping one breast in his hand, he wrapped his lips around her protruding nipple and sucked.

She watched his cheeks hollow, felt the tug clear to her womb and made that noise again. Thrusting her fingers into his hair, she held his head in place. Then she immediately reversed herself, trying to tug it away as the sensations grew almost more than she could bear. "Oh, please," she whispered. "Please, please, please."

"Christ." Dev looked up at her, saw the flush riding her cheekbones and the need weighing down her eyelids. He felt the slight slope of her breast in his hand, the spear of her nipple shifting against the roof of his mouth beneath the firm pressure of his tongue. And he nearly went off in his jeans like a teen getting lucky for the first time with the girl of his dreams.

Jane obviously needed a Truth in Advertising warning slapped on her. Because God have mercy.

So, what did you think, that the way she dresses indicates her hotness factor? Clothing has jack to do with a woman's sexuality. Jack. It was a no-brainer, but apparently he was a slow learner, because while the fact might be self-evident, it caught him by surprise all over again as *this* woman moved against him and made those sexy little take-me sounds deep in her throat.

Reluctantly, he released the sweet spike of her nipple, which seemed to be Jane's personal detonator, and pushed back to kneel astride her legs. They had sprawled wide and he narrowed his knees on the outside of her thighs to push them back together again. He watched her hips perform a little bump and grind against the spread as he unbuttoned and unzipped her slacks.

Man, she was killing him here. "Lift up, honey."

She did and he slid her pants down her hips, revealing little hip-hugger panties that matched her bra. He almost had her divested of the slacks, but couldn't prevent himself from pausing to run his thumb up the damp satin-covered furrow of her sex.

"Dev?" Her voice rose two octaves and her newly bared thighs pressed hard against the knees trapping them closed.

He swore and ripped the slacks off. Luckily they had wide legs because he'd forgotten about her shoes.

And holy shit, she looked hot wearing nothing but a minuscule pair of panties and those black-and-tan ankle-strap high heels. Wrapping his fingers around her ankles, he raised them in the air and yanked, bringing her sliding down the comforter and up over his knees. Spreading her legs, he scooted her a little higher up his thighs and leaned into her until his cock, straining the fly of his jeans, brushed the V beneath those pretty little panties.

She arched into the contact, but he could see he had her at an impossible-to-maintain angle and he sat back on his heels and pulled her up to straddle him.

She promptly crossed her ankles behind his back and wound her arms around his neck, bringing their chests into full contact. "Ooh."

No shit. He slid his hands up her bare back, then stroked his way down to grasp her gently rounded hips. He rocked her on his hard-on. "Dev's gotta give Legs a ride."

The crook of her lips was like no expression he'd ever seen on her face. This Jane wasn't embarrassed at hearing him repeat Finn's earlier words. *This* Jane looked carnal and knowing.

And that was before a sultry laugh burbled out of her chest.

"Jane's going to be the one doling out Dev's rides, pal," she informed him, and, planting those cork platform-sole-and-high-heeled shoes into the mattress next to his hips, she raised and lowered her hips infinitesimally. She was slow and meticulous and her rhythm threatened to drive them both to madness.

His own hips started rocking, slowly at first, then faster and harder until he was lifting her higher on her feet and then slamming them back down with his hands grasping her hips to hold her to him. "Can't take this much longer," he panted. "Gotta get inside you."

"Good idea. I hate to admit this, but my legs are giving out anyhow."

Laughing, he rolled them over, kissed her roughly, then pushed back to stand at the side of the bed while he kicked free of his boots, socks and jeans. "Love the undies," he said, watching as she lounged back on her elbows, her legs sprawled without an atom of self-consciousness and her beige nipples pointing at him like little missiles locked and loaded, semaphoring *Come and get me* loud and clear. "Lose 'em."

"You lose yours."

He hooked his thumbs in the waistband of his boxers and thrust them down to the point where gravity could do its job.

"Oh, wow." Without taking her gaze off his dick, which had sprung free and was pointing at her as if she were the magnet and it the iron shavings, she sat up to remove her panties. Licking her lips, she glanced up at him. "I'm sorry, I know I'm staring. It's just…been a while since I've seen one of those."

His cock was bobbing like a dashboard hula dancer and he wrapped it in his fist to hold it still. "Babe. I'm doing some staring of my own." At five and a half feet of flawless skin, flushed pink and clad in nothing but a pair of sexy heels. At slumberous blue eyes and shining, stick-straight hair that tumbled over her right shoulder and graced her sex in an oh-so-Jane tidy little stripe. "You oughtta go naked more often. It's a very good look on you."

She gave him a droll smile. "I bet you say that to all the girls."

Actually…he didn't. He'd dated a lot of women in his time and probably plenty with more spectacular bodies. Yet every one of them had dressed to advertise the goods; there'd been no surprises. Jane was all surprises and looking at her set him to slowly stroking his cock. He didn't even realize he was doing it until her gaze lowered to watch.

Looking back up at him, she crooked a finger. "C'mere."

Hey, nobody had to ask him twice. He stopped himself from diving on top of her, but just barely. And the fact that he found it necessary brought him up short. *She's a rank beginner, and you've been around the block a time or two,* his ego whispered. *You gonna let her lead you around by the dick?*

Hell, no.

He lowered himself alongside her and set out to demonstrate who was boss. He poured on the expertise, kissing her until she panted, touching her until she moaned.

But he was fooling himself if he thought he was the master seducer here. "Aw, Jane," he whispered, catching her earlobe between his teeth while he stroked his fingers down her silky stomach to the beckoning little touch-me strip of hair down between her legs. "You just undo me. So honest. So fearless." He slipped the pad of his forefinger between slippery feminine lips and watched her eyes blur as he slid it lazily up and down the slick furrow. "So hot."

"Oh God, Dev." Her head ground into the coverlet and her hips rocked beneath his hand. "Please. Won't you—"

He gently patted her clitoris. "What do you want me to do, Janie?" He'd heard her friends call her that, and what he'd once written off as wildly out of character he now saw as suiting her to a T.

"Put this—" her hand snaked out to wrap around his cock "—inside me. Now. Yes?"

"You got it." Because how stupid would he be to argue? Two more minutes with her hand on the goods and he'd go off like a Fourth of July rocket. Unpeeling her fingers, he rolled to the side of the bed. A second later he'd fetched a condom from the nightstand drawer and was ripping it open. Efficiently, he suited up.

Rejoining her, he propped himself over her and set about bringing her back to the state of arousal she'd been in when he'd pulled away to take care of business. It didn't take long. He was beginning to realize that Jane was a powder keg of passion.

He licked her nipples and sank his forefinger into that sweet heat between her legs, flattening his palm against her mound. The sheath he probed clamped down on his finger and his patience imploded. Sliding his hand away, he kneed her legs apart and insinuated himself between them. Thumbing down his dick, he eased the head inside her.

Jesus. She was slick and wet and so freakin' tight. He looked down at her. "Janie."

Her eyes, which were glazed and inward-looking, slowly focused on him. "Hmm?"

"I want you to know I've got a clean bill of health."

"'Kay." She raised her legs up over his hips, which sent his cock sliding into her a couple of inches. "Me, too."

Like it had even occurred to him to think otherwise. Before he could decide whether he should mention that or not, she planted her feet on the mattress and pushed against him, ensconcing him even deeper within the kiln-hot sheath.

His breath exploding from his lungs, he drove himself all the way home. When Jane's throat arched and a sound of appreciation wafted out on a shuddery sigh, he pulled back, then slammed forward again.

"Oh!" Her hands gripping his biceps, her short nails digging in, she stared up at him with a furrowed brow. He feared he'd gone too fast, was too rough. But her hips contracted when he started to pull out and she propelled them ceilingward to meet his next thrust, which he tried without noticeable success to soften. And she panted, "Full. God, Mary, I feel so full."

"Too much?" He eased back. *Saynosaynosayno*. Because the saints help him, he wasn't one hundred percent certain he could do the right thing and back away if it was.

"Uh-uh." She licked her bottom lip. "Want more."

He went a little crazy. He should have considered her relative inexperience and kept it gentle, but instead…

He dug his toes into the mattress and pushed up on his palms and he hammered into her with long, hard strokes. Looking down at where they were joined, he watched himself pull almost all the way out of her, then slam back in. Pull back and slam forward. Then he looked up at her face.

Her cheeks were flushed and her eyes heavy-lidded as she watched him in return. "Omigod, omigod,

omigod," she panted and raised her hips as she'd been doing all along to meet him move for move. "Feels… so…good."

Bending his elbows, he lowered his head to kiss her. "You feel good," he said when he lifted his head once again. "So hot and tight and—*damn,* Jane!"

She pulsed around him—one hard, fast contraction—and he made himself slow down a bit to provide her more sensation. "That's it, baby, come for me. Come for me, Janie." Hunching his back to reach her breast, he gently sucked her nipple.

She exploded, contraction after contraction kneading him, pulling at him, trying to coax forth his own orgasm. "That's it. God!" Letting go of the tight rein he'd imposed on himself, he felt his testicles pull up as his hips picked up speed once again. Jane's little after-orgasms continued to pull at him and he was lost, lost, lost.

Losing track of everything but his own drive for release, he thrust deep and threw back his head, his teeth clenched tight against the roar crowding his throat when the world around him suddenly turned red. He exploded in pulsation after hot, spine-jarring pulsation.

Minutes or maybe a hundred years later, he collapsed atop her. "God Almighty," he breathed and his voice sounded as if someone had taken a sandblaster to it. Wrapping his arms around Jane, he carefully scooped her close. One of her arms escaped his round-up and flopped limply to lie, fingers curled up, upon the coverlet. "I'm amazed you don't do this twenty-four hours a day," he said. "You were made for this."

"Oh, yeah," she agreed without opening her eyes. She looked as if he'd rode her hard and put her away wet. "I'm a freaking love machine."

CHAPTER FOURTEEN

What am I, a yo-yo? Dev should have just picked a stance and stuck with it.

"Sorry about hustling you out of bed the minute I got mine."

Jane glanced over at Devlin, who was busy checking his side-view mirror and changing lanes. She could feel color heating her cheeks. "I wouldn't exactly call it the *minute* you got yours," she murmured. Once he had recovered enough to slide off her, in fact, he'd gathered her against him and held her for a good ten minutes, silently finger-combing her hair, stroking her back and placing random kisses on her forehead, cheeks, temples and nose.

She'd felt wrapped up in care and security.

It was probably best not to dwell on that, however, as a sense of security wasn't something she could afford to grow accustomed to. "And, honestly," she assured him instead, "I understand. I heard what Finn said before we left—your brothers need you back at the mansion."

He made a noncommittal noise and, feeling a little unnerved by the continued silence, she rushed to fill it. "Hey, I'm under a deadline myself. So this works out all the way around."

Actually, she was kind of relieved. Because what did

one *say* in the wake of apocalyptic sex? Her entire view of an activity she had always considered overrated at best had just gone up in a mushroom cloud. She didn't quite know how to act, let alone what to talk about.

So wasn't it kind of silly, then, to let it bother her that Dev wasn't expending any effort to make conversation?

They remained quiet the rest of the ride to the mansion. Once through the kitchen door, Jane was more than ready to be by herself and, leaving Devlin to deal with the alarm code, she hotfooted it down the hallway to the parlor.

He caught her arm just before she escaped inside the room. "What's this?" he demanded wryly, handing her her car keys. "Can't wait to shake my dust from your shoes?"

"You haven't exactly been Mr. Chatty yourself. I assumed you wanted your dust shaken." She looked at his weathered hand on her silk organza sleeve and just wanted to go into the parlor, slide the doors closed and immerse herself in Miss Agnes's collections. She knew what she was doing with them, unlike this new-to-her relationship business. Yes, she understood that it wasn't a real relationship, just a quick and dirty fling, here one day, then gone the next. But there still ought to be some sort of rule book a girl could refer to. For all she knew the last hour and a half might have been it. Maybe she was supposed to remove herself gracefully.

"Have I been quiet?" he murmured, moving close. "Probably because I'm blown away by this afternoon and wondering when I get to see you again."

"Oh." The bottom dropped out of her stomach. Okay,

so it hadn't been just a one-shot deal. *Good.* "Um…you could come to my place tomorrow night if you want."

He moved closer yet. "Not tonight?"

"No." Her heart was thundering in her chest and she was tempted, really tempted, to cancel the plans she'd already made for this evening.

But one didn't blow off one's girlfriends for a man; that was a sacred pact that harked back to the days when she, Ava and Poppy were still in training bras. Well, she and Poppy had been, anyhow—Ava had been an early bloomer. "I have tickets to a play this evening."

"Tomorrow night it is, then." And, hooking his hand around the back of her neck, he hauled her in for a hot, hard kiss.

He set her free almost as quickly as he'd grabbed her, and the next thing she knew she was staring dazedly at the muscular bunch and flex of his rear as he strode from the room.

Shaking her head, she closed the pocket door, hung up her coat and, pushing up her metaphorical sleeves, got to work.

Except it was almost impossible to concentrate, and after catching her mind wandering for the umpteenth time, she finally granted herself a short break. Maybe if she took a few minutes to quit thinking, to not dwell on the way her world had just spun on its axis or worry about what she was or was not accomplishing, her head would clear and she'd start to focus.

After dragging a chair to the back of the room, she went to the kitchen and made herself a cup of cocoa. Plopping down with it a few minutes later in the southeastern corner of the parlor, a section she'd seen precious

SUSAN ANDERSEN   207

little of lately, she sipped her drink as she feasted her eyes on the Lalique glass collection, the Daum Nancy winter scene miniature vases and stoppered bottles, the fragile linens and her personal favorite: the glass display case of antique cameos.

Her nerves slowly settled.

She nursed her cocoa until it started to get cold, then drained the dregs and rose to her feet, feeling refreshed. Maybe now she could get something done this afternoon.

Except, as she walked toward the front of the room to do just that, something scratched at the back of her brain. She couldn't put her finger on the exact problem, but the idea that she'd registered something "off" niggled, itching for attention.

What, though? An item in one of the collections she'd just finished using as her tranquilizer of choice was the obvious answer. Except she couldn't consciously recall seeing anything to produce this edgy feeling.

So give yourself a minute or two to figure it out, a voice inside her suggested. *Then you can put it out of your head and concentrate on your real work.* She about-faced.

"Hey, Jane!"

Work boots thundered down the stairs and after a final conflicted glance toward the far corner of the room she shrugged and headed back up front.

There was a knock on the pocket door. Then, without waiting to hear an invitation to come in, someone began sliding it open. In seconds the breach had widened.

"Jane, you in here?" David's voice asked. "Ja— Oh. Hey. There you are."

All three of Devlin's brothers crowded the partial opening David had created. She couldn't help but smile at them, for they looked so friendly and pleased with themselves as they grinned back at her.

"What's up?" She directed the question at David, but found her attention drifting past him to Devlin when he suddenly appeared behind his brothers. She raised her eyebrows at him.

Apparently he didn't know any more than she did, because when he returned her look over Bren's right shoulder, he essayed the facial equivalent of a shrug.

"How would you like to come to a party?" Finn asked.

"Hey, I was gonna ask her!" David protested.

"When, tomorrow? The woman's got a job to do—she doesn't have all day to stand around waiting for you to spit it out."

"Um, a party?" The unexpected invitation had jerked her attention away from Dev, but without thought she glanced at him again. His face had gone expressionless and he gazed back at her with shuttered eyes.

Something inside her curled in on itself. She didn't have to be a card-packing member of Geniuses 'R' Us to see he wasn't thrilled by his brothers' invitation.

Lifting her chin, she returned her attention to the other Kavanagh men. "Whose party? When?" If she was reading Devlin correctly, she wouldn't be attending no matter where or when. But damned if she'd just shoot down three men who had been nothing but nice to her without at least coating her refusal in the social niceties.

"Saturday," David said. "At our folks' house."

"Oh, no," she protested in genuine horror. "I'm not barging in on your parents' party."

The three men threw back their heads and roared, and even Devlin's mouth quirked up in a wry smile.

"Ma and Da don't consider a party a party unless their house is bursting at the seams," he said.

"That's right," Bren said. "And this will give you the perfect chance to meet my Jody. I've told her about you and the work you've been doing here for your museum. She's dying to meet you in person. C'mon." He flashed her a charming smile. "Whataya say? You'll have a good time."

"Absolutely," David agreed. "One thing you can count on with the Kavanaghs, they know how to throw an event you won't forget."

"Yeah, fistfights on the lawn tend to stick in your mind," Devlin muttered.

"Shut up, Dev," all three brothers said in unison.

"You can tell you've been gone a long time," Finn added. "We haven't had a lawn brawl since the mid-nineties."

Dev scowled and Jane gave them all a tight smile. "Let me check my calendar at home, okay? I'd love to come but that date sounds familiar. I think I may already have booked something for the evening."

"Sure," Bren said. "Just let us know."

They all left, even Devlin, whom she'd half expected to stick around long enough to make sure she turned down the invitation. Nerves jangled in her stomach but at least she'd demonstrated reasonably quick thinking in an awkward situation. Her reply had sounded as if she really wanted to attend the Kavanagh party, which, okay, she did. She'd love to see a family that big in action. Clearly, however, Dev thought she was good enough for a hot tussle between the sheets, but planned to keep her as far as he could from any relatives she hadn't already met.

She plunged into cataloging the designer clothing in an attempt to blow off the resentment that bubbled and burned just beneath her surface composure. But her teeth were clamped tight.

Three solid hours passed before she remembered her earlier disquiet regarding the collections in the back of the room. She'd accomplished much more with the couture collection than she had expected to do when she'd first returned from her escapade with Devlin. Deciding anger was an excellent motivator, she checked to be sure that every item she'd logged into the database this afternoon had been transferred to the rolling rack for transportation upstairs to the secret closet. Then she headed for the back of the room once more to see if she could figure out the source of her earlier unease.

She gave everything a quick, comprehensive onceover, then concentrated on the case of cameos. "Damn, damn, damn," she muttered as she tried to recall its contents as she'd last seen it. "Why couldn't Miss Agnes have kept records of her collections?"

"She did. The problem is, she kept them in her head."

With a choked screech, she whirled to face Ava. "You scared the crap out of me!" Giving her thundering heart a comforting pat, she blew out a gusty, "Hoo."

"Sorry." Not sounding overwhelmingly contrite, her friend strolled into the room, her hips rolling as if they moved on oiled ball bearings. "Since Poppy drove, I just assumed you heard the car. That girl is in serious need of a new muffler."

"That *girl* has a Jack Sprat–lean bank account," Poppy said, joining them.

"Well, for heaven's sake. We inherited a huge estate and probate is officially over," the redhead replied. "There must be enough in the coffers for a muffler."

Poppy shrugged. "Miss A. was long on collections of rare artifacts but short on cold, hard cash. And the executor of her estate ran through what she did have to pay the lawyer and the estate taxes and things like those notice-to-creditor ads he placed in the newspapers to satisfy probate. Then there was our down payment to Kavanagh Construction for the remodel."

"It's probably anti-American of me to admit this," Ava said, "but it just chaps my hide to have to pay estate taxes."

Jane snorted. "Can you say Boston Tea Party? I think it's American squared to think paying taxes sucks," she said. "Still, ours could have been a lot worse. Except for the jewelry and silver, the guy the court hired to assess Miss A.'s stuff vastly undervalued her collections. I'm guessing he probably considered most of it froufrou girly stuff."

"Idiot," Poppy muttered.

"Yes, he was, which was a huge boon for us. If he'd had any idea what most of these little beauties are worth we would have had to sell a third of the collections just to handle the taxes."

She'd been quickly backing up her day's work as they talked, and she shut down the computer before turning her full attention back to her friends. "We haven't discussed cash disbursements for ourselves. That's something we should probably sit down and talk about in more depth. We need to figure out how much to set aside for the rest of the renovation, for Miss A.'s taxes for the quarter she was alive this year and the cost of running the mansion, plus any other expenses we can think of to keep from being caught by surprise. Then I can put out feelers to sell some things to free up some cash. But that's not going to happen right away, so until I have time, we could always sell the antique linens collection. I can think of three prospects right off the top of my head who would be hot to buy it. That might solve your short-term cash-flow problem, Poppy."

Except…where was the oval, twenties-era, openwork, embroidered tablecloth and its six matching tea napkins that Miss A. had used the very first time she'd had the three of them over for tea? It occurred to Jane that she hadn't seen the set among the other linens this afternoon. Perhaps that was what had been gnawing at her. Miss Agnes had set the small table in the morning room with it every time they'd gotten together; it had become as much of a tradition as her yearly gift to them of a brand-new leather-bound diary.

Of course, it was entirely possible that the constant use had worn the fragile fabric to the breaking point. Hauling her focus back on point, she made a quick calculation of the worth of the collection. She'd have to give it a closer inspection than she had done during her break. But still— "There must be fifteen to twenty thousand dollars' worth, so split that three ways—"

"And it's peanuts," Ava said.

"Speak for yourself," Poppy snapped. "Unlike you,

Miss Trust-fund baby, five or six thousand dollars is a nice chunk of change that will tide me over for quite some time."

"Aw, Pop." Ava slung her arm around the blonde's shoulders and gave her a conciliatory squeeze. "I'm sorry. That was thoughtlessly said."

"S'okay." Poppy rested her head on Ava's shoulder for a moment. "I know you didn't mean it in a bitchy way. You're just so used to being Miss Moneybags, you're a little out of touch with what the rest of us consider a princely sum." Still standing in the drape of her friend's arm, she narrowed her eyes at Jane. "There's something different about you today. Did you treat yourself to a facial?"

"Huh?"

"Your skin's all glowy." There was a heartbeat of silence, then, looking like a cartoon character who'd just had a lightbulb flash on over her head, Poppy stared at her. "Omigawd. You've done the humpty-hump with Dev!"

Heat flowed into Jane's face as Ava looked at Poppy, then slowly turned her head to gape at her. "Janie?"

Hearing men's voices weaving under and over the sounds of construction going on upstairs, she glanced up at the ceiling, then back at her friends. "I am not discussing this here."

"You DID!" Ava's arm dropped from around Poppy's shoulders.

The blonde boogied over to the hanging rack of cataloged outfits. She pulled Jane's coat off its hanger and tossed it to her. "Put that on. Ava—" she gathered up an armful of the couture clothing "—come help me take this stuff upstairs to lock up for the night. Then the three of us are going to go grab a drink before the play." She leveled a look on Jane. "And one of us had better be ready for a little show-and-tell."

"I NEVER DID LIKE show-and-tell," Jane muttered twenty minutes later as they sat in the back of a bar near the Paramount Theater where the Best of Broadway show they were slated to attend was playing.

"Liar." Poppy made a face. "You always loved demonstrating how smart you are."

"But only when she could talk about the origins of whatever it was she'd brought in to show," Ava said quietly. "Janie's never been big on exposing her emotional side."

No fooling. And since she was tied up in knots six ways from Sunday, this was about as emotional as it got. Knowing her friends wouldn't rest until she told them something about her unprecedented sexual encounter with Devlin, however, she shared the part she was actually kind of proud of. "When I ran into Dev in the kitchen this afternoon, I asked him if he wanted to have no-strings sex with me."

Both women's mouths dropped open. Poppy was the first to recover. "You did not!"

"Did so." She adored the image of herself as fearless and bold. Trouble was, these were her best friends and they knew her better than that. So she came clean. "Of course, I damn near passed out the minute the words left my mouth."

"Oh, my, God," Ava breathed. She went silent as the waitress arrived. The minute the woman placed their drinks in front of them, collected the tab and left, however, she leaned toward Jane across the small table. "Did he jump your bones right then and there? What were his very first words?"

"'Grab your coat.'" She explained with as much detail as she could remember up to the moment when Devlin quit covering her in kisses in front of his family photo and whirled her onto his bed. She wasn't about to disclose the really intimate stuff, but just describing that much brought back all the sensations with a moist and prickly immediacy. She pressed her thighs together against the renewed tug of desire pulsing deep between her legs.

"I'm guessing he was good," Poppy said wryly, observing her.

"Oh, man." She blew out a noisy breath. "I never knew."

"Yeah, that time I visited you at college and met your academic-type boyfriend, what's-his-name—"

"Eric."

"—he didn't strike me as the Mr. Lusty type. But this thing between you and Dev... Are you sure you're okay with the fact that it's only until he goes back to Europe?"

"Yes. That was a big selling point, in fact."

"Jane, Jane, Jane." Ava sighed, shaking her head mournfully.

Poppy's lips crooked, but she didn't allow the aside to detour her. "So a finite shelf life is a good thing, in your estimation. And the sex is out of this world." She took a sip of her wine and set her glass back on the table. Twirling its stem, she watched golden liquid climb up and down the goblet's sloped bowl for a few seconds.

Then, fingers stilling, she raised her eyes and pinned Jane in place with a look. "So why don't you seem over the moon?"

Crap. Jane actually would have liked getting their take on the situation. She simply cringed, however, at the thought of exposing her emotions or—worse—her insecurities. She much preferred putting a good face on things and letting it go at that.

Did Poppy know her, or what?

Lifting her glass of club soda, she gazed at the bubbles popping above the surface for a second, then set it back on the table, untasted. She sighed. "I expected it to last longer than a single afternoon. Now that I know what sex can be like with someone who knows his stuff, I was looking forward to screwing my brains out for a couple of weeks or a month or…I don't know how long. But for a while, anyhow." Picking up her glass again, she stared into it and said in a low voice, "I figured this would be a good way to dip my toes into the passion pool without drowning in the stuff until I wound up as psycho as my mom and dad."

"I think your folks' drama-queen and -king personalities and hefty quantities of alcohol have had more to do with the messes they've made than passion," Poppy said.

Ava reached across the table to press cool fingertips against the back of Jane's hand, which until that moment Jane hadn't realized was fisted against the sleek wood. She relaxed it beneath her friend's touch.

"What happened?" the redhead asked. "Does Devlin have to go back sooner than you thought?"

"No."

Ava's slender brows met above her nose. "Then why

was the sex restricted to only this afternoon?" Her eyes flashed with sudden fire. "Did that son of a bitch give you the boot once he got what he wanted?" Then she shot upright in her chair. "Oh God. Did he *tell his brothers?*"

A kiss-and-tell incident during their senior year at Country Day had permanently colored Ava's tolerance for men who shared private moments. She'd gifted her virginity to a boy she believed to care for her—only to discover that he'd slept with the "fat" girl in order to win a bet with his friends.

"Ah, Av, no." Jane turned her hand over to grip her friend's. "It wasn't like that." She explained about Devlin's silence on the ride back to the mansion, his apparent turn-around once they'd reached it, then the invitation from his brothers that had sparked his ego-shattering lack of enthusiasm for the idea.

"It sounds a little schizoid," Ava agreed. "But is there any chance you're worrying about nothing, maybe jumping to conclusions?"

"How am I supposed to know without a little down-home communication? He didn't talk to me in the car, but when he said it was because he'd been thinking about how soon we could get together again I thought *my misunderstanding*—but one that was now cleared up. Yet if it was, then why did he just stand there stone-faced while his brothers asked me to a party that their parents are throwing? It's true he didn't yell, 'Over my dead body.' But he sure as hell didn't say, 'Yeah, you gotta come,' either." And she felt the cold ache of his unspoken rejection all over again.

The fact that she let it get to her stiffened her spine. "If he doesn't want me there all he has to do is say so," she said with all the dignity she could muster—then admitted glumly, "I'm not built for all this drama. In the space of a few hours, I've gone from being out-of-my-skull filled with wonder over the fantastic sex to being made to feel like Dev's dirty little secret. I just want to know where the hell I stand."

"Jane has to know the rules," Ava murmured.

"Yes, I do, and damned if I'll apologize for it."

"Communication cuts both ways, though, Janie," Poppy said. "Does *he* know it's over between the two of you? Because it sounds to me like he still thinks he's getting together with you at your place tomorrow night."

"Well, I guess if he's dumb enough to turn up after treating me like the dirty mistress," she said, meeting her friend's eyes squarely, "I'll just have to communicate with crystal clarity so Devlin Kavanagh won't have the least doubt how I feel about being his closet lover."

CHAPTER FIFTEEN

Wow. Helluva difference between a Kavanagh party and the ones my parents throw. I always felt—I don't know—sort of lonely and out of step at Mike and Dorrie's parties. Who knew it was possible to feel so much a part of the festivities?

DEV KNEW HE'D SCREWED UP well before he knocked on Jane's door, saw the peephole shield slide open and heard her mutter, "You're a ballsy peckerwood, I'll give you that."

He winced. She had cause to be pissed, given his blank-faced reaction to his brothers' invitation. Coming in the wake of his silence in the car yesterday, he could hardly blame her for being put off and confused. Hell, he'd been a tad confused himself, confused and stupefied by the sex they'd shared.

But thinking about that now was merely a way to avoid dealing with his latest screw-up. He squared his shoulders. "Let me in, Jane."

Her sigh filtered through the door. "Fine." The peephole shield fell back into place, the tumblers from two locks clicked and she opened the door.

She stood on the other side in a pair of black capri leggings and a gray baby-doll top, with one bare foot stacked atop the other and her eyes dangerous slits of

blue behind narrowed lashes. But that was the only
expression that warned of her mood. Eating coffee-
flavored ice cream from a pint-size carton, she gazed at
him with a blank face.

"I'm sorry about yesterday."

She shrugged as if it didn't matter, but he'd seen the
flash of betrayal that had crossed her face when he'd
shut down in the parlor yesterday. Yet even witnessing
her withdrawal, he hadn't uttered the few words that
would have erased the rejection she'd felt.

In his own defense, she had no idea what she'd be
letting herself in for.

All the same, he tried to explain himself. "I heard
Finn invite you to my folks' party and I panicked."

"Sure. Can't have your down-and-dirty fling buddy
mingling with your family," she said carelessly and
spooned up another bite.

"I don't know about down and dirty. I just heard the
invitation to a family do and I flashed on Mom asking
whether you preferred spring or fall weddings. I heard
my aunt Eileen demanding your thoughts on having kids
before your eggs got too old."

Blinking, she lowered the spoon. "What?"

"My family's not big on respecting other people's
privacy, babe. And there's nothing they like better than
seeing one of their own walk down the aisle. Then when
we *do* settle down and marry, the baby issue rears its
ugly head. Why aren't there babes on the way? When
are you going to have one? We love babies. The more
the better."

She snapped upright. "You've been *married*?"

"Hell, no. But I've watched it happen to my sister

Maureen and to my sisters-in-law and my cousins or my cousins' girlfriends or wives." Hands in his pockets, he shifted his shoulders. "Me, I quit bringing dates to family functions when I was seventeen."

"But why would they ask any such thing of me? No one even knows about the two of us."

"Oh, they will. The women in my family have radar like you wouldn't believe when it comes to this sort of thing."

Jane studied him a moment, then stepped back from where she'd been blocking his way. "Come in." She offered him the Häagen-Dazs carton. "Want some ice cream?"

"Sure." Accepting the container, he pulled out the iced-tea-length spoon stabbed into the frozen concoction and dug himself out a bite as he followed her down the short hallway.

Glancing up from the carton, however, he stopped short. Because Jane's apartment was chock-full of the last thing he expected to see—a riot of color.

The combination living-dining room walls were painted a buttercream gold that made the hardwood cherry floors gleam in contrast. A short forest-green velvet couch heaped with colorful throw pillows and two burgundy leather chairs formed a conversational area around a small coffee table, and vivid prints hung on the walls. Colorful mosaic towers of varying height held chunky candles on the narrow library table behind the couch, and brightly patterned pottery canisters sat atop the small ell of black granite that comprised the kitchen countertops.

"Wow. This is great."

"It's tiny, but I love it."

The place was probably no more than six hundred square feet, but a clever floor plan made the most of every inch. "Hey, I spend most of my time on boats. Compared to all but maybe three or four supersize yachts I've sailed, this is downright palatial."

It was shipshape as any boat he'd been on, too—except for a mess of papers strewn across the breakfast bar. He glanced from it to her. "Am I interrupting your work?"

"No, it's okay. I'm just checking some of Miss Agnes's collections against the itemized inventory list the estate assessor made." Her brows creased for a second, then went smooth and expressionless. "It's nothing that can't wait."

He indicated the door at the end of the living room. "Mind if I take a look?"

"Go ahead."

He strolled over and opened it into a tiny solarium. That in turn opened onto a narrow deck, and he stepped out onto it. The brisk late October wind tugged at the ends of the knit scarf he'd wound around his neck, but he ignored it to brace his hands on the tubular metal railing. City lights gleamed to the south and east, while Elliott Bay spread like pooled black satin in front of him. The lights of the West Seattle peninsula shimmered along the bay's far boundary line and although it was too dark to see the Olympic Mountains across the Sound beyond it, he knew they were there. "Great view."

"I know." She came out to stand next to him, hugging herself against the cold. "Isn't it gorgeous?"

Unzipping his old leather bomber jacket, he hooked

an arm around her waist and tugged her in front of him, tucking her back against his chest. He wrapped the sides of his jacket around her and propped his chin atop her head. Warm, slick hair shifted against his skin.

She settled in and for a moment they gazed out at the view in silence. Then Jane curled her hands over his leather-clad forearms. "I'm not sure I understand why you're so worried about your family," she said, staring at the bay. "At least they sound somewhat normal. Now, a party at *my* folks' place would be a guaranteed booze-and-drama fest. But if it helps, I'm not interested in weddings or babies and I don't mind making that clear to your family if it will get them off your back." She tipped her head back and to one side to look up at him. "I don't want to own you, Dev. Just lease you for a while."

Which pretty much made her every man's perfect woman. So why did a tiny kernel of discontent make him tighten his arms around her as if to keep her from breaking away?

He gave himself a mental shake and eased his hold. He should grab some dinner pretty soon; low fuel was making him fanciful.

She'd put all his doubts about mixing their relationship with his family to rest, however, and he rubbed his jaw against her hair. "So," he murmured. "Wanna go to a party with me?"

GORDON WAS PERFORMING his sacred Saturday-morning grooming ritual when the phone rang. Massaging moisturizer into his freshly exfoliated cheeks, he strode over to check out the caller ID read-out.

It was Jerry Waskowitz, an old friend from the 'hood.

He hesitated, his hand suspended above the wireless unit. He'd pretty much forsaken all of his old Terrace friends, but he and Jerry went way back. Plus, Jere was the only person he knew who shared his love of poker. He hadn't seen or talked to the guy since the fiasco at the Vegas Challenge.

He snatched up the receiver. "Hey."

"Hey, Gordie—" Even as a frown was forming between Gordon's brows at the diminutive use of his name, Jerry amended, "Gordon, I mean. How's it goin'? Long time no see."

"Going great." And it was. He was officially off the hook, in the clear, a free man. He'd paid off the last of the interest he'd accrued with Fast Eddy.

"Glad to hear it. Play any poker lately?"

"No, I've had my nose to the grindstone." And getting his kicks from helping himself to bits and pieces of Jane's collections. Of course, now that his debt was paid off, he'd pretty much decided it would be best to quit while he was ahead.

"Yeah, them daytime jobs can sure get in the way of a guy's fun time, can't they? I haven't played as much as I'da liked, either. How's your gig at the museum going?"

"Fan-fucking-tastic." If one ignored the fact that it would probably be years and he'd be old, gray and— he shuddered in distaste—wrinkled before he ever got his hands on a collection of his own the caliber of that bitch Kaplinski's. "How about you, man?" he inquired in return. "How's your job going?" Not that he gave a particular rat's ass. Jerry was a mechanic—did it *get* any more plebian than that?

"Rough and greasy," his friend replied amiably.

"Pretty much the same ol' same old. Which is the main reason I'm calling. You wanna go down and catch us a card game at the Muckleshoot tonight?"

His first inclination was to say no. And with an unpleasant jolt, he realized that he'd been avoiding the Indian casinos and card rooms where he'd played hours and hours of poker these past several years. What the fuck was that all about?

He was a gambler. An ace poker player. Yeah, sure, he'd hit a rough patch. But shit happened to the best of them.

And he *was* one of the best. Hell, he was destined for greatness.

But one didn't reach greatness by avoiding one's proving ground. Hell no. One tested it. Again and again. And since when did he choose the safe route, anyway? Why was he backing off from that mansion full of treasures when he had a gold mine right at his fingertips? That was just plain chickenshit.

Yes, it was a risk he didn't need to take now that Fast Eddy was finally out of the picture. But when you were born with balls of steel, you didn't sweat the small stuff. Fast Eddy was only a big deal if Gordon put himself in the position of needing his help again. And that wasn't going to happen—not when he had the mansion's contents as his secret ace in the hole.

Then there was the extra-added bonus of getting to screw Kaplinski.

Not literally, of course. His lip curled. Slipping the sausage to that little stiff would be like fucking a blow-up doll that had been kept in the freezer. But anytime he could screw her over figuratively, he planned to be there with bells on.

"Gord, you still there, bro?"

"Huh? Oh, sorry. Got distracted by a neighbor across the way taking her shirt off in front of her window."

"No shit? She stripped right down to bare titty?"

"Yep."

"You live the high life, man. So, you wanna go play a little poker tonight, or what?"

"Sure. Why not?"

"I'll swing by and pick you up. What time sounds good to you?"

"How about nine?" He thought of the green pulled-feather Steuben art glass shade he'd noticed the last time he'd been in the mansion. It would probably fetch in excess of eleven hundred dollars on the open market and probably seven or eight hundred from a fence. A small smile pulled up the corners of his mouth.

"I'll have to drop by my bank for a quick withdrawal first. Then I'll be ready whenever you are."

JANE HAD NEVER SEEN so many people crammed into one medium-size house. "Are you sure you don't want to just let me go in by myself?" she asked Devlin beneath the babble of the dozens of voices that had rolled out to greet them when he'd shoved open the front door to his parents' house. "Your family doesn't need to know we've got something going."

"Too late," he said with a subtle jut of his jaw toward the living room. "That's my mother over there." Before she could locate the woman he'd indicated, his arm wrapped around her shoulders and he whisked her around a couple of smokers already lighting up as they pushed their way out the door, ushered her past two men arguing the merits of backpacking stoves and dodged a group of kids who darted past, whooping at the top of their lungs. "Anyway, like I told you before, the Kavanagh women have state-of-the-art radar when it comes to this sort of thing. Hey, Ma."

Releasing Jane, he gave a plump woman with hair a faded shade of his own rich, dark auburn the Devlin special, a rib-cracking hug that lifted her off her feet. Setting her back down, he kissed her on the lips, then stepped back. "This is my friend Jane. Jane, my mom, Erin Kavanagh."

"How do you do," Jane said, offering her hand. "Thank you so much for having me."

Ignoring Jane's hand, Erin pulled her in for a hug. "Oh!" Jane said, standing very still within the other woman's embrace, not knowing quite what to do. The only people she was accustomed to receiving hugs from were Ava and Poppy. Tentatively, she raised her hands and gave Erin's shoulders an awkward pat.

"You're more than welcome," Devlin's mother said, first stepping back to hold her at arm's length while giving her a friendly appraisal, then releasing her. "I'm so glad you came. I've heard a lot about you from my other boys, so it's nice to have an actual face to put to the name." Then she waved her hand toward the back of the house. "There's beer and wine and soft drinks in the kitchen and a buffet in the dining room. Go. Enjoy. Make Mr. Loose-lips-sink-ships here introduce you around."

Devlin did precisely that. He introduced her to two sisters she hadn't already met, Kate and Maureen. He introduced her to a plethora of cousins and aunts and uncles. Made her acquaintance to many, but apparently not all, of his nieces, nephews and second cousins, most of whose names she didn't have a prayer of keeping straight. He led her deep into the living room to meet his grandmothers Hester and Katherine, then over to the sideboard in the dining room where his grandfather Darragh and his father were enjoying a dram of whiskey. When they ran into David coming in the front door as they were passing by, Devlin introduced her to his wife, Julie, and their son and daughter.

He didn't introduce her to Bren's Jody, but that was only because when Bren spotted them, he dragged her off to perform the introductions himself. She'd met so many people in such a short space of time her head spun.

"This is like that family photo of yours—on steroids," she said at one point as she squeezed into a corner of the crowded kitchen while Devlin bent over the selection of beverages in the refrigerator. "Is everyone here a relative?"

Pulling a beer out for himself and a Diet Coke for her, he slammed the door and straightened, cocking his head at her. "What's that?" he yelled.

She raised her voice to be heard above a group of men singing the Irish national anthem over by the sink. "Everyone you've introduced me to. Are they all related to you?"

"Most of 'em." Grabbing a fistful of ice cubes from the freezer, he dropped them in a glass and handed it to her along with her can of soda. He gave her a grin as he twisted the cap off his beer. "Told you, Legs. It's a big freakin' family."

"No kidding." She couldn't even imagine. But that didn't stop her from experiencing some serious family-envy. Everyone she'd met today seemed so connected, so easy in their history with each other.

"C'mon," he yelled, grabbing her hand. "I can't hear myself think. Let's go find Hannah and Finn. They're probably hiding out in the basement. And if I know Hannah, she'll have scored an assortment of the best the buffet has to offer."

They were weaving their way through the crush to an interior door at the back of the kitchen when an older woman strode into the room. She had flaming red hair that Jane was pretty sure had been given a helping hand from the finest chemistry that money could buy. It should have clashed with her burnt-orange unstructured jacket but somehow didn't. With her chin held high, her shoulders squared, her considerable bust thrust front and center by her erect posture, she had a presence that could be felt clear across the room.

"For Gawd's sake," she bawled at the singers. "Take it outside! The damn windows are rattling."

They shoved away from the kitchen counter and took it outside.

In the relative silence that followed their departure, the woman stood with her hands on her hips, survey-ing the crowd that remained. Her gaze stopped at Dev-lin and Jane and she marched over. "Hello, Devlin, luv. Gimme a kiss, then."

He bussed the cheek she presented. "Hey, Aunt Ei-leen. How's it going? This is my friend Jane."

"How nice to meet you," Jane said. "I saw a wonder-ful photo that you took of Devlin's family."

"Did you, now? In our Dev's apartment?"

"Uh…huh."

The older woman gave her a comprehensive up-and-down. "You must be—what?—twenty-eight, twenty-nine?"

"Aunt Eileen…"

Jane's lips curled up slightly at the warning in Dev's voice. But she said politely, "I'm thirty."

"So what are your thoughts, then, on babies? Are you planning on having one or two before your eggs get too old?"

She couldn't help it. A gut-busting laugh exploded out of her.

Eileen's eyebrows drew together. "Did I say something amusing?"

"Only in that it was exactly what Devlin said you would say."

"That would have been when I was explaining why I'd hurt her feelings by not being awash in enthusiasm when Finn invited her to this party," Dev said. "Knowing she'd get the third degree and all."

"One question hardly constitutes the third degree, boyo," Eileen informed him coolly.

"But it is a bit early to be asking me my goals toward parenthood," Jane said quietly. Reaching out, she touched Eileen's sleeve. "Ma'am, counting today, I've had a grand total of one date with your nephew."

"Hey!" He straightened beside her. "What about the Noodle Ranch?"

"Sitting down at the same table with you with my take-out bag does not constitute a date, Kavanagh. Now, if you'd like to take me back there and actually buy me some noodles—"

An arrested expression crossed his face and she wondered if the same thing she was suddenly thinking had occurred to him, as well—that they'd had burn-up-the-sheets sex together, but had never actually been out on a date.

Apparently so, because he said, "How about we give Mama's Kitchen a try instead? That is, if Mexican tickles your fancy. Or if you'd rather have seafood we could hit the Belltown Bistro."

She took a sip of her soda. "Either one sounds great."

"Monday night?"

Unexpected warmth bloomed in her stomach and a pleased smile curled her lips. But getting all mushy over him wasn't in her game plan and for one second it froze her in place.

Then she shook off the concern. It was a fling that would be over when Devlin went back to Europe. There was no need to second-guess every stray emotion it brought forth. The idea was to enjoy it while it lasted. "Monday would be good."

Hooking her neck in the crook of his elbow, Dev leaned in to give her a brief, hard kiss. "Excuse us, Aunt Eileen," he said without taking his gaze off Jane when he'd lifted his head once again. And, lacing his fingers with hers, he set off toward the basement door, deftly winding through the crowd.

"Just answer me this, Jane," Eileen raised her voice to say. "Do you prefer spring or summer weddings?"

"I thought that was supposed to be your mother's question," she murmured to Dev.

He shrugged. "Mom was amazingly reticent today. Maybe she's scaling back on her daily allotment of interfering."

Jane twisted to look over her shoulder at his aunt. "I haven't really given the matter much thought," she said. She let the silence stretch out for a moment. "But I do have my bridesmaids picked out."

Dev laughed and tugged her through the door he'd just opened.

Neither of them saw his aunt's satisfied grin.

CHAPTER SIXTEEN

I have got to learn to trust my instincts. Because sometimes, when something doesn't feel right, it truly isn't.

JANE WAS PUMPED. She'd stopped at Kits Camera at Westlake Center on her way in to work and, even riffling quickly through the shots, she'd known she had something good. Something *really* good. She boogied down the sixth-floor hallway toward her office.

Gordon Ives stuck his head out his own doorway as she danced past. "*Some*body is feeling perky."

"I am so jazzed!" she agreed, waving her envelope of prints at him without stopping. "I took pictures of the gown I've chosen for my Couture for the Ages focal piece, and they turned out even better than I had hoped. If the other pieces photograph even half as well, my catalog is going to pop!" She halted midbop and grinned at him. "You've got one of the best eyes in the business. Wanna see?"

"Absolutely." He followed her down to her office.

"Yesterday I dropped off a memory card to have some prints made," she told him, striding into the room and heading straight to her desk. Pulling out the bottom drawer, she dropped her purse inside. "Then, like an idiot—" she closed the drawer with her foot "—I forgot about them until I'd squeezed my car into a parking space that felt two sizes too small and hiked half a mile to the Wolcott mansion."

She tossed her manila folder with the mansion's multipaged inventory list that she'd been poring over for several days now onto the desk and shimmied out of her coat. She knew she had no business going over it on company time. But she intended to do so all the same, if she could squeeze a minute out of her insane schedule.

"Bummer," he murmured and grabbed for the folder as it slid across the desktop with too much momentum. The top flipped back and the entire stack of papers sailed out and over the side.

"No kidding," she agreed, rounding the desk to help as he bent to pick them up. She hadn't been willing to trek back to her car and wrestle it from its spot, let alone drive back downtown. In the end, however, she might as well have made the extra trip. She'd spent the entire night worrying how the pictures had turned out, anyway.

She stooped down to assist in rounding up her papers. The photos were definitely worry-worth. If the Dior didn't have the visual pop she expected, she'd have to go back to the drawing board for her focal piece. She was so committed to this gown that the prospect of choosing something different would be very difficult and cost her time she couldn't afford.

She held a hand out for the papers that Gordon had gathered off the floor but was simply gazing at blankly. Stacking them atop the pages she had rescued, she rose to her feet.

"Well, that was clumsy of me. Thanks, Gordon." Glancing down at the top sheet, her eyebrows furrowed briefly at the sight of two items that were highlighted in yellow. "This is turning into a worry of a different nature," she said, knowing she had to pull her head out of the sand and do something about what she was now convinced were stolen items.

"Anything that I can help you with?"

"No—but bless you for asking. I'm beginning to believe only the cops are going to be able to help me with this one." Then the Kits Camera envelope caught her eye and she brightened, temporarily shelving her anxiety over the missing items. "You could give me your expert advice on these, though," she said, waving him to a seat in front of her desk as she spilled the prints onto it. Swiftly she arranged them for Gordon to peruse. "Here, take a look."

"Holy sh—" His voice trailed away as he bent over the desk, looking at print after print of the champagne-colored, glass-beaded crepe gown. He studied the prints of it by itself, then those of it coupled with the ermine evening cape. "Christian Dior," he murmured. Tearing his gaze away from the photographs, he glanced up at her. "Late fifties?"

"Yes."

"It looks to be in incredible shape. And it photographs beautifully."

"Oh God." It took every bit of self-control at her disposal not to do a quick dance around her desk. "That's what I thought. I am so pumped about this piece." She waved toward the snapshots as she sedately circled back to her side of the desk. But her hips apparently hadn't received the command from control-central, for they performed a few victory swivels before she collapsed in her seat. "The cape, too, of course, but it's the gown that's going to make the collection." Her desk phone rang and she excused herself to answer it.

"Hey, Legs," Devlin's voice drawled in response to her hello. "Sorry to call you at work but I know what a social butterfly you can be."

She snorted. Her insides, however, lit up.

"And always so gracious and ladylike, too," he observed. "I like that about you."

She refused to give him the satisfaction of making her laugh, but she smiled as she rocked back in her chair. "What can I do for you, Kavanagh? As you mentioned, I'm at my place of business and I do have work to do."

"I just wanted to get hold of you before your calendar fills up. You free tonight?"

"So far. But the day is young."

"Which is why they call me Mr. Early Bird, babe. Want to catch the worm—er, that is, have dinner with me?"

"Why, Mr. Bird." She found herself fluttering her lashes as if he could see and felt heat rise in her cheeks at her foolishness. "Are you asking me for a...date?"

"I suppose I am. At least, rumor has it that's what it's called when a man takes a woman out for a meal. We're not talking one of those promlike dates, though. I'm not springing for a wrist corsage first time out of the gate. Not unless you promise to put out."

A laugh sputtered out of her. "Right. Like I'm planning to discuss *that* on my work phone."

"You're right. That's more dessert-type conversation. You in the mood for Mexican? We can gaze into each other's eyes over a plate of beans."

This time her laugh rolled straight up from her belly. "You're such a romantic fool."

"Babe. You have no idea. So we on for Mama's Kitchen?"

"Yes. Sounds good."

"Sweet. I'll see you this afternoon at the mansion to firm up our plans. We can decide then what time I should pick you up."

Oooh, it really was an honest-to-goodness date, she thought as she replaced the receiver. Door-to-door pickup and delivery and everything. It was all she could do to keep from squirming with pleasure in her seat.

But she'd displayed a big enough lack of professionalism in front of Gordon for one morning—as evidenced by the first words out of his mouth.

"Hot date?"

Her initial inclination was to freeze him with a few well-chosen words. But it was hardly fair to blatantly flirt with someone in front of a man, then punish him because he'd noticed. Besides, her lips were already curling up in an anticipatory smile. "Well, a dinner date, anyhow."

"Tonight?"

"Uh-huh."

He sighed. "Lucky you."

She looked at him, wondering for the first time about his love life. She wasn't even sure of his sexuality. She thought he was straight. But given his preoccupation with grooming, his general fastidiousness and the fact that she'd never once seen him with a woman…maybe not.

Then again, it wasn't as if she'd ever seen him with

a man, either. "How about you?" she heard herself ask. "Do you have anyone special?"

"Nah."

"Someone you see occasionally?"

"Not even that right now. I'm pretty much wedded to the job at the moment."

"I hear that." Boy, did she, considering she'd been like that, too…until Dev. The thought fired off tiny synapses of shock throughout her system. But it was true. Fooling around with Devlin had added some balance in her life she hadn't even realized was missing. She'd had Ava and Poppy to keep her well-rounded and figured that was all she'd needed. But avoiding anything that smacked of passion as assiduously as she'd done had left her perhaps the slightest bit top-heavy on the straight-and-narrow side of life. Perhaps passion wasn't such a bad thing after all.

Provided it came in the form of a guy who'd be gone before she got so sucked under its spell that she'd turn as obsessive as her parents.

Gordon abruptly rose to his feet. "Well, I'd better get back to my own stuff."

"Of course." She, too, rose. "Thanks for taking the time to look at my pictures. I really do value your eye for quality. And if I haven't mentioned it enough, I also appreciate all the hard work you're putting into the Spain exhibit."

"Not a problem," he said. "I'm always happy to help."

I'D BE HAPPY to help you right off the observation deck of the Space Needle, in fact. Gordon marched back to his own office and gently closed the door behind him.

It wasn't nearly as satisfying as slamming it so hard it cracked all the hinges, but he was a civilized man. He didn't lose control; that was what separated him from the Neanderthals he'd grown up with in the Terrace.

He needed to think. Kaplinski was obviously both brighter and quicker than he'd given her credit for if she'd already tumbled to the missing treasures. He, however, had his usual luck on his side. One might not think so on the face of it, considering he'd just discovered his cash cow was about to dry up. But what were the odds that he'd be in place to field Jane's folder when it went flying? Gathering the papers that had escaped, he'd recognized several of the highlighted objets d'art on them as items he'd liberated for the cause. His.

So the bitch intended to call the cops, did she? Apparently, then, all that was left for him to do was make one last foray into the Wolcott mansion. Tonight, while Jane was on her date. (And who the hell would have dreamed there was a man out there who actually wanted to screw her? He would have said it was impossible, but that was sure the impression he'd gotten from listening to her side of the conversation.)

But he digressed. The point here was that if his secret stash was about to be shut down he might as well give the police more items to look for.

And as long as he was at it, he'd throw a spanner in little Miss Hotshot's oh-so-important plans. Yes, sir. One final *fuck you* to demonstrate his regard for her.

It wouldn't add any income to his coffers. But it would ruin the bitch's week.

And that all by itself made him feel a whole lot better.

"You got us the Elvis room!" Jane smiled over her shoulder as the hostess of Mama's Kitchen led them into the dining room filled with Elvis memorabilia. "How did you manage that?"

Dev dragged his gaze from the sway of her hips, which he'd been staring at, wondering what color her panties were beneath her navy-blue skirt. "I've got pull."

"Do you now?" She raised her eyebrows at him. "I thought Mama's didn't take reservations for parties under six."

"Sure, shoot me down." He cocked a black brow at her. "So maybe it was just blind luck." He'd put in the request for a table in the Elvis room but there had been no guarantees, since the restaurant gave first priority to large parties. After they'd been seated and the hostess who had been listening to their conversation with a wry smile walked away, he leaned over the table and ran his fingertips down the back of Jane's hand, between her fingers, then down them until his fingertips pressed against hers. She had such soft skin. "I told them nothing but the finest for my date," he murmured.

"Ooh. I *love* a big shot."

"In that case, don't be afraid to live large. Order the Virgin Strawberry Margarita and a combo plate."

She did, and when their drinks had been delivered and the waitress had left, he leaned back in his chair and watched Jane take a sip. "How come you never drink anything alcoholic?"

She hesitated, then said, "I do have an occasional drink. But mostly I steer clear because my folks are… heavy drinkers." Her eyebrows furrowed in delicate creases. "No, that's prettying it up. They're alcoholics."

His knee-jerk reaction was to reach out and touch her. To offer comfort. He maintained his indolent pose with an effort, because he sensed comfort was the last thing she wanted. "Both of them?"

"Yes."

On the other hand, this wasn't something you yawned and said "Ho-hum" over. Watching her fingers tap the tabletop in time to "Livin' on a Prayer," which was playing over the speakers, he took his cue from her.

Or tried to, anyway. Because still he heard himself say, "I'm sorry, Janie. That's gotta be rough."

She shrugged but he could see it wasn't something she cared to discuss over chips and salsa. Appreciating that she'd told him that much—not to mention that this was supposed to be a date and therefore fun—he said, "Tell me you weren't a Bon Jovi fan when you were a kid," and curled his lip to demonstrate his opinion of that eventuality.

"What do you mean *were,* Gonzo? I remain a fan." She fanned her face with her fingertips. "I mean, have you ever *looked* at Jon Bon Jovi?"

"Can't say that I have. He's not exactly my type."

"Ah." She took another sip of her drink, then, setting the glass back on the table, gave him a knowing look. "Don't go for blondes, huh?"

"Cute, Kaplinski."

Her lips curled up in a pleased-with-herself smile. "I try. And really. One hundred million fans can't be wrong. I suppose *you* were a Van Halen or a Guns N' Roses fan." Planting her chin in her palm, she gazed at him. "So, how about your fashion sense during that era? Were you strictly a blue jeans guy? Or, wait. I bet you wore parachute pants and were one of those break-dancing kids. I can definitely visualize you spinning on your head."

He grinned. "Finn was the break-dancer in the family. And I attended parochial school, sweet thing, so that meant a uniform. I mostly wore jeans at home. But I admit to a year of strutting my stuff in parachute pants. I looked *hot,* too. All the girls wanted me."

"I'm sure you were a legend in your own mind." She gave him a slow, thorough up-and-down, then diluted the sizzle factor by shooting him a Huck Finn grin. "Actually, I liked those pants. I think they might be making a comeback, too. At least, I saw something awfully similar on a girl downtown the other day. I just might have to get myself a pair."

"In a nice bright red?"

She laughed. "Probably not."

"So what is your favorite color? No, wait, don't tell me." Closing his eyes, he pressed his index and forefingers to the spot between his brows. "I see…black."

"No, smart-ass. Green."

He opened his eyes, sat straighter. "No shit?"

"Yeah. I really like green, especially the soft, sagey shades."

"Like your bedroom walls," he said. He'd become intimately acquainted with that room the other day and it had been painted a soft gray-green that presented a sharp contrast to the pristine white woodwork. The color scheme had carried over in the palm-leaf printed comforter and the numerous throw pillows piled against her shams.

"Yes," she agreed. "How about you? What's your favorite color?"

"Blue. Like your eyes, babe."

She made a rude noise.

Grinning at her, he looked at her shiny hair and remembered a style his sister had worn years ago. "So, did you wear your hair in those tall-ass big bangs in high school?"

"Please." She gave him a look down the length of her nose. "You're obviously years older than I am. I was, like, eleven or twelve when that fad hit."

"Right," he scoffed. "And prepubescent girls never follow the hot styles of the day or anything." Studying her sleek and slippery hair, he gave her a knowing look. "Ah. Couldn't get your hair to achieve those heights, huh?"

"No," she promptly admitted. "And it just chapped my hide, too. Poppy had an amazing swoop, but mine and Ava's fell flat every time."

"On the other hand, you and Ava won't have any embarrassing pictures for future generations to ridicule."

"There is that," she agreed.

Dinner arrived and as they ate they continued to exchange stories from their teenage years. That segued into a discussion of their early twenties, which segued into their work.

"So, you planning to sail boats until you're old and gray?" she inquired at one point.

"Probably not. Part of me loves it and can't visualize giving it up. But another part is getting tired of the constant living out of a duffel."

"I can't even imagine your lifestyle," she admitted.

"I'd love to see some of the world, but for maybe two or three weeks at a time. I'm a Seattle woman at heart. Poppy and Ava are here and so is my work." She forked up some rice, but didn't carry it to her lips, leaving it suspended instead over her plate while she gazed at him across the table. "Tell me about some of the places you've been to, though. Which did you like best?"

Their dinners cooled on their plates as they shared bits and pieces of themselves. And the more they talked and laughed, the closer loomed a realization in Devlin's mind.

He really liked this woman. Liked her a *lot*. And not just for the stunning sexual chemistry that threatened to burn them alive whenever they happened to rub up against each other. They meshed on so many levels, it was almost scary. And the more time he spent with her, the more levels he seemed to discover.

A long while later, after the waitress had taken away their plates and returned with Jane's flan and Mexican hot chocolate and his cup of coffee, he leaned back in his chair and watched her take a bite of the custard. "So… about you putting out on a first date—"

Taking her time licking the spoon, Jane gazed at him, her eyes through her lashes mere glints of pale blue ringed in a darker hue. Then she dipped her chin and gave him a demure smile. "I'm not that kind of girl."

"I can't tell you how sorry I am to hear that."

The toe of her high heel suddenly stroked his ankle beneath the table. "A really determined man might be able to change my mind though," she murmured while giving him another of those contradictory I'd-never-dream-of-having-sex smiles. "I like highly motivated men."

He shot his hand up for the waitress. "Check please!"

Jane laughed and moved her foot back to her side of the table.

His cell rang as they were walking back to the sports car he'd reserved for their date. Checking the readout, he shrugged and said, "I'm sorry, I've got to get this." Flipping the phone open and bringing it to his ear, he said, "What can I do for you, Finn?"

"Did you already take the chop saw to the mansion?"

"Yeah, I'm going to need it in a few days."

"Change of plans, bro. We need it at the Morris job tomorrow. I'm on my way to the mansion now—where will I find it?"

"In the cupboard in the room next to the sunroom. The one that connects on the north wall. Is that all you need?"

"Yep, that'll do me."

"Good. I'm on a date—don't call me again."

"Got it." Finn laughed. "Give Legs a big, hot kiss from me."

"Right," he said, deadpan. "That's gonna happen." Flipping the phone closed, he dropped it back in his jacket pocket and slung an arm around Jane's shoulders. "Babe. I'm yours for the rest of the night."

Crossing the courtyard between the two buildings that comprised Jane's condominium complex a short while later, Dev stopped, pulled her into his arms and kissed her. He didn't lift his head again until he felt her sag bonelessly against him. "Invite me in for coffee," he ordered.

One of the things he really liked about Jane was that she was nobody's pushover. Slowly straightening against him, she unlocked her hands from behind his neck and lightly scratched her fingernails down his nape. "Well... I don't know."

He kissed her again until those same nails dug in to hold him in place. He ripped his mouth free. "Invite me in—"

"Would you like to come up to my place for—" licking her lips, she smoothed her fingertips over the little crescents she'd left in his nape "—coffee?"

"Oh, yeah."

They strode through the lobby to the elevator like a couple of business associates. But the minute the doors closed, Dev leaned back against the wall and hooked an arm around her waist, yanking her to him. He welded his lips to hers. When he lifted his head this time, Jane was leaning heavily against him, one leg sliding up the outside of his thigh.

He blew out a harsh breath. "This car have a security camera?"

"I don't know."

"Then it's probably best I don't rip your top off. I'd hate to see you turn up on the internet on a Best Candid Camera Underwear Shots site."

She dropped her head to his chest. "Why, oh why didn't I buy that unit I looked at on the third floor?"

The car arrived at their destination seconds later and they raced each other down the hallway. Crowding close behind Jane at her door, he rubbed his palms down her thighs and kissed the back of her neck while she fumbled with the lock. When the knob suddenly turned beneath her hand, they tumbled into her apartment.

What should have taken seconds to make it down the hallway took them much longer, because they kept getting sidetracked by kisses and attempts to remove each other's clothing. Jane pulled free from his kiss as they came abreast of the kitchen. "About that coffee," she panted.

He choked on a laugh and, picking her up, carried her into the bedroom, where he tossed her on the bed. He dropped down alongside her. Propping himself up on his elbow, he reached out to unbutton her top.

"Babe. I've got a tip for you. Never trust a guy who's dying to see what color underwear you're wearing beneath your Darth Vader getup du jour. We'll say anything to make that happen." Spreading open her top, he sucked in a shallow breath.

"Ah, man," he breathed, bending his head to press a reverent kiss to the sweet, sweet delicate cleavage he'd just exposed. *"Green."*

CHAPTER SEVENTEEN

*I used to think Poppy's folks calling the cops The
Man was just one of those leftover sixties things.
A hippie affectation against authority, not a genuine indictment against that particular branch of
it. But maybe they were onto something.*

"HEY, WHAT'S THIS?" Devlin murmured several minutes
into their postcoital snuggle. "You're tensing up." He
rubbed his work-roughened hand in small, soothing circles on Jane's naked hip. "And I think I smell circuits
frying. What's got you thinking so hard?"

"I've been ignoring my instincts," Jane told him without a second's hesitation. It was a relief to share her concern. With a slight adjustment, she settled against him
more firmly and stroked her cheek on his chest, feeling
muscles glide beneath his warm skin as he tightened his
arm around her. "I've told myself that something I know
on a gut level is happening isn't—and now I have to do
what I should have done right away and call the cops."

"Whoa." He turned onto his side, rolling her off
him but then hooking an arm around her waist to slide
her across the small stretch of sheet separating them.
Once they were face-to-face, he pillowed his head on a
brawny, up-drawn arm and studied her. "What do you
mean, call the police? What the hell's going on?"

Mirroring his pose, she explained about the missing items from Miss Agnes's collections. "I first noticed something was off several days ago. But I convinced myself I was imagining things."

"Sure—you live in a concrete world." Lifting his head from his biceps, he rocked forward the few inches necessary to kiss the curve of her neck. Then he settled back. "Which is merely an observation, by the way. I don't mean it in a derogatory way."

"And I don't take it as such. It's true. I do like things black or white."

"Mostly black," he said sotto voce.

She ignored that, but his unrelenting teasing when it came to her color-in-fashion choices drew a faint smile from her all the same—and a definite lightening of her spirits. "So, as I was saying before I was so rudely interrupted, I thought I was imagining things. And I was kind of impatient with myself, you know? I thought I was just being fanciful. Because there could be any number of explanations why a good part of the stuff I remembered was no longer there."

His fingertips brushed the side of her neck as he tucked a lock of hair behind her ear. "But?"

"But when I hunted up the inventory list compiled by the probate appraiser and checked, all the items I couldn't locate were on it."

"Meaning someone's lifted them between then and now."

"Yes. And when I double-checked the entire list, there were other things missing, as well. So I have to call the police. Not to mention Poppy and Ava, who I should have informed first thing. I kept putting it off, though, hoping the situation would somehow fix itself." She made a face. "Which is ridiculous. Which is why I have to quit ditching my responsibilities and call. Everyone."

"But not right this minute," he said, snuggling her closer until they were body-to-body. Sliding down, he opened his lips over the point of her chin. Then he scraped his strong teeth down her throat before locking onto the curve of her neck where it flowed into her shoulder. "It's late."

She shivered at the sexual threat against her vulnerable skin…and tilted her head for more. "It's barely after eight."

"It's after eleven in New York," he murmured, moving lower. His left hand slid with a whisper-light touch down her stomach and between her legs. "Five a.m. in Spain."

She arched into his touch. "So you agree with that old philosopher Jimmy Buffett?" she panted. "That it's five o'clock somewhere?"

Dev shifted her even closer. "Damn straight. There'll be plenty of time to call in the morning."

GORDON STOOD in front of the Dior gown with a freshly honed knife in his hand and a pillowcase full of stolen booty at his feet.

This was the third time he'd found himself planted in this spot and he was growing annoyed with his procrastination. His plan had been simple—get in, liberate as many collectibles as he could fit into the pillowcase without clanking like the ghost of Christmas Past, then slice the Christian Dior to ribbons and get the hell out. Fast and efficient, with the extra reward of knowing he'd destroyed half of old lady Wolcott's gift to the Met—and along with it Kaplinski's credibility in the museum world.

Well, okay, the plan had been to demolish the *entire* collection, not merely this gown. But this would have to do, because he'd hunted throughout the mansion while he was collecting his loot and the rest of the haute couture clothing was nowhere to be found. Skaggy bitch had probably transferred it to the museum already—although it was a mystery to him why she would leave behind what she herself had proclaimed her central piece.

Well, whatever the reason, it just went to show that the Ives luck remained kissed by the gods. They clearly loved his ass, because while he couldn't annihilate Kaplinski's collection entirely, having the Dior gown still here at least provided him a golden opportunity to make her scramble to find another focal point for her exhibit. And he was just aglow knowing she'd be devastated. That was the bonus that put the bloom in his cheeks.

It was also something he'd be wise to gloat over later. He hadn't maintained a spotless record all these years by pushing his luck. He was a gambler, yes. But there was a big difference between taking a well-thought-out chance—and pushing that chance beyond good sense. When it came to possibilities and probabilities, he'd learned to pay close attention to the latter.

So it was time to do what he'd come to do and hit the road. The gown's golden beads gleamed in the soft light of the desk lamp he'd turned on and, stepping up, he raised the knife.

Only to leave it hovering above the gown for a moment before dropping his hand to his side. "Fuck!"

He couldn't do it. The piece was beyond stunning and in incredible shape for a textile half a century old. He simply could not take a knife to it.

Didn't mean he was going to walk away and just leave it for Kaplinski, though. He might not be able to bring himself to destroy a piece so beautiful, but she hadn't won. Pulling the gown off its padded satin hanger, he carefully folded it and placed it atop his treasures in the pillowcase.

Hell, this was even better. He'd mount it behind ultraviolet light-filtering glass—with spacers, of course, to keep it from touching—and add it to his collection of pretties.

Over the years he'd liberated an item here and an object there from various museums where he'd interned or worked. It was surprisingly easy to do, if you had the nerve. One didn't pick the museum's most prestigious or popular items, obviously. He'd wait for one of the periodic purges where long-stored collections were weeded of pieces that were broken or otherwise badly marred, then make a list of the damaged pieces with two or three perfectly good, carefully chosen items mixed in. When he took it to the curator in charge to be signed off on, it was always with a cheery, "But you'll want to check these for yourself, I'm sure," as he'd handed it over.

As if. Most senior curators didn't want to muck around in dusty storage rooms. Only once had one taken him up on it, and it was with genuine regret that Gordon had beat him back to the storage room to inflict the damage he'd claimed the pieces had sustained.

Since he'd known better than to dip into the same

pool more than once, he didn't have an abundant treasure trove. But that merely made the enjoyment of those pieces he had gained by outwitting the system all the sweeter.

And it was sure as hell more than freaking *Jane* had had before she'd been named heir to the Wolcott fortune. He'd never mentioned his collection to her, of course, but its existence had been a powerful secret he'd hugged to himself as they'd vied for supremacy on the exhibits Marjorie assigned.

Then she'd suddenly shot right past him on the ownership front, and it was so fucking unfair he could spit. Breathing hard, he stared down at his sack of goodies.

His agitation eased.

At least he'd have this. So big deal if his personal collection was modest. Kaplinski's Christian Dior gown would be given place of honor in it. And he would smile every damn time he looked at it, remembering how he'd screwed her over.

He'd also enjoy the memory of besting her when the pieces he took tonight funded the poker tournament that would finally set his feet firmly on the road to the high life. One day he was going to own collections with impeccable provenance. Museums that had failed to appreciate his genius when it might have benefited them would beg for the chance to display his possessions.

And it would all depend upon his mood whether or not he granted them permission.

He didn't exactly whistle, but his step was light as he turned out the light and set off for the kitchen. Then, just steps from its entrance, he heard men's voices at the back door and the sound of a key in the lock.

Son of a bitch! Ducking into the dining room before whoever was out there could open the door and see him, he looked around, a danger rush pumping through his veins as the back door opened and a voice suddenly said clearly, "...though why you'd want your cabin—excuse me, *chalet*—right on I-90 is beyond me. Granted, it's probably quieter when there's snow up there, but now I'm going to forever associate the word *chalet*—which *ought* to bring to mind a stacked blonde with that braid-wrap-thing around her head—with the sound of jake brakes going down the hill. All. Friggin'. Night. Long."

Grateful for the moonlight filtering through the tall mullioned windows, he glanced around. With the possible exception of a built-in cupboard, there was nothing in the dining room with the potential to fully conceal him. Keeping close to the wall, he crossed to it on silent feet, hoping to hell it wasn't jammed full. He could use a place that afforded better cover than the long mahogany table.

When he opened its fir-paneled door however, he discovered an old dumbwaiter, the floor of its movable cubby misaligned a good foot and a half below the opening. For a nanosecond he merely stared at it, thinking that didn't make a damn bit of sense when the kitchen was across the hall.

Then he shrugged impatiently. Who gave a fuck—no doubt the kitchen had been in the basement at one time. The important thing was the dumbwaiter wasn't big enough to climb into even if it were lined up right, and he wouldn't trust its ancient pulley system to bear his weight if it had been. But he slipped the laden pillowcase into it when he heard the men's voices growing closer. Then he eased closed its door and stepped out of sight behind the dining room door.

If these were workmen, hopefully they'd merely come back for something they'd forgotten. And if that were the case all he had to do was sit tight until they went upstairs. At which time he'd grab his sack—which in retrospect he realized he should have kept with him— and be on his way.

"I'll get the saw and be right back," said a man who was suddenly inches from where he stood, and Gordon's breath froze in his throat. They were divided by so little space that he could almost have stuck his fingers through the gap between the door hinges and plucked a strand of the burly man's hair from his head.

"Excellent," said another from the direction of the kitchen. "It's a happy day when I can get someone else to do my work for me. I'll just put my feet up and wait right here."

Laughing, the brunette continued down the hallway but Gordon's mind shrieked, *Shit! ShitfuckSHIT!*

Panic he hadn't felt at the men's appearance grabbed him by the throat, and muscles jumped and twitched beneath his skin in an adrenaline-fueled demand to flee. But he took a deep breath, eased it out and gave himself a mental shake.

You're stronger than a random primal urge, he assured himself sternly. *Hang tough.* He did, refusing to allow instincts that should have been eradicated about the time man hit the Industrial Age to jolt him against the door. That would not only alert a couple of brainless working stiffs that they weren't alone, but act like a freaking neon arrow pointing the way to his position.

His muscles settled and he smiled grimly. All he had to do was outwait them. This might not be the most secure hiding place in the mansion, but if the men had been working here for a while it would be just another room in the house to them and one they probably never even glanced in anymore. So it was okay. Everything would be just fine.

He stood statue-still behind the door for what seemed like hours but was likely only minutes. Then the man upstairs yelled down, "Didn't Dev say he left the saw in the room next to the sunroom?"

"Yeah, the one on the north side," Kitchen Man called back.

"What?"

"For Cri'sake, David." Muttering something about how all he'd ever wanted was a puppy but had gotten a useless little brother instead, a dark-haired man marched past the dining room with long-legged strides. A second later Gordon heard him loping up the staircase. "I said the one on the nor—"

He didn't wait to hear more. Moving back to the dumbwaiter as quickly as he could and still maintain silence, he had his hand outstretched toward the cupboard knob when the one called David said something and Gordon heard the unmistakable sound of footsteps pounding back down the stairs.

Get out! GET OUT! His flight impulse kicked in with a strength that wouldn't be denied and, panicking for real this time, he fled the room, dashing across the hall into the kitchen and out the back door before the man he heard pounding down the stairs could reach the bottom.

He arrived at his car three blocks away and had his

hand on the door before his panic finally subsided. His first instinct then was to go back. To give the workers a little time to vacate the joint, then go retrieve his goodies.

Except it was too late. He'd burned his bridges by not deactivating the alarm before he'd left.

He knew a lot of guys from the 'hood who would have attempted it anyhow, who would have taken the chance that the workmen hadn't reset the alarm for a quick stop and gone in, snatched the hidden loot and taken off again with no one being the wiser.

Then again, three-quarters of them probably started and ended each day worrying about dropping their soap in one of the state pens' shower rooms.

He had no intention of joining them.

With a contemptuous curse, he climbed into his car and drove away.

DEV AND JANE WERE raiding her freezer for ice cream when his cell phone rang. Reading the ID information, he shook his head, flipped the phone open and drawled, "Don't even tell me you couldn't find the saw, dude, because I know where I left it."

"We've got a problem here, Dev," Finn said and the grimness of his tone wiped the smile from Devlin's face.

"At the mansion?" He pushed away from the counter. Jane turned to look at him and he held a finger up in the universal "Hold on a second" signal. Silently, she returned the half gallon of ice cream to the freezer and shut the door.

"Yeah. The alarm went off while David and I were upstairs."

"Is it possible the door didn't latch behind you when you came in?" But he knew better; his dad had hammered conscientiousness and respect for the owner's property into their heads from the moment they were big enough to pick up their first hammer. Not to mention Jane's certainty that items were missing. "Sorry. Dumb question."

"We talked to the people monitoring the alarm, and they called the cops. They're on their way."

"So are we."

Jane was holding herself tensely when he flipped his phone closed and shoved it back into his pocket. *"What?"*

"Finn and David think there was a break-in while they were there. They've called the cops."

"Dammit, I knew it!" She raced back into the bedroom. "Let me put some clothes on," she said, kicking out of the pajama bottoms she'd pulled on when they'd rolled out of bed. She donned a pair of jeans and threw on a little black cardigan over her tank top, then sat on the bed to slip on her shoes and socks.

He put on his own footwear and shirt and they were out the door within five minutes.

When they pulled into the driveway a short while later, the mansion was lit up like Macy's on Thanksgiving Friday. Letting themselves in, they found David and Finn waiting for them in the kitchen.

Both men rose to their feet. "I'm sorry, Jane," Finn said.

"For what? It's not your fault."

"We think maybe someone was in here when we arrived. David and I should have been more vigilant."

She waved her folder of inventory papers. "If it's anyone's fault, it's mine," she said. "This was not a one-shot deal. I just told Devlin tonight that I've noticed things missing. But because I didn't want to believe it, I put off calling the police."

"Yeah, yeah, and when you mentioned calling them earlier I talked you into waiting until morning, so it's my fault, too." Dev gave his head an impatient shake. "We can play the blame game all night long but it's not going to get us anywhere."

"True," she said ruefully. "So I'll go do something concrete. I'm gonna take my inventory list into the parlor and see what else is missing."

Finn watched her leave the room. "I feel like crap about this."

David nodded his agreement.

"It sucks," Dev granted.

"NOOOOOO!" Jane suddenly wailed and there was such anguish in her voice that he and his brothers nearly trampled each other in their haste to get to the parlor first. They skidded through the open pocket door scant seconds later.

Jane swung around when she heard them arrive, hugging herself against a room that suddenly felt thirty degrees cooler. "They took the Dior," she said, hysteria threatening to overtake her. "Oh God. *They took the Dior!*"

"What's a Dee-ore?" David asked, and she unwound an arm long enough to point a shaky finger at the now-empty hanging rack as if that would somehow answer his question.

"That gold dress that's always hanging there?" Dev

asked and even if he were just making a calculated guess she appreciated that he at least had a clue what she was talking about.

She nodded, forcing a tremulous smile for his acuity. Then, to all three men's obvious horror, a big fat tear escaped her best efforts to hold it back and rolled down her cheek.

"Aw, man, don't cry," David begged.

Finn averted his eyes, his jaw clenched.

Dev crossed to her in two giant steps and wrapped an arm around her shoulders. "Who would want a dress?" he demanded with calm male logic. "Maybe you put it away in the secret closet with the rest of the dresses and stuff and just forgot. You think?"

A bark of humorless laughter escaped her. "No, that would have been the *smart* thing to do. I was so careful with everything else, but the Dior was my...I don't know, my touchstone or talisman or something. I left it out to inspire me to make this the best damn exhibit the Metropolitan Museum has ever seen." She wiped her eyes with quick, surreptitious movements against the swell of Devlin's chest. "Now I have to tell the director that a vital part of Miss Agnes's bequest was stolen because I was arrogant and careless."

A bell rang in the foyer and they all looked at each other blankly for a moment because no one ever used that door. Then Finn rolled his shoulders. "The cops," he murmured and went to let them in.

As it turned out, it wasn't a "them" but rather a lone patrolwoman—a severe, no-nonsense-looking dishwater blonde. She and Finn spoke briefly as he escorted her into the room, then he brought the woman over. "This is Officer Stiller, Jane. Officer, Jane Kaplinski."

She had stepped away from Dev to promote at least the illusion of standing on her own two feet and, functioning on autopilot, she started to offer her hand. Before it rose halfway Stiller gave her a brusque nod, ignoring the budding invitation to shake. Her holster creaked as she pulled a notebook from her hip pocket. "You're the owner?"

Feeling clumsy, Jane stuffed her hand into the pocket of her jeans. "Co-owner. Along with Ava Spencer and Poppy Calloway." She turned to look at Dev, blinking uncertainly. "I need to call them."

Officer Stiller turned to him, as well. "And you are?" she demanded.

"Devlin Kavanagh. You've already met my brother Finn, and this is David. We're Kavanagh Construction—we're doing an extensive remodel on the Wolcott mansion."

"At nine-forty-five at night?"

He narrowed his eyes at her, but said in a neutral voice, "I'd brought a company saw here yesterday that my brothers need for another job, so they stopped by to pick it up. The alarm went off while they were here, indicating someone who was already inside got spooked by their presence and ran."

"Or that your brothers failed to reset the alarm or fully close the door when they came in."

Finn stepped forward. "The alarm is set to automatically reactivate," he refuted in a cool voice. "You might want to call the security company to verify the time the alarm was disarmed."

Jane's head snapped up. "They can do that?" she demanded.

He nodded at her. "This system is state-of-the-art."

"Then I need to see all the times the alarm has been armed and disarmed since the system was installed," she said. "I've got a list of things I noticed missing before tonight's incident."

The policewoman pinned her with a stern look. "And you didn't think it was important to report that?"

"I've been around these collections most of my life and wasn't positive at first that some of the items I thought were missing hadn't simply broken or worn out. But when I checked them against the inventory list it showed I wasn't imagining things. I talked to Devlin about it tonight and planned to file a report in the morning."

Stiller studied her for another second then turned back to Finn. "Accepting for the moment that the security company can verify you set the alarm, how can you be certain you didn't fail to completely latch the door behind you?"

"Aside from the fact that our da would skin Davy and me alive if we were ever that sloppy, you mean?"

Officer Stiller actually smiled a little and Finn said seriously, "The system doesn't allow you to enter the code when a door or window is open. Plus I stayed in the kitchen while David ran upstairs to get the saw—long enough to have an improperly deactivated alarm go off."

"So how did anyone get past you?"

"When David couldn't find it—"

"Because I went to the room south of the sunroom instead of the one to its north," his brother inserted.

"—I headed upstairs to help. But he'd already realized he was in the wrong room while I was still on my way up and he located the saw right where Dev said it would be just as I reached the top of the staircase. So I turned around and came down again. The kitchen felt drafty when I walked back in and that's when I noticed the back door was ajar. The alarm went off about five seconds after that."

"Who has the code for the alarm?" Stiller asked.

"I do, of course," Jane said, "and so do Poppy and Ava. So do the Kavanaghs."

Stiller looked at Devlin. "Does your company ever hire illegal aliens?"

"No. Our employees are all U.S. citizens. We're also bonded with the state for each worker. Check out our history—we've never had a claim filed against us."

"And the security code for this house? Is it posted anywhere so your workers can let themselves in and out if you're not available?"

All three brothers' eyes narrowed and Finn said, "We *are* the crew on this job. The rest of our men are tied up on another project."

"And why would we do something so irresponsible even if they were here?" Dev demanded coldly, stepping forward. "Are you trying to suggest that this was an inside job?"

Jane jerked, because that possibility had never once occurred to her. She considered it for maybe five seconds, gave an additional few to mulling over what she knew about Devlin and his family—and dismissed the notion as ludicrous.

"You have to admit that what you've told me so far

makes it appear that way," the policewoman said with a gentleness she hadn't displayed up until now.

"That's crazy," Jane said. "Poppy investigated Kavanagh Construction thoroughly before she hired them. They've been in business since 1969. That's nearly forty years without a single blemish on their record. Why would they risk a hard-earned reputation for a fistful of collectibles that are admittedly worth a fortune— but only if you have some idea how to market them?"

"You appear pretty knowledgeable," the officer said. "Do you know how to market them?"

"I'm a curator at the Metropolitan Museum, so yes, I do. But if you're suggesting that I took this stuff, let me remind you that I already own it. And you're welcome to look into my background. You'll find I don't have any debts or addictions in need of fast cash."

"Can you supply me a list of what's missing?"

"I can give you what I've compiled so far, but it'll take me another day or so to figure out what was taken tonight. The only thing I'm certain is gone is a Christian Dior gown." Her stomach cramped and, shoveling her fingers through her hair, she blew out a breath. "That's a huge kick in the head for me."

"You're most stressed out over a *dress?*" Officer Stiller's tone didn't leave any doubt what she thought of getting all worked up over the loss of something so frivolous.

Jane's shoulders squared and she looked the other woman in the eye, tired of her lack of sensitivity. She was the victim here, not the villain—and certainly not some empty-headed fashion-mad nitwit. "I'm stressed about the theft of a vintage haute couture fifties-era gown that's worth over twenty thousand dollars and didn't belong to us—to Poppy and Ava and me. The Dior is part of a bequest to the Met that I've been cataloging in preparation for an exhibit, and I failed to secure it with the rest of the collection. So not only is its loss a blow from an aesthetic standpoint, it's a blot against me professionally. This is probably going to take my career a big step backward."

"Then I agree you probably should have taken more care securing it," Officer Stiller said.

"Hey!" all three men snapped, and David and Finn grabbed Devlin when he took a hot step toward the officer.

"Well, thank you for pointing that out," Jane said with all the dignity she could summon. "Because I hadn't figured out on my own that I screwed up. Good God, lady. I didn't think it was possible to feel any crappier about this." She looked the policewoman in the eye. "Guess I was wrong about that, too."

"Sorry," Stiller said stiffly. Dull color climbed her face, but she looked at Jane without flinching. "I should have phrased that more diplomatically, but it's been a rough day. I'll write it up, of course. And we'll run a check of the local pawn shops to see if anything's shown up. But it looks like you've got people in and out of here all the time and in the same way that we look at family first in a homicide, we look at those in possession of the security code in a burglary where there's no sign of a forced entry, particularly since you claim tonight isn't the first time you've suffered a loss. So I'm going to have to check out everyone who had access. Aside from that—well, unless you can come up with someone else who had an opportunity to catch a peek at the code, I'm not sure what else I can do."

"Let me show you around to give you an idea what we're dealing with and why I didn't recognize right away that things were missing."

After spending an additional twenty minutes showing the policewoman through Miss Agnes's collections, she supplied her with a list of the items that had gone missing before tonight's burglary. "I'll get you the rest by the day after tomorrow," she promised as she ushered Officer Stiller out the front door.

Closing it behind the woman, she turned and leaned back against it. She scraped her hair off her forehead with a weary hand and looked at the three Kavanagh men who had followed her into the front foyer.

"Well, that was fun. Anyone else feel in need of a good primal scream?"

David took a step toward her. "The officer had a point about the way this looks," he said carefully. "You really don't blame us?"

She blinked. "Of course not. I don't know what the hell is going on, but I do know none of you would steal from us."

Grabbing her, Finn planted a big kiss on her lips. His ability in that department had nearly the same off-the-Richter-scale impact as his brother's, and she blinked as he set her back on the ground and turned to look Dev.

"Marry her quick, boyo," he advised him. "Or I will."

CHAPTER EIGHTEEN

Thank God for girlfriends. What a screwed-up world this would be without them.

POPPY AND AVA WERE at the mansion within twenty minutes of Jane calling them. "I am so sorry, you guys," she said after explaining the evening's events in greater detail than she'd gone into over the phone. "I let you down, big-time."

"No shit," Poppy said. "Here I thought you were God, but it turns out you're not."

"She's *not?*" Ava demanded incredulously. Then she gave a philosophical shrug. "Ah, well, in a way that's a relief, isn't it? Because God doesn't make mistakes, and just look how she screwed up." Wrapping an arm around Jane's shoulders, she tugged her to her side in a warm, lush hug and said seriously, "Get over yourself, Janie. It doesn't all rest on your shoulders."

Poppy nodded her agreement. "You managed to figure out that pieces of Miss A.'s collections are missing. That's more than Ava or I ever would've realized."

"Yeah, whoop-de-do for me," she said morosely. "I discovered them—then dithered about trying to convince myself I didn't know what I knew."

"Of course you did. We have a brand-new state-of-the-art security system—why *would* you think someone slipped past it to rip us off?"

Dev entered the parlor, looking tough and competent, all hard shoulders in the soft sweater he'd donned for their date.

A date that felt like an aeon ago.

"Finn and David took off, and I set up the alarm system to change the code," he said. "Do you remember what to do once you've entered the new number?"

"Yes." She turned to her friends. "We just have to come up with a new one. Any ideas?"

He turned away. "I'll leave you to it."

"No," she said. "We'll be giving you the new code as soon as we decide what it should be anyway. That is—" She turned to her friends. "You do agree that it couldn't be any of the Kavanaghs, right?" Her own belief was a gut certainty. But it didn't stop her from awaiting Poppy and Ava's verdict with a certain amount of anxiety. The three of them weren't always of one mind, but generally it was the small stuff they squabbled over. If they had doubts about *this* it would constitute their first real major difference of opinion.

"Actually, I do agree with you," Poppy said, and Jane almost sagged with relief. She turned her head to look at Ava.

The redhead set her loose and fastened a level gaze on Devlin. "I haven't been around you or your brothers as much as these two have," she said. "But I trust Jane. She has good instincts." The corner of her mouth tipped up in a wry, crooked smile. "And people might look at Poppy's big brown eyes and blond curls and those hippie-dippy skirts she's so fond of wearing and think 'hot little marshmallow.' But Jane and I can attest to her tenacity and attention to detail. She spent considerable time researching your company before we hired you."

"Yes, I did," Poppy agreed, but she obviously didn't feel the need to belabor the point, for she immediately turned her attention back to her friends. "And you know what bugs me most about this whole situation—aside from Janie losing her exhibit centerpiece, of course? It's the cop's attitude. Because *somebody's* helped him- or herself to this stuff. And if we didn't lift it and the Kavanaghs didn't lift it—but the police insist on concentrating their entire search only on us anyway—then they're basically granting whoever did take it a license to steal. And the idea of that really burns me up."

"I couldn't agree more," Ava said. "And I believe I'll have a talk with Uncle Robert about it. He and the mayor play eighteen holes together almost every Wednesday." She flashed a cool shark's smile that contrasted sharply with the Earth Goddess impression her warm coloring and abundant curves usually conveyed. "I think it's time they had a little chat about something more important than the finer points of chasing balls around the greens with a stick."

"REMIND ME not to get on Ava's bad side," Dev said as he drove them back to Jane's condo half an hour later. "That was kind of like watching Marilyn Monroe suddenly grow gator teeth." He glanced over at Jane, who had been staring silently out the car window. "Does she really have the ear of the mayor?"

She turned toward him, making an obvious effort to erase the brooding expression furrowing her delicate eyebrows. "Yes. Her folks aren't the most warm-and-fuzzy people in the world, but they do have connections to a good portion of the Seattle/King County/Washington State political machine."

"Handy."

"I suppose," she agreed glumly. "If you can't have a Mom-and-apple-pie-type family like you've got, a politico in the dynasty pocket is almost the next best thing."

Okaaaay. But when he thought about where that had come from, he reached across the console and squeezed her thigh. "I'm sorry about your dress, babe."

"Yeah, me, too." She grimaced. "And I'm being a real baby about it." She sat a bit straighter in the passenger seat. "I suppose I oughtta get over it. As Officer Stiller pointed out, it's only a dress. It's not as if I overheard the solution for world peace then lost the piece of paper I wrote it on."

"Officer Stiller is an ass. And I think you oughtta allow yourself tonight to wallow in it. You can always get over it tomorrow."

"Oh. I like that." She gave him the first real smile he'd seen since the discovery of the Dior's theft. "Thanks. I'll do that—I'll get my act together tomorrow."

He found a parking spot right in front of her condo. As he draped his arm around her shoulders to walk her in, she leaned against him as if she were too tired to support her own weight. And he realized anew how depressed she was over the thefts. A funny, warm protectiveness suffused him.

Marry her quick, boyo, or I will.

His step faltered for a second, then he picked up his pace, a soft snort escaping him. *Yeah, right.* He wanted to shield her from the type of blow she'd taken tonight, not shackle himself for life to a woman he was only now beginning to know.

They were almost to the lobby and Jane was digging through her purse for her key when voices charged with drama and passion filtered through the glass-doored vestibule. She jerked to a stop, her head snapping up. "Aw, *shit*," she muttered. "This night just keeps getting better and better, doesn't it?"

He looked from the older couple arguing in the lobby to her. "Neighbors of yours?"

"Oh, no, it's better than that. That's Mike and Dorrie, stars of the Battling Bickertons' Always Amazing Traveling Road Show." He must have looked as blank as he felt, for she added, "Mike and Dorrie *Kaplinski*."

"Oh. You mean—?"

"My parents, yes." She squared her shoulders. "Look, why don't you head home? Trust me, you don't need this—and I promise I'll call the minute I finish dealing with whatever tonight's imaginary crisis is."

Standing on her toes, she gave him a goodbye kiss, then slid out from under his arm and pushed open the doors into the lobby.

I don't think so, babe. He followed in her wake.

The twenty-something woman behind the curving counter of the security desk greeted their appearance with a little too much white showing around her eyes. "Oh, look," she said with palpable relief to the couple who hadn't stopped arguing long enough to notice they were no longer alone. "Here's your daughter now."

Jane gave Sally an apologetic look. "They came separately, I assume?"

"Yes. Your father first, then your mom. Please. Would you take them up to your place?"

Jane sighed.

A florid-faced man with Jane's shiny brown hair rose from the wide leather bench across from the desk. "We've been waiting over an hour for you, Jane Elise," he said.

The woman with hair streaked orangey-red remained seated, her hands on the bench behind her. The position both propped her up and thrust her chest forward, and she crossed and uncrossed her electric-blue-spandex-clad legs, whichever foot that ended on top tapping an impatient rhythm in the air. "Not only that, but that young woman," she said, thrusting her chin toward Sally, "*refused* to let us to do so in the comfort of your apartment."

Jane grabbed Dev's hand and headed for the elevator. It opened the moment she punched the button, and, glancing behind him, he saw her father quick-stepping after them and her mother scrambling off the bench to follow.

"If you had called to let me know you were coming," Jane said coolly as everyone piled into the car, "I might have been able to give you an estimate on what time I'd be home. Although with all the crap that's gone on tonight—"

Cutting herself off, she shook her head. "But what am I thinking? You aren't interested in my troubles."

Dev looked at her in surprise. Of course they were interested; they were her parents.

Except…neither her father nor mother asked a single question in response to that provocative lead-in. So maybe he should extend Jane the courtesy of acknowledging she knew them a whole lot better than he did.

"As for Sally, Mom," she continued. "She didn't let you into my apartment because I've instructed everyone who works the front desk not to."

"You'd deny your own mother a bit of comfort? Well, if that's not the chilliest thing I've ever heard! But of course we're talking about you, aren't we, Miss Cold Fish?"

His presence apparently registered on the older woman's radar as the car reached Jane's floor, for she suddenly looked at him. "Who are you?" she demanded as Jane led them down the corridor to her apartment and unlocked the door. The older woman gave him a swift, comprehensive once-over. "You look too hot-blooded to be Jane's date. You two work together at the museum, or something?"

A flush crept up Jane's throat at her mother's dig and icy anger settled in the pit of Dev's stomach. That was a hell of an attitude to have about your own kid. "No, ma'am." Draping his arm over Jane's shoulder, he snuggled her close, his hand dangling over her chest. Plucking up a hank of her hair, he stretched it over his index finger and caressed its satiny texture with his thumb, his knuckles brushing her breast with each stroke. "I'm Dev—Janie's boyfriend."

"*Are* you now?" Dorrie lifted her eyebrows at Jane. "So much for hightailing it in the other direction the minute you see a hint of passion headed your way."

Jane returned a noncommittal look. "You know nothing about my arrangement with Devlin."

"That's not the important thing, anyhow," Mike cut

in, and Dev stared at him in amazement. A father just learns his daughter's carrying on a hot-and-heavy affair with a guy he doesn't know squat about and he doesn't think it's worth commenting on?

Apparently not, for Mike said, "You've got to talk some sense into your mother, Jane."

"No, Dad. I don't," she disagreed, rubbing her fingers against her temples. "Am I the only one who remembers our last twenty-five conversations on this very subject?" Neither parent answered and she sighed. "Guess so. Well, let me refresh your memories. Take your drama to your mama, as we used to say in school. I'm not interested in being your audience any longer."

Dev could see why this was her twenty-sixth take on the same conversation, because her father barely allowed her to quit speaking before he said, "Jane, we're putting on *Cat on a Hot Tin Roof* and she wants to be Maggie the Cat! Will you for God's sake tell her she's too old? I've told her myself until I'm blue in the face, but you know how pigheaded your mother can be."

Jesus. He scowled at Jane's old man. How was she supposed to answer that? he wondered in disgust. Talk about a no-win situation. If she agreed, she was condemning her mom. At the same time she could hardly disagree and hurt her father.

But Jane was either made of sterner stuff than he'd given her credit for or just plain accustomed to crap like this, because she said, "And I assume you think *you're* young enough to play Brick?"

"You got it," Dorrie agreed. "So tell the old fool he's the one who's—"

"I've got a news flash," Jane said, ruthlessly cutting

her mother off. "You're *both* too old for those roles. Just as you were too old last season when you wanted to play Oberon and Titania in *A Midsummer Night's Dream.* So cast yourselves as Big Daddy and Big Mama. Or—here's a thought—find a play that's actually age-appropriate for a change. *Arsenic and Old Lace,* maybe."

"I'm not sharing the starring role with another woman!" her mother said with the horror another might reserve for a suggestion she turn her child over to white slavers.

"Then do *Who's Afraid of Virginia Woolf!*" Jane snapped.

There was an instant of silence. Then—

"Ooh," Dorrie said thoughtfully.

"That's not bad," Mike said. "In fact, that's damn good." He looked at his daughter. "Got any gin? We oughtta sit down and talk about this."

She rubbed her temples more strenuously. "When have I ever had gin here, Dad?"

"True. You're not the best hostess."

"I'll say," Dorrie agreed. But she smiled at Jane. "This is brilliant, though, darling."

Dev watched pleasure chase across Jane's face at the praise, but her mother had already turned away to touch Mike's arm. "There're only six actors in the entire play and we could probably get students to play the road-house waitress and the—what was the other one? The bartender? Oh, the manager, I think." She shook her head. "Anyhow, that's not the important thing. My point is that we could get the kids to play them for peanuts."

"My head is gonna explode," Jane muttered and Dev abruptly reached his limit. It was as if they didn't see her unless one had need of her as a weapon against the other. Whipping his wallet from his back pocket, he pulled out a twenty and offered it to Mike. "Here. Go get yourselves a cup of coffee and talk it over. Jane's had a rough night and she needs some rest."

"And aspirin," she murmured. "I could really, really use a couple of aspirin."

Her father didn't hesitate to pocket the cash. "Thanks, son. Come on, Dorrie. Let's go down to the El Gaucho and toss some ideas around."

"I'm not sitting in any stinky cigar lounge," Dorrie said. "Let's go to the Viceroy."

"You're kidding, right? The crowd there is Jane's age."

Jane herself appeared to be invisible to them as she walked them to the door, still arguing, and saw them on their way. Dev realized that neither Mike nor Dorrie had hugged or kissed her—not in greeting, not in goodbye. In his family no one got in or out of a relative's house without one or the other—and in the case of his mother, grandmothers and aunts, both. Up until tonight he'd taken that for granted, never giving it a helluva lot of thought one way or the other, aside from occasionally wishing that Aunt Eileen would wear one of those nontransferable lipsticks. Suddenly, however, he had a new appreciation for his family that he hadn't possessed half an hour ago.

Taking Jane at her word, he headed for the bathroom across from the kitchen and had two aspirin and a cold glass of water waiting for her when she came back down the hallway. He handed them to her.

"Oh God, thank you." She tossed the pills back and chugged the water, draining the cup of its last drop.

"You want more?" he asked, indicating the glass.

"No, this was perfect. All I want right now is to go to bed."

"Go get ready, then, and I'll give you a neck rub before I tuck you in."

She gave him a tired look. "You don't have to do that."

"I know I don't have to. I want to."

"Look," she said, meeting his gaze as her jaw tilted with pride. "I won't apologize for my parents. I know I should probably be embarrassed that you saw how erratic they can be, but I gave up thinking years ago that anything Mike and Dorrie do reflects on me."

"Hell, yeah," he agreed emphatically.

"Well, it was either that or live in a perpetual state of embarrassment," she added with her usual honesty, then grimaced. "Okay, the truth is I really, really wish you hadn't witnessed our screwed-up family dynamics and I'm sorry you had to be involved in their melodrama. It was sweet of you to stand up for me—"

"Babe," he interrupted, reaching out to sweep away a strand of hair that had fallen over her eye. "I don't do sweet. Your mom clearly doesn't know jack about you if she thinks you're somehow lacking sexually, and I just thought she should understand that. But, Janie," he added gently, "all families are a little messed up."

"Oh God." She rested her forehead against his collarbone. "Don't be so understanding. Please. I don't think I can take it tonight."

"Okay." Turning her around, he pointed her toward

her bedroom and gave her butt a smack. "Go get ready for bed."

She didn't argue, just disappeared into her bedroom bath to follow his suggestion.

While she was gone he lit the candles on the library table behind the green velvet couch and turned out all the lights except the one on the microwave over the stove. That, he put on its night-light setting.

Back in the living room, he flipped the switch for the small gas fireplace, and watched blue-tipped orange flames poof to life along its fake logs. He kicked off his shoes and sat down to wait. Propping his back against one of the couch's overstuffed arms, he stretched his right leg along the cushions, his left leg sprawling wide, knee bent and foot braced against the hardwood floor. He gazed out the window, absentmindedly cracking his knuckles as he watched a lighted ferry glide into Elliott Bay between the candle flames reflecting back at him from the darkened glass.

Jane, too, cast a dim reflection a short while later when she walked into the living room, dressed in boy shorts and a matching skinny-rib tank, wrapping a fleece robe around her waist.

Widening his bent leg even farther, he patted the cushion between his thighs, reaching for her wrist when she came within grasping distance. Her scrubbed face looked soft in the candlelight, and the flames cast red highlights in her shiny hair as he pulled her between his legs. Situating her with her back to him, he instructed her to loosen her robe, and slipped its collar to the edge of her shoulders when she complied. Once he had a clear playing field, he began massaging her neck.

Groaning, she promptly bent her head to give him more room to maneuver.

He kneaded with his fingers, pressed with his thumbs, and with each manipulation she emitted a rhythmic gravelly-voiced little *uh* deep in her throat, her head rocking in sync with the tempo of his thumbs. Little by little, however, the sound ceased and her breathing evened out as she slipped into slumber. Her neck lost the last fraction of tension holding it upright and her head drooped limply, her chin almost to her chest.

Easing her back against his chest, he gazed down at her. He could see in the candlelight that her shorts and tank were gray, something he hadn't been able to tell in the night-darkened reflection. Smiling wryly, he carefully lifted a strand of hair away from her bottom lip. If her mother had always dressed in the electric hues she'd worn tonight, he thought maybe he understood Jane's penchant for dark and neutral colors a little better.

He shifted her inch by inch until he was able to get an arm around her back and one under her thighs, then he straightened off the couch with her carefully cradled against his chest. He carried her into her bedroom, stooped to fold back the covers with the hand beneath her legs and slid her into bed. He would have liked to remove her plush robe. It hung open but he feared all the maneuvering necessary to get it out from under her would wake her up again, and God knew she could use her rest after the evening she'd had.

As he straightened from his bent-over position, however, her eyes slitted open and she raised her arms to flop them over his shoulders. "Where y'goin'?" she demanded sleepily.

"I'm gonna head home, let you get some sleep."

"No." Her arms inched inward to loop around his neck, the navy fleece a luxuriant caress against his skin. "Stay here." She yawned, long and wide-mouthed, then rubbed her lips together languidly, her eyes heavy-lidded as their gazes met. Her mouth curved up at the corners. "Let's make love."

He knew he should resist the temptation of her warm, sleepy smile. Knew he ought to simply knead her shoulders until she fell back asleep, which would only take minutes.

Instead, he bent and softly kissed her.

With a lazy hum, she arched in his arms and he lowered himself onto the bed, settling half on top of her and kissing her long and deep.

Sex between them had generally been all flash and fire—feverish, but with a bite to it that kept them hovering on the edge of control. Tonight, he loved her tenderly, carefully. He peeled her out of her robe, pulled her tank top off over her head, slid her shorts down her long legs and over her feet, dropping the discarded clothing over the side of the bed. He stripped off his own clothes and tossed them to join hers on the floor.

Once he'd settled back atop her, skin to skin, he alternated between bracing himself above her with an inch of dead space between them, connected by nothing but their lips and tongues and Jane's arms, and bending his elbows to rub his chest against her breasts, his hair-roughened inner thighs against her smooth outer ones, his cock glancing off her stomach, her thigh, the moisture between her legs. He moved with deliberate, patient, drawn-out sensuality, and it cost him. Sweat began trickling down his temples and he had to grit his teeth tighter and tighter to remain in control.

"Inside me," Jane whispered, her hips following when he pushed himself up off her for the umpteenth time. "Oh God, Devlin, inside me now." Hooking her heels behind his knees, she lifted herself.

And suddenly wet, soft folds were pressed against his scrotum. Adjusting their positions, he drew back his hips and gave her what they both wanted, sliding into her with one sure, firm thrust. Simultaneously, they sucked in their breaths.

Janie had circles under her eyes, though, and he'd be damned if he'd go at her like a sailor on shore leave. So, planting his elbows on the mattress, he stroked her hair away from her temples with gentle fingertips and rocked inside her. He alternated shallow thrusts with long, slow, deep ones and her eyes went half-mast. Moments later her breath went shuddery, and her nails dug into his shoulders. Then she arched beneath him and a seemingly unending, undulating contraction worked his dick like a gel-filled fist, dragging him over the edge with her.

Marry her, boyo, or I will.

He hadn't even had time to collapse upon her prone body when his brother's words whispered through his brain, and he tensed, his hands braced against the mattress and his elbows locked. *Dammit, Finn, get out of my head.* But try as he might to shrug the words aside, they kept repeating in his mind.

It was ridiculous. He wasn't ready to marry anyone. But he had to admit, he felt protective of Jane after seeing her with her parents. And something about this lovemaking had left him feeling raw and unguarded, yet shielding and strong.

He stared down at her, at her rumpled hair dark against the silvery green sheets, at her thick lashes resting upon sex-flushed cheeks, at the soft smile that curled her lips.

And he lowered his forehead to hers, filled almost against his will with abrupt purpose. "You know what?" he said. "You oughtta come to Europe with me when I go back."

CHAPTER NINETEEN

I hate, hate, hate *it when people change the rules on me!*

"WHAT?" All the lovely lethargy, that warm feeling of floating in a pool of well-being disappeared, and Jane tensed all over. She shoved at Devlin's hard shoulders. "Get off."

He rolled onto his side facing her, and she scrambled upright, sitting erect and jerking the linens up. The nudity she hadn't given two thoughts to a moment ago suddenly made her feel vulnerable and she tucked the thin sheet under her arms. "What did you say?"

She knew, of course. She just couldn't quite wrap her mind around it.

"Nothing." He shifted upon the mattress, his indolent sprawl perhaps not quite as relaxed as it appeared. "Forget it."

She started to exhale.

Then his dark brows snapped together. "No, dammit." He pushed up on his forearm and scraped his dark fire-colored hair off his forehead with his free hand as he stared at her. "It's not nothing. Come with me to Europe when Bren's better."

"I can't do that!"

"Sure you can." Sliding prone once again, he bent

his elbow to prop his head in his palm. The position thrust his biceps into prominence and even lying still, she noted, he radiated an animal energy that drew her. "Look, I'm not asking you to jump into something right this minute," he said in a reasonable tone. "I have no idea when Bren's going to be well enough for me to leave. But just think of all those dynamite museums. You'd love Europe. I can show you all kinds of wonderful things."

"Hey, little girl, want a ride?" she mocked. "I've got *can*-dy." The laugh that tumbled out of her, however, verged on hysterics. "Oh God. Your timing leaves so much to be desired."

"Because…?"

"Hello, you just met my folks! Oh, I bet you thought tonight was a unique, one-off situation. No, no, no, no, no." She could feel her hair whipping around her face as she shook her head and feared she looked like a bobblehead. She sucked in a calming breath. Blew it out. "This evening's farce was pretty much a microcosm of my entire life, Dev. I can't even recall how old I was when I vowed never to get sucked into the kind of all-consuming passion for another person that their world seems to revolve around."

"Too late."

Panic clawed at her throat and she tried swallowing it whole. "It's *not* too late!"

"I think it might be for me. Because, babe, I feel a shitload of passion for you."

"Well, you sweet talker, you."

He merely looked at her. "I'm not trying to get you to sign off on a marriage contract, Jane. I don't know if this thing between us will last. But I do know I feel something for you that I've never felt before and I wouldn't mind exploring it." He inspected her while she tried desperately to keep her expression neutral. "So, you're not even tempted to run away with me?"

She almost strangled on a bitter laugh. Because, look at him. His hair was rumpled, his jaw was shadowed with black stubble and his skin stretched taut over well-defined muscle and hard bone. The man was dangerous, with a capital *D*.

And that was merely the physical. The emotional danger was even more volatile to her peace of mind.

"I am tempted," she admitted. "That's what scares me. I'm rooted in Seattle. Poppy and Ava, who I consider my real family, are here and so is my career, which is just starting to take off. Well, if the theft of the Dior hasn't blown it all to hell, that is. But even so I'm tempted to head off to Europe with you, to sail around the Mediterranean and see the museums of the world. But I will *not* throw away everything I've worked for to satisfy a few rebellious hormones."

"It's more than just hormones, and you know it."

"Do I?"

"If it's anything like what I'm feeling, you do. But you go ahead and play hard to get. I've got lots of time." Reaching out, he stroked a finger down her inner arm, his knuckle grazing the outer curve of her breast as it cruised past on its trek from shoulder to wrist. Goose bumps rose in its wake, but that was nothing compared to what she felt when his eyes met hers and she saw the confidence shining in them.

That rattled her right down to the bone.

As did his self-assured tone when he said, "I'm going to wear you down yet. Count on it."

GORDON WATCHED from the end of the sixth-floor corridor as Jane knocked on Marjorie's door, then went inside. When their supervisor's door closed behind her, he marched down the hallway to his own office, went in and eased his door closed.

Then did an end-goal victory dance in front of his desk.

Yessss! How does it feel, hotshot, having to tell Marjorie you allowed the Dior to get ripped off? How high and mighty are you now?

Stupid bitch.

Still. He flopped down onto his desk chair. He wished to hell he'd hung on to the Dior when he was beating feet out of the mansion. It didn't bother him so much that he'd had to leave the rest of the things behind—he was a big boy and those were the breaks. A gamble was a gamble—it was the risk that gave it that extra punch and made it so exciting. But the Dior...

That was a piece of art and it ought to be in a climate-controlled closet or behind ultraviolet-light-filtering glass the way he'd planned. Not moldering away in that cold dumbwaiter shaft.

And yet...

Whataya gonna do? Rolling his shoulders, he reached for the folder containing the frigging Spain exhibit. The situation was what it was and there wasn't a damn thing he could do to alter it now. There wasn't a hope in hell that Kaplinski hadn't changed the security code and he wasn't going to luck into it a second time.

But at least he had the satisfaction of knowing he'd corrupted her shiny reputation at the Met. The thought of the reaming out she was undoubtedly getting at this very minute tugged a very pleased smile from his lips.

Because that was work well done.

"THIS IS REALLY LOUSY timing, Ava." Dismayed, Jane stared at her cell phone later that afternoon, then dropped onto the Wolcott parlor love seat and rubbed at the tension tightening the back of her neck. No, not merely lousy; it was incredibly crappy timing.

"I'm sorry about that," Ava said. "But I didn't have a lot of input in the matter. Uncle Robert obviously got on the horn with the mayor, who then must have gotten in immediate touch with the police chief, because the next thing I know this Detective—" there was a rustle of paper at her end "—de Sanges is calling and telling me—*telling,* mind you, not asking—that he'll be at the mansion at five to take a report. I plan to get there before that, and I'll be sure to tell Poppy to arrive early, too."

"Okay, whatever," she said dispiritedly.

"Well, that's what I like to hear—a positive attitude." Exasperation laced Ava's voice. But almost in the next breath it turned contrite. "Oh, Janie, I'm sorry. You were going to tell your supervisor today about the Dior, weren't you? That didn't go too well?"

"Well, let me put it this way—if I were a dog, I'd have my tail tucked firmly between my legs."

"She *blamed* you?"

"Not out loud. Marjorie said all the right things. She insisted it wasn't my fault. I'm just not sure she really believes it."

"I'm sure she's not delighted to hear the Dior's gone. At the same time, she has to know how responsible you are. No one who's been around you for any length of time can seriously believe you wouldn't have done everything in your power to protect those exhibits."

"Yet I didn't, did I? I left the damn thing out, night after night, instead of locking it away with the rest of the collection."

"In a locked mansion with a high-tech alarm system!"

"I know, I know." She waved her hand, even though her friend couldn't see. "And I don't mean to keep flogging that cadaver Equus. I'm just going in circles trying to wrap my mind around the need for a different focal point. I had beaucoup ideas invested in the Dior for both the catalog and publicity, but I've got to let it go and change my focus. In any case—" she got herself back on point "—I'll be ready when you get here."

She heard Devlin working upstairs when she hung up and was sorely tempted for a moment to take her woes up there and unload them on him.

Bad idea. Bad *idea!* Angrily shelving it in the far, dark corner of her mind where she stored all her more ill-conceived inspirations, she went into the library with the intention of going through the photograph albums where she'd first discovered the snapshot of Miss Agnes in the Dior. Maybe a photo of her in a different gown would suggest a new direction to take.

But she'd forgotten how many albums there were. Deciding she'd take a stack home and look at them tonight, she glanced up at the ceiling where she could hear Devlin banging around. She might as well ask him to help her. Trying to avoid him hadn't worked; he just kept showing up despite her best efforts.

And the real kicker was that she was always happy to see him. So maybe if she engaged his attention in her search for a new exhibit centerpiece he'd leave off with the follow-me-to-Europe talks, which he'd been pushing pretty steadily since the other day.

But she couldn't afford to think about that. There was too much emotion attached to the subject; it was better left for a time when she could devote herself to giving it the attention it deserved. Like…

Well…

Never.

Okay, that wasn't fair. Still, for this moment in time at least, she was shoving the damn thing out of her mind.

She plunged into entering data for the uncataloged clothing in the secret closet. She was getting closer to completing this segment of her undertaking, which would finally push her over the hump and onto the downhill slide. Well, if the research on some of the pieces went as smoothly as she anticipated, that was.

It was all she was prepared to think about right now.

Poppy and Ava arrived at four-thirty, their cheeks flushed from the sudden cold snap. They had barely removed their coats and unwound their scarves from around their necks when the front doorbell rang. All three women exchanged a look. It had to be the detective, but he was a full half hour early.

"Must be a cop trick," Jane murmured and went to answer the door.

She really, really didn't want to deal with this today. But she had no choice, so as she entered the foyer she strove for an attitude adjustment. It wouldn't be fair to let the detective see she was less than happy about their appointment. After all, she and her friends were responsible for dragging him out here. Pasting a polite smile on her face, she opened the door.

Then had to crane her head way, way back in order to look up into the face of the man on the steps.

Oh. Wow.

He wasn't handsome, exactly. But there was sure something compelling about his dark eyes, ax-blade cheekbones and prominent, arrogant, bony nose. It was that whole hawk-predator thing, she thought. The guy was the sheikh from the Sisterhood's all-time favorite fantasy: *you, big, strong, dominant man. Me, quivering little slave to your smallest command.* They used to weave all sorts of outrageous stories around that general theme as teens. For the first time today she almost grinned.

Then she pulled herself together. "Um, hello." *Good God.* As if the purple-prose-induced images they'd once created at an age when their sexuality was first beginning to bloom had *any*thing to do with the matter at hand. "I'm Jane Kaplinski. You must be Detective…?"

"De Sanges," he supplied, a chilly, all-business snap in his voice. Clearly he was not thrilled to be here.

Well, swell. A disgruntled cop was *just* what she needed to round out her day.

On the other hand, it was hardly his fault she'd had a crappy day or that he was the embodiment of the fantasy man she and Poppy and Ava used to whisper about in the dark back in the seventh grade. Keeping her expression professional, she stepped back. "Please. Come in."

She led him to the parlor where Ava and Poppy were waiting.

After the introductions, he took the seat she indicated, pulled a battered notebook from the inside breast pocket of his suit coat and promptly got down to business. Taking notes as Jane talked, he occasionally asked for clarification of a point or posed a question that Officer Stiller had not.

Other than that he didn't waste breath on chitchat. And once he'd gathered all the info he needed for his report, he merely sat for a long silent moment, staring down at his ratty-edged notebook.

Leaving Jane with the sinking feeling that he wouldn't be extending any hope of solving their case.

She jumped when Poppy suddenly demanded, "You aren't going to help us any more than the patrolwoman did, are you, Detective?" The blonde climbed to her feet and paced impatiently behind the love seat she'd been sitting on with Ava. Gripping the back of it, she watched de Sanges through narrowed eyes. "Does our case seem like too much work to you? Or just the opposite, perhaps? Do we bore you?"

He looked at her from his club chair, and for an instant the male admiration Poppy usually garnered glowed in his dark eyes. But it was gone so quickly, Jane was left wondering if her imagination had run away with her again the way it had at the door with that insane flash of the sheikh and the kidnapped virgin.

"No, ma'am," he said with chilly civility. "I'm neither lazy nor bored. I am wondering why I was called off a case where an elderly lady was assaulted and put in the hospital by a mugger to come hold the hands of three women who've apparently lost their silver spoons."

Oh. Jane had to hand it to him. He was good. He'd managed to call them spoiled rich girls without actually saying the words.

Well, he certainly wouldn't be the first to mistake her and Poppy's financial circumstances. And hearing about the elderly woman in the hospital, she could even sympathize with his displeasure in what was clearly politically motivated coercion to take on their case.

Poppy apparently didn't feel the same. Whipping back around the love seat, she crossed the rug in a few ground-eating strides so long, impressions of her thighs should have been permanently imprinted on her filmy skirt. Slapping her hands down on the arms of de Sanges's chair, she leaned over him, electrified from head to foot with displeasure.

"I'm sorry as can be that none of us was injured," she said between her teeth, her nose almost touching the detective's. "Had we known that was a requirement to make our case worthy of your attention, maybe we could have thrown ourselves in harm's way. And leaving off for a moment your assumptions about us—which is pretty ironic, really, coming from a cop who doesn't want to do his job—"

"I do my job just fine," he said flatly.

"Do you? Or do you simply jump to conclusions based on preliminary evidence, without bothering to dig any deeper?"

He surged to his feet, forcing Poppy to straighten and backpedal out of his way. For a moment they stood toe-to-toe, locked in a stare-down. Such was their concentration on each other that Jane half expected to see smoke curling within the few inches of space that separated them.

As if growing aware of it himself, de Sanges's red-hot aura suddenly iced over, and he took a large step back. "I've been on the job for almost thirteen years, Ms. Calloway." Hands on his lean hips, he was all cold authority as he gazed down the length of his nose at her. "You don't get to disparage my professionalism."

"Why not?" she demanded, not even bothering to throttle back the heat. "What respect have you shown us as the victims of this burglary? While you and Officer Stiller run around trying to prove that we, or maybe the Kavanaghs, stole our own possessions—"

His shoulders stiffened as if her antagonism pushed at his control. His voice, however, was cool and civil when he said with an edge of dryness, "Right this minute I'm leaning more heavily toward you."

"Of course you are. Because God forbid anyone should have the temerity to ask you to do your job. And meanwhile the real thief is skating scot-free."

"Then give me something to work with!" he roared and once again heat seemed to pump off him. He flicked up a long, olive-skinned finger. "There was no forced entry." Another finger joined the first. "Nobody had the code except you and the construction people." A third finger joined the other two. "The three of you just insured the joint for a fortune—"

"When do you propose we should have taken out our insurance policy, Detective?" Ava interrupted, her coolness a marked contrast to Poppy's passion. "Considering we just inherited this house and all its possessions."

"Or maybe you think we're responsible for Miss Agnes's death, too," Poppy snarled.

He took a step toward her. "Listen, Blondie—"

"Hey!" Jane and Ava snapped in unison.

Color rode his sharp cheekbones and he stepped back once again. "I apologize, Ms. Calloway. That *was* unprofessional."

Jane and Ava looked at Poppy.

"What?" she asked.

They gave her a harder look and she shrugged. "Oh, all right." She turned to Detective de Sanges. "I apologize, as well," she said with a palpable lack of sincerity. "My last remark might have been uncalled for."

Ava rolled her eyes but said calmly to the detective, "We're not stupid women, you know. If we'd wanted to steal from ourselves, we would have done it before we upgraded the security system."

Jane nodded. "And I sure as hell wouldn't have shot my career in the foot by including a twenty-thousand-dollar gown that belongs to the Metropolitan Museum in the list of stolen items."

"What?"

She explained the circumstances of how the two exhibits had come to be in the mansion.

He looked interested and pulled out his notebook again. "Does anyone at the museum have anything to gain by messing you up with your employer?"

She blinked at the notion, as it was both new and unexpected. But after a moment's thought, she could only sigh with regret. "No. Not really."

De Sanges rubbed his eyes with the thumb and forefinger of his left hand. "You're not giving me much to work with here." Then he dropped his hand and looked at them. "But I'll look into it, okay?"

He asked a few more questions, extracted a few more details, then rose to his feet. Jane got up, as well, to see him out.

The instant she came back into the parlor she walked over to Poppy. "What the hell was that all about?"

"Wasn't it obvious?" her blonde friend returned blandly. "He was stonewalling us and I called him on it."

"Yes, you did," Ava agreed dryly. "But your body language was more 'Daddy, do me.' And he looked more than willing to oblige, too. For a minute there I feared the two of you were going to start going at it in the middle of the room."

"Don't be ridiculous—"

"Right in front of Janie and me."

Jane saw a very real potential for this conversation to quickly disintegrate into a squabble and said, "So, did anybody else think de Sanges looked exactly the way we imagined our old seventh-grade honey, the sheikh, would?"

Ava whirled to stare at her. Then she broke into a wide, dimple-producing grin. "*Yes!* Omigawd, that's it! There was something so familiar about him—except this guy is titillating, which pretty much eliminates most of the men we know." She turned to Poppy. "Explains your plunge into feisty virgin mode, doesn't it?"

"Please." Poppy snorted. "Virgin, my butt." She essayed a sheepish shrug, however. "But okay, I admit something about him struck sparks off me above and beyond our being yanked around by the Man, as my folks would say. And I might have overreacted a little."

"A *little?*" Ava asked, auburn eyebrows raised.

And Jane laughed. "Ya think? You've never hesitated to speak your mind, but I've never seen you jump down anyone's throat with quite the gusto you showed Detective Sheikh."

Poppy's color was high, but her brown eyes went serious when she regarded Jane. "What about de Sanges's question regarding the people you work with? *Is* there anyone there who wouldn't mind screwing you over with the brass?"

"Well, Gordon Ives and I compete for assignments. But it's always been a friendly rivalry and he's been really helpful taking over my Spain exhibit while I've worked on this. Plus, until the Dior went missing, none of the gone-astray pieces had a thing to do with my exhibits. And even if they had, how could he have gotten in here?"

"It's a freakin' mystery," Ava said dolefully and collapsed back on the love seat she'd sat upon earlier. A saw abruptly roared to life upstairs, then almost as quickly whined into silence, and she pulled her attention away from the ceiling to look at Jane.

"That reminds me. What's the story with you and Dev? Are you avoiding him, or something?"

Her heart suddenly lodged in her throat, Jane gave her friend a carefully blank look. "I have no idea what you're talking about," she said blandly. "No idea at all."

CHAPTER TWENTY

Thank God Devlin finally stopped all that go-with-him-to-Europe stuff. And bless him, bless him, for saving my butt tonight!

JANE WAS AVOIDING HIM. How the hell did she do that? Dev wondered as he sat in her apartment, watching her pore over a photo album from the stack of them she'd brought home from the mansion. She was sitting not three feet away in the same goddamn room with him and somehow she still managed to avoid him. Maybe it was the way she'd waited until he'd taken a seat on the short couch before pointedly choosing one of the burgundy leather chairs for herself, the small coffee table firmly between them.

Whatever it was, he'd handled his campaign to take her back to Europe with him all wrong. He should have paid more attention when she'd tried to tell him about her parents' constant drama making her want nothing to do with passion. He wasn't quite sure what passion had to do with it, but he'd seen how they focused on each other to the exclusion of their own daughter, so maybe it was something along those lines. Maybe Jane equated passion with getting so tied up in another person that it made you selfish and stupid. If so, he'd been way too quick to blow off her emotional response. And he should have had the sense not to hound her.

Not right off the bat, at any rate.

Well, no one had to hit this boy over the head to show him the error of his ways. So he had one thing in his favor tonight—he'd changed his strategy. He just hoped to hell it wasn't too late.

Pretending things weren't strained between them, he'd shown up on her doorstep with an order each of the Peking Beef and Snow Pea Chicken she liked so much and a liter of club soda. He hadn't once mentioned Europe, his going back or the prospect of her accompanying him. And after they'd killed off the cartons of Chinese food and she'd set him to work going through albums in search of a good visual that might spark an idea for her new focal point, he'd fallen in with the program with gusto. This was important to her, and he gave the hunt the same concentration he would have put into getting a customer's yacht to safe harbor.

And—speak of the devil—hello!

Stopping halfway into the current album he'd been flipping through, he studied a photograph. Damn. That was pretty cool. "How about this one?" Twirling the album around, he pushed it across the coffee table at her, stabbing his forefinger at the ruffle-edged photograph in question.

It featured a young Agnes Wolcott in a long gown, being handed out of a vintage limousine. To his admittedly less than trained eye, the dress she wore was sexy, yet ritzy-looking in that old-time Hollywood glamour kind of way. "You have this getup in your collection?"

She leaned forward to study it. "Yes," she said slowly.

"That's the Mainbocher. It's from the fifties, the same era as the Dior. And oh, my God." She bent her head to give the photo an even closer inspection. "I think this necklace she has on is part of the jewelry bequest to the Met, as well. And how cool is that car? The whole thing's very visual and very close to what I had with the Dior photograph that gave me the idea to showcase it in the first place."

Looking up, she gave him the first stress-free smile he'd seen in a couple of days. "This will work!" Jumping to her feet, she dumped her album onto the coffee table, leaned across it and, balancing one hand on his shoulder, gave him an enthusiastic, smacking kiss on the lips. When she pulled back, he grasped her wrist and tugged, and she let herself be pulled toward him, circling the table to collapse on his lap.

"Devlin, *thank* you." She smiled down at him. "This will work very well. You can't tell by the black-and-white photo, of course, but the gown's bodice and skirt are alternating ivory and a pastel peach in the front and a pale dusty rose and blue in the back. And the skirt has that wonderful heavy-silk flow to it."

"I like the top part. That is seriously hot."

She grinned at him. "You go for the strapless look, huh?"

"You bet. Not to mention that—" he cupped his hands under his pecs as if holding up breasts "—pleated stuff offering up her rack. Very Madonna/Gwen Stefani."

She grinned. Then sighed, and rested her cheek against his shoulder. "Thank you," she repeated quietly. "I've been so worried about what to build the exhibit around since the Dior disappeared. But this is an excellent substitute. What a huge relief."

Something inside him went all loose and warm. But he kept his voice casual when he replied, "Glad to be of assistance."

"Yeah?" Rising onto her knees, she swung a leg over his lap and watched herself settle, wiggling a little when the seams bisecting the crotch of her jeans aligned with his fly. "Oh," she murmured. Then she raised her gaze to meet his and wiggled with a little more force. "Then assist *this*."

His hips lifted accommodatingly, but he managed to keep his hands at his sides and summoned up a sorrowful look. "You just want me for my body." He turned his face away from her. "I feel so cheap."

"Aw, nooo," she crooned and bent her head to press soft, openmouthed kisses against the side of the throat he'd exposed.

He tipped up his chin to give her more room, heat curling through his belly, his dick.

His heart.

Cupping his jaw in her hands, she turned his face back to hers and pressed a sweet kiss upon his mouth. "You're my big, strong guy," she murmured once she'd raised her mouth again. The soft smile she gave him sent warmth through his veins like a crackling fire on a chilly night. Then she bestowed a butterfly-light peck on each eyelid. "So funny." She kissed his nose. "So warmhearted."

Her hips kept swiveling. "Did I mention giving?" Reaching down, she laced her fingers through his and brought them up, pressing the backs of his hands against the plush velvet of the couch.

Then she scooted back onto his knees so she was no longer rocking upon him. "And a whole lotta work," she said dryly. "So hardly cheap, Charley. It would be more economical in the long run to just go out and rent myself a stud."

He laughed, disengaged their hands and grasped her hips. Pulling her forward, he slapped their bodies together, readjusting her seat upon him until they were lined up exactly the way they'd been a minute ago. He gave her a cocky smile. "You wouldn't have nearly as much fun."

Raising her arms in the air, she crossed them until her little two-bite breasts thrust forward and her elbows pointed at the ceiling. "Maybe. Maybe not." She swiveled her hips again. Gazed down at him. "We've got on way too many clothes."

"I can fix that," he said. And did.

Okay, so he didn't quite manage to get everything off, but he did remove or rearrange the essentials. They both sucked in a sharp breath when she suddenly took him into her body with one sure downward slide, sheathing him deep.

She rode him slowly at first, almost languorously, uncrossing her arms and lowering her hands to press his to her breasts. Little by little, however, their rhythm began to pick up speed as he drove more emphatically upward and she slapped down to meet each thrust. Then her head dropped back, her hair brushing her back and the muscles in her long, pretty thighs standing in relief beneath her skin as she lifted and lowered herself upon him.

Sweat trickled down his temples, along his neck, and he eased his hands out from under hers to sink his fingers into her hips once again. He was close—hell, he was damn near cross-eyed, he was so near to the edge—but he wasn't about to go over without her. So he gave a little lick here, slicked his forefinger over a straining little bundle of nerves there, and they both plunged fathoms deep into a screaming sea of release.

It was a long while later before they disengaged themselves and reordered their clothing. Several minutes after that, while leaning on the breakfast bar watching her assemble a pot of coffee, he suddenly remembered the purchase he'd made earlier and snapped his fingers. "I got you something," he said. "I'll be right back."

"What?" Jane's head snapped up, but she was questioning thin air. Devlin had disappeared not just down the hallway but clean out of her apartment. Her slightly ajar door was the only indication that he'd return. "You got me...a gift?" she murmured anyhow. She couldn't remember the last time anyone besides Ava or Poppy had bought her anything.

By the time he let himself back in, she'd turned on the fireplace in the living room and assembled a plate of cookies she hoped he wouldn't notice were slightly stale to go with their coffee.

"Sorry," he said, striding straight over to the fire, slapping at his arms. "I forgot I'd had to park a couple of blocks away. I should have put on my jacket—it's freezing out there." He pulled out the bag he'd had tucked under his biceps and tossed it to her. Then he crossed over to sit in the leather chair opposite where she sat. "I saw this in the window of a store when I was downtown collecting a package my mom asked me to pick up for her," he said. "It all but screamed your name when I walked by the window where it was displayed. That's how strongly it reminded me of you and an earlier conversation the two of us'd had."

"What is it?"

"Babe." Lounging back in his chair, he crossed his arms behind his head. "Only one way to tell, isn't there? Open it and see."

She looked from his face to the package in her lap and felt a smile tugging at the corners of her lips. Widening the mouth of the bag, she reached in and pulled out a soft tissue-wrapped bundle. She spread the tissue open.

"Oh! Pretty color." She wasn't yet sure what it was, but it was constructed of a soft sage-green fabric with a satiny finish. Picking the garment up, she shook it out. "Oh!" she said again. And laughed. "You found me some parachute pants!"

He hooked a cookie off the plate and grinned at her. "You'll notice they're not black."

"Hard to miss," she agreed, and had to swallow against a lump in her throat, "when they're my favorite color."

"Yeah. Try them on. See how I did fit-wise. I saved the receipt in case they don't fit or you don't like them or want 'em in black or something."

"I love them just the way they are. Thank you." And, standing up, she kicked off the leggings she'd worn and stepped into the pants, tugging them up her legs and zipping them. "Wow." She grinned at him. "They fit perfectly."

"I told the saleslady your waist was about yay big."

He curled his fingers to demonstrate. "And your hips about this. She went and found a pair that fit that criteria."

She never would have guessed he'd paid such close attention to her body type. It scared her a little to know he'd focused so single-mindedly on her.

Mostly, however, it warmed her right down to her toes to know she was important enough to someone to have them note the details that way.

"Dev! Have you heard the news?"

Dev held the telephone receiver away from his ear the next afternoon as the unexpected volume and pitch of Hannah's voice threatened to punch a hole in his eardrum. Cautiously returning it, he said, "I'm guessing not. But just tell me, okay? Don't yell."

"I'm sorry, I'm sorry, but I'm just so excited! Jody just called. The doctors said Bren's tests came back today with the best results they've seen since he was first diagnosed. They're 'cautiously optimistic' about him beating this sooner rather than later, which in doctor speak is almost like saying he's got a clean bill of health. Okay, not really, but it's very, very good."

"Holy shit." He grinned. "Holy shit!"

Hannah laughed. "I know! Is this the *best* news ever, or what?"

"No fooling."

When he hung up a short while later he just wandered his apartment smiling, not only at Bren's excellent diagnosis, but at the speed at which this particular bulletin would travel the family grapevine. It was several minutes before he realized he would soon be able to return to his life on the Continent.

And couldn't for the life of him have said why the smile dropped from his face.

A HUGE GUST OF WIND hit the Metropolitan Museum. The blast of air didn't rattle the well-constructed building's windows, exactly. But it did buffet the double panes with an explosiveness that made heads in the crowded cafeteria lift to cast them a wary glance.

Gordon wasn't one of the gawkers. He noted the sudden howl and fury beating at the windows, as well as the uneasy shifting of the diners around him, in a far corner of his mind. Vaguely he marveled at the contrast of today's unsettled weather with the chill stillness of a couple of days ago. But he was deep in thought, so he didn't spare either more than a distracted second of his attention. It wasn't until the women at the table behind him started yammering on about the escalating storminess of Seattle's late fall weather that he realized this morning's wind, which had already been blowing like crazy, had grown even fiercer.

"Did you hear the weather forecast today?" asked a woman with a particularly piercing, attention-grabbing voice. "They're predicting a storm along the lines of the Inaugural Day Storm we had in the nineties."

Another woman snorted. "Oh, there's a big surprise. They predict something like that every time we get a more-than-gusty wind. Boys and their toys," she scoffed. "Is there anything Seattle weathermen—excuse me, *meteorologists*—like better than predicting disaster with their Doppler radars?"

"They are actually right sometimes, Virginia," yet another woman said mildly. "I was one of the million and a half people who were without power for almost a week during that December storm they predicted a couple years ago. I about froze my tushie off with only my gas fireplace to keep me warm. Trust me, it's not that efficient when temperatures are in the thirties and there's no electricity to run the fan."

"I know, and I'm not trying to minimize your ordeal. I'm just saying that nine times out of ten *WIND STORM whatever-the-year*—" She invested the words with plummy-voiced drama before dropping back to her normal register "—turns out to be a big nonevent."

Gordon tuned out again when they segued into a debate about the effectiveness of predicting weather when you live between two mountain ranges as opposed to a place like Kansas where you could see it coming from a hundred miles away. Closing up the plan-o-gram he'd been pretending to study while he ate his lunch, he climbed to his feet and gathered up his tray. He hadn't been able to concentrate on it worth shit.

Not when all he could think about was the sound of Jane's voice out in the sixth-floor hallway this morning when she'd asked Marjorie if they could talk for a minute about the centerpiece gown she'd selected to replace the Dior for the couture exhibit.

She'd been wrecked by the Dior's loss—he knew she had been—yet in just a matter of days she'd found another fucking gown that was good enough to infuse her voice with enthusiasm. He was having a tough time wrapping his mind around that. Because accepting it meant his sacrifice of the Dior, which he deserved ten times more than Kaplinski did, had been for nothing. He'd left it to rot in the dumbwaiter and now he didn't even get the satisfaction of its loss tanking her career? Jesus. The bitch was like a cat with nine lives. She kept landing on her feet no matter what he hit her with.

Hands in his pockets, head down, he strode through the museum toward the employee elevators, trying not to scowl at the biscuit-colored marble floors as discontent circled through his brain.

"Gordon!"

He looked over his shoulder and saw Marjorie walking down the corridor toward him. She waved a hand when she saw she had his attention. "I need a minute of your time," she called.

He glanced at the tall, olive-skinned, black-haired man at her side and his normally facile mind went blank…except for one word.

Cop.

Ice coated his entrails but he wasn't a poker player for nothing. He didn't so much as blink. He wasn't some rank amateur with a raft of "tells" to give him away.

But how the hell had they caught on? He hadn't left anything at the mansion to connect him with the break-ins. Of course, fat lot of good that would do him if the cop had a warrant to search his apartment. If that happened he was well and truly toast. Most of the pieces in his special room wouldn't stand up to close scrutiny.

But it was ridiculous to even think that way. There wasn't an iota of probable cause to get a warrant.

Unless the cop knew a judge who wasn't too fussy about following the exact letter of the law.

Christ, Ives, enough, already! No need to jump the gun.

His mental ping-pong of I'm-screwed-there's-nothing-to-worry-about had raced through his mind at the speed of light and, secure in the knowledge that his expression hadn't shown a hint of his thoughts, he pasted a pleasant smile on his face as he waited for his boss and the cop to catch up.

"This is Detective de Sanges," Marjorie said as they walked up to him. "He's looking into the burglary at the Wolcott mansion that cost us the Christian Dior gown. Detective, this is Gordon Ives, whom I was telling you about."

Telling him what, *Marjorie?* But ignoring the question screaming in his head, he merely said, "Yeah, that was a really lousy break." He extended his hand to the cop.

The detective's grip was firm and he studied Gordon with unreadable eyes. "Is there somewhere quiet where we can sit and talk?"

Confidence growing with the knowledge his own grip was as dry and firm as the cop's, Gordon gave de Sanges an easy smile. "Sure. Come up to my office.

"I apologize for the accommodations," he said a short while later as he cleaned a stack of folders off the visitor's chair in his office and offered it to de Sanges. "Junior curators only rate these closets." He circled the desk to take his own seat then gave the detective his solemn attention when he was settled. "So. The Wolcott robbery. I've never been in that mansion, so I'm not quite sure how you think I can help."

De Sanges merely looked at him for one long, silent

moment. Then he pulled a battered notebook out of the inside breast pocket of his surprisingly well-made suit jacket. "Your supervisor said you and Ms. Kaplinski vie for exhibits?"

"Sure." He shrugged. "There's two of us in the junior position, we're both ambitious and there are only so many exhibits that the senior staff is willing to let us do on our own. Not to mention that the only chance for advancement for several years is when Paul Rompaul retires next fall. So we compete."

"It must have seemed pretty unfair, then, when she inherited that mansion just crammed full of cool collectibles," the detective said sympathetically. "*And* got to be in charge of not one but two collections just because she knew the Wolcott woman. Talk about the competition being slanted in her favor."

Yes! But just in time, he recognized de Sanges's unexpected intelligence, his insight and sensitivity, for the ploy it was. The man was pretending to understand the rank unfairness of Gordon's plight in order to soften him up for the kill.

Well, the cop hadn't yet been born who could get the best of Gordon Ives. He was too smart to fall into that trap. "Yeah, it was tough," he admitted. "It's almost impossible not to be envious. But the rivalry between Jane and me has always been a friendly one. And she gave me the Spain exhibit, which had gone to her in our most recent competition, so that took quite a bit of the sting out."

"What do you think of her personally? Do you have any theories about the burglary at the mansion?"

"Jane?" *Aside from the fact she's a boring, stuck-up,*

know-it-all rich bitch, you mean? "She's smart. And dedicated. But I don't have a clue about the burglary. That's more your area of expertise, wouldn't you say?"

"Sure." The detective lounged on the narrow office chair, the ankle of one big foot propped on his opposite knee as he regarded Gordon with friendly curiosity. "But my theories are still evolving at this point, which is why I'm always interested in another person's point of view—especially if he has more expertise in the area I'm investigating than I do. See, I was leaning in one direction when I was first pulled into this case. But then I talked to your supervisor and you—and I find myself doing a one-eighty and leaning in an entirely other direction." He consulted his notebook. "You've never been in the mansion, you say?"

"Nope. My relationship with Jane is entirely professional, so I've never been invited."

"So none of the prints we lifted at the scene are going to match yours then, right?" De Sanges raised his head to look at him and there was no friendliness in his expression now. He regarded Gordon with cool, hard cop eyes.

Shit! He'd touched all sorts of things in the mansion and hadn't given the issue two thoughts, because he'd never expected it to matter one way or the other. Panic threatened, but he forced himself to be cool, to think things through.

And gave himself a mental pat on the back for his insouciance when he met de Sanges's gaze and said, "Nope. Hard to leave prints in a place you've never been."

"That's true. So I'm sure you wouldn't mind letting us take yours to eliminate you from the suspect list."

"Actually, I would. I fail to see why I would even be on your suspect list, and I believe in protecting my civil rights. I also believe in that presumed-innocent-until-proven-guilty point of law."

The cop held his gaze for just a second longer than was comfortable. Then he lifted one shoulder in a negligent shrug. "Yeah, that's a good one," he agreed and rose to his feet. "Thank you for your time. I'll be in touch," he said and sauntered from the room.

Gordon watched him go, then rubbed at the headache brewing behind his eyes. Well, that was just a whole lotta fun. But he was okay. He was cool. Because he was probably imagining the detective even suspected him. Why would he? And, hell, even if de Sanges did, he couldn't prove a damn thing. Because Gordon had played it smart. He'd adhered to the golden rule of gambling and quit while he was ahead.

So, no. There was no good reason for his heart to be pounding like a jackhammer this way.

He was in the clear.

CHAPTER TWENTY-ONE

*God, what a day. It started out with the storm—
and that was just the beginning.*

"THIS IS ONE MOTHER of a wind," Devlin said as he and his sister let themselves out of the Wolcott mansion. "You shouldn't have come out in it to get me." Then he shot her a grin. "But I appreciate that you did."

The howling air tried to suck them into the yard and he put Hannah between himself and the back door as he locked up. "Christ. It must be blowing seventy-five miles an hour," he yelled over the noise. "Gimme your keys. I'd better drive."

"Ooh. 'Cause you're such a big, strong man and poor little me is just so helpless." Her sarcasm projected nicely over the freight-train rumble of the wind. But she handed him her keys.

"Hannah, you're about as helpless as a barracuda," he muttered as they bent into the blasting air to cross the short distance between door and car, dodging small downed limbs from the trees at the corner of the lot.

She shouldn't have been able to hear him, given the clash and fury of the weather. But either she had ears like a barn owl or the wind created a direct line that carried his words to her. "Damn straight," she called.

They climbed into her car and slammed the doors and

the decibel levels dropped dramatically. But his sister, not being one to simply leave well enough alone, gave him a look as she buckled up and went right back to the subject he'd kind of hoped they'd finished. "I'm the one who bucked the elements from Fremont to get you home safe, boyo."

"Yeah, and why is that?" he asked with sudden suspicion. "What brings you out on a Saturday? It's not like you to give up your day off—let alone get your hair all mussed just to save me a little inconvenience. Not to mention I'm a helluva lot closer to my place than you are to yours."

"Why is it people always mention the very thing they're 'not to mention'?" She flipped down the visor and studied herself in the mirror. "Well, hell, that's a ratty look. I put a lot of effort into getting the artfully windblown look. It's not supposed to be whipped into a grievous mess by *real* wind." She took a brush out of her purse and started working out the snarls.

"Which doesn't really answer my question, does it?" Putting the car in gear, he backed out of the driveway.

She shrugged. "You don't have a car and it's nasty out. I didn't want you to get blown into the Sound."

"Uh-huh. That sounds real good—on paper. But I know that *you* know I'm perfectly capable of getting myself where I need to be if conditions allow—or stay put in the mansion if they don't. So what's the real story?"

"Okay, fine." She snapped the visor closed and shifted in her seat to look at him. "I want to know when you're going to move home for good."

He turned to stare at her for a moment before the wind tried to tug the car out of the lane he was fighting the steering wheel to keep it in. Returning his attention to the road, he said incredulously, "And you drove across town on the windiest damn day of the decade to ask me that?"

"Yes. And for the opportunity to talk to you without everyone else around." She let him navigate steep Queen Anne Avenue but gave him a steady look the minute it leveled out. "It's time for you to come home, Dev."

Watching the signal light turn green, which wasn't an easy feat considering the thing was blown almost horizontal, he opened his mouth to reply.

She must have read his mind, however, for she said before he could, "And don't say you are home. You know what I mean." She sighed, then added in a reasonable tone, "You look happier these days than you have for the past several years."

"And you know this *how?* You've only seen me on sporadic visits."

"My point exactly."

"Look." He shook his head. "I appreciate the fact you want me back home again. I really do. But Bren is getting better. And sooner or later I'm going back to Europe."

"Why?" she demanded. "Because you love living out of a duffel so much?"

No, he really didn't, and in truth, moving boats around the Mediterranean far from everyone he loved had worn a little thin during the past couple of years.

What the hell? He squared his shoulders. Where had *that* come from? He shot across Denny and, thanking God for the nearly nonexistent traffic, steered Hannah's car like a heat-seeking missile toward his apartment.

He liked his life on the Continent just fine. Sure, he got a little restless every now and then. And maybe occasionally he even grew a little homesick. So, big deal. It happened.

But having his sister's words lend weight to what were momentary dissatisfactions and, worse, make him doubt himself, if only for a moment, pushed all his buttons. "Back off, Hannah," he snapped as he double-parked in front of his building. A ferocious gust of wind rocked the car. "You know I can't take the lack of privacy that comes with being around the family full-time. It's like living in a fucking goldfish bowl."

"Oh, for God's sake, Dev," she snapped back. "Get over it! What are you, still nineteen? Living with this family is exactly what you make of it."

"Well, thank you, Dr. Phil, for making me see the light. Hallelujah. I guess now my life can finally get on track." He battled the wind to open the door, climbed out, then took a deep breath and blew it out. He leaned into the car as she clambered over the console into the driver's seat he'd just abandoned. "You want to wait out the storm here?"

"No," she said sulkily.

"Don't pout. We're just not gonna see eye to eye on this subject."

"We would if you weren't such a frickin' idiot."

He grinned at her.

But when she added seriously, "You're breaking Mom's heart, you know," the smile dropped from his face and he straightened smartly away from the car.

"Oh, good, Han. Great. That's real nice." Guilt was a thousand insects crawling beneath his skin, but he was damned if he'd give his sister the satisfaction of seeing she'd hit the target smack in the center of the bull's-eye. He was furious with her for laying this trip on him, but he gave the roof of her car a slap, stepped back and in carefully uninflected tones said, "Drive careful, sis. It's a bitch out here."

"I SHOULD GET GOING," Ava said to Jane, gripping the tails of the knit scarf she'd just that moment unwrapped from around her neck. "Coming over the floating bridge in this wind unnerved me big-time and, okay, I kind of panicked. I mean, I know it's not much farther to my place from the I-90 interchange than it is to here, but I saw the north exit for I-5 and just jumped on it instead of the southbound. And…I've already told you all this. Wonderful. Now I'm repeating myself."

"Of course you are," Jane said soothingly, taking her friend's scarf from her hands and easing Ava's coat off her shoulders. "You're still shook up. Come sit down. Have a cup of tea."

Ava did as instructed, but after seating herself at the breakfast bar she watched with a puzzled pleat forming between her auburn brows as Jane rummaged through the cupboards. "Since when do you have tea?"

"You remember Joyce Hammermaster who works at the Starbucks corporate office down in SoDo? She gave me a couple of boxes when I attended a thingie at her place." Now if she only had a clue what she'd done with them she'd be in business. Wait a minute, was that—? "Aha! I knew I'd put them in here somewhere. Calm or chai?" She shot Ava a grin. "Calm, I'm thinking."

"Definitely."

They sat down with their cups in the living room a few minutes later, sipping tea and eating Jane's emergency stash of chocolate. Despite the roaring wind outside—or perhaps because of it—it felt cozy and safe inside.

Until Ava looked at her and said, "So has Dev mentioned anything more about you going back to Europe with him?"

She stiffened, wishing, wishing, wishing, as her sense of safety fled, that she hadn't told her friends about that. "No. Not for three days now."

"Hmm." Her friend propped her chin in her palm, tapped one beautifully manicured fingertip against her temple and regarded Jane like a psychologist—if they came built like fertility goddesses. "And how do you feel about that?"

"Well, I'm not bothered by it, if that's what you're asking."

Ava merely raised a brow at her, and Jane said, "What? I'm *not*. I'm…relieved, really." Okay, even she could see she was protesting too much. Yet she couldn't seem to prevent herself from reiterating, *"Really."*

"On a scale of one to ten on the bullshit meter, I give that a thirteen."

"Yeah." Exhaling with a whoosh, she curled herself protectively around her teacup, her shoulders hunched. "I *want* to be relieved, okay? But mostly I'm just riddled with paranoia. I mean, what's the story here? He went from hounding me without pause about how I should go to Europe with him to complete and utter silence on the matter. And why do I care? This was supposed to be a short-term relationship, anyway."

"But…?"

"Am I suddenly not good enough or something? Has he lost interest?" She sighed. "I don't know, maybe he's just tired of the sex."

"Yeah, right." Ava's voice was derisive. "On the off chance there's a guy out there somewhere who tires of sex, I think I can guarantee you Dev's not the one. I've seen the way he looks at you."

She hated her own junior-high-school impulse to demand *what way* and tried to disguise it with mockery. "So, like, Lenny told Jimmy, who told Carole Lee, who told me that Bobby Joe is really, really hot for Tiff."

Ava merely looked at her and that was all it took for Jane to roll. "Okay, I'll bite," she said with a show of indifference so unconvincing she was embarrassed for herself. "How does he look at me?"

"Like he's the shark and you're the chum, sugar."

"Oh. Well. That's a lovely image." She dropped her head in her hands. "You couldn't have said like the sheikh looks at the virgin? Chum, my ass. Chump, more like."

"Aw, now you're just having a woe-is-me party. Well, I'm ready to get back to my own place, anyhow, so I'll leave you to it." Rising to her feet, she gathered their cups and plates and carried them to Jane's kitchen. Then she went to fetch her scarf and coat from the closet.

Starting the process of wrapping herself in her outerwear, she crossed over to Jane and gave her one of her warm, lush hugs. "Thanks for the tea and company, Janie. I appreciate it big-time."

"I wish you'd stay," she answered, looking out at the wind whipping Puget Sound into a fury outside her windows. The afternoon was growing preternaturally dark. "I don't think it's safe to be driving. They're saying the wind's blowing at God-only-knows how many miles per hour."

"It felt like a hundred, if you ask me. I've seen footage of Lake Washington blowing those big, mondo waves over the bridge before, but I'd never experienced it for myself until today." Ava shivered. "I can die a happy, happy woman if I never experience it again."

"So why put yourself at risk? I know you're not crossing the lake again, but a wind this strong could knock your little Beemer clean off the high-rise on the West Seattle bridge."

"Which is why I plan to go along Alaskan Way and take the low span."

"Did you hear they even closed Coleman dock to the Bremerton and Bainbridge ferry runs? That *never* happens. Stay here, Av."

"Thanks, but I kind of want to be in my own place."

The lights dimmed, then came back bright. Jane looked at her friend. "Awful dark there on the beach if your lights go out."

"You downtown dwellers aren't the only ones with underground wiring, pal. I'll be fine."

"Well, call me when you get home, at least. Have you heard from Poppy today?"

"Yeah, she called to say she dropped in to check on her folks and they talked her into staying over."

"I wish I could talk you into doing the same," Jane said wistfully.

"I'll be fine. I'll call when I get home, okay?"

"You'd better."

She closed the door behind her friend and headed for the kitchen to clean up. It only took minutes, and once the area was tidied she had nothing to do. She turned on the television, then turned it off again ten minutes later, tired of the ceaseless storm coverage. She tried to read but gave up after rereading the same paragraph for the umpteenth time. She straightened things that had no need of straightening. Cursing her own neat-freak streak that denied her something to occupy her attention, she prowled from room to room like a caged cat.

Ava called as promised but still Jane felt edgy, so she went out into the tiny solarium to watch the wild churn of Elliott Bay and Puget Sound. She could relate to all that storm-tossed turmoil.

Because it hadn't been strictly worry for her friend that had her feeling all restless and reckless. It was brooding over the subject Ava had raised.

Why *had* Devlin quit asking her to go to Europe with him?

Her chin came up. Well, there was only one way to find out, wasn't there? As a concession to the wind she plaited her hair into two braids. Then she grabbed her coat out of the closet, snatched up her purse and let herself out of the apartment.

She had second and third thoughts the moment she drove out of the underground garage and turned onto Western Avenue. Gale-force winds buffeted her car.

This was nuts. She hadn't even called to see if Devlin was home. He'd talked about getting a few things done at the mansion this morning, and for all she knew he was still there. He could get just as caught up in his work as she did in hers.

On the other hand, it was a measly half mile to his place, one that she generally just walked, and she was out now, anyhow. She turned up the hill toward First Avenue.

Between trying to find a parking place when clearly anyone with an ounce of sense was staying inside today and questioning what on earth she was doing, her temper was on the iffy side by the time she squeezed into a space up near Regrade Park. It was odd seeing the small, fenced-in space next to Dan's Belltown Grocery without a single yapping dog racing around. As one of the few off-leash parks in the city, it was usually packed with them, but of course this wasn't exactly a day for taking your dog for a stroll.

She had no comprehension how strong the wind actually was, however, until she climbed from the car.

Holy crap! She staggered against the onslaught as the stormy weather, like a giant unseen hand on her chest, tried to push her backward. It was one thing to watch it from the safety of her home, she discovered; another to be out in it.

"Me and the scarecrow, baby," she muttered. "If we only had a brain." Well, too late now. Bracing herself, she bent into the wind to make her way the two and a half blocks to Devlin's apartment house.

His building was an older brick three-story with no security desk, so she let herself in and climbed the stairs to the top floor. "You'd better be here," she grumbled as she knocked on the door. She'd gotten herself all jacked up and needed an outlet for all this emotion that roiled inside her with more force than the storm tearing up outside. When there was no immediate answer, she pounded her fist against the panels.

"Hold your horses!" Devlin snapped from the other side of the door and Jane blinked. He sounded even testier than she felt. She hadn't thought that was possible.

The door whipped open and Dev stood on the other side, staring down at her. For a second, pleasure shone out of his eyes. Then his dark brows snapped together.

"What the *hell* are you doing out in this weather?" he demanded, wrapping his hand around her forearm. "Get in here!" Pulling her across the threshold into his apartment's hallway, he reached over her shoulder to slam the door shut behind them.

"Hey!" Her temper flared, happy as a pig in slop for the opportunity to cut loose. "No manhandling!" She twisted her arm out of his hold.

"Sorry," he said, sounding anything but. "I'm a little on edge. This seems to be my day for chicks who don't have the sense to stay out of the elements. But hey." He shrugged. "You're here now. Come on in." Turning on his bare heel, he headed for the living room.

She faltered. "You've got another woman here?" Oh God, oh God, she hadn't even thought of that. No wonder he sounded less than welcoming.

"What?" He looked at her over his shoulder. "No. Hannah came all the way from her place just to give me a ride home from the mansion, but she's gone now. And it turns out it wasn't overwhelming concern for my safety that made her risk coming to see me, anyway. What she really wanted was to talk about when I was coming home."

Jane's breath eased out. *Hannah, not a new honey.*

Relief rushed through her veins like champagne. But her brow pleated. "You are home."

The lift of his hands toward her mimed *exactly!* But he clarified, "To stay. She wants to know when I'm coming home to stay."

He rolled his shoulders like it was no big deal, but temper still rolled like thunder in his eyes. "I guess because she and Finn used to know me best of anyone in the family, Han suffers under the illusion that she knows what I want better than I do."

He made a visible effort to shake off his bad mood. "But enough about my sister. What the hell are you doing out in this crappy weather?"

The savvy part of her, the part that dealt with ego-driven senior curators and foreign dignitaries who wanted the best for their museums first and her needs second told her to back off, to shelve her concerns until Devlin had a chance to truly calm down.

But where she should have bitten her tongue until it bled, if necessary, his cranky demand instead served to loosen the restraint on what little common sense she had left. She stepped up to him. "Why have you quit asking me to go to Europe with you?"

He blinked down at her. "What?"

"Did you change your mind about wanting me to go?"

"No." He moved in close and bent his knees to bring their eyes to a common level. Pleasure edging out the anger in his eyes, he rubbed gentle hands up and down her coat-clad arms. "I was giving you room to make a decision without me browbeating you into it. You've decided to come with me, then?"

That's when she realized she should have thought

this through. "Um, no," she stuttered. "That is, I don't
know." All she'd wanted was an answer. She hadn't
thought beyond it to the reply she might be expected
to give in return.

"What the hell?" He jerked back, temper flaring back
to life in his eyes. "What's it gonna be, Jane—are you
in or are you out? Or did you just come here to fuck
with my mind?"

She was in the wrong and knew it. So she did what
any right-thinking woman would do.

She made it his fault. "Don't you take that tone with
me," she snapped. "I just came to find out why you suddenly quit asking me to go with you. Don't blame me if
I'm confused—you're the one who hounded me for days
on end to give up everything I've worked for to follow
you to the Mediterranean, then suddenly no longer had
a word to say about it."

She was right in his face and it struck her that she was
all revved up from arguing with him. That she actually
liked it—she who eschewed all commotion. Fear trickled
an icy finger down her spine and she backpedaled fast.

"God!" She edged toward the door. "I knew this
wouldn't work between us. It was a dumb idea to think
it would. So why don't we just admit it and call it a day."

He took a step toward her then stopped, his hands
shoved into his jeans pockets. "You want to just give
up?"

"I prefer to call it making an intelligent decision
based on the facts."

Color rode his cheekbones and his eyes were dark,
dangerous. "Fine," he said flatly. "If you can't take one
minor fight without cutting and running back to your

safe little life, then let's do that, Jane. I don't have the patience today to deal with a woman who's too damn chickenshit to step outside her comfort zone because she has some dumb idea she'll suddenly turn into her parents."

She felt sicker than if he'd kicked her in the stomach. That was so unfair.

Maybe he's right, a little voice whispered in her head.

No! He wasn't. Heart thundering, stomach churning, she tipped her chin up at him.

And returned fire. "At least I acknowledge my hang-ups. But, hey, you just keep fooling yourself, Devlin. Trot on back to Europe as soon as Bren is better so you can pretend your issues don't exist. Go back to that world where it's all your family's fault for daring to care about you."

Dear God. A tiny clear-thinking corner of her mind was appalled at herself. How had everything turned so nasty so fast?

She opened her mouth to say—she wasn't sure what. But something conciliatory that would vanquish all this drama. She'd handled everything wrong. All because she was really, really afraid of what might happen if she dared to admit she wanted to be with him.

Before she could utter a word, however, to dial back all the fight and fury, he folded his arms across his chest and regarded her with indifferent eyes. "Don't let the door hit you in the butt on your way out, babe."

And just

like

that

It was too late.

For a second she simply stared at him while pain radiated deep within her. Then she did what she'd done all her life; she regrouped.

Well, fine. It was just as well, considering wild surges of destructive, all-consuming passion too reminiscent of her parents were trying desperately to rise in her. She wanted to *force* Dev to love her, she realized with a shock she felt clear down to her toes.

Oh God. To *love* her.

Pressing her lips tightly together to keep the words he wouldn't want to hear and she didn't want to acknowledge locked deep inside her, she turned and walked back down the hallway.

Conscious with every fiber of her being that he didn't say a word to stop her as she let herself out of his apartment.

CHAPTER TWENTY-TWO

I've had lousy days before, but I had no idea it was possible to feel this mad, bad and sad. Or be so freakin' scared on so many levels.

SHE COULDN'T GO HOME; it was the only clear thought in Jane's head. She made her way back to her car, then merely sat in it for a long, blank moment, staring blindly through the windshield. She'd go nuts if she went home, just her in the apartment without a damn thing to take her mind off Devlin.

She could always take her woes to Poppy at the Calloways' or to Ava at her condo on Alki, she supposed. Except her throat felt swollen with unshed tears, her heart was tight with grief and her emotions were simply too raw to throw on the table for discussion.

She could work, though. A brittle laugh escaped her. Hey, her love life might implode, but she always had the job. God knew she had spent a lifetime burying herself in her work ethic whenever the going got rough. In fact, today's blowup had probably merely hurried along the inevitable. She never would have gone to Europe with Devlin, anyway.

Because, face it. That would have meant giving up everything she'd worked for. And without her work, who the hell was she?

No one. Absolutely no one at all.

Oh, for— Okay, even for a woman in the grip of the worst heartache she'd ever known, that was too pitiful. Pitiful and diametrically opposed to everything she believed, if she could allow thwarted *passion* of all things to drive her to such depths of self-pity. *No whining!* she commanded herself sternly, sitting taller in her seat. *You* do *have work that you love. That's more than a lot of people can claim. So just suck it up and go put your back into the one thing you still have some control over. Make this exhibit the best that it can be.*

She started the car and headed for the mansion.

WHAT THE HELL just happened here? Dev stopped his restless pacing when it brought him back to his front door for the third time. He thrust a hand through his hair as he scowled at its panels. What the *hell* had just happened?

He'd kicked Jane out into the storm.

His shoulders stiffened and his scowl deepened. That was her own damn fault. She'd built his hopes up only to cut them off at the knees. But had she been content to leave him bloody and just walk away? Hell, no. Not until she'd talked trash about his relationship with his family. Psycho*babble* trash.

Dude, his conscience barked. *Stay on target. You. Kicked. Her. Out.*

IN A STORM!

His fingertips went numb—a thankfully temporary phenomenon he'd experienced since childhood whenever he admitted to a wrongdoing he was particularly ashamed of. Crossing his arms over his chest, he tucked his hands into his armpits. No matter what the provocation on either side—and thinking about some of the trash he'd talked about *her* family, he knew he wasn't blameless in that regard himself—he'd behaved completely out of character.

He didn't have the fabled redhead's hair-trigger temper and as a rule it took a lot to nudge him to his flash point. Once he was pissed, however, it also took a bit to cool him down again. And between his sister and Jane today he'd been seriously riled.

Still. This wasn't the way he'd been raised to treat a woman. If his da ever found out about it, Dev could count on a trip to the woodshed—and it didn't matter if he was a grown man.

He snorted. Because who was he kidding? This wasn't about his treatment of just any woman. It wasn't generic. This was about Jane, who had been turning him inside out since the night they met. Who'd been driving him crazy. Making him laugh. Making him snarl.

Making him love her.

He stilled. Aw, shit, that was it in a nutshell, wasn't it? Jane Kaplinski had gone and made him fall in love with her.

A sudden knock at the door had him whipping around to face it, a rush of relief coursing through him. He took a giant step forward, ripping the door open. "Good, you came to your senses—"

"Didn't know I'd lost them," Finn drawled, strolling in.

"What the hell *is* this, Kavanagh Sibling Day?" Dev slammed the door and all but tromped on his brother's heels, conscious of a leaden disappointment deep in his gut. "What the hell are you doing here?"

Finn glanced over his shoulder as Dev stalked him into the living room. "*O*-kay. You weren't expecting me, obviously. Nice to see you're filled with delight at the thought of my company, though. I have that effect on people. Usually it's women, but—"

Dev gave his brother a hard shot to the shoulder with the flat of his hand.

"Bro. Chill. Jesus, what a killjoy." But Finn shrugged. "You said you were going to work this morning, so I stopped by the mansion to see if you needed a ride home." Flopping onto the couch, Finn looked up at him. "But since that whole block's without power, I figured you'd probably hoofed it on back here, so I decided to swing by to see if you were home."

"Let me get this straight," he said suspiciously, Hannah's visit fresh in his mind. "You came out in this weather to act as my chauffeur. From—what?—the goodness of your heart?"

"No." Finn's eyes narrowed. "I had a date last night with a woman who lives on the eastern slope of Queen Anne and since I was in the 'hood—"

"So you're not here to tell me it's time to give up Europe," he interrupted, skeptical.

Yet…this was Finn who, unlike their sister, had never interfered in his business. Dev was beginning to suspect he was making a fool of himself—and still he couldn't stop himself from adding, "You're not here to tell me it's time to move home for good?"

Finn rose to his feet. "Mood you're in, bro, I don't give a fuck if you ever move home. What the hell is your problem?" Then, his face clearing, he gave a sage nod. "Ah. Had yourself a fight with Legs, did you?"

"Big-time."

Finn regarded him with the wariness of a male faced with the prospect of a conversation about *feelings*. "You don't want to talk about it, do you?"

"Hell, no. But I can tell you I was suave. I was cool. I told Jane not to let the door hit her in the butt on her way out."

Finn stared at him. "You threw her out in this storm?"

"Yeah." He dug his thumb and fingers into the stiff muscles at the back of his neck. "And you should take off, because I need to track her down."

His brother nodded. "Make it right."

"I don't know if that's possible, Fineas. But I can at least make sure she got home all right. And maybe attempt another talk. One where my temper doesn't play a part."

"Not often it does. I wouldn't have minded being a fly on the wall to see what got you to that point."

Dev just shook his head.

"You want a ride down to her place?"

Why the hell would he want his brother tagging along when he came face-to-face with the woman he'd just had the biggest fight of their relationship with? Then the lightbulb went on over his head. "Shit, no Flexcar today. I miss the European subway system—and I imagine the bus service is bound to be spotty today. Let me try calling her first—see if she's home."

He dialed Jane's number but it rang four times before switching to her answering machine. Something deep in his gut clenched at the sound of her voice telling him she wasn't there but to leave a message and she'd get back to him.

"Jane?" he said when the machine beeped. "Pick up if you're there. Uh, please?" He sighed at the lack of response. "Look, I'm not calling to fight. I just want to make sure you got home okay. It's blowing like hell out there." He gave her another moment to answer, then disconnected and tried her cell phone. After leaving the same message on its voice mail, he swore and pocketed his phone.

"Not home?" his brother asked.

"I don't know. She's not answering either of her phones, but she could have turned the volume off so she wouldn't have to deal with it." His jaw clenched. "With me."

"Only one way to find out," Finn said in a brisk, don't-even-get-emotional-on-my-ass voice. "Let's roll."

JANE DID A REASONABLE JOB of blanking her mind and focusing on her driving until she reached the mansion. Such was her concentration, in fact, that she didn't even notice the neighborhood was dark until she turned into the drive. A mass of small branches topped by one large, jagged, forked one blocked her way, so she pulled back onto the street. That was when it hit her. None of the houses were lit.

"Well, great." She found a place to park a few houses down the block anyhow, because no way in hell was she going back to her empty apartment. She had her Maglite in the glove box; better to get a few things done by flashlight than to twiddle her thumbs at home.

The only problem with that plan was it took forever to accomplish even the smallest task working strictly by her flashlight and the little bit of illumination she gained from opening the drapes in the upstairs room that hosted the secret closet. Her Mag wasn't one of the puny pen-size ones, but it was still a far cry from a nice big meaty light such as the one Officer Stiller had worn. What she wouldn't give for one of those right now.

But of course that wasn't the real problem. *That* would be the vignettes of her encounter with Devlin that began popping up on her mind's screen when the fast-paced barrage of work she'd envisioned failed to materialize to keep her brain occupied.

It started with colors for some reason: the gold of his henley hugging his strong shoulders and skimming the swells of his chest, making his hair look redder and his eyes a truer green. Then the exact shade of blue from the spine of one of his Sudoku puzzle books—a book she didn't even remember seeing while they were arguing—popped into her head. It was ridiculous.

Too damn chickenshit to step outside your comfort zone because you have some dumb idea you'll suddenly turn into your parents.

Devlin's voice in her brain made her hand freeze in the midst of scribbling notes on the items of apparel still needing further research. Dropping her hands to her lap, she drew a breath, then blew it out.

Okay, she'd rather think about the puzzle book. It might be ridiculous but it was preferable to *this*.

It was too late, however; his accusation roared in her head and it was either face it or beat on her own temples until the voice quieted.

She *was* a coward. The truth hurt, but she couldn't deny she had spent most of her life avoiding non-work-related passion for the sole reason that she had been exposed to her parents' skewed version of it. Yet the funny thing was, it wasn't actually their never-ending, zealous fervor for one another that was the real issue. At least not in the way she had always believed.

Her tablet and pen dropped to the floor and she climbed to her feet, where she stood staring down at the faded carpet, her hands dangling limply by her sides. *My God.* Why had she never seen this before? *Passion* wasn't the glitch to be avoided. She had just wanted, just once, for their unswerving attention—their passion—to be on her.

Dammit, kids had needs that should be met, but hers rarely had been because her mom and dad were always so involved with each other. She'd always felt like a shadow in the family portrait and hadn't known how to go about changing that. She hadn't known how to say, "Look at me. Notice *me*."

And of course without prompting from her—and Dorrie and Mike being Dorrie and Mike—they hadn't. So after a while she'd said, "Fine, I don't need that, anyhow. It's passion and it sucks and I don't need it."

Only passion hadn't been the problem. And the real deal didn't suck.

And she thought maybe she did need it.

The awful knot in Jane's stomach began to unravel. She closed up the closet, pulled the drapes back over the windows and headed out. She was going to gather her courage in both hands and go back to Devlin's. She was going to give it another try, only this time without using any of the tricks she'd devised over the years for shielding herself.

And if that didn't work, if it still wound up as messed

up as their earlier encounter had been? Well, at least it wouldn't be because she'd been too chickenshit to take a chance.

Reaching the midpoint of the staircase, which was illuminated by murky daylight coming through the front entry's leaded-glass sidelights, she thought she heard a faint, rhythmic squeaking noise coming from the back of the mansion. She froze, then leaned cautiously over the banister. The gloomy hallway below was empty and she heard nothing further over the howl of the wind and the creak of the trees. Her ears must be playing tricks on her, she decided. Given the ferocity of the weather, it was more likely a sound from outside than one from within. Maybe a branch scratching across a window.

She snapped off her flashlight, but kept its comforting weight in her hand. She couldn't recall how long the backup battery was supposed to keep the security system working in a power outage, but going on the hope-for-the-best-but-assume-the-worst theory, she crept down the hallway, cautiously peering into each room she passed. As she suspected, there was nothing untoward in any of them and she relaxed a bit more with each area that turned out to be unoccupied.

But what the hell was she doing, behaving like one of those women in the horror flicks that you yelled, "Don't go in the basement!" at? It wasn't as if she were the least bit prepared to confront an intruder. And if she really believed there was one in the house, she should have beat feet out the front door at the first suspicion instead of sticking to her usual routine and heading for the kitchen door to make her escape.

She shook her head, pretty sure she was scaring herself unnecessarily, the way she, Ava and Poppy used to do with ghoulish stories at summer campouts in Poppy's backyard. But her immediate goal was nevertheless to get out of the house ASAP. Without electricity the place was spookier 'n hell.

She ran lightly past the dining room with just a quick glance inside and whipped into the kitchen.

Stopping dead with the door in her sights.

Omigawd. Horror crawled up her spine, culminating at the nape of her neck where fine hairs she hadn't even known were there stood on end. It *wasn't* her imagination; she'd seen something—someone—over by the old dumbwaiter cupboard. Heart pounding, she dashed for the back door, where she scrabbled to turn the knob, almost sobbing with relief when it finally twisted beneath her stiff fingers and the door opened.

Then a masculine hand suddenly shot over her shoulder and slammed the door shut.

And Jane screamed down the house.

"Do you think I'm breaking Mom's heart?" Dev asked Finn as they circled the area near Jane's condo, looking for a place to park. His sister's accusation had been gnawing at him almost as much as his worry over Jane.

"What?" Finn took his gaze off the road for a split second, then focused his attention back on his driving. "No. Why would you think so?"

"Hannah said—"

"Ah. Well. Hannah. Your living so far away hit her hardest. She misses you, Dev. So does Mom, but I think Mom has a better understanding of why you need to be away from us. I'm sure you've noticed how hard she's been working to stay out of your business since you got back."

No, he hadn't. Which just went to show what a self-absorbed ass he was. Because thinking about it, he realized that while Aunt Eileen had made the usual when-you-gonna-settle-down-and-have-babies push when he'd shown up at his folks' party with Jane in tow, his mother hadn't. Nor had she so much as hinted in that direction the other times he'd seen her.

Looking back, in fact, he suddenly recognized that damn near everyone in his family had grown beyond that. *He* appeared to be the only one who was still reacting the same way he had when he was nineteen. "Shit."

"What, you *want* to break Mom's heart?"

"Grab that spot!" He pointed to a parking slot that had just opened up and Finn whipped across two lanes, beating out a woman in a Mini to claim it.

"Of course I don't want to hurt Mom," Dev said, going back to their conversation. "Why do you think I lost my temper with Han in the first place when she suggested it? But I'm just beginning to realize that I've been holding a grudge against a family attitude that doesn't even exist anymore." His mouth crooked. "Well, if you don't count Aunt Eileen, that is."

"Yeah, she's never gonna change. And don't kid yourself—Mom wants grandkids from you. But you quitting college and striking out for Europe, then staying instead of just having a quickie rebellion threw the fear of God into her. She won't hound. I think she's just grateful for every day you spend here."

"But, hey, no pressure," Dev said dryly.

His brother grinned. "Yeah. No pressure."

They battled the elements to reach Jane's condo, where the young woman at the desk buzzed them in. "Hey," she said cheerfully, recognizing him from previous trips through her territory. "Lousy weather, huh?"

"No kidding. Jane up in her apartment?"

"Oh." She looked startled. "No. I assumed you were meeting her here. She left about forty-five minutes ago."

He breathed an obscenity under his breath, then shot her an apologetic grimace. "Sorry. Okay if we wait for her up in her apartment?" he asked. "I have a key." Jane was bound to have an address book where he could find numbers for her friends.

"I'm sure it would be fine, but let me just check." She made a few strokes on her keyboard, then leaned forward to read the document she'd pulled up. A flush climbing her cheeks, she looked at him across the counter. "I'm so sorry, but you're not on the list. I know you and Jane are tight—I've seen you coming and going together. But we're not allowed to permit guests beyond the lobby if they're not on the list."

"I understand," he said, even though he wanted to disregard everything she'd said and just bulldoze his way into Jane's apartment. "Do you mind if my brother and I stay here while I try to track her down? It's a mess out there."

"Of course. Stay as long as you like."

Dev and Finn chose the bench farthest away from the front desk and he pulled his cell phone from his jacket pocket and punched in a number.

"Who you calling?"

He opened his mouth to reply only to have the ringing abruptly stop and his sister-in-law answer. "Hey, Jody."

The line crackled ominously and he said briskly, "It's Dev. Bren there?"

His brother was summoned, but in the short time it took for him to reach the phone, the connection grew even more tenuous. Bren's voice hiccuped in and out when he picked up.

"Can you hear me?" Dev demanded and when he got what he thought was an affirmative, said, "You dealt with Poppy when we bid on the Wolcott mansion. You got a phone number for her?"

"Le…ee…get…" The phone went dead.

"Shit!" Dev resisted the urge to hurl it across the lobby. "I lost him," he said to Finn.

"Let me try mine. I've got a different provider."

"If you get through, see if he has Ava's number, too. And the mansion's."

"Power was out up there." Finn scrolled up Bren's number and punched the call button.

"So you've said. But I've seen an old landline phone there, so it might still work. Of course, with the way everyone's got a cell phone these days, chances are Jane and her friends didn't bother opening an account with Ma Bell."

Finn flipped his phone closed. "Mine's down, too. Now what the hell do we do?"

"I go upstairs—and screw the list I'm not on. We need a phone that works."

The desk girl murmured behind them and they turned as one to see if she'd overheard them. When they noticed she was talking on the phone, however, they looked at each other.

Then crossed the lobby to the desk.

CHAPTER TWENTY-THREE

I thought I had issues, but Gordon? He takes the cake. How can anyone be that screwed-up and have nobody even notice?

HYSTERICAL WITH FEAR, Jane screamed and screamed. The intruder was yelling in her face, but she couldn't hear a word he said. She stared at him in horror but couldn't have described what he looked like to save her soul. Terror ruled her.

Then he backhanded her across the face, and the shock of being struck cleaved through her fire-siren shriek like a Samurai sword through chiffon. She swallowed hard and the tiny amount of saliva she managed to work up slid down throat tissues that felt as if they'd been worked over with a cheese grater.

"Damn," the man murmured in a voice so self-satisfied she registered it even over the fury of the storm outside. "I don't know about you, but that was sure as hell good for me."

Why, you— For the first time she looked at her prowler and really saw him. And another shock shot through her system. *"Gordon?"* She blinked, but the features she'd seen were still the same.

Her coworker's brows snapped together. "You didn't know it was me?"

She shook her head, aware she still wasn't operating on all cylinders.

"Well, that's just fucking great. I knew coming back here was a mistake."

"What do you mean, back? You've never been here before—" Her brain kicked in. "Oh my God, it was you? *You're* the one who's been pilfering Miss Agnes's stuff? *The one who took my Dior?*"

He didn't need to reply; she saw the answer on his face. He'd picked a lousy day to dump this on her, and with an inarticulate growl of rage, she launched herself at him, punching, gouging, kicking at any body part within reach, ruled by an unthinking, pain-driven fury. She wanted to inflict some pain of her own. "You rat! You goddamn, lousy, gutter-born bastard *rat!*"

"That's enough!" he roared, grabbing her wrist as she threw another punch and stopping her fist inches from his nose. "God, you make me want to just kick the shit out of you."

"You can try." She sneered. Then, watching his face darken, she came to her senses. Okay, *not* the best thing to say to someone bigger and packing more upper-body strength than her.

But even as she braced herself for another blow, he yanked her deeper into the kitchen and jerked a chair away from the table, shoving her in it. "Sit down and shut up!" he snapped. "I gotta think."

She had little option concerning the former command and thought it prudent to follow his decree regarding the latter, as well—at least until she could figure out what was going on. Pressing her lips together, she slumped in her seat and folded her arms across her breasts.

"That's more like it," he muttered. "Smug, stupid bitch."

"Hey!" She shot upright, good sense forgotten. "You're a stone thief who robbed me blind, but *I'm* the bitch? You've got a hell of a lot of nerve, pal."

"You tried to kick me in the jewels! And look at this!" He slashed his hand angrily along the lines of his designer-label, all-black clothing, which was several rumples beyond its usual pristine condition.

She saw he wasn't kidding—that he was actually furious about the state of his apparel. A chill chased down her spine. This didn't look promising. She was alone in a mansion that was way spookier in the dark than she ever would've imagined with a clearly unstable man who had a lot to lose—and she was on her own. Just like she'd been on her own all her life. She was starting to see copping an attitude wasn't going to improve the situation.

"I'm sorry. It's a bit of a shock seeing you here," she said in as reasonable a voice as she could muster. "Maybe you and I have never been bosom buddies, but we are coworkers and I thought we at least respected each other's dedication to the exhibits. Yet here I am, discovering it was you who stole the Dior." She looked at him in sincere puzzlement. "You knew how much that gown meant to me, Gordon, so I kinda feel like I'm the injured party here. Yet you're the one calling me names. What's with that? What have I ever done to you to warrant being called a smug bitch?"

"Well, let's see—aside from you stealing exhibits that rightfully should have gone to me, you mean, and believing I'd just smile and think that was *okay?* You called me a gutter-born bastard rat. But, hey, I guess it's okay for the princess to call the peon names. After all, you were born with a silver spoon in your mouth and had every advantage handed to you on a goddamn matching platter while I had to fight for everything I've ever accomplished."

Her mouth dropped open. She knew she should address the gutter-born crack. He seemed to be getting all twisted out of shape over it.

Yet it was his misconception regarding her birth that grabbed her attention. "What are you talking about? I grew up just off Highway 99 out by the airport!"

He blinked, looking uncertain for an instant. Then he gave a *yeah, right,* scoffing laugh. "You went to Country Day. I've heard Marjorie rave about it."

"Yeah, on a *scholarship.*"

"I heard you went to Radcliffe, too."

"Again, on scholarship. Gordon, my parents are actors. And not the red-carpet-walking, Broadway or Hollywood kind. On their best year they maybe pulled in thirty thousand dollars."

His eyes hardened. "Which is about eighteen grand better than my old lady ever did."

"Still, that was one year on a combined income and you have to agree it's a far cry from rich."

"Yeah, poor you. You just inherited *how* many hundreds of thousands of dollars in priceless artifacts?"

"Interesting you should mention that, considering *you're* the only one to profit from it so far." *Shut up, Jane. Just. Shut. Up.* It had been a mistake to mention money at all, a poorly thought-out attempt on her part to illustrate how far removed she was from the trust-fund baby he apparently envisioned.

Because clearly the amount of money her family'd had when she was growing up was of much less interest to Gordon than the simple fact that she'd *had* more than he'd had—more money, more advantages, and never mind that the latter hadn't come from any huge influx of the former, but rather from her own hard work. Accepting that getting him to see he'd misunderstood her background wouldn't gain her any ground, her mind ticked through ways out of this mess.

She didn't foresee a happy ending to this situation. Gordon didn't strike her as the violent type, but then she'd never suspected him of stealing, either. And now she was in the position of being the only one who could identify him. Who knew what he would do to keep her from unmasking him? There was a resolution about him that didn't bode well for her—as if he'd do what he had to do and never mind that it was outside his comfort zone.

She kept coming up empty in her search for a way out of this mess. She sat near the back door, a mere few feet from freedom. But Gordon was nearer. Same thing with the front entrance—unless she could devise a way to get a head start, he'd be on top of her before she could unlatch the dead bolt, let alone get the door open. So without stopping to think it through, she asked the question that had been itching at the back of her mind. "Why didn't you just…*wait?* Wait for me to leave the house and then leave yourself?" God knew that would have been *so* much simpler all the way around.

"Whataya think, because I *like* putting myself in no-win situations?" He rubbed his hands over his face and gave her a look of disgust. "Obviously, I thought you recognized me. You looked right at me in the dining room."

He didn't add, "And now I'm gonna kill you for it," but his eyes were flat and sort of…soulless, and she swallowed dryly.

"I didn't see you. I was rattled about being in the mansion in this storm, even though I'd almost managed to talk myself into believing I was panicked over nothing. I just wanted out of here at that point, so I didn't really take it in." Oh God. She really needed to come up with a strategy, she realized, fighting a rising tide of panic.

One, preferably, that had her coming out of this alive.

Unfortunately, the only thing she could think of was to stall him. It wasn't much, considering she didn't expect anyone to ride to her rescue, but a girl had to work with what she was given. Guys liked to brag, didn't they? Well, Gordon was a guy and if she could get him talking, maybe, just maybe she could put off whatever it was he had in mind while she came up with a better plan for getting her butt out of the sling it was in. She licked her fear-stiffened lips.

"How on earth did you ever get the code to the security system?" she asked with a downright decent imitation of admiration. Who *said* the acting gene had skipped her by?

Well, okay, Mike and Dorrie had. But they were wrong.

Only an actress could listen with every indication of ingenuous, wide-eyed, aren't-you-just-the-*smartest?* awe as Gordon answered her question in a tone loaded with contempt for the very air she breathed.

My butt I can't act.

"CAN I USE your phone, love?"

The girl behind the desk blinked up at Dev. "Oh. I don't know…"

He didn't rip it out of her hands. He was going to give her one chance to do the right thing. "Look, I know you're worried about the rules and all, but I'm worried about Jane. She might be fine at one of her friends' houses but I don't know that, and I don't have their numbers to even check. I'm not trying to bust your chops but it's either let me use your phone to try to track her down or I'm going upstairs and I don't care who you call to stop me. I can get what I need and be gone long before anyone of real authority shows up."

She lifted the phone off her desk and placed it on the counter.

"Thanks." Punching in Bren's number, he thought he should have used the threat right off the bat. There was a downside to being raised to do the right thing.

His brother answered so fast he must have been sitting on his phone. "Dev, that you?"

"Yeah."

"Good, Jody was starting to get worried." Translation: Bren was. "I've got some numbers for you. Are you ready to write them down in case we get cut off again?"

Reaching over the counter, he scooped up a pen. "Shoot." He wrote Poppy's home number on his palm, then her cell number, as well, although he held out no great hope of that being active.

"I'm sorry," his brother said. "I don't have a number for Ava, but here's the mansion's."

Dev wrote that down, as well. "Thanks, Bren. This helps a lot."

"Give me a call when you find her, hey?"

"Will do." Disconnecting, he immediately dialed Poppy's home number. Getting her machine, he hung up without leaving a message and dialed the cell number. As he suspected, he got the out-of-service screen, so he tried the mansion. It rang and rang and after about the eighth or ninth he got a recorded intercept message telling him that the number he was dialing was not answering.

Thanks, Ma Bell. I couldn't figure that out for myself. He returned the receiver to the cradle with a briskness that was just this side of slamming and looked at the young woman across the desk. "I'm sorry, but I need Ava's number. I'm going upstairs. Finn?"

The last thing he saw as he strode to the elevator was his brother reaching across the counter to press one lean hand against the telephone receiver, talking softly to the rattled receptionist as she struggled to get it away from him.

THE SUDDEN STRIDENT RING of the seventies-era phone on the kitchen wall made Gordon jump. He whirled to face the sound and Jane took it as a sign. One that read RUN LIKE HELL WHILE THE RUNNING'S GOOD. This was far from ideal but it was probably her one and only chance. She slid silently out of her chair.

She was barely through the door when he yelled out and she ducked into the dining room and grabbed a chair, holding it over her head as she hid to one side of the doorway. A heavy black garbage bag over by the open dumbwaiter caught her eye and a fierce frown creased her brow as she wondered what he'd snatched today.

Gordon stuck his head through the door and she brought the heavy chair swinging down at his head with all her strength. He must have caught the motion from the corner of his eye, because he ducked down, his arm curling protectively over his head. The chair nevertheless connected with a thunk and knocked him skidding across the floor on his butt. He bellowed in rage or pain or maybe both, but Jane didn't stick around to see how he fared. She sprinted for the front door.

She was fumbling with the dead bolt when she heard him swearing with vicious creativity and—more ominously—what she thought were the sounds of him dragging himself to his feet. Abandoning the dead bolt, she took the stairs two at a time to the second floor.

She slammed shut every door she passed in the hope that she could create a little confusion to buy herself an extra minute, then ducked into the sitting room to Miss Agnes's suite. Closing that door much more quietly, she loped across the room to the secret closet and sped through the opening ritual. She slid inside, closing it just as she heard Gordon calling her name from the hallway. It was darker inside than the devil's soul and her breath hitched.

"Where are you, you bitch?"

It was quiet for a moment except for muffled noises that she took to be Ives kicking doors to the various rooms on both sides of the hallway.

The door to the bedroom next door suddenly slammed against the wall. "Olly, Olly, Oxen free," he crooned.

"Come out now, Jane, and we'll call it square. I'll take my sack and go home."

Yeah, right. His lips were saying one thing, but his actions said he wasn't leaving until he'd eliminated the one person who could identify him. Nerves screaming, her senses drenched in what would ordinarily be the bracing scent of cedar, she stood stiffly in the closet, hoping the rapid tha-THUMP, tha-THUMP of her heartbeat wouldn't give her away like the old man under the floorboards in "The Tell-Tale Heart."

Okay, it had actually been the protagonist's insanity that had conjured the sound. Fair enough, since she couldn't swear she was all that far from going nuts herself.

She heard Gordon banging around in the bedroom next door. Then the connecting door crashed open and she could have sworn she heard his ragged breathing— a distinct unlikelihood given the ferocity of the storm buffeting the house.

He swore. Then his voice went so cheery it made her flesh creep. "You know what, bitchy-poo? It's probably for the best if you stay in your little hidey-hole. I don't exactly want to do this face-to-face. But I know what I gotta do now, anyhow." His voice had been growing fainter as he moved farther away. "See you around, Kaplinski! Or maybe not." Laughter that chased goose bumps down Jane's spine floated in from the hallway.

Then it grew quiet. Carefully, she eased down to sit on the floor, hugging her knees to her chest and wondering when she dared crawl out of the closet. He was probably waiting for her to do exactly that.

Or so she thought. Until, terror streaking through her, she smelled the smoke.

CHAPTER TWENTY-FOUR

...and for a minute all I could think was, Where's Devlin? OhGodohGod, where is he? I need him!

ADRENALINE WAS A DEVIL in spurs riding Gordon's shoulder as he left the big pile of scrap lath he'd found in a torn-apart room upstairs smoldering beneath the filmy under-draperies in the master bedroom. Skin twitching, he loped down the stairs, heading for the dining room on the first floor.

Screw everything. Let the place burn to the ground and Bitch Kaplinski with it. He'd grab the bag he'd left behind the last time he was here, start a few more strategic blazes and wait a few minutes to see if he'd flushed her out. Then he was getting the hell out of here. What a cluster fuck this had turned into.

He'd known better than to come here today. He was always so careful, and he'd *known* better! But he'd been fretting himself sick over the thought of the Dior quietly rotting away in that dumbwaiter. And when the storm had hit it had just seemed like a God-given opportunity to go retrieve it. Even if the mansion's security system wasn't knocked out, he'd figured the cops would be up to their eyeballs in emergencies. A burglar alarm wouldn't even be a blip on their radar when a whole shitload of them were likely to be set off by all the power failures both intermittent and long-term. So even when his instincts for self-preservation had screamed *Don't do it!* he'd ignored them.

Which just went to show he should always listen to his instincts. Because now he'd been put in a position of having to do something about Jane.

Hooking his finger in the neckline of his designer windbreaker, he tugged, craning his head in first one direction, then the other. He was no killer. But Jane hadn't left him any choice. She could identify him as the Wolcott mansion burglar and he knew damn well that little Miss Holier-than-thou would rat him out in a New York minute. Then that big, dark cop who already suspected him would get a warrant for his place and find not only the items he'd stolen from here but his goodies from the other museums he'd worked for, as well. And he'd go to jail, an institution he'd worked his entire *life* to avoid.

His determination to steer clear of it was a powerful motivator, so when it came to a choice between Jane or him going down? He chose Jane.

The smell of smoke grew stronger. This place was old and dry and was probably gonna go fast once the flames really sank their teeth in. He wanted to leave in the worst way, but he had to stick around to make sure Jane didn't stroll out. Fucking bitch had displayed more luck than any one person who wasn't him ever oughtta have.

Then he brightened and his nerves settled a fraction. Because as long as he was just hanging around waiting anyhow, why let all the Wolcott goodies go up in smoke? The old lady had accumulated some of the finest collections he'd ever seen and the real crime would be letting them just melt into unrecognizable puddles of steel, glass and ash. Besides, if the entire joint burnt to the ground, who would know what was missing?

He took his bag to the kitchen and set it next to the door. Then he grabbed another trash bag from under the sink and headed for the parlor.

OhGodohGod! Gordon had set the house on fire? Jane cracked open the secret closet and peered out. No one was in sight, but for all she knew he could be right outside the door. A thin haze of smoke filled the sitting room and she dropped to her stomach, keeping her nose close to the floor where the air was freshest. Dear Lord, she wished Devlin was here. She could really use his solid, no-bullshit strength right now.

But he wasn't here, and that was her own damn fault. God, she was an idiot; why, oh why had her pride seemed more important than the way she felt when she was with him?

Just the thought of him, however, seemed to imbue her with a little strength of her own. It steadied and focused her, and cautiously she pulled herself across the room on her elbows, propelling herself with the toes of her boots, until she reached the doorway to Miss Agnes's bedroom.

A pile of lath that she'd last seen in the sunroom smoked and smoldered between the bed and the chaise, and even as she watched, a long, translucent tongue of flame rose from it to lap at the illusion curtains hanging behind tied-back drapes.

They burst into flame.

With a squeaky yelp, Jane jumped to her feet and ripped the curtains down, dropping them to the floor and grabbing up the little throw rug at the side of the bed to beat out the blaze. She was *not* letting that weasel burn down Miss Agnes's house.

Hoping this was the sole source of the fire and that he hadn't started others throughout the house, she kicked apart the teepee-stacked kindling. Then, snatching up a wastebasket, she ran into the attached bathroom to fill it with water from the bathtub faucet. Picking up a pair of scissors from the vanity, she shoved them into her waistband, then carried the wastebasket back to the bedroom and emptied its contents on the fire. A hiss of steam rose from the smoldering remains.

She had to go back for more water twice before she was certain the fire was extinguished. Wiping the back of her wrist across her sweaty forehead, she stared at the mess of Miss Agnes's once-pristine bedroom and breathed in the acrid stench of burnt, wet wood that permeated the air.

She really wanted to crawl back into the safety of the secret closet and pull the paneling closed behind her. But if Gordon had set one fire to keep her from exposing him, chances were he'd set more to ensure the mansion burned to the ground quickly. She went back to the sitting room to close up the closet against the smell, then sidled up to the room's door to the hallway. She pressed her palm against the wood, relieved to find it wasn't hot to the touch. Cautiously opening it, she peeked around the jamb. The hall was empty.

She peeked into the other rooms on the second floor, but to her surprise there were no other fires. Just setting the one seemed a pretty iffy proposition if Gordon's ultimate goal had been to prevent her from blowing the horn on him. But what did she know of his reasoning processes? As she headed for the staircase she could only be grateful for the way they had worked in this instance.

Déjà vu, she thought cynically as she paused halfway down the stairs. She had been here, done this, before. If she thought she'd been wound tightly earlier, however, it was nothing compared to this time, since she now knew that the Boogie Man was real and not merely a case of her imagination running wild. Mouth tight, the sharp-bladed scissors she'd filched from the vanity clutched in her fist, she kept to the left side of the sweeping staircase where the shadows were deepest and descended as quietly as she could, bypassing the third riser from the bottom that squeaked.

Not that anyone was likely to hear over the raging wind, but she wasn't taking any chances. And this time she used her head when she reached the bottom; she raced directly to the front door.

She scrambled to unlock the dead bolt, exhaling softly when it unlatched. She eased the door open.

Only to have Gordon's arm reach over her shoulder to slam it shut again just like he had done earlier in the kitchen.

"Surprise, bitch. Déjà vu."

"Shit!" she screamed. And, whirling, she plunged the scissors into his stomach with all the force she could muster.

"There's her car!" Relief flooding him, Dev leaned forward in his seat. He'd been starting to believe he'd never find her, even though Ava had assured him that Jane always, but *always,* turned to work—especially if other parts of her life were going to hell. He remembered the way the redhead's voice had hardened to honed steel when she'd added that she had better not find out he'd hurt Jane or he'd have her and Poppy to deal with—and he would not like what that meant for him.

But Jane's friends were the least of his worries at the moment and he mentally brushed the conversation aside. His brow furrowed. "Why is she parked on the street?"

"Because the driveway's blocked," Finn said as he turned into it. He pulled the car as far forward as it would go before a pile of branches put a halt to its progress, then shoved the gearshift into Park. "Good enough, yeah?"

Dev was already scrambling from the car. He sprinted for the back door without waiting for his brother, who caught up with him anyway when he opened the door.

"Jane!" he hollered, then wrinkled his nose as a faint acrid scent reached his nostrils. He gave Finn a puzzled glance. "Why does it smell like a three-day-old campfire in here?"

"I don't know, but look at this." Finn straightened from the black garbage bag he'd been bent over, an evening gown in his hand. "Isn't this the dress Legs had hanging in the parlor? The one she was so upset about being ripped off?"

"Yes. What the hell's going on?" He went to a drawer and pulled out a couple of butcher knives. "Here's hoping if we run into someone, he's not packing." Handing his brother one, he eased his head around the corner of the doorway to peer into the hallway. "What the—?"

He could see feet and the bottom part of someone's legs at the base of the stairway up the hall. Finn looked over his shoulder. They exchanged a glance then eased down the hall toward the figure.

When they got closer Dev saw a man sitting sprawled on the second riser of the staircase. Hands that looked too smooth to have ever done an honest day's work cupped the handles of a pair of scissors that stuck out of the man's side near his stomach. He looked at Dev and Finn with dull eyes. "She ruined my Helmut Lang," he said. "I paid six hundred dollars for this jacket."

"Where is she?" Dev demanded, then raised his voice to yell up the staircase. "JANE!" When neither the man nor Jane responded, he looked at his brother wild-eyed. "Oh God, Finn. Where the hell is she?"

A noise he'd been too preoccupied to notice before caught his attention and he whirled to peer behind him into the foyer. The open entrance door was banging in the wind.

"Keep your eye on him," he yelled over the sound of the storm and headed out into the front yard. The last thing he heard was Finn saying, "You spent six hundred bucks on that? Dude, that's seriously whacked. No wind-breaker's worth that kind of green."

Dev didn't see any sign of Jane in the front yard and headed for the back, yelling her name.

He almost tripped over her as he raced around the side of the house. She was kneeling in the shadows, throwing up in the bushes.

He dropped to his knees behind her. "Janie?"

She started, and with a choked scream tried to scramble away.

He snaked his arm around her chest and pulled her back between his spread legs. "Are you okay?"

"Devlin?" Her head craned around to stare up at him over her shoulder. A sob escaped her and she turned in his hold to wrap her arms around his neck, hanging on as if her life depended on it.

"Did he hurt you?" he demanded, hoisting her up.

"No. No, I'm all right," she assured him shakily, twining her legs around his waist.

"Thank God." Hands grasping her butt to hold her in place, he strode with her around the house to the back door, where he let them in. The noise level dropped the minute he closed the door behind them.

He set her on her feet, but kept her close in his arms, so damn grateful that she was all in one piece he could barely breathe.

She looked up at him, her face bleached of color. "Oh God, Dev, I stabbed him. Gordon Ives. From work. Is he still here? Did I kill him? I could feel the scissors punching through his skin and it made the most awful wet, squelchy sound." Gagging, she raced for the sink, but apparently had nothing to bring up.

When her back quit heaving and she rested her head on her folded arms on the counter, he turned on the faucet and wet a dish towel. He gently wiped her face, then poured her a glass of Coke from the fridge. While she sipped it, he pawed through the cupboards for the box of saltines they'd bought to have on hand for Bren's chemo days.

"The guy's in shock, but I think it's just a flesh wound," he told her, handing her a short stack of crackers. Not that he was a medic, but no guts had been spilling out, there had been no foul odors and the man's color had been decent. "Finn's with him in the other room. What the hell happened here?"

When she told him, it was all he could do not to go rampaging down the hallway to beat the shit out of Ives. Instead, he reached for the phone on the wall, breathing a sigh of relief when he got a dial tone. He punched 911. Next he called the number for Detective de Sanges from the business card stuck between the phone's sturdy plastic chassis and the wall. Then he stuck his head out into the hallway to let Finn know what was going on. "Tie the bastard to the banister and come in here. And don't waste your time being gentle."

THE MANSION HAD BRISTLED for hours with police, paramedics, the fire marshal, a couple of Devlin and Finn's family members and Poppy and Ava. By the time Jane was able to escape with Devlin to her place, she was feeling pretty raw. The second she'd hung the recovered Dior gown safely in her coat closet she turned to him.

"I'm sure I'm going to be happy about getting this back tomorrow," she said dully. "But right now I need a shower. I just feel kind of…besmirched." She held her breath, fearing he'd suggest joining her. She didn't think she could handle that right now. She'd figured a few things out this afternoon, and as a result she could no longer bear the idea of having their relationship be defined solely by their sexuality—even if she had been the one who'd proposed the idea in the first place.

But Dev merely nodded and said, "I'll make a pot of coffee—or would you prefer cocoa? Too bad you don't drink—if ever a day called for a shot of something strong, this would be the one."

The bare breath of a sardonic laugh escaped her. "No fooling." She dragged herself into the bathroom and shut the door behind her. After turning on the shower, she shed her clothes, forgoing her usual tidiness to just let them lie where they dropped, then stepped into the tub. She stood under the spray, letting the hot, rhythmic pulsations work the tension from the back of her neck.

She knew she had to put herself on the line when she went back out there, something she generally tried to avoid at all costs. But if today had taught her nothing else, it had brought home the fact that life could change on a dime and you had better ask for what you wanted today, because you might not get a tomorrow.

She procrastinated as long as she could, but eventually she had to turn the water off, step out and dry off. She applied lotion, climbed into a black tank top and the parachute pants Dev had bought her and combed out her hair. She gave herself a once-over in the mirror, inhaled a deep breath and blew it out.

Then left the steamy comfort of the bathroom.

Devlin had turned off the lights, started the gas fireplace and lit her candles. Diana Krall crooned on the CD player and he met her by the breakfast bar, where he promptly pulled her into his arms.

"I don't ever want to go through another day like today," he said in a hoarse voice.

A choked laugh escaped her. "Oh God, me, either." She inhaled the scent of him, the Lever 2000, fresh laundry, all-man Dev smell. Then she stepped back. She tugged on the short hem of her tank, took a breath, then glanced up at him. And took the plunge.

"Look, I don't know how you're going to feel about

this, since I was the one who said no strings to our relationship and now I want to change all the rules. But the thing is…I think I'm in love with you."

He narrowed his eyes. "You *think* you are?"

"Okay, I am." She thrust her chin up at him, her stomach in knots. But she owed him her honesty. "The thought of you—of us—was what gave me strength this afternoon when I was playing mouse to Gordon's cat and—" She squealed in an embarrassingly girlish way when he suddenly swept her off her feet and whirled her around. "What the—?" She smacked his solid shoulder with the flat of her hand. "What are you doing? Put me down!"

He set her back on her feet, but kept his arms looped around her waist, leaning back to grin down at her. "I thought I was gonna have a heart attack over that weak-ass *think* business. Because I am so in love with you, Jane."

A feeling she had never experienced unfurled inside her. It felt as if she'd swallowed the sun, all bright and hot, and she blinked up at him. "You are?"

"Oh, yeah. *God,* yeah! Why do you think I acted like an ass this afternoon when I thought you were messing with me? I've got all these *feelings* for you and when I thought you didn't give a shit about me—"

"I do. I give a really big—" She shook her head impatiently. "That is so not how I want to say this." She drew a breath in. Quietly blew it out. And smiled up at him, unafraid for perhaps the first time in her life to let someone see every speck of emotion in her eyes.

"I have all these feelings for you, too." Plucking his hand off her hip, she brought it around to press it over her heart, allowing him to feel its thunderous beat beneath his palm. "My God, Dev, my emotions are so *big* I feel as if I can't possibly contain them all, as if they just want to spill out over everything in their path. All this time I thought my *job* was the big love of my life, but it sure wasn't my career I was thinking of today. I was scared to death I might never see you again and I realized my position at the Met's not nearly as important to me when stacked up against that.

"So, to answer the question I did my best to avoid this afternoon—if you still want me to go to Europe with you, I will. I'll follow you anywhere."

"Oh. Yeah. Huh." A short laugh rumbled out of his throat and he rubbed a hand over his mouth. "About that." Encircling her wrist, he led her to the couch, where he dropped down and pulled her onto his lap.

She immediately scooted up to sit, back erect, on his knees. "Have you changed your mind?"

"About you? Never. About going back to Europe? Possibly." He plucked a strand of hair away from the corner of her lips. Then his mouth firmed and he sat a little straighter. "Okay, listen up, because I'm about to say 'You were right,' and it's the only time you will ever hear that from me."

She grinned at him. "Wanna bet?"

"Prob'ly not." He gave her a smile so open and sweet that Jane's heart clenched. Then he sobered. "You were right."

She nodded solemnly. "I usually am. Which particular time would you be talking about?"

"When you virtually told me to man up and face my issues with my family. I've been avoiding doing that for the past fifteen years—but I realized today that the only person they still even *are* an issue for is me." He slid her down his thighs back onto his lap, then bent his head to kiss her. When he raised it once again, he stroked a gentle thumb over her damp bottom lip. "We don't have to go to Europe, Janie. You've got a job and friends that mean a lot to you and I'm perfectly happy to stay right here."

"Then maybe we should discuss the pros and cons. But not right this minute." This time she initiated the kiss and when they came up for air she rested her head on his shoulder. "It's not something we have to decide immediately, right?"

He pressed his lips to the top of her head. "Right."

Jane's heart continued to feel full to bursting. "The important thing is that we've got a definite future together."

"Babe." He tipped them over onto the couch cushions and propped himself above her. "Our future's so bright, we gotta wear shades."

EPILOGUE

Barcelona, Spain

> *I have a brand-new mantra. Happiness is a bride
> with a naked groom.*

JANE TIPPED DOWN HER shades to look over the rims at
her husband. Her *husband,* for cripe's sake. "My God,"
she murmured, still not used to the idea, given that the
marriage was only three days old.

"What can I do for you, doll?" Dev snapped her picture, then looked up from the viewfinder where he'd
been setting up her shot with the Catalan Art Museum
in the immense National Palace building in the background. He laughed when she rolled her eyes. "Oh. I
thought you were practicing my title."

"In your dreams, hotshot."

"Definitely." He returned his attention to the screen.
"Show us a little leg, love."

She lifted the long, colorful flounced skirt he'd
bought her and struck a flamenco pose. "I was just mar-
veling anew about how fast you got me to the altar."

"Like that was a hard sell." He gave her a smoldering glance. "You wanted me bad."

"Uh-huh." She returned a little smolder of her own.
"And I knew I could have you, too. Any time, any place.

Just. Like. That." She snapped her fingers at him. "I didn't need to marry you for it."

"True. But I was too suave and determined for your feeble powers of resistance to defend against."

"Pfffft. I just got tired of the incessant begging and decided to save you from embarrassing yourself."

"So you say, babe. But clearly I swept you off your feet, because here you are, aren't you? Mrs. Kavanagh."

"I know!" She grinned. "And I luvvv my name. It is so much cooler than Kaplinski." Then, thinking about their quickly assembled, fairly private wedding and the big reception Dev's parents had thrown them, her brows furrowed. "I'm just not sure how well I'm going to fit in with your family."

"What are you talking about? My family *loves* you. Ma's already bragging to everyone she knows about the hot new exhibit at the Met and telling them *her* daughter-in-law, the newly promoted full-fledged curator, is responsible for it. I wouldn't be surprised if she hasn't done a one-stop shop and bought the entire Kavanagh clan season passes for Valentine's Day."

"They're always *hugging* me, Dev. I've never met a family so big on all that hugging stuff." She wondered if she would ever get used to it. Not that it wasn't kind of nice in some ways, but— "They hug me when we arrive at one of your family get-togethers, then they hug me again when we leave. And not just, like, your mom, either—*all* of them. Is that really necessary?"

"Yep. 'Fraid so."

"But I never know how to respond or what to do with my hands!"

"Yet still you hang in there, letting them do their

stuff." He hugged her himself. "And you're getting lots better at it, too. You were so stiff at first I considered canceling our flight, rigging you up with a sail and just surfing you to the Med."

"Ha-ha." She smacked his arm. "You are such a comic." But she had to swallow the appreciative snort tickling her throat.

He wrapped an arm around her shoulders. "You'll get used to it. You don't have a problem with Ava or Poppy hugging you, so just loosen up and go with the flow." He stroked his thumb along her cashmere-clad upper arm. "Seen enough Romanesque art for one day?"

"Yes."

"Good. What do you say we blow off the funicular and get a cab back to the hotel?" He wiggled his dark brows at her. "I've got a little wifely duty for you to perform before we go out for some tapas and maybe catch the Purple Line to the Segrada Familia."

"Would this wifely duty have anything to do with beating your shirts against the rocks in the plaza fountain? Because, I gotta tell ya, I've been dying to give that a go."

She felt his lips curve where they were pressed against her temple. "Yeah. Right. Laundry," he agreed dryly. "That tops my honeymoon to-do list."

Señora Landazuri hailed them when they entered their small hotel a short while later and handed Jane a slip of paper. *"Liamada,"* she said, cocking thumb and pinky to her ear and mouth in the universal sign for phone call.

"Gracias," Jane murmured and, reading the number on the slip, said to Devlin, "It's from Ava."

Up in their room, Dev felt what he was pretty sure was a fatuous grin spread across his kisser as he watched Jane peel off her cardigan, pick up the telephone receiver and punch in a series of numbers. She smiled at him over her shoulder.

The sun pouring through the window picked highlights from her hair as she talked to Ava, but he quit admiring the effect long enough to take note when her eyebrows momentarily furrowed. A while later she replaced the receiver in its cradle and crossed over to him. Hitching up her skirt, she climbed onto the end of the bed where he sat to straddle his lap.

"Gordon copped a plea today," she said. "He agreed to fifteen years."

"That's not even close to long enough," he growled, wrapping his arms around her hips and burying his head in the shallow cleavage between her breasts. When he thought of what Ives had been willing to do to cover his tracks—

"I know." Wrapping her arms around his head, she rested her cheek against his hair. "It seems like he ought to be put away forever. But Ava said the D.A. says this is a reasonable sentence. If not for the fire, it would have been a lot less. He had no previous record and carried no weapon. But the fire, even if it was ineptly set, turned it into attempted murder."

"And thank God for the inept part. What about all the stolen items they found in his condo?"

"That helped, too, I imagine." Her shoulders hitched. "Anyhow, it's done. I'm just glad that it's over and I won't have to testify. But let's not talk about that ass anymore. This is our time."

"I hear that." He nuzzled her dainty cleavage for a moment before coming up for air. "So, what do you think of Europe so far?"

"It's got a great bedroom."

He grinned, because it was true: they'd only been here for two days and they'd probably spent more time in their room than the average tourists. But, what the hell. They were on their honeymoon. "I love you big-time, Mrs. Kavanagh."

"I love you more, Mr. K."

"Not possible." He flopped onto his back with her atop him. "But I do have a couple of things I could do that might inspire you somewhere near the vicinity of my magnitude of emotion."

"Why, I do believe I feel that magnitude," she marveled, wiggling against his erection. "And talk about a small world—I have a suggestion of my own that might inspire you somewhat nearer *mine*." Jane lowered her head to whisper it in his ear.

"Babe." It took every ounce of self-control to hold his hands wide of his body in a negligent attitude of unconcern, when what he really wanted was to yank up her skirt, pull down her panties and seat himself in his favorite spot in the world. He looked at his bride pushed up on her forearms, giving him a cocky little smile that said she knew damn well what he was thinking.

Inserting his hand beneath her skirt, he gave her ass a light slap. "By all means, then," he said huskily. "Ladies first."

* * * * *

Don't miss Susan's brand-new book,
SOME LIKE IT HOT,
coming soon from Harlequin HQN!
Turn the page for a sneak peek...

CHAPTER ONE

Oh, my God. Is he coming here?

Before Harper Summerville glanced out her front window to see Max Bradshaw striding up the sun-dappled trail between the evergreens on the inn grounds, she'd been enjoying her day off. It was fun puttering around the little playhouse-size one-room-plus-loft cottage that was part of her employee compensation as the summer activities coordinator for The Brothers Inn. She loved, loved, loved the glimpses she could catch from back here of the fjord that was Hood Canal and the soaring Olympic mountains beyond it. The spectacular scenery was what brought people to the little resort town of Razor Bay, Washington.

Seeing a huge unsmiling man bearing down on her, however, made that enjoyment falter. And her heartbeat inexplicably pick up its pace.

He looked different than he had during their previous two brief meetings. Plus, the first time she'd seen him, as well as on the handful of occasions when she'd glimpsed him around town, he'd been wearing his deputy sheriff's uniform. But there was just no mistaking a guy that big, that hard-looking, that intense and *contained* for anyone else.

She blinked as he suddenly left the path and disappeared from view, then shook her head at herself.

Alrighty, then. Conceited much? Because despite her cottage being the only one up here before the trail wound into the woods behind it, it apparently hadn't been Bradshaw's destination. Breathing a sigh of relief—right?—she plugged in her iPod earbuds and turned back to the couple of boxes she'd put off unpacking.

Within moments, she'd revived her earlier enjoyment. She loved seeing new places, loved meeting new people and diving into jobs that were never quite like any other. Because she'd structured her life to do exactly that, she was generally a happy woman.

Harper sang along with Maroon 5 as they played through her earbuds. As she efficiently unpacked the boxes of odds and ends her mother had insisted on sending her, she swiveled her hips and bopped in place in time to the music.

Thoughts of her mother's hopes and expectations for her, however, elicited a sigh in the midst of her crooning. Gina Summerville refused to believe that Harper could live very contentedly without a permanent base or a host of belongings, since making a home had been *her* way of coping with the constant moving from place to place that had been part and parcel of her husband's work. Neither Gina nor Harper's brother Kai had loved the adventure of seeing new countries and meeting new people the way Harper and her dad had.

Still, Harper had to admit that she adored the throw pillows and candles her mom had sent. They added a whole new touch to her minuscule cabin. Admitting as much certainly didn't take away from how she chose to live and honor her dad's memory.

All the same, when the song ran its course, she

thumbed through her playlist and pulled up her father's one-time theme song.

"'Papa was a rolling stone,'" she sang along with the Temptations, as she focused on finding a place to put the other items her mother had sent, given that storage space was at a premium in the tiny cottage. "'Wherever he laid his hat was his—'"

Something warm brushed her elbow. Her heart climbing her throat like a monkey riding a rocket, she jerked her chin downward. She stared at the rawboned, big-knuckled masculine hand touching her.

And screamed the house down.

"Shit!" Max Bradshaw's voice exclaimed as she ripped the earbuds from her ears and whirled to face him.

He was in the midst of taking a long-legged step away from her. His big hands were up, palms out, as if she had a Howitzer aimed at his heart.

"Ms. Summerville—Harper—I'm sorry," he said in a low, rough voice. "I knocked several times and I heard you singing, so I knew you were here. But I shouldn't have let myself in." Slowly lowering his hands, he stuffed them into his shorts pockets and his massive shoulders hunched up. "I sure didn't mean to scare the sh—that is, stuffing out of you."

Even through the embarrassment of knowing he'd seen her shaking her butt and singing off-key, it struck her that this was probably the most words she'd ever heard him string together at one time in her presence. Drawing in a deep breath and dropping the hands she'd clasped to her heart like an overwrought silent film heroine confronted by the mustache-twirling villain, she pulled herself together. "Yes, well, intention or not, Deputy Bradshaw—"

"Max," he interjected.

"Max," she agreed, wishing she'd simply said that in the first place. After all, not only had they been introduced on the day she'd interviewed for her job at the inn, but they'd attended the same barbecue just a couple weeks ago. "As I was saying—"

Her already open front door banged against the living room wall and they both whirled to stare at the man barreling through it. From the corner of her eye, Harper saw Max reach for his right hip, where his gun no doubt usually resided.

The stranger's forward momentum carried him across the threshold and into the small room, the screen door slapping closed behind him. As he left the glare of sunlight flooding the porch, he coalesced into a tall, gangly man in his mid-thirties.

Then he was blocked from view as Max stepped in front of her. She leaned to peer around him.

"Are you okay, miss?" the man demanded, glancing about wildly. She assumed his eyes had adjusted to the dimmer interior lighting, for it was obvious from the way they suddenly widened that he'd gotten his first good look at Max. His prominent Adam's apple rode the column of his throat as he swallowed audibly.

For good reason. Max was six-four if he was an inch and probably weighed in the vicinity of two-twenty.

Every ounce of it solid muscle.

But Harper had to give the resort guest credit. He was clearly outmatched, yet while he looked as though he'd give a bundle to go back out the way he'd come in, he instead moved closer and ordered firmly, "Step away from her, sir."

"Oh, for God sake," she heard Max mutter, and hysterical laughter bubbled up Harper's throat. She swallowed it down as she watched Max do as directed.

Then she looked at the resort guest. "I'm okay," she said soothingly. "It's really not what you must think." She ran him through her mental database. "You're Mr. Wells, right? I believe your wife is in my sunset yoga class."

"Sean Wells," he agreed, shedding some of the tension that caused him to all but vibrate.

"This is Deputy Bradshaw," she said. "I screamed because I had my earbuds in and he startled me."

Sean relaxed a bit more, but he shot Max a skeptical look as he took in the bigger man's khaki cargo shorts, black muscle shirt and the tribal tattoos that swirled down his right upper arm from the muscular ball of his shoulder to the bottom of his hard biceps. "You don't look like a deputy."

The dark-eyed gaze Max fixed on him froze the other man in place. "It's my day off," he said with his usual "Just the facts, ma'am" directness.

Harper had no idea why she found that so damn titillating.

"I just came by to ask Ms. Summerville to dinner," he added and shock whipped her head around.

She gaped at him. "You did?" *Crap.* Was that her voice cracking on the last word? She hardly ever lost her poise. But in her own defense, during their previous encounters she'd gotten the impression Max viewed her as a mental lightweight. She would have sworn, too, that she hadn't even registered on his Attraction-O-Meter.

"Yes." Dull color climbed his angular face. "That is, Jake sent me. Jenny's having a dinner party tonight and wants you to come." Glancing away, he leveled an are-you-still-here? look on Sean Wells.

The man immediately mumbled an excuse and melted out the door.

"Thank you," Harper called after him, then quirked an eyebrow when the deputy turned back to her. "You sure know how to clear a room."

"Yeah." The shoulder with the tattoo lifted and dropped. "It's a talent of mine." He gave her his default let's-cut-through-the-bullshit look. "So, what do you want me to tell Jenny? You in or you out for tonight?"

"I'm in. What should I bring?"

"You're asking me? I'm the guy who usually shows up with a six pack of beer."

She grinned at him. "I'll call Jenny."

He didn't smile back—yet something in his expression lightened, which might be his version of one. Hard to tell, since his deep voice contained its familiar all-business crispness when he said, "Good idea. I'll leave it to you to let her know you're coming, then. So." He gave her the terse nod she remembered from their earlier encounters. "Sorry about scaring you. I guess I'll see you tonight." He turned for the door.

"I guess you will," she murmured to his already re-treating back. She trailed in his wake as far as the screen door and watched through it as he strode down the path. She didn't turn away until he disappeared around a bend.

Wow. Nothing, not even the photograph she'd seen of

him in the dossier the Sunday's Child's investigator had sent her, could adequately describe the sheer impact of the man in the flesh.

Then a small smile curved up the corners of her lips and she shook her head. "But at least this time he didn't call me ma'am."

REQUEST YOUR FREE BOOKS!

2 FREE NOVELS
FROM THE ROMANCE COLLECTION
PLUS 2 FREE GIFTS!

YES! Please send me 2 FREE novels from the Romance Collection and my 2 FREE gifts (gifts are worth about $10). After receiving them, if I don't wish to receive any more books, I can return the shipping statement marked "cancel." If I don't cancel, I will receive 4 brand-new novels every month and be billed just $6.24 per book in the U.S. or $6.74 per book in Canada. That's a savings of at least 22% off the cover price. It's quite a bargain! Shipping and handling is just 50¢ per book in the U.S. and 75¢ per book in Canada.* I understand that accepting the 2 free books and gifts places me under no obligation to buy anything. I can always return a shipment and cancel at any time. Even if I never buy another book, the two free books and gifts are mine to keep forever.

194/394 MDN F4XY

Name	(PLEASE PRINT)	
Address		Apt. #
City	State/Prov.	Zip/Postal Code

Signature (if under 18, a parent or guardian must sign)

Mail to the **Harlequin®** Reader Service:
IN U.S.A.: P.O. Box 1867, Buffalo, NY 14240-1867
IN CANADA: P.O. Box 609, Fort Erie, Ontario L2A 5X3

Want to try two free books from another line?
Call 1-800-873-8635 or visit www.ReaderService.com.

* Terms and prices subject to change without notice. Prices do not include applicable taxes. Sales tax applicable in N.Y. Canadian residents will be charged applicable taxes. Offer not valid in Quebec. This offer is limited to one order per household. Not valid for current subscribers to the Romance Collection or the Romance/Suspense Collection. All orders subject to credit approval. Credit or debit balances in a customer's account(s) may be offset by any other outstanding balance owed by or to the customer. Please allow 4 to 6 weeks for delivery. Offer available while quantities last.

Your Privacy—The Harlequin® Reader Service is committed to protecting your privacy. Our Privacy Policy is available online at www.ReaderService.com or upon request from the Harlequin Reader Service.

We make a portion of our mailing list available to reputable third parties that offer products we believe may interest you. If you prefer that we not exchange your name with third parties, or if you wish to clarify or modify your communication preferences, please visit us at www.ReaderService.com/consumerschoice or write to us at Harlequin Reader Service Preference Service, P.O. Box 9062, Buffalo, NY 14269. Include your complete name and address.

ROM13R

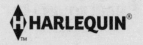

PORTIA DA COSTA

When it comes to diamonds—like their men—some women prefer them rough

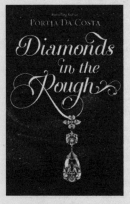

Thanks to her grandfather's complicated will, Miss Adela Ruffington, along with her mother and sisters, is about lose her home and income to a distant cousin, the closest male heir to the Millingford title. For Adela, nothing could be more insulting—being denied her rightful inheritance for a randy scoundrel like Wilson, the very man who broke her heart following a lusty youthful dalliance years ago.

Still smarting from the betrayal of his latest paramour, Wilson Ruffington never anticipates the intense desire Adela again stirs within him. Despite his wicked tongue and her haughty pride, their long-ago passion instantly reignites at a summer house party, the experience they've gained as adults only adding fuel to the flames.

Wilson and Adela are insatiable, but civility outside of the bedroom proves impossible. Determined to keep Adela in his bed, Wilson devises a ruse—a marriage of convenience that will provide her family with a generous settlement, as well as prevent scandalous whispers. Their plan works perfectly until family rivalries and intrigue threaten to destroy their arrangement…and the unspoken love blooming beneath it.

Available wherever books are sold!

Be sure to connect with us at:
Harlequin.com/Newsletters
Facebook.com/HarlequinBooks
Twitter.com/HarlequinBooks

HARLEQUIN® HQN™
www.Harlequin.com

PHPDC811

Susan Andersen

77691	THAT THING CALLED LOVE	___ $7.99 U.S.	___ $9.99 CAN.
77589	PLAYING DIRTY	___ $7.99 U.S.	___ $9.99 CAN.
77457	SKINTIGHT	___ $7.99 U.S.	___ $9.99 CAN.
77419	HOT & BOTHERED	___ $7.99 U.S.	___ $8.99 CAN.

(limited quantities available)

TOTAL AMOUNT	$ _____
POSTAGE & HANDLING	$ _____
($1.00 FOR 1 BOOK, 50¢ for each additional)	
APPLICABLE TAXES*	$ _____
TOTAL PAYABLE	$ _____

(check or money order—please do not send cash)

To order, complete this form and send it, along with a check or money order for the total above, payable to Harlequin HQN, to: **In the U.S.:** 3010 Walden Avenue, P.O. Box 9077, Buffalo, NY 14269-9077; **In Canada:** P.O. Box 636, Fort Erie, Ontario, L2A 5X3.

Name: _____

Address: _____ City: _____

State/Prov.: _____ Zip/Postal Code: _____

Account Number (if applicable): _____

075 CSAS

*New York residents remit applicable sales taxes.
*Canadian residents remit applicable GST and provincial taxes.

H HARLEQUIN® HQN™
™ www.Harlequin.com

PHSA0613BL